FIRE IN THE MOUNTAIN

FIRE IN THE MOUNTAIN

AJ ABERFORD

This edition produced in Great Britain in 2023

by Hobeck Books Limited, Unit 14, Sugnall Business Centre, Sugnall, Stafford, Staffordshire, ST21 NF

www.hobeck.net

A CIP catalogue for this book is available from the British Library.

ISBN 978-1-915-817-07-5 (ebook)

ISBN 978-1-915-817-08-2 (pbk)

Cover design by Spiffing Covers

www.spiffingcovers.com

Printed and bound in Great Britain by Clays Ltd, Elcograf S.p.A.

To my wife, Janet, who has given me unwavering support and hours of hard work to help this, and the other George Zammit books see the light of day. I thank you for everything. And yes, I'll go and open the wine!

PRAISE FOR THE INSPECTOR GEORGE ZAMMIT SERIES

BODIES IN THE WATER

'I thought I knew everything about murders in the Med – not so – this series is a fantastic read!'
Robert Daws, bestselling author of the *Rock* crime series

'What a fantastic debut thriller from AJ Abeford! *Bodies in the Water* gives the real lowdown about crime and corruption in the Mediterranean, in an adventure that ranges from the tourist enclaves of Malta to the war-torn deserts of Libya and weaves together an intricate tale of murder, human trafficking, money laundering, terrorism and organised crime. In the centre of it all is Detective George Zammit, an intriguing new character on the crime thriller scene who is sure to become an instant fan favourite. Meticulously researched by someone who clearly has a deep understanding of the subject matter, *Bodies in the Water* rattles on at a supercharged pace, leaving the reader waiting expectantly for the next novel in what is destined to be a hugely popular new series.'
J.T. Brannan, bestselling thriller and mystery author

'I am definitely a fan of George and 100% will look forward to reading the next in the series.' Alex Jones

'… a cracker. Organised crime, people smuggling, run ins with ISAL and the hapless Detective George Zammit. Tricksy as a Zen novel.' Pete Fleming

BULLETS IN THE SAND

'Wow another cracker of a book from AJ Aberford! The book travels from Malta to Libya and Italy and the characters are brilliantly written!' Sarah Blackburn

'I cannot wait for the next book, the good news, it's out soon and there are more to follow!' Ken Usman-Smith

'This is one hell of a book! It has everything under the sun, murder, humour, romance and especially action and plenty of it!' Gibbo The Great

HAWK AT THE CROSSROADS

'Mr Aberford can't write quick enough for me.' Handbag Lover

'I found myself unable to stop reading, eager to find out how all the twisty double-crossing, outsmarting threads were going to play out.' Kerry Young

'Another great read from AJ Aberford.' Irene Smith

AUTHOR'S NOTE

Although the plot points are inspired by the political circumstances and certain events at the time of writing, the story is the product of my imagination and not intended to be an accurate account of any such real-life events or a comment on any of the people who may have been involved in them.

Malta is a small island and three-quarters of the population share the same one hundred most common surnames. As a result, there's a chance I have inadvertently given a character the same name as someone alive or maybe dead. If that is the case, I apologise. The events, dialogue and characters in this book were created for the purposes of fictionalisation. Any resemblance of any character or corporation to any entity, or to a person, alive or dead, is purely coincidental.

ARE YOU A THRILLER SEEKER?

Hobeck Books is an independent publisher of crime, mystery, thriller and suspense and we have one aim – to bring you the books you want to read.

For more details about our books, our authors and our plans, the chance to enter competitions, plus to download *Crime Bites*, a free compilation of novellas and short stories by our authors sign up for our newsletter at **www.hobeck.net**.

You can also find us on Twitter **@hobeckbooks** or on Facebook **www.facebook.com/hobeckbooks10**.

ARE YOU A THRILLER
SEEKER?

PROLOGUE

It was a long walk up the hillside. Even the sturdy legs of the elderly labourer felt the incline and the altitude working against them. He had been told to make sure he followed a slightly different route every day – perhaps via a terrace to the left of the valley one day, along the right the next. He never flattened the vegetation, scuffed the moss or polished a path onto the stones beneath his feet. When he smoked the fake Marlboro cigarettes he bought online, he carefully collected the filters in an old screw-top jar.

Dressed in a straw hat, frayed khaki cut-offs and a faded, sweat-stained green cotton shirt, he blended perfectly with the patches of light and shade on the grey soil and lumpy basalt outcrops.

He had been doing this for many months, and another winter would soon arrive, adding to the difficulty of the daily journey. He was paid well for his efforts, but he did not like the quarry owners. They owned his house, his labour and, now, his conscience. He told himself he did not need to like them, but knew he had no option other than to do their bidding. His wife never asked where he went every morning, nor what he did to earn the extra euros. But her studied silence told him she knew that it was happening again.

After thirty minutes of climbing the hillside, he stopped, dropped his canvas rucksack by his feet, and took a moment to get his breath back. The ascent was the easy part. He set his jaw and pushed on, to tackle the unpleasant part of his task. Ahead was a narrow gulley where bristling thorn bushes barred the path. It was where he took the most care not to disturb nature's defences. Satisfied he was unobserved, he took off his straw hat and wrapped a long purple cotton scarf around his head and brow for protection.

At the head of the gulley, he turned his attention to a horizontal fissure in the rock, about a metre high, partially concealed by grasses and shrubs. Looping the rucksack straps around his feet, so he could pull it behind him, he strapped a head torch on top of the scarf. When his preparations were complete, he lay on his belly and eased himself through the crack in the rock, into the tunnels beyond. After a minute of creeping like this, he checked above his head with his hand and gently raised himself to his feet.

Beyond the patch of light from the head torch was the pitch black of a tunnel. The only sound was the distant dripping of water. The air was dank and clammy, and smelled of mouldering vegetation. He picked his way over the uneven floor, counting for twenty paces, staring down into the brilliant white pool of light at his feet. A twisted ankle in that place was something he could not allow to happen.

Edging forward, he sensed, rather than saw, the drop. It was only just discernible as an area of deeper, more intense blackness. He opened his rucksack and took out a plastic carrier bag containing two litres of water, half a loaf of bread, an apple and a pack of boiled ham. Behind a nearby rock was a coiled ten-metre line. He attached the carrier to the rope and gently lowered it over the drop into the darkness below. He waited for a minute or so, listening intently. Eventually, he heard the gentle clatter of rocks shifting below him and then a rustling of the plastic, as the bag was taken from the rope. There were no words spoken today. He feared for the person below. It had been too long. When they became quiet, it meant they had given up hope.

The man had learned to remain silent and shut his mind to what was happening there. Once the delivery had been made, he retrieved the rope, coiled and replaced it, ready for the next day's drop. After making his way down to his rough stone house, he thought nothing more about it until the following morning, when it was time to begin the journey once again. But the one thing he could never get used to, no matter how many times he made the drop, was the worsening smell of human excrement and filth that rose to meet him every time the bag was taken from the rope.

CHAPTER 1

INSPECTOR GEORGE ZAMMIT

VALLETTA, MALTA

I<small>T HAD BEEN ONLY</small> a couple of months since Inspector George Zammit, of the *Malta Pulizija,* had returned from his last trip to Libya, and finally, only now was he starting to put the memory of those disturbing experiences behind him. His dreams of sinking ships, sleek attenuated nuclear missiles and those concrete boxes in the desert, filled with contorted human bodies, had started to fade, much to his wife's relief. His yelps and twitches had disturbed her sleep for weeks, and she had not held back on making her displeasure known.

"Not only are you gone for months – you bring these nightmares home with you! And still no word of a promotion... what does someone have to do to impress Gerald Camilleri? I thought he was such a gentleman after he more or less promised me he would promote you..."

George had been demoted to the rank of inspector in the Community Affairs section when he had defied Assistant Commissioner Gerald Camilleri's invitation to join his own Organised and Financial Crime squad. This punishment had rankled with Marianna more than it had with her husband. The loss of status amongst the senior officers' wives had been hard for her to bear, particularly the loss of the invitation to the commissioner's summer garden party. While George had been away in Libya, his boss had paid a welfare visit to Marianna, to assure her of her husband's wellbeing and, more importantly, to confirm the special hardship payments that she would be relying on to fund the family holiday to Spain. Marianna had got it firmly into her head that, on his return, George would be restored to his former rank of superintendent. As yet, that had not happened.

After a short period of leave, and the much-discussed family holiday to Nerja, George reluctantly returned to active duty. On his first day back, he strolled into the office where he had previously spent a few pleasant, stress-free years: putting boots on the streets to increase police visibility, giving lectures to schoolchildren and advising on traffic-calming measures. He read the note on his desk, telling him to report to Assistant Commissioner Camilleri's office, and any pleasure he had taken in returning to duty immediately disappeared.

In the past, any visit to the assistant commissioner's office would have brought George out in a nervous sweat, as he tried to think what Camilleri might want of him next. Over the years, Camilleri had bullied, blackmailed and coerced George into all manner of situations, many driven by his superior's association with the Bonnicis, who owned Malta's largest energy and online gaming companies. Camilleri also habitually smoothed the path for the Bonnicis' deep involvement with a long-established, pan-European crime family, based in Milan.

Over the years, George had gradually become aware of his boss's involvement with the so-called 'Family', but politics, business and policing were often interconnected in Malta, and George was frequently required to tread a difficult path between what he knew and his obligations as a police officer. Assistant Commissioner Gerald Camilleri was a complex man who had established, and now maintained, an uneasy equilibrium on the island. His connections, they said, went right to the top of government, evidenced by the fact that he appeared to run the Pulizija, despite his relatively low rank. The assistant commissioner had long since realised the elimination of high-level crime was a futile ambition, tolerating a certain amount of criminality, so long as it was committed with his full knowledge and by disciplined, professional criminals, who ensured neither the general population nor the tourists were disturbed.

Camilleri permitted white-collar crime, yet forbade drug smuggling. International tax evasion and money laundering were considered victimless crimes; the narcotics trade, human trafficking and terrorist-related activities were not. Privately, he hated politicians, but accepted that their fingers were often to be found in the public purse. He was reconciled to the fact that the island was awash with Russians, Chinese, Arabs and dubious Eastern European business types, who had taken advantage of the Maltese government's 'passports for cash' scheme, so they could gain easy access to other EU countries. If his political masters wanted to flood the island with that sort of person, Camilleri did not consider it his job to police their activities.

However, if violence spilled over onto Malta's streets, Camilleri would act quickly and decisively. If anyone took him for a fool, they quickly paid the price. All in all, George conceded that Camilleri's approach had its benefits and brought a measure of calm and prosperity to the island. Criminals, who might otherwise have disappeared *sub rosa* and created all manner of trouble unseen, were given a measure of leeway and respect; in turn, they helped to maintain order on the streets. If such unwritten rules were broken, then the game was over. Corradino, Malta's Victorian hellhole of a prison, was full of those who had gone beyond what Gerald Camilleri was prepared to tolerate.

George Zammit, however, was a much simpler character. He was, at heart, a family man, and, although he suffered endless chiding and criticism from his wife and their daughter, Gina, he knew it was well meant and without malice. Gina was shortly due to marry Giorgio, who worked in the local butcher's shop and, now that the Spanish holiday was over, the forthcoming wedding was the main topic of family conversation, to the silent exasperation of George and his son, Denzel. Marianna had insisted on that name!

Thanks to the influence of Gerald Camilleri, Denzel was now a constable in the Immigration Section of the Pulizija and looked and acted the part of an up-and-coming young officer. George was secretly filled with pride every time he saw his son, resplendent in his pale blue uniform, confidently walking the corridors of police headquarters. He and George had worked together briefly, bringing down a drugs ring being run out of the docks at the western end of the Grand Harbour, and George secretly hoped that father and son could work together again in the future. He would like that.

So, this was his narrow world, and he was perfectly happy within it. Sitting in his wicker chair in the back yard, where he would take a brief nap in the afternoons, he often wondered if what he felt was contentment. The only thing that interrupted the deep calm of his preferred way of life was work. It had a nasty habit of throwing George into the most challenging of circumstances. In recent years, he had been shot, beaten, held captive in a concrete cell by Islamic terrorists, cast adrift at sea... and any number of other terrible experiences. Once he was back home, however, terrors subsiding, he righted himself and sailed calmly on.

George ambled down the third-floor corridor to the corner office overlooking Marsamxett Harbour. He never looked forward to a private interview with Gerald Camilleri, but was confident he had not been back long enough to have done anything to cross the mercurial assistant commissioner. He rapped on the door, realising belatedly he had used too much force.

"Come!"

"Assistant Commissioner. Good morning. You wanted to see me?"

"Yes, George. Sit, and there is there no need to beat the door like that. I am not deaf."

As usual, the office was uncluttered, with no papers or files to be seen. No photographs, no certificates of merit, no plants – no statement that might give a clue as to the AC's character or personality. That was no accident. Gerald Camilleri was an intensely private man. He was sat to one side of the large, highly polished rosewood conference table. He steepled his hands and placed them under his chin. George immediately recognised that this was not a good sign. It meant the assistant commissioner was preparing to broach something unpleasant.

"First, I have good news." He paused for effect. "I am restoring your rank to that of superintendent, in my own Organised and Financial Crime squad."

George's face dropped.

"But I already…"

"Yes, George, Organised and Financial Crime. I am not having you languishing in Community Affairs any longer. Or, you can choose redundancy if you prefer? I am sure I can arrange a suitable package for you. Which is it to be?"

Gerald Camilleri was well into his sixties and well past retirement age, although normal rules did not apply to the assistant commissioner. He had the body of a stork, with long, stick-like legs and arms. His pale skin had started to develop liver spots and his silver hair was thin, leaving the scalp beneath visible. His red-rimmed, pale blue eyes appeared to have no lashes. Camilleri never smiled. Colleagues often discussed this fact and they all agreed that none of them could recall ever seeing him *really* smile or show any sign whatsoever of genuine mirth or pleasure. That was not to say he never tried. Occasionally, he would twitch the sides of his mouth and screw up his eyes for a moment, which was clearly expected to be an overture of friendliness.

It was that flicker of a smile George noticed now, as Camilleri delivered the veiled ultimatum.

"Well, in that case, I suppose I'd be honoured to serve in your unit, sir."

There it was again, the flash of a smile... or was it a grimace?

"Good. Welcome to Organised and Financial Crime, Superintendent. So, that is the good news. Your wife will be delighted, I am sure. She will not make the garden party this year, but the commissioner's Christmas drinks party is still to come. Now, for the less good news. I am afraid there is no post immediately available, so until I can make some changes and move a few people around, we have to find something for you to do."

The long thin hands were still steepled. George sensed trouble.

Camilleri stood up and buttoned the jacket of his grey pinstripe suit. He walked across to the window overlooking the marina below and assumed the position he usually took when he wanted his subordinates to know he was deep in thought. Without breaking his gaze out over the waters of the harbour, he did something remarkable. He started to talk about himself.

"You will not be aware of this, George, but I have a family."

"I always assumed you came from somewhere, sir."

"Do not be flippant, George. This is hard enough for me to talk about as it is." The AC recovered himself. "I have a sister, who has a daughter, my niece and god-daughter, Silvia. I am very fond of her. Unfortunately, she has gone missing. It has been over a fortnight now. Naturally, my sister is distraught."

George remained silent.

"Silvia is a marine biologist, studied in Bologna. A very bright girl. She is also an environmental activist. Very involved in the climate issue... that sort of thing. Last seen in Catania. She had been protesting outside the geothermal plant on Mount Etna. You have heard about it? Fracking causes earthquakes, and drilling into a volcano… well, it is like sticking a pin into a bear, is it not? Anyway, my niece is now missing."

George pondered for a moment, then said: "But, sir, she's a grown woman. And two weeks without making contact isn't unusual for a young person. She's probably gone off with a boyfriend or something. Is your sister the worrying kind, maybe?"

"George, you may not believe this, but as far as Silvia is concerned, I am the worrying kind."

Camilleri paced the room, gently drumming his fingers against his thighs as he walked the length of the office.

"Listen, I do not usually discuss my private affairs, as you well know, but since I am asking your advice and your help, I will explain our family a little further. My sister, Carmella, and I are very close. I am some years older than she and, after our father was killed, I suppose I became the man of the house, even though I was only twelve at the time. I like to think I helped to raise her. Hence our closeness."

George nodded along but could not resist asking: "You say your father was killed?"

"Yes. He too was a policeman, but, unfortunately, he did not have my light touch and made himself several significant enemies." Camilleri looked off into the middle distance, remembering a disturbing time. "It was 1974 and Malta was independent, but seeking to establish the republic. Tempers were running high and he got himself shot. To this day, I do not know why, or by whom, and I do not suppose it really matters now."

"My word! I 'm sorry."

"No need. The man was a brute and a bully – inside and outside the house. The three of us were better off without him. So, you see, when an older man took advantage of my little sister and refused to do the right thing by her, we closed ranks again. Together, my mother, Carmella and I brought up the baby.

Perhaps you will understand now why I look upon Silvia as a daughter."

For a moment, Camilleri looked out of the window, gaze focused on nothing except maybe the past. He turned to face George again, bringing himself back into the moment.

"Naturally none of what I have just told you must ever pass your lips or you will join Ivan Cassar in a hole in the ground in Libya," he said conversationally.

George was confused.

"I'm sorry... Who's Ivan Cassar?"

"The man who abused my sister. A merchant seaman who was stupid enough to agree to meet a contact of mine in Tripoli."

George swallowed noisily. He would very much rather have never heard that confession.

Camilleri seemed oblivious to the implications of what he had just said. He went to his desk and took a buff envelope from a drawer. He returned to the conference table and spread a small pile of photographs in front of George.

In the first, George saw a sepia-coloured image of a very young-looking woman, in a full-skirted summer dress, carrying a baby wrapped in a white shawl. Alongside her stood a much younger Gerald Camilleri, in a heavy-looking woollen suit. He had a head of shiny dark hair, Brylcreemed to his scalp. His thin face was split by a broad, beaming smile of genuine pleasure – an expression George had never seen on him before. The next photograph showed what must have been the same woman, Carmella presumably, many years later, older and slightly care-worn. Standing alongside her, a strong-featured vital young woman had one arm draped around her mother's shoulders. The young woman George assumed to be Silvia had multiple piercings, bushy shoulder-length brown hair, exaggeratedly flared retro denims and a Rainbow Pride vest.

Camilleri leaned over George's shoulder: "This is Silvia. She must have been in her early twenties when it was taken."

George quietly wondered why the usually intensely private assistant commissioner was taking him into his confidence and showing him these intimate family pictures.

The last photograph was a recent studio portrait of Gerald Camilleri, his sister and Silvia. Camilleri was standing straight-backed, immaculate in his dark blue suit and brilliant white shirt, while Carmella stood on the other side, wearing a plain, service-able, dark-blue dress and jacket, looking slightly sheepish in a frivolous-looking hat. Between them was Silvia, in her academic gown, and holding a scroll. From what George could see, she was a tall woman, nearly as tall as Gerald himself, with long limbs, but broad shoulders and hips. She had cappuccino-coloured skin, dark smoky eyes and strong, but not unattractive features. Her eyes seemed to blaze out from the photograph, the intensity of their gaze almost accusatory.

Camilleri said: "That is the most recent family picture, taken last year after Silvia received her doctorate. We can crop it so that it just shows her. To return to the point: my sister is adamant Silvia is missing and that something is wrong. I believe her. I have spoken to the Questura in Catania and they are idiots. I have no confidence in them whatsoever, but at least they have agreed we can send an observer to work alongside them in their inquiry."

"Mela, that's something. Who..." Belatedly, the penny dropped. "Oh, no, sir, not me! I've only just got back from Libya."

"Catania is hardly Libya, George. It is forty minutes by plane. You could commute, for God's sake! Look, do this as a personal favour to me. Sad to say, you are the only one around here I can trust with such a delicate matter. Take the family shopping for the weekend in the retail parks, that will keep them happy. The department will pay for the flights – not the shopping, of course! Then, afterwards you stay on. I want you out there immediately – *Superintendent*."

CHAPTER 2
GIANNI DEL BOSCO
NATIONAL INSTITUTE OF GEOPHYSICS AND VOLCANOLOGY, ROME

GIANNI DEL BOSCO sat in silence in his office at the INGV, National Institute of Geophysics and Volcanology, a few kilometres south-west of Rome's city centre. Even there, he thought he could detect the aroma of sulphur seeping in, making its way through the dust motes that swirled in the clear sunlight of an Italian autumn. Without noticing, he twisted a lock of his long greying hair around one finger. Outside, the unseasonal heat baked the surrounding parkland. Inside the air-conditioned office, the windows were closed and the atmosphere hung heavy. He took his glasses off his domed forehead and started cleaning them with the end of his tie. He looked up at the woman sitting opposite him, face taut and expectant.

"No change, Lucy?" he asked.

The young woman shuffled in her seat and looked at her laptop, shaking her head slightly at what she was seeing. She had to tread carefully with her boss. He was unpredictable, jittery and as prone to eruptions as the volcanoes they studied.

"Not for the better. Today's mapping confirms more surface deformation on the south side, by centimetres, not millimetres. Then, this morning, at four a.m., we recorded more seismic swarms. There's mounting concern among those on site – and I don't blame them!"

Lucy Borg was a volcanologist from the British Geological Institute who Del Bosco had seconded to his team when he realised he had a serious problem on his hands. She spoke English with a strong Maltese accent that he had found amusing when she had first arrived. These days he was not finding much to laugh about.

Lucy continued the update.

"Yeah, it's degassing rapidly – CO_2 and sulphur levels are increasing day by day and vented steam temperatures are still rising." She looked up at him. "The magma reservoir is building fast. I'd say very fast – unlike anything we've seen in the past."

She sat back and adjusted her spectacles.

"It's becoming a significant problem, Gianni."

Del Bosco looked at her and said, with a note of incredulity in his voice: "A problem? Is that what you call it – a problem? Jesus! When will people start taking this situation seriously? Do we have any readings on the magma chambers, the shallow and the deeper one?"

Lucy sighed deeply and looked at her tablet.

"Yeah. Again, it's not good news. The shallow chamber continues to grow. It's now six kilometres beneath sea level, around 20 kilometres long by five wide." Seeing Del Bosco's enquiring expression, she paused, before adding, "Twelve months ago it was half the size and mostly solid. About five to fifteen per cent melt. Today we're at twenty-five per cent molten rock. The lower chamber is worse." She sat back, pushed the tablet away from her and shrugged helplessly.

"Gianni, I know it's serious!"

Del Bosco clasped his hands in front of his face as if in prayer. He started to rock gently in his chair. Lucy watched him warily. Abruptly, he slapped his hands down on the desktop, making her jump.

"It looks to me like there is a possibility, in fact a strong possibility, the pressure could flood the upper chamber. If it does, the roof will not withstand the pressure increase. And that will be it... the beginning of the end!"

Lucy fiddled with her pencil and tapped the table in a show of resolve.

"OK, I'm not sure it's as bad as that, but you're right – it *is* bad! Just to get the full picture out there, I believe this is being caused by a significant movement of the tectonic plates. Our thinking has always been that the heavier African plate is pushing forwards and magma directly from the Earth's mantle is being sucked into the space left behind. Right? Or that's what we've always seen, historically speaking.

"Now – I'm not sure it's the only scenario. I think it's just possible that the African plate might have cracked and there's a new window that the magma is flooding through. It's the only reasonable explanation for the volumes that have suddenly appeared."

Del Bosco stared at her.

"So these magma flows could continue for some time. How long exactly?"

Lucy shrugged.

"Until we have further eruptions that'll release the pressure. Then, the new caldera can start to cool and seal the chambers."

"I meant, how long until the eruptions?"

They both stayed silent while she calculated. Eventually, Lucy said: "A week? A month? I don't really know for sure. But, if this continues, the volcano will have to release the pressure. It's just a question of whether it'll do it gradually or there'll be one big blow out. Either way, we're in for a rocky ride."

Del Bosco slumped back in his chair, considering this. Finally, he clapped his hands together and said: "Those idiots in Catania. Why do they not see what is right in front of them? Are they completely stupid?"

The Catania Section – Etna Observatory was an offshoot of the INGV. Recently, Catania and Rome had been at loggerheads about what was happening in the mountain. Catania claimed superior local knowledge, insisting that real-time studies conducted on the volcano itself contradicted the analytical conclusions coming out of the Rome HQ. Lucy Borg could not understand how two scientifically based teams, employed by the same institution, could hold such different views on something so important.

Mount Etna lies in the region of Catania, Sicily, and dominates the landscape for over 1,000 square kilometres, in plain view of over 600,0000 people. The island of Sicily, as a whole, has a population of six million. The southern half of Italy, or Mezzogiorno as it is known, is home to 14 million people. A huge volcanic eruption would have serious consequences for all of these people.

At 16:00 that afternoon, Gianni Del Bosco had a conference call scheduled with Luisa Marongiu, Italy's Minister of the Interior. He was uncertain what he should recommend. In the worst-case scenario, which he knew was unlikely, they should plan for an evacuation of the city of Catania and even the eastern area of Sicily. In addition, they should advise civil authorities throughout the whole of Southern Italy to prepare to face the fallout from a possibly catastrophic eruption. He doubted his advice would be well received. If there was to be an eruption of the size he dreaded, life as they all knew it would be dramatically affected, and not for the better. If he put the minister on full alert, and there was no such eruption, his own reputation would be ruined. Either way, he could not win.

CHAPTER 3

LUCY BORG
TRASTEVERE, ROME

Lucy had been raised on Gozo, the sister island to Malta, 200 kilometres across the Mediterranean Sea from the south face of Mount Etna. On clear winter days, when humidity was low and the atmospheric haze disappeared, the upper sections of Etna became visible from her home, ominous and mysterious, its snow-topped peak picked out against the intense steel blue of the sky.

When she was a child, she had asked her father how a mountain made of fire could have snow on top. He had explained the ice-capped volcano was like a giant *panettone*, dusted lightly with icing sugar, while inside, the cake and the fruit lay waiting to be discovered. He told her there was nothing to worry about. The volcano made good soil and warmed the earth so that people could plant vineyards and orchards, for oranges and pistachios. Mount Etna was their friend. And, even if sometimes it became angry, there was always time for the people who lived nearby to run away and wait until its temper had cooled. Then, they could return to their houses in safety, happy that the volcano had fallen back into one of its long slumbers.

Sometimes, during the day, a thin plume of smoke would be visible, rising vertically from the South Eastern Crater into the untroubled sky but, when there were eruptions, from vents on its southerly and eastern sides, turbulent gases would hurl debris and clouds of dust high into the atmosphere. Then, the teenage Lucy would press binoculars to her eyes, watching the orange glow, fascinated and terrified to see light bursting from the molten rock that oozed out of the volcano's crevices, sliding and tumbling down the side of its colossal bulk. By that time, she knew the smoke was gas, being expelled from deep within the earth's crust, and that the molten rock came from a terrifying reservoir of magma, not so far below the earth's surface, on which human beings made their homes. She also knew what her father had told her about Etna was not true. The volcano never slumbered – it just waited, biding its time, growing in strength, until one day it could hold back no longer. Then it would strike.

Unsurprisingly, her obsession with Etna had set the direction of her future studies. Leaving Gozo, she had gone first to Utrecht for a bachelor's degree in geoscience, then had taken a master's at Fairbanks in Alaska, and finally a research fellowship at the University of Bristol School of Earth Sciences, where she published several well-received academic articles in her area of special interest: Mount Etna.

When Lucy had first gone to Rome, to work at the INGV, she had taken a small apartment just behind the Piazza Santa Maria, in the trendy district of Trastevere on the west bank of the Tiber. In the mornings, it took her over an hour to fight her way through the Roman traffic to the INGV building. Despite the stressful commute, she felt it was worth it for the pleasure of living in the bohemian inner-city district, with its lively squares, narrow cobblestone streets and colourful buildings.

About a year later, Silvia had moved in. They had met in a bar and had immediately recognised each other's Maltese accents. Lucy had thought Silvia was wonderful; bold, colourful, prone to impulsive outbursts and acts that excited and horrified her in equal measure. It was Silvia who had grabbed the more timid Lucy, only an hour after their first meeting, and boldly kissed her in the middle of the bar, to the cheers of the other customers.

Lucy had blushed and told her not to dare do that in Malta, where there were still places where they would be lynched! Secretly, Lucy loved Silvia's daring and was happy to be swept along by her enthusiasm and energy. Silvia had been immediately struck by Lucy's sense of inner calm and quiet confidence. Lucy had pale blue watchful eyes, that were rarely still. She was not tall, some 15 centimetres shorter than Silvia, with a narrow, pointed jaw and nose. She hated her hair, which was straight and mousey, pale brown, hanging to just above her shoulders. She was attractive, rather than pretty and had been surprised when the tall, super-confident Silvia, had first approached her.

Lucy was more reserved, and came across as being slightly shy, while Silvia exuded confidence and loved voicing her many, strongly held, convictions to anybody who would listen to her. Lucy would sit back and enjoy watching, as Silvia naturally took the floor in discussions, the warmth of her deep voice, pulling people towards her point of view. But when the two of them were alone together, it was Lucy who provided the aura of calm and quiet that Silvia needed to balance the other side of her nature.

It was unsurprising therefore, that when Silvia committed herself to something, she did it with every fibre of her being. So, it did not take long before Lucy found herself enthralled by the ardent relationship with the tall, passionate, environmentalist. In matters of love, Lucy, usually reluctant to lead, was happy to be swept along, instinctively trusting, and eventually matching, Silvia's willingness to pledge themselves to each other and share the flat in Trastevere.

Three weeks ago, Silvia had announced she was going to Mount Etna, to spend a few weeks at the protest camp, outside a geothermal electricity plant, halfway up the volcano. Lucy knew she could not and should not try to stop her but, despite Silvia's arguments that the public had to be made aware of the dangers of fracking on a volcano, Lucy had been upset and a little annoyed by her rushed departure.

At first, Lucy heard from her regularly, and Silvia gave useful on-the-spot accounts of the volcano's activity, but a week later, silence descended. Every text and phone call Lucy sent suddenly went unanswered. She was worried. Her days buzzed with a low-level anxiety that surged into full-blown panic attacks when she thought about what might have happened. She made herself consider the possibility that Silvia had just left her. Walked out. Had enough of living with a quiet, nerdy volcanologist from a Maltese backwater. She rang Silvia's phone incessantly and left endless messages, pleading for an explanation. So far, she had received no reply.

Lucy knew little about Silvia's home life, except that she had previously lived with her mother in the working-class district of Paola, to the south of the Grand Harbour. Her father had disappeared abroad when her mother announced she was pregnant and Silvia had never met him. That was all the family background Lucy knew. Eventually, she contacted the Questura in Catania to report Silvia as missing and sent them an email with photographs of her. She waited on the line for twenty minutes, until a disinterested *agente* took some cursory details and scrutinised the photographs she had emailed. Lucy told him that Silvia had last been seen at the protest outside the geothermal plant, on the north side of Etna.

"She's a *manifestante*? An *eco-attivista*? Pah!"

Lucy argued that, even if Silvia was a protester, that did not make her a troublemaker and, either way, she was still missing.

Even down the line, she could sense the *agente* shrug dismissively, implying it was no surprise if a person such as that did not reply to texts or answer their phone.

"Maybe she's moved on to another protest somewhere?

Following a boyfriend... or a new girlfriend perhaps? I know the type, there's nothing to worry about here."

In most people's estimation, Silvia was a radical: she had facial piercings and tattoos, she was out and gay, had strong environmentalist views. She preached and argued and became frustrated when others did not share her passion for the environment, the ocean and the climate. At university in Padua, she had studied marine science and witnessed the destruction caused by overfishing, bottom trawling and pollution in the Mediterranean Sea. She argued passionately that damaging human activity was making the Mediterranean's marine ecosystem one of the most endangered in the world. Those she spoke to were often decent, thoughtful, liberally minded people, who would shake their heads and nod along sympathetically. But, after a while, their eyes would glaze over and they would start glancing around the room. Silvia knew they would do nothing to help. It drove her on to protest even more loudly against the destruction of the natural world, and that was why she had gone to the camp on Etna.

CHAPTER 4
MINISTER OF THE INTERIOR LUISA MARONGIU

PALAZZO DEL VIMINALE, ROME

MICHELE TOMMASINI WAS a senior ministerial adviser and part of the Italian government's permanent bureaucracy. It was his job to encourage his minister to do the right thing and curb any behaviour that might damage the reputation of an office of state. In the case of the current minister of the interior, Luisa Marongiu, this often proved a testing responsibility.

In the vast Palazzo del Viminale, the minister's office was situated at the end of a long corridor, decorated with marble panels, stucco, and elegant glass inserts. The room itself boasted several large three-light windows, elaborate chandeliers and a refined corner balcony. The long internal windows were open, but the shutters were closed to keep out the low autumn sun, causing the slats to spread thin bands of light across the polished wooden floor. Michele was trying to get the minister's attention, saying: "Personally, I'm not convinced. I can't just go along with all this on the word of one man. I know Del Bosco will say WOVO... I've explained who they are to you, you know the World Organization of Volcano Observatories... have reviewed the numbers, but still... it's all a bit, you know, hysterical. It's been three weeks since we last spoke to him and what's he got right so far? Nothing. Still waiting!"

The minister, a well-built, middle-aged woman, whose appetite for self-promotion was only matched by the regard in which she held herself, tossed her long, glossy brown hair over her shoulder and looked up from the pile of papers in front of her, fluttering her eyelashes over the top of a pair of severe black-framed spectacles.

"Tell me again who WOVO are?"

Michele knew Luisa Marongiu was super-bright and an extra-ordinarily hard worker, but he found her habitual eye fluttering and hair tossing unnecessary and distracting. He sighed, knowing she could not help herself.

"Minister, WOVO stands for World Organisation of Volcano Observatories. It's a worldwide network of volcanic fire hunters, primed, as far as I can see, to spread general despondency and panic. Del Bosco's considered a bit of a big cheese among them, I'm afraid, so they're all on board with this. But I don't know... it just feels wrong. Anyway, his own people on the ground, in the Etna Observatory in Catania, refute his findings – categorically. And I mean, they should know, shouldn't they? Privately, they tell me Del Bosco is considered, well, to be blunt, a little excitable."

He walked across the expanse of polished parquet floor and looked out of the tall window onto the square below. He considered his options. The best way to get the Minister's full attention was to give her a decision to make. The trickier the call, the more focus she applied to it.

"I suppose, if you want to start a full crisis-response exercise and start planning for the evacuation of millions of people, on the basis of Del Bosco's report, that could be an option?"

Her head jerked up from the papers in front of her. She took off her spectacles and studied him closely.

"Well, let's not be too hasty. If Etna has already erupted, it doesn't seem to have done much damage. I don't want to set hares running if I don't have to, and I certainly don't want to evacuate half of Sicily on the word of someone, you say, is... unstable, and whose own people disagree with him."

"Minister, what we've seen recently aren't eruptions! Volcanoes don't just go pop! They rumble on for weeks, months even. The magma beneath the volcano pushes upwards and when the pressure gets too much, gas and lava escape. That's what we're seeing now. And then, if Del Bosco is to be believed – the big bang."

"Hmmm. Give me Del Bosco's worst case."

"Do you really want to hear it?"

"Michele, of course I want to hear it. If you don't mind"

"OK. You'll have heard of the Krakatoa eruption of 1883?"

"I have."

"That was ten thousand times more powerful than the Hiroshima bomb. The reduced sunlight ruined harvests, led to colder winters, starvation and plague."

"We're not talking on that scale, surely? People will definitely panic if that sort of message gets out."

"Just hang on. Now the eruption in Yellowstone, Wyoming, half a million years ago, was even more powerful than Krakatoa. It probably covered half of the US in a couple of metres of ash and blocked out the sun for years."

"Really?"

She sat back in her chair.

"You weren't listening on that call with Del Bosco, were you?"

"Yes, I was, it's just I don't remember all the details. That's your job."

Michele glared at her, but continued.

"What Del Bosco is saying, is that the next eruption of Etna could possibly be even bigger than Yellowstone."

The minister furrowed her brow and pouted her lips.

"You're not being serious, are you? What on earth can we do?"

"I don't really know. Stockpile food, ground airplanes, mobilise an operation to clean up the ash, bring farm animals indoors, close the borders, evacuate Sicily, tell the rest of the country to stay indoors and shut their windows – pray? None of it would make much difference in the end."

"For Christ's sake, Michele, this is complete nonsense. No wonder the Observatory people in Catania have called him out. You don't believe it, do you? Why is he still in post? You have to do something! The man's a bloody danger. He could start a national panic. Shut him up – send him to Iceland or somewhere."

"I tend to agree it's all a bit alarmist but, even if he's half right, it would be a catastrophe."

"Well, if we're all going to die, or become homeless and starve to death, getting fired will be the least of my worries, I suppose. So, keep him quiet! We're not going to scare the public. Can you imagine the press headlines? 'The End of the World'… and I'll be the one they blame. They'll want somebody's head, that's for sure. So no more Etna talk, please. Just keep that Del Bosco character quiet.

"Now, can we talk about something more important? My TV interview tomorrow. It's a Saturday so… a business suit or something less formal? What do you think?"

CHAPTER 5
SUPERINTENDENT GEORGE ZAMMIT

CATANIA, SICILY

GEORGE ARRIVED at Catania's Fontanarossa airport along with Marianna, Gina and Giorgio, who were all feverish with excitement. He had made it clear that he was expected to work, but the others had two days in the shops, to find their outfits for Gina's forthcoming wedding. George had promised to keep a few hours spare so he could try on suits and Marianna had agreed that was the end of his obligations.

They checked into a budget hotel, only a couple of kilometres from the airport and even nearer to the retail parks and shopping malls. Before George had time to change into more formal clothes, so he could introduce himself at the Questura, he heard the door of their room open and saw his wife's back view as she stepped out into the corridor and, with a cheery "Bye!", she left to fetch Gina. Round one of their buying expedition was about to begin. With a sigh, he lay back on the bed and waited for his family to clear the hotel.

Fifteen minutes later, George was sitting in a taxi taking him to the Questura of the Polizia di Stato, in central Catania. The driver was a portly bald guy in a baggy white T-shirt, the hair that sprouted from his shoulders reaching to just above the neckline. He spoke in a thick Sicilian dialect that George barely understood.

They travelled due east until they hit the main coast road and then directly north, passing the coastal resorts, while heading for the city centre, seven kilometres away. George was idly looking at the signage for various hotels and lidos when he realised he kept seeing the same beaming face, gazing down at him from the roadside hoardings. The man was in his early forties, with a chiselled, tanned face and a full, perfectly coiffed head of wavy black hair. His open smile said 'Trust me'; his slightly hooded eyes read, 'You'd be a fool to trust me'. It looked like his large, brilliant white teeth had either been Photoshopped or were the result of some expensive dental work, but they were certainly not the ones God had given him.

George leaned forward and spoke to the driver.

"Who's that then? The bloke with the teeth?"

"Vito Amato?"

"Yeah, him."

"He's the Mayor. Up for re-election soon. He'll get back in."

"Left or right?"

"Well, sort of left, but with a bit of right. Hard to say, you know? He's for the people, but also for business and law and order."

George was confused.

"Left, with a bit of right, eh? OK."

"*Sì, sì,* he takes the votes in the countryside, but in the city, they love him, too. He understands the farmers, the volcano but, in the city, he brings the jobs and the new green stuff."

"What 'new green stuff'?"

"Well, the volcano makes the cheap electricity, and that makes the hydrogen, and that's now fuel for the city and all the ships and trucks. We've got the shipyards, doing the hydrogen conversions, making a lot of jobs, and then there're the trucks, all getting converted and running on the green! Look, this taxi? It's a hydrogen taxi! Clever, no? So, there's work and Vito Amato, he makes that work. We love him!"

"OK!"

"And, in the country, he understands the ordinary people, the workers. They say he's not a Catholic, but he's holy. He's got his own religion. He talks to the people in their own way. The old way. He's a crazy man, but we love him! Yep! But when the Pope came here, Amato kissed the ring, crawled around at his feet and bowed like we all did – like you have to! He's not stupid, he's a politician! You don't want a stupid man for Mayor, no?"

George returned to looking out of the window. Sicilians… madmen, the lot of them. A few moments later, in the centre of Catania, the taxi pulled up and the driver released the door locks.

"Signore, arrivato! La Questura di Catania!"

George paid the driver, careful to get a receipt. On entering the grey façade of the police headquarters, he found himself in a very familiar world. The half-tiled walls, the sage green, heavy-duty resin floors, the echoes of voices and footsteps in the corridors and the raised wooden reception desk with the scratched Perspex screen. He could have been back in Pulizija HQ in Malta, or any police station in southern Europe.

Like many Maltese, George was fluent in Italian, the language of their nearest neighbour, and quickly found himself directed to the office of Vice Questora Cristina Capozzi. She was a good-looking, slightly built woman in her late thirties, with neat, medium-length dark hair, deep brown eyes and an unsmiling, thin-lipped mouth. When she stood to greet him, he was surprised to see she could not have been more than 160 centimetres tall.

She examined George, as though he was a foreign species.

"So, Superintendent Zammit, you've come all the way from Malta, have you, to teach us Sicilians how to find a runaway?"

George plonked himself uninvited into the chair in front of her cluttered desk.

"I was hoping it wouldn't be like this," he countered to the implied rebuke. "The woman concerned is the assistant commissioner's niece." He shrugged. "You know how it is."

"Of course. But it doesn't make me like it any better. A stranger coming here to peer over my shoulder."

"OK, I understand. Listen, I'm not here to make trouble. I just need to report back on the circumstances of the disappearance and what inquiries are being made."

"Oh, that's all, is it?"

George looked at the stubborn set of her jaw and saw he was going to get nowhere with this woman.

"Oh, well, if that's the way it's going to be, maybe I can start by seeing the files? Then, I'll have a chat with the person leading the missing persons team and, after that, I'll report back and we'll see where we are. How's that?"

George raised his eyebrows and held up his hands, in a gesture of openness and cooperation.

The stony face of the vice questora stared back at him.

"When we realised who the missing woman was, I personally assumed command of the inquiry, Superintendent. That's how seriously we take things when we know a fellow policeman is concerned about the outcome."

"*Mela.*" George used the all-purpose Maltese filler word that started many a conversation. "In that case, I can only thank you and assure you my visit won't be a distraction to you."

"I hope not, we've a lot on at the moment. What with the election, then protests at the power plant and Mother Etna not behaving herself currently."

"Mother Etna?"

"Yes, we call her that sometimes. The volcano; the Mother. Sorry, it's a local thing, a bit strange really."

"OK, understood. The files?"

"I have them ready for you. Follow me, please."

George was led down four sets of stairs until they were in the basement of the Questura. The vice questora ushered him into a small, stuffy room where rows of shelves were filled with cleaning materials, toilet rolls, and four or five galvanised buckets holding long-handled mops. A steel desk had been shoe-horned into most of the available floor space. On top of it was a neat stack of three buff files, each containing no more than two or three sheets of paper, by the look of them.

Capozzi did not reveal the slightest trace of embarrassment.

"Space in this building is tight," she said with a shrug.

George picked up the flimsy files and weighed them in his hand.

"Well, the upside is, I won't be here for long, will I? Do you have a car I can borrow? And a designated contact in the Questura? You don't want me bothering you day and night, I take it."

"I'm sorry, we don't have a car to spare, but Agente Diego Russo will be at your disposal. He's young but shows promise."

"Well," said George, with a forced smile, "I'll make a start there then. You wouldn't be so good as to send young Diego down, would you?" He let the files flutter onto the desktop. "I should have finished reading these by the time he gets here."

CHAPTER 6
LUCY BORG
CATANIA, SICILY

AFTER THE DISCOURAGING conversation with the Questura, Lucy asked Del Bosco for permission to go to the INGV Etnean Observatory in Catania and check their core data, to try and discover whether the differences in opinion were due to a foul up in the information chain. She said she had contacts there who were reasonable people and might agree to help. She also felt that, since Silvia had last been seen on the island, she herself had to visit it and do some investigating on the ground – but Del Bosco did not need to know about that.

He was feeling frustrated by the regular shouting matches he was having over conference calls with the senior team at the Etna Observatory. He could never get hold of Andrea Costa, the director in Catania, who seemed to be adept at avoiding him. Del Bosco did not understand what was going on and how such a fundamental disconnect had arisen. Lucy persuaded him that a low-level visit, from a well-mannered, unassuming Maltese woman, might be a less confrontational approach. Del Bosco pushed his spectacles on top of his head and sighed. He took an expenses form from his desk drawer and scribbled a signature.

"Go and find out what the hell is going on. I've tried, but nobody's listening."

When Lucy arrived in Catania, late the next afternoon, she immediately went to the offices of the Etna Observatory, in the derelict Piazza Roma, where she presented her INGV pass at the reception desk. The security guard studied the pass and, with a smile, politely denied her entry, asking her to wait to one side. A tall woman eventually arrived, wearing a beautifully cut lilac trouser-suit and oversized wire-framed spectacles. She looked Lucy over.

"Hello, and you are?"

"I'm Lucy Borg, senior analyst at INGV, working under Gianni Del Bosco in Rome. I've come to meet with some of your analysts, to look at the data sources behind the latest reports."

"Really? That's interesting. Didn't you know things have changed around here recently? I'm Ornella Mancini, I've taken over from Andrea Costa as the new *directrice*. Please have a copy of this. I'm surprised Gianni didn't keep you better informed."

She showed Lucy a copy of a letter dated the previous day, from Luisa Marongiu, Minister of the Interior, addressed to Del Bosco in Rome, informing him that, as part of the policy of devolving more powers to the metropolitan cities, the management and control of the Catania-Osservatorio, Etneo Section of the National Institute of Geophysics and Volcanology (INGV), had been transferred to the Mayor's Office in Catania.

"I've told Gianni that all visits from Rome must be pre-authorised by me, and I'm afraid I've heard nothing about your visit." Ornella Mancini smiled sweetly.

Lucy's mouth fell open.

"Well, I'm here now. What shall I do?"

"I'm sorry, but after all the recent arguments with Gianni, I don't want my team being distracted by his hysterics, for want of a better word."

Ornella Mancini twisted her face and looked at the steely faced woman in front of her, who refused to break eye contact.

She knew of Lucy by reputation and had heard she was a competent and well qualified resource.

"Listen Lucy, we've got our plate full here and can always use the help of a good analyst. Leave it with me for a day or two and I'll talk to Rome and agree a brief for you. How would Gianni, and you, feel about a short secondment?"

Lucy could only imagine Del Bosco's reaction to the letter. He would consider it the equivalent of giving responsibility for monitoring Etna to a bunch of high-school students. Nevertheless, Lucy nodded her agreement and left the Observatory. As soon as she was outside the door, she called Gianni's office and left a message, telling him what had just happened and that she was going to wait in Catania until he and Ornella Mancini had agreed the terms of reference for her secondment.

Outside on the street, through a gap in the buildings, 30 kilometres away to the north the top of Etna's crater was just visible. The sky around it was calm and clear that day, with no plumes of smoke or steam. Some 15 kilometres closer, on the southern flank, she could make out the patch of buildings that was Nicolosi, halfway up the mountain. There, 5,000 people lived symbiotically with their "Mother Etna", as they called her. Mother bombarded them with lethal showers of glassy rocks and black cinder-like grit from time to time, but the stubborn townspeople kept indoors when she was fractious, only emerging later, with brushes and shovels, to clean their houses and streets. Even at its most benign, the volcano was dark and menacing. Lucy could not understand the mentality of people who were content to live in its malevolent shadow. And never more so than now.

Her thoughts were interrupted by the ringing of her phone, buried deep in her handbag. For a moment, she thought it might be someone in the Etna Observatory, contacting her to commiserate on the stupidity of it all, but then she saw it was a Maltese number.

"Lucy Borg?"

"Yes?"

"Hello, this is Gerald Camilleri, Silvia's uncle. Her mother asked me to ring you. As you can imagine, she is deeply worried about Silvia's disappearance. I gather you are in Catania?"

Lucy was stunned. She had no idea Silvia had even mentioned their relationship to her mother and was surprised that she would give out Lucy's number without saying something to her. Although the relationship was intense and committed, they had agreed it was not yet time to play 'Meet the Families'.

"Well, Mr Camilleri, you've caught me by surprise! I've never met any of Silvia's family, but it's nice to hear they know all about me. Did she give her mother this number?"

"Well, not quite. You see, I am a senior policeman in Malta and it is amazing what we can find from someone's phone records. Carmella, my sister, knew Silvia was seeing someone, but did not know what he, or rather she, was called. It did not take me long to find out who it was Silvia rang most often. I apologise for the subterfuge. And please do not worry – my sister and I are aware we live in modern times. We do not judge, although our parish priest may not be quite so understanding."

"Well, Silvia and I have got nothing to be ashamed of, so he, and you, can think what you like. I suppose you found me using 'location tracker' or something?"

"Something like that. My apologies, I did not mean any offence, I mis-spoke. But now that we are in touch, I was hoping we could work together and try to find out what has really happened to my niece. The Catania police do not seem to be making much progress, despite my efforts to lean on them."

"Of course. I've felt so bloody helpless!"

"Well, can we start by you meeting up with a superintendent I have sent over to work alongside the Catanian state police? Tell him what you know, who Silvia's friends are, what she was involved in etc. Try to find out if there were any recent problems or confrontations... that sort of thing. He is called Superintendent George Zammit and he is a nice chap, with no edge to him at all. But effective, mind you. Do not be fooled. Zammit may appear a little slow but he is very resourceful. I am texting your number to him now."

CHAPTER 7

FATHER GRECO
CHURCH OF ST JANUARIUS OF NAPLES, MALETTO, ETNA

VITO AMATO, the man in the posters, was in his early forties, of medium height and build, with a body hardened by regular gym work. His wavy dark hair was well groomed and regularly tinted, his nails manicured, and the flashing white veneers that filled his smile had cost him over four thousand euros. In the summer, he darkened his sallow skin by spending time at his beach house near Acireale and in the winter he used the sunbed in his conservatory. Appearances were important to Vito. He could not be Mayor of Catania and not take care to look his best – people expected it.

He favoured slim-fit suits and tight white shirts, which he knew flattered his figure. The Mayoral car was a black Maserati because, after all, it made sense to buy Italian. He did not trust politicians who drove around in an inconspicuous Mercedes or Range Rover, like they had something to hide. He was born on a small farm on the green western slopes of the volcano, not far from the medieval town of Maletto. The town stood on a steep hillside, at an altitude of 1,000 metres above sea level, nearly one third of the way up the volcano. Vito's earliest memory was of the ever-present tang and pithy essence of citrus oil, from the family's blood orange groves. His father had died when he was young and the farm had passed to his uncle, forcing his mother to take a two-roomed apartment in the town. She had found work in a small shoe shop and Vito, as the eldest, looked after his two younger brothers. It was in the village that he had first met Father Greco.

The middle-aged priest had a reputation as a renegade and spent much of his time outside, roaming the foothills of the volcano on foot. Even in the blazing summer heat, armed only with a bottle of water and a battered black umbrella, from some long-gone outfitters in Palermo, he would pick his way across the basalt outcrops and grainy volcanic soils of pumice and ash, which comprised his far-flung parish. He would call at the more remote farms, baptising the newborn, giving last rites to the sick, counselling and offering comfort where he could to those who struggled. Whenever his black umbrella was seen, moving across the cultivated lower slopes, a tractor would blow its horn, or there would be a shout and a wave, followed by an invitation to the nearest farmhouse for simple refreshments.

When he would disappear on his wanderings, often for several days, nobody could ever say where he slept. Many would testify to feeding and watering the spare, craggy-faced priest with the long white beard, but nobody reported that he had taken a bed, a barn or shelter from them of any kind. This was strange as the weather on the volcano was changeable and violent storms were not unknown, even in the summer months. Up to 1,000 metres above sea level, the sides and valleys of the volcano were cultivated; above that height, there were forests of white oaks, birch and chestnut trees. Some farmers would recount seeing the priest making his way towards the tree-line at dusk, leaving the comforts of the lower slope behind him, perhaps to seek shelter in the caves and tunnels that ran beneath the volcano, or to sleep alongside bears and wolves, as the children preferred to believe.

Father Greco recognised intelligence and ambition when he

saw them and accordingly took an interest in the young Vito. His mother was not entirely happy about the priest's close involvement with the boy, though she eventually conceded only good had come from their connection. Father Greco persuaded him to make the daily trip on the Ferrovia Circumetnea railway to attend the Jesuit College in Catania. Vito did well and in other times would have gone on to study for longer, but there was little money in the Amato household so, when the boy was sixteen, Father Greco used his influence to get him work in the council housing department in Catania.

Over time, Vito became aware of the gossip that had developed around Father Greco's interest in Maletto's young boys, but he rejected the stories and said, in his experience, it was only the priest's help and encouragement that had enabled him to better himself and support his family in those difficult years.

It did not take long for Vito to begin his inexorable rise to become the proud owner of four thousand euros' worth of veneers and to ride around the communes of Catania in a spacious black Maserati. But what Father Greco also taught him was the strange blend of mysticism and Catholicism that was all-important to the people who lived on and around the volcano.

At a Sunday school held in the stuffy back room of the unfashionable Church of St Januarius of Naples, Father Greco had offered bowls of pasta and introduced his small class of bored *scugnizzi*, or street boys, to the hidden secrets of the cult of the volcano. Their church in Maletto, he said, was named after the patron saint of volcanoes, whose dried blood magically liquefied in front of thousands of people, three times a year, in the Cattedrale di San Gennaro, Naples's cathedral.

The small crowd of ragged street boys would stop fidgeting and start to take an interest as Father Greco told them, in hushed tones: "The crowd in Naples watches the two small glass ampoules, one containing a solid red mass, the other a fine red powder. The Archbishop of Naples places them on the altar itself, alongside all the church's other sacred relics. They have bits of bone, splinters of finger, a black withered leg… then, through the power of prayer alone, they see the blood of St Januarius turn from solid to liquid, as if the blood itself is being reborn." The priest would go glassy-eyed as he spoke, at the sheer wonder of the story. He would turn his head upwards, opening his hands in front of him. "When the miracle occurs, the bishop tips the ampoule, so the crowd can see liquid blood move inside the glass. They cheer and clap as if they have enjoyed a magic trick.

"And why is St Januarius a saint?" Greco would go on. "Januarius himself was beheaded at the Solfatara volcano, north of Naples, during a period of persecution of Christians, and his headless body cast into the flames for the ultimate glory of resurrection. You see, another volcano, just like ours!"

When he had the attention of the class, with these stories of vials of blood and beheaded saints, the priest would drop his voice still further, as if to impart a secret. The group of shifting, scratching boys would edge forwards to hear what came next.

He told them about the Greek philosopher, Empedocles, who had climbed to the top of Mount Etna and thrown himself into the fires below, so that he could be consumed and reborn! Father Greco taught them that there were many ways to achieve eternal life and maybe Empedocles was not such a fool as he was afterwards made out to be. Like all of us, he sought immortality, although Empedocles had had the arrogance to proclaim that he would return as a God! Such a thing could never happen, of course.

Rebirth, the priest told them, was only available to those who had undergone Confirmation and received the gift of the Holy Spirit. But for the people who lived under the shadow of the threatening volcano, it was only a small step to acknowledge Mother Etna, engage in dialogue with her, put their fate in her hands and ask her for salvation. For who was to say that the Holy Spirit did not reside within her, the Mother? And why should those who dwelt on a volcano, and were always at its mercy, not recognise its deep, magical powers?

Vito had been terrified when he first heard this teaching, but in time he became a politician and understood the meaning of oratory, the power of stories, how to keep a sceptical crowd happy by the timely offer of a free meal. Vito grew up to be the sort of man who believed in everything yet nothing, at the same time. Belief was important to him, because beliefs were something held by others, and those 'others' voted. First there were the locals who voted him onto the communal council in Maletto in his early twenties and later made him their mayor. And, from there, he was on his way to becoming Mayor of the Metropolitan City of Catania.

But, at the local feast of Santa Maria del Carmelo, held each July in Nicolosi, half way up the south side of the volcano, Vito would not bid the hundreds of euros necessary for the honour of heading the procession of sixteen bearers, carrying the weighty statue of the saint around the village. He would pay more, in order to carry the silver, bejewelled model of Mother Etna. The icon of the Mother was the height of a small child. The structure was made from sheets of silver, fixed over a wooden frame. On the very top of the crater, beads of black jet, onyx and agate were interspersed with blood-red rubies representing its fiery crown. Further down, small tiles of jasper and grey marble denoted the flanks, with raised beading of smoky quartz and red and orange sardonyx marking the lava flows. Rust-red spinels gave way to a multi-coloured base where brassy yellow pyrite, mint-green jasper and lavender amethyst represented the vines and citrus groves of the lower slopes. Between the rare showings of the icon, its vast worth in gems alone meant it was kept safely in a locked vault, in the crypt of the eighteenth-century Church of Santa Maria del Carmelo, that had been cleared of the bones of the old monks who had rested there for centuries.

In the early evening of the Friday nearest to the 16 July, a huge crowd in Nicolosi would watch the procession featuring the wooden simulacrum of Santa Maria del Carmelo. The band would play, and the priests in their vestments followed the ornate gilded wooden cross around the narrow streets. Behind them, keeping careful time with their steps, sixteen sweating men would take the saint on her heavy stretcher, held high on their shoulders, for her annual walk around town. The crowd would press back to let the procession through, then join the rear of it to follow the saint back to the church. When the priests had finished their prayers, and the good lady was back in her place in the west transept, a smaller but more fervent group of worshippers would linger. The parading of the icon of the Mother was held in secret, always late in the evening. Father Greco had been told by higher authorities in Rome, no less, to disassociate the parading of the Mother from the yearly appearance of the saint. Vito had laughed when Father Greco had told him that.

"Be careful, father, they're on to you and your Brothers of Etna. There'll be charges of heresy next!"

"Oh, do not laugh," said the old priest, "we have already been threatened with those charges! On several occasions! The Orthodox see shadows everywhere."

"They're right. When I look, I see shadows, too."

"Well, that is why we pray, Vito, that is why we pray."

In the long run, Father Greco had fallen foul of some of his parishioners, not because of any finding of heresy by the modern inquisitors of the Holy See, but due to his fondness for teaching the town's *scugnizzi* and the other young boys from Maletto. As it became generally known that those commissioned with the Holy orders of the Catholic Church could no longer be trusted to uphold the absolute good, and were capable of committing fundamental evil, this led to malicious rumour and gossip, that was eventually fed back to Father Greco by the boys themselves. Whether Father Greco had any sinful desires or thoughts would never be known, but the shame he felt that people might see him in this light had a profound effect upon the devout clergyman.

His disappearance from the church of St Januarius of Naples, to take refuge in the mid and upper reaches of the volcano, was viewed as an admission of guilt by his accusers. The arrival of a new priest, who delegated the management of the Sunday School to an elderly nun, confirmed their suspicions about the previous incumbent's relationship with his young charges. Not even public protestations by Vito Amato that, in his time with the priest, nothing had occurred that should concern the town's busybodies or sully the reputation of a devout and charitable man, could reverse the impact the gossip had on Father Greco.

The priest never turned his back on Catholicism but, high up in the solitude of the volcanic landscape, he sought to understand the mystic ways of the Mother. He found that by mixing the familiar liturgy of the Catholic Church with the pagan incantations of those who had worshipped the volcano, he stumbled upon on a belief system that eased his wounded mind. This new form of worship seemed to satisfy the needs of others too. Those who lived around the volcano, and were in awe of it, sought to address both the ancient and the modern deities in their prayers. He was not the first to follow this path, but the jealous dictates of the organised Catholic Church ensured such freedom to explore had been all but lost. The question Father Greco asked was not whether a man believed in God, but rather which gods he believed in.

His disappearance delighted the self-righteous gossip-mongers of Maletto. The vanishing priest became the subject of ever-more scurrilous stories. He had gone to the forest and been eaten by wolves, who now marauded around the lower slopes of the volcano, emboldened by his bad blood. Others said he had thrown himself into the volcano, in his shame, in the hope of redemption. Some said he remained alive and practised black magic and witchcraft, exerting supernatural power over the volcano itself, that acted according to his whim. Another commonly held belief was that he had died, early one morning, while at prayer on the volcano's rim. Whether the fall was a terrible accident or, like Empedocles, a leap in search of eternal life, they would never know.

This latter story greatly amused Father Greco. Upon hearing that the tale was widely accepted, he never graced the town of Maletto again, but remained on the mountain, working amongst those who shared his beliefs and living as a virtual recluse, on and within the volcano.

CHAPTER 8

SUPERINTENDENT GEORGE ZAMMIT
QUESTURA DI CATANIA

GEORGE HAD BEEN RIGHT; it did not take him long to work through the slender buff files on the case of the missing Silvia Camilleri. There was a partially completed front sheet, with an address, date of birth, religion and ethnic indicator. Inside was a report made by Agente Alfredo Marino of a phone conversation with one Lucy Borg, of an address in Trastevere, who had reported Silvia as missing. Agente Marino had recorded that Silvia Camilleri was a regular protester at the demonstration outside the Pirao power plant and had been arrested several times for obstruction and trespass. She had outstanding fines of three hundred euros and one caution for obstructing the police.

Agente Marino went on to comment that Silvia Camilleri was a research marine biologist and an activist on a range of environmental causes. Hence, he surmised, her eco activities probably took her all over the world. He also noted the outstanding charges against her and unpaid fines and concluded: *'It is likely therefore that she would leave one place to arrive at another.'*

He recommended the missing person report be given a low priority.

George shook his head and snorted in disgust. His first reaction was that it seemed unlikely a committed activist and a professionally trained, independent woman would run from such a fight, let alone behave so irresponsibly towards her partner, flatmate, lover or whatever Lucy Borg was. He took photographs of the paperwork on his phone, so that Assistant Commissioner Camilleri could make his own assessment of the quality of the inquiry to date.

Almost as soon as he had finished his photography, the door opened and Vice Questora Capozzi entered, followed by a solid tub of a man. Despite his youth, he had no discernible waist, causing his heavy police belt to be strapped precariously around the widest part of his almost spherical torso. George wondered how this boy had ever managed to pass the police recruit's basic fitness test. The agent's jet black hair was plastered across his head with some sort of preparation. A heavy lock hung down over his forehead, accentuating the red blotches of adolescent acne on his cheeks. On his face was the bright, hopeful smile of someone who yearned to be liked.

Capozzi introduced them and almost immediately turned away, shooting George a sardonic grin over her shoulder. She left them standing looking at each other.

A second later, the young policeman bumbled over with one hand outstretched.

"*Come va?* Are we partners now? Oh, I'm Agente Diego Russo, by the way. Great to be working with you."

"Er, no, we're not partners. I'm a visitor from the Maltese Pulizija. You're here to help me in my inquiries surrounding a missing person, Silvia Camilleri, a Maltese marine biologist."

"Oh, OK then. Great! Missing person, though? Bummer."

George pushed the files towards Diego.

"Take a look, then you'll know as much as I do."

Diego took a small notebook and an expensive ballpoint from the breast pocket of his shirt. He made elaborate preparations to record the key details before George stopped him.

"You don't need to do that, these are our files and we can take them with us."

"Yeah, right, *ho capito*. I just want to be thorough; you know? Anyway, you haven't asked me yet…"

"Asked you what?

"You know… about my name? Most people ask me, nearly straight away."

George was confused. "Your name? What about it?"

"Well, where it comes from?"

"I've no idea, Diego, where does your name come from? I assumed it was Spanish."

"I'll give you a clue: who played for Napoli until 1992 and scored one hundred and fifteen goals?"

"Diego, I have no… oh, OK, so you're named after Maradona the footballer?"

"You got it!"

Diego beamed at George, his broad open smile clearly indicating he expected something more to be said.

"Well, that's great!" George obliged him. "But Maradona was the world's greatest footballer, and you…" he looked at the unlikely figure in front of him "… well, do you even play?"

Diego's face fell.

"No, I'm no athlete, that's for sure. I only made it through the police assessment centre because my mother knew the inspector in charge of recruitment. She gives him eggs and some chickens every Christmas. It's not a bribe though, more like a present. She's got a yard out back where we keep a pig and the chickens. So, there we go. What's the plan now?"

The expectant beam was back on his face. George understood what was behind the vice questora's glance back at him, as she left the room. She had palmed him off with a well-meaning idiot. However, there was something about this boy that George liked and found strangely familiar. After all, he had been just such a naïve flounderer himself when he had first joined the Maltese Pulizija.

"Well, Diego, the first things we need to do are to contact Miss Borg, who filed the report that her friend was missing, and then we need to go and talk to the protesters at the geothermal plant and find out what they know about Silvia. After that, other than wandering the streets looking for her, I haven't got a clue."

Fortunately, at that moment, his phone rang and, when he answered it, a hesitant female voice said: "Is that Superintendent Zammit? I've been given your number by Gerald Camilleri, I'm Lucy Borg."

"A happy coincidence, Miss Borg, I've just copied your number from the Questura files and was about to ring you. We need to meet. Where are you now?"

"I'm in the street, outside the offices of INGV, not far from you. They won't let me in!"

George told her to hang on and he would find somewhere for them to meet.

"Diego, where around here sells good coffee?"

"Well, that's a hard one! Some say Romero's, but I don't like it personally. Then others say, if you walk a bit further, there's Prestipino's on the piazza in front of the Duomo, but they can be surly in there, you know? Now, I'm not sure about this but others say…"

"Diego, stop! Lucy, can you find Prestipino's? It's a café in front of the Duomo. Walk over there now and we'll have a coffee and a chat. It's been recommended."

George put his phone back in his pocket and started gathering his files, making ready to leave. Diego was standing looking at him, clearly put out.

"Hey, that's not fair! I didn't exactly recommend it. Don't blame me if the service is annoying, I did say. Just wait a minute, I'll have to get my coat, it's upstairs."

George did not hesitate to try and rid himself of the overweight youth.

"It's OK, thank you, Diego. I can handle this by myself."

What George was not ready for was the expression that flooded Diego's face. It was like looking into the eyes of a betrayed child.

"But you don't know where it is and I'm here to show you places. You said so?"

George sighed and relented.

"OK then, go and get your coat."

As Diego puffed up the stairs, his lank black hair bouncing up and down and his cheeks turning scarlet from the effort, George wondered what revenge he could inflict on Capozzi for dumping Agente Russo on him.

————

Lucy Borg was calm and collected while she sat across the table from them with her arms folded, retelling her story, details of which Diego scribbled furiously into his brand-new notebook. She had very little to say about the facts of the disappearance that were not covered in the *Polizia* files, but what impressed George was her certainty that something 'not good' had happened to Silvia

"I can tell you, here and now, she'd never have walked out of my life without a word. Even if she's fallen for someone else, at the protest – and I've thought about that because she'd been there before – she'd have come back and told me so to my face. She wasn't frightened of hard conversations."

Lucy stopped to dab her eyes with the back of her hands. Diego produced a crumpled ball of a handkerchief from his pocket and offered it to her. Lucy wisely waved it away.

"So, those stupid comments in the file – they don't know her. Who she is. This just isn't like her."

Lucy sniffed and blew her nose on a paper napkin. Diego stuffed his own grimy rag back into his pocket.

"Anyway, she'd never have quit the protest just when it was starting to get attention. There was nothing else she was interested in. God knows, I'd listened to her go on about it for long enough! I just don't know where she could have gone." Lucy took a sip of her coffee.

Remembering where she was, she looked up at them.

"Good coffee. Good recommendation... Davide, is it? Sorry, I forgot."

"No, it's Diego, actually."

"Oh, like the footballer?"

Diego beamed at George.

"Exactly. You see, *she* got it!"

Lucy cradled the coffee cup in both her hands, the warmth spreading along her fingers, oblivious to Diego's delight. She looked out into the Piazza del Duomo. Slightly off-centre, stood the Fontana dell'Elefante, the small, smiling, black basalt elephant that was the symbol of the city. On its back was a large obelisk, several metres tall, which was said to have magical power over the volcano, though where the story originated from, nobody seemed to know.

Lucy continued in a low voice, as if speaking to herself.

"Sometimes I thought Silvia was only with me because I'm a volcanologist and could help her with the technical stuff. She was so committed...practically obsessed... to what's happening on Etna! There was a TV crew coming up to talk to her and a British company was doing a documentary on the new Green Revolution happening in Catania. Silvia wouldn't have missed that – not voluntarily anyway."

George was inclined to agree. After they had finished their coffee, he suggested that the next morning they should visit the protesters' camp, on the north side of the volcano. Lucy said Silvia had spoken to her about two friends she had there, in particular, Monica and Aldo, the long-standing co-organisers. Lucy was sure, if they could catch up with them, Silvia's friends would be able to help.

They set off to walk slowly back through the city's old town with its baroque buildings, just as the afternoon was drawing to a close. The sun was sinking, casting Etna's eastern slope into deep shadow. It seemed to glower at them. Diego must have felt the ill will coming from the mountain.

He said: "Look at the volcano. There are times when it's just spooky, you know? In fact, there are locals here who pray to it… call it Mother and stuff. Isn't that weird?"

George said nothing, hoping Diego would turn up a side street and find his way home, or anywhere else.

Lucy said quietly: "If I were them, I'd start praying too. That thing is a monster and it's quite capable of killing everyone in this city, pretty damn' soon. Believe me!"

Diego looked at her, his mouth hanging open.

"No way? No one told me anything about that!"

George had heard enough.

"I'll see you tomorrow, Lucy. And, please, don't frighten the children with these stories or poor Diego won't sleep a wink tonight. Agente Russo, can you get us a car of some sort for tomorrow?"

"Er, yeah. Sure thing. I think so. A car?"

Lucy looked at George, straight-faced.

"Superintendent, tomorrow I'll tell you precisely what's going on with the volcano, and I promise you, you won't like it."

CHAPTER 9
VITO AMATO

BENEVENTI WINERY, MOUNT ETNA, SICILY

ITALY'S DENOMINAZIONE *di origine controllata* was introduced in the mid-1960s to stand alongside the French system, the *appellation d'origine contrôlée*. But, unlike the French system, Italy's DOC specifies not only the production area and methods to be used for each wine, but also guarantees the quality of certain wines, which must pass a government taste test. The area of the Etna DOC is semi-circular in shape, running at an altitude of between 400 and 1,000 metres around the volcano, from Randazzo in the north clockwise, including Milo and Zafferana Etnea in the east, skirting Nicolosi in the south, to finish above Adrano, in the south-west.

It is indisputable that, for the last 100 years, the finest wines from the Etna DOC have come from the Beneventi Winery in the north, to the east of Randazzo. Here, on the mid-slopes of the volcano, the perfect combination of temperature range, altitude, soil, sunlight and rainfall all work together to produce red wines from the world-famous Nerello Mascalese grape.

Behind the bustling reception area of the stone-built, hacienda-style winery, where the tasting trips and the cellar tours form up, was the two-storey west wing that was home to the Beneventi family. Seventy-year-old Alberto Beneventi, known to all as Albi, and his Dutch wife, Anna, lived there together with their two adult children, Benedetta and Bastiano. Three stylish apartments were set away from the day-to-day bustle of the office workers, the production facilities and the never-ending stream of tourists, drawn by the Beneventi brand and the spectacular location of the winery.

Albi had inherited the business from his father and had run it successfully for most of his adult life. It had long been his plan to hand over the management of the winery to Bastiano, supported by his sister Benedetta, but things had become much more complicated when he had acquired some new business partners and diversified his interests into the energy sector. The new partnership required him to become the face of the Nuovi Modi geothermal energy plant, built on some of the family's land at Pirao, on the north side of Etna. This facility had become the target of the demonstrations where Silvia Camilleri had last been seen.

Albi had asked Bastiano to join him and become a director of the energy business that included the geothermal electricity plant and the associated hydrogen plant. Benedetta was then left to run the winery single-handed. She was thrilled at the prospect of being out from under her brother's shadow, while Bastiano was stunned by their father's sudden and unforeseen change of direction.

The geothermal plant provided electricity to nearly all the transmission and distribution companies in northern Sicily. The Metropolitan city of Catania had access to some of the cheapest power in the world, for which Vito Amato shamelessly, and incorrectly, claimed the credit. This abundant low-cost electricity also ran the energy-intensive hydrogen-production facility. The electricity generated courtesy of the volcano allowed a giant electrolyser to convert water into oxygen and hydrogen. The hydrogen was then processed for use as fuel in Catania's commercial vehicles, buses and taxis, and now powered a new generation of ships, built for a sister company of Nuovi Modi in the Far East. The first three of these ships had arrived and would become the standard-bearers for the inaugural net zero-carbon fleet in the world, based in Catania.

Albi was now the figurehead of it all and had become a celebrity in Sicilian and Italian industrial circles. He appeared at energy conferences, dressed in black, like some American tech entrepreneur, and read pre-prepared scripts. He did heavily managed presentations to politicians, regulators and others, as well as voicing scripted platitudes to the media. But, he did it with such cool charm and aplomb, nobody questioned his obvious lack of deep technical knowledge.

Despite his rapid rise to fame as the supposed father of the 'Green Catanian Revolution', Albi still preferred to spend as much time as possible in the winery, getting under Benedetta's feet and offering unwanted advice. The winery boasted a kitchen that was renowned throughout Sicily. Dinners were served in sumptuous private rooms, overlooking the formal gardens at the back of the house. While most visitors enjoyed tastings of contemporary wines, with modest culinary pairings, in the more exclusive sessions, historical vintages, from the company's 100-year-old cellar, were accompanied by dishes the equal of any to be found in fine-dining city restaurants. In one of these rooms, that enjoyed a private entrance away from the inquisitive gaze of the visitors, Albi was currently entertaining Vito Amato.

Three walls of the room were lined, floor-to-ceiling, with unlabelled bottles of vintage wines, lying on old heavily varnished, wooden shelving and locked behind black-painted wrought iron grilles. The fourth was papered in a heavy red flock, with two gilt-framed oils from the early nineteenth century displayed against it. A low light illuminated a dazzling white tablecloth, on which stood nothing but a bottle of mineral water in a wine cooler, from the winery's own, sulphur-heavy spring, and two glasses.

Vito was disappointed. He shrugged his shoulders and gestured at the bare table.

"Albi, I was hoping for more than a glass of water! I can smell the cooking from the finest kitchen in Sicily, yet the table is empty!"

"You're late, Vito, I said twelve thirty and it's now after two. I've already eaten in the house. I can ask for antipasto and bread, if that suits you? I can't waste away the afternoon eating two lunches."

"And I'm running the city, Albi. I can't be at your beck and call. I came as soon as I could."

"Hmm. Listen, Vito, they're getting concerned up at the plant. They're telling me the signs and the data are not good. We're getting daily earthquake swarms and the temperature and volumes of gas are off the scale. We're thinking of reducing the drilling, to let things settle down."

Vito flicked his wrist dismissively.

"Relax, I've now got a direct line into the Etna Observatory and I get a daily update from the director, Ornella Mancini. She says Mother's going through one of her phases, nothing more. For God's sake, don't slow down the generators! You know they don't believe the fracking has any impact on the behaviour of the volcano."

Albi asked: "What happened to Andrea Costa? I thought he ran the place?"

"Don't worry about him. He's not our concern anymore."

Albi Beneventi looked at him.

"Just because you've bullied Rome into handing over the Observatory to you, it doesn't make the problem go away, Vito. You're a local, you know the signs, we could be looking at a 1669 event here, or worse."

In 1669, nearly a million cubic metres of lava was thrown out along a fissure, above the south-facing town of Nicolosi. The blast formed the double cone known as Monte Rosso and the lava destroyed a dozen villages on the lower slope and submerged the western part of Catania in molten lava. The frantic townspeople had dug trenches in a vain attempt to divert the flow. It was Etna's worst explosive event of 'modern' times, but nothing compared to the possibilities Lucy was predicting.

Vito rocked back in his chair, clasped his arms behind his head and flashed his veneers in a grin.

"Albi, you're getting old. Every rumble or fart sends you into a panic. I can see what you've built here," he waved his hands around, "it's remarkable. But what we've built up the hill at Pirao, is even more remarkable. We're the stars of Europe's Green Movement! Catania can become the first carbon-neutral city in the world! Three-quarters of a million people, living and working at net-zero!"

"Hah! You mean, think of the contracts! Building Nuovi Modi drill heads two, three and four? The electricity supply contracts, across all of Sicily? The whole island served by hydrogen buses; fuel for private vehicles; the haulage fleet converted within three years? And the ships... we can't forget the bloody ships! Yes, it's wonderful, but remember who owns them, eh? These are not businesspeople, not as we know them. I've warned you already – we're puppets and one day they'll cut our strings."

Vito's face hardened.

"Albi, as I recall, a lot of your money is in this too, don't forget that. I know what you owe them. Your family are in this up to their necks. The future will judge you on how it all plays out. This is no time to get old man's cold feet. We're thinking big here. Big ambition, big goals and, yes, big money! If you wanted to sit in the conservatory and write yourself into the family history, you should've done it while you had the chance. Our partners can't blame us for what happens with the volcano, but they certainly won't understand you shutting down operations every time there're a few judders. Especially if Ornella Mancini tells them there's nothing to worry about! *Capisci?*

"You get it? I'll have that antipasto now. And you can do me some bread, to go with it. I'm starving."

Thirty minutes later, Vito was in his car driving down the coast road back to the city, with the taste of artisan wild boar salami still on his palate. He rang Bastiano Beneventi.

"Ciao, ciao, Bastiano! Come stai?... Sì, sì, bene, bene! Listen, I've just had lunch, if you can call it that, up at the winery. Your father's in a funny mood. What's eating him?"

"Oh, don't worry about it! He's in one of his mystic phases; talking about the Mother and disappearing off into the woods to smell the gases. He reckons he can forecast eruptions by sniffing the air. He's worse than a dog, wandering around with his nose in the air. He gets freaked out. "

They both laughed.

"But seriously, Vito, you've got to remember, he's a farmer at heart. The family have been on the land for generations. He's still got a lot of traditional beliefs, deep down."

Vito was silent for a moment, then said: "Hey, I understand totally, I was brought up by Father Greco, remember. He got me schooled."

"Really?" asked Bastiano, "that crazy priest who lives up in the caves and preaches the old religion?

"That's what I'm saying: Dad sometimes goes to his Masses."

"I know he does. Don't knock it, it gets to you. Just watch him, that's all. Albi's involved with the Brothers of Etna and they can get a bit edgy when the Mother starts to play up. Watch him, is all I'm saying."

Bastiano was only too aware of his father's involvement with the Brothers, people who lived in the shadow of Etna and followed Father Greco in mixing traditional Catholic beliefs with Ancient Greek mysticism, focused around the volcano.

Bastiano said: "I think he goes to a few of their things, but he's not hard core. He might be a bit superstitious, but he's not a complete lunatic."

Vito replied: "I still show my face at their Masses sometimes. They're voters too, you know. Got to cover all the bases! Anyway, how's the beautiful Benedetta? Have you told her how much I adore her?"

"You've made that pretty obvious. But she's not biting."

"*Porca miseria!* What can I do? Help me, Bastiano."

"Look elsewhere! Anyway, I thought you were having a thing with that Ornella Mancini woman at the Etna Observatory?"

"Strictly tactical, Bastiano, strictly tactical! But Benedetta, oooh, that's something else!"

"Oh, well, Vito, tough shit. I'll keep an eye on Dad, make sure he stays onside, but leave my sister alone, she's not interested."

Vito cut the call and drove the car into the congestion of the city. It was a shame about Benedetta; he did not like her that much, but with the family name and fortune, he believed he could learn to put up with her.

CHAPTER 10
SUPERINTENDENT GEORGE ZAMMIT

MOUNT ETNA, SICILY

GEORGE HAD SPENT the evening with Marianna and Gina, inspecting the pile of purchases made on their sorties to the retail parks. After dinner, he went to the hotel lounge with his laptop and browsed the internet for information on the volcano and the geothermal power plant there. A whole new view of the world opened up before him. He could not get over how thin and fragile the earth's crust was. The thought that humans rattled around on this scab, while beneath them the earth boiled and churned, deeply unsettled him.

The geothermal plant drilled through the surface layers of rock to release the reserves of heated water kilometres beneath the surface. On rising, this hot water vapourised to form steam, which then powered the turbines in the generating halls. It was simple, yet amazing. An unlimited, free source of energy, lying right beneath his feet.

As George pondered the mysteries of geothermal energy, Giorgio, his future son-in-law, watched a Serie A game at the other end of the lounge, with some other excitable and increasingly rowdy guests. Upstairs, the ladies were sorting their goods into the ones they intended to keep; the ones to be returned the next day; and the ones they liked, but weren't quite sure about the sizes. George gripped the arms of his chair at the thought that, only 30 kilometres away, one of the world's most active volcanoes was bubbling, belching and weeping tears of molten rock at 1,000°C. It was all most unsettling.

The next morning, he looked out of his hotel window, up towards the mist-shrouded mountain. He felt as if he was departing on a major expedition. He had abandoned his dark business suit for walking boots, light flannel trousers, a thick checked shirt and a heavy winter coat, which he held over his arm.

By eight o'clock, he and Lucy were outside the Questura waiting for Diego and his car. It was a glorious late-autumn morning and the summer's lingering humidity had finally been blown away by a fresh offshore breeze. At 8:20, an ancient red Fiat 500 clattered over the dark grey basalt paving of the square. Diego was visible inside, appearing to fill the entire two front seats of the tiny car. The vehicle seemed to list slightly to the left, as the suspension absorbed its unusually heavy load. George was speechless with dismay. Lucy kept her hand over her mouth, to suppress her laughter, as they watched Diego try to squeeze himself out of the driver's seat.

Finally freeing himself from the grip of the Fiat, he seemed delighted and surprised to see them.

"Hey, what's happening? We all good then? What's the plan?"

George was having none of it.

"The plan is, I'm going to hire a half-decent car, not one that looks like it's been stolen from a 1950s scrapyard! And one that's capable of taking three human beings, safely, halfway up a 3,000-metre volcano! And you're going straight home to dump that red thing and change out of uniform, so you don't scare the life out of our soon-to-be talkative protesters."

"Yeah, right. Good plan!" Diego paused momentarily and his smile dropped away. "So, the car's no good then?"

Three hours later, a newly rented VW saloon, with only 1,000 kilometres on the clock, was taking the climb up the side of the volcano with ease. Diego was in the passenger seat. He clasped his hands behind his head and decided to break the silence.

"Some ride, yeah?"

George sat, stunned. Lucy had just delivered a 30-minute lecture on what was currently happening kilometres beneath them. It was even worse than he had thought. He was trying not to dwell on the image of a lake of boiling molten rock, slopping around in an enormous, hellish cavern, no further away from them, than they were from the beach at Taormina. Unbelievable! And nobody seemed to be doing anything about it.

"This isn't all just theory, right? This is real?" he had to ask.

"Sorry, George, it's as real as we are, sitting here in this car. What we don't know is when the next eruption will come, but Silvia and her friends argue that fracking will accelerate it."

"And what if they drill into the chamber itself? Isn't that like pricking a balloon?"

"It depends on the pressure in the chamber. At low pressure, the magma will slowly rise and cool, effectively plugging the borehole. But, if the pressure is high, there can be a blow out, which would not only kill everyone on site, but would create a new volcanic vent, letting the molten lava flow through. The gas and steam already coming out of those boreholes was increasing rapidly and temperatures were rising – and that was a month ago, before the Catania observatory stopped releasing data to us. So, we don't know what's currently happening. That's the worst part of it. The flanks could be splitting apart as I speak."

Diego was peering out of the window.

"Scary. But it's kind of pretty up here too."

George wasn't in the mood to be diverted from the thoughts currently running through his head.

"It is for now, but you just imagine this hillside on fire, with millions of tonnes of molten rock pouring down. It wouldn't be so pretty then! I can't believe we're driving on top of all that."

"Yeah. No. You're right!"

Lucy tried to divert them to the task in hand.

"Look, what we're doing here is trying to find Silvia, so put all this to the back of your minds for now, OK?"

Diego nodded.

"OK, yeah, back of our minds. Done it. It's there, right at the back. Aaaand… it's gone."

George had been thinking. He decided he did not want Diego with them when they started talking to people at the protest. The boy was a liability, but there could still be a use for him.

"So, Diego, have you ever worked undercover?"

"Undercover? What, like Serpico?"

"Yes, just like Serpico. Have you?"

"Well, no!" He laughed, that short nervous bark of his. "No, I haven't. Not like that. Lying on stairs, pretending to be out of it? No, I don't do drugs and stuff… I mean, yes, sure, I've smoked a little weed – who hasn't, right? But no."

"OK, so now is your chance."

"Really?"

"I'm going to drop you off, a kilometre or so before the site, and I want you to walk on and start talking to the protesters up there. Tell them you've heard some scary stuff about what's going on with the fracking and you'd like to know more. Not from the fake news in La Sicilia, but from people who really know. Tell them you live in the city and you and your friends are concerned about the environmental impact of what's happening and are thinking of joining the protest."

"But I'm not."

"Not what?

"Not concerned about the environmental impact. I mean, they make the hydrogen up here and it's doing good things. It's really green. I mean, it's greener than grass! It's like petrol from water. How much greener can it be?"

"But to do that, they need all the cheap electricity they get from free steam, powered by this bomb under our feet that's about to explode! Look, just *pretend* you're interested. You know, going undercover!"

"So should I say I'm a policeman?"

Luckily, Lucy intervened, before George could reply. She bent between the front seats and looked back at Diego, saying gently: "Don't mention you're a policeman. When we show up, pretend you don't know us. And when we've left, say you'll think about things some more. Then walk down and meet us back where we dropped you. It'll be fine."

She peered up the hillside, through the deciduous forest where the leaves were just starting to thin as autumn lazily drifted in. A little higher up, they had their first sighting of the grey steel, windowless buildings of the plant and a large number of process tanks.

They were over 1,000 metres up the north side of the mountain, having driven up the autostrada, skirting the eastern flank of the volcano, with the Mediterranean Sea to their right. Then, turning inland, they had started to climb, until they hit the medieval tourist town of Randazzo, where they turned south, to continue their ascent of the north face of the volcano. Behind them, the spectacular view of the Alcantara Valley and the rest of northern Sicily opened out; verdant, undulating, a spectacular patchwork of ordered vines, squares of yellow and brown fields, bordered by hilltops of palest grey rock, woods and small copses of oak and chestnut, just changing from summer green to the lemon and saffron of autumn.

It was here that they left Diego.

Lucy waited until the car door had clunked shut and George had started the engine, before she spoke.

"I was wondering what you were going to do with him."

George laughed.

"Mela! Who knows? He might actually stumble across something."

Lucy flashed him a smile.

"'Stumble' is the word." She paused. "I'm starting to feel nervous. I'm not sure what we're going to find."

George gave her a tight-lipped smile.

"I know it must be hard for you. I'm sorry."

Five minutes later, they arrived at the entrance to the plant, a formidable pair of galvanised steel gates. These were set into a boundary fence made up of three-metre paling, hung with razor wire, that disappeared off into the woods in each direction. The gates were open, but a red-and-white barrier arm regulated traffic entering the plant. Warning signs were attached at eye-level, all across the gate and at 50-metre intervals along the perimeter fence. A zigzag motif suggested the risk of electrocution. There was a well-appointed and well-manned gatehouse to control access to the site.

Protesters' placards were tied to the fence while sheets of fabric, printed with the messages and symbols of the environmentalists, fluttered gently in the cool mountain breeze.

Lucy immediately saw the protesters' camp, set back from the road in woods to the left of the gate. The air was filled with the smell of wood smoke. The verge of a service road, which ran around the plant, was home to a cavalcade of vehicles, including several old camper vans and converted, hand-painted buses and trucks. On the edge of the forest, there were a dozen or so large tents, some linked by sheets of plastic that collected dew and rainfall, of which there was plenty. The water was channelled through runs of grey plastic pipes, tied to the trees, into two raised plastic 1,000-litre containers. In the background, a diesel generator rattled away, supplying the camp with electricity. Washing hung between the trees and Lucy felt a lump in her throat at the thought of Silvia's clothing suspended, wet and life-less, from those lines.

They parked the car and stepped out, fastening their coats against the cool mountain air and the damp of the forest. Every-thing seemed quiet, as they walked along the flattened and muddy verge towards the camp, to find Monica and Aldo.

CHAPTER 11
NATASHA BONNICI
CASTELLO BONNICI, MALTA

LATE AUTUMN WAS Natasha Bonnici's favourite time of the year. The intense heat of the summer and the unbearable humidity of Malta's August were both behind her and the pillowy mounds of cumulus clouds were piled high into the sky, shading the island from unremitting direct sunlight. The occasional deluge washed away the summer dust, filled the wells and freshened the streets. In October, the tourists' presence became less evident and the beaches and restaurants were reclaimed by the locals, who made the most of the pleasant 'second-spring' season, as they called it. Malta lies 100 kilometres to the south of Sicily. But, whereas the Italian island enjoyed its share of green landscape and cooler, higher ground, for most of the year, Malta was a hot, treeless platform of limestone. It was no wonder the locals called it *the Rock*.

Castello Bonnici stood on a high northern ridge, above the tourist resort of St Paul's where it could catch the north-easterly sea breezes. The fortified *castello* was the Bonnici family seat, nestling quietly in the hills behind the tiny village of il-Wardija and virtually unchanged for 200 years. The building had long corridors of smooth polished stone and unplastered limestone-block walls, hung with tapestries interspersed with suits of armour. Its forbidding double front doors were made from thick weathered hardwood, with black iron nails securing the planking. The vaulted entrance hall contained a grand marble staircase, which split into two halfway up, accessing the galleries running around the first and second floors. Crenellated towers and the adjacent chapel gave the castello a fortified look, although, in fact, it had always served as a family home.

Natasha Bonnici had not needed to lay siege or storm the walls to gain control of the building. Her father had unknowingly sold it to one of her holding companies when he exiled himself from the island, disgusted by the ruthless way she had murdered her way to the top of the Family, a long-established organisation that operated across Europe, beyond the law, for many generations. Once in power, she had begun the process of turning it from an old financial guild into a modern conglomerate, with interests in energy, finance, property and transport. She had deliberately exited sectors where the Family might run up against the less sophisticated organised criminal groups, rife in areas like construction, waste disposal and property development.

To help her in this, she had recruited an inscrutable Turkish power broker and member of the new pro-Western Turkish government, Hakan Toprak. An energetic man in his forties, Toprak had an impressive track record. He had run the Turkish Oil and Gas Corporation, before, with a little sleight of hand, negotiating the Turkey–Libyan treaty of 2019, where Turkey gained the lion's share of the maritime rights to exploit the seabed between the two countries. As a senior officer in the Turkish state intelligence agency, the Millî İstihbarat Teşkilatı, or MİT, he ranked alongside the generals who had seized power from the last political-Islamist president.

Toprak had won his seat at Natasha's side by engineering a long-term agreement, entitling the Family's companies to exploit Turkey's maritime oil and gas reserves, generating enormous profits for them, the Turkish generals and, of course, himself. Toprak's involvement with the shadowy Family was not known to the generals back in Turkey, but he saw no problem with the arrangement. He had the valuable knack of turning every situation into one that benefited all parties. He remained a trusted member of the inner cabal that comprised the new Turkish government and was also the first Muslim to join the Family. Natasha and the Turk had become allies; the first woman and the first Muslim in an organisation of predominantly white, Catholic, occasionally blue-blooded European plutocrats. For the time being, the Family accepted their leadership, still reeling from the ruthlessness with which Natasha had seized control, but fear and suspicion of the newcomers continued to linger.

In the Eastern Mediterranean, Toprak was known as 'the Hawk': a man of honour, a fixer of problems, a shrewd businessman, an arch political manipulator and someone who preferred to work alone. In Ankara, it was accepted that Toprak did his best work when given a long leash. His political instincts were not born out of ideology, but sheer pragmatism. He remained a practising Muslim, but privately despised the more extreme elements of political Islam. He believed the restrictions and restraints imposed on the population by the clerics had no place in modern commercial life and had no intention of allowing his country to be dragged back into the Dark Ages. Kemal Ataturk had enshrined secularism into the constitution when he became Turkey's first president in 1923, and Toprak the Hawk sought the freedom to fly wherever he wanted, whenever he wanted, unconstrained by politicians, mullahs, borders or convention.

It was still warm enough to sit on the rear terrace, gazing out over the Marfa Ridge, towards the channel that separated the islands of Malta and Gozo. Natasha was looking relaxed, wearing flared denims and a loose silk shirt, along with her usual oversized black sunglasses. She always dressed carefully when she was due to meet Hakan Toprak. He was a trim, good looking man, with salt-and-pepper hair and a bristling moustache that, on the one occasion they had kissed, late on a balmy evening earlier that summer, Natasha had found to be soft to the touch. She was disappointed that the relationship had gone no further than that. When their lips had parted, they were left in a loose embrace, standing on St Barbara Bastions, overlooking the Grand Harbour.

Hakan had dropped his arms and said: "You are a remarkable and truly beautiful woman, Natasha Bonnici, but I will do us both a favour and take my leave. I would never wish to offend you, but in the morning you will thank me for it."

Still with her arms around his neck, the soft menthol scent of his skin flooding her senses, she looked into his unblinking, prominent brown eyes.

"Hakan Toprak, you're a bloody mystery to me. Go on then, turn me down! I can live with that."

Natasha was in her late thirties, with shoulder-length, tumbling dark hair, long limbs and a taut, lithe body. Her skin had the typical Mediterranean olive complexion, and a little cosmetic dentistry had ensured a sparkling, winning smile. As well as running the Family, she had become a celebrity in European business circles, as chair of MalTech Energy, the successful start-up that had burst onto the European oil and gas markets. She had featured in all the major business magazines and, as a highly eligible, single woman, had been pursued by a wide variety of admirers, both married and unmarried. In private, she could be fun and witty. She was extremely rich. But she was also insecure, jealous, vindictive, and, when it suited her, a cold-blooded killer, who seemed able to act totally without conscience. That was what made Hakan wary of her.

He knew her last relationship, with Luke van der Westhuizen, a South African diamond dealer, had ended with him hanging himself in a Turkish prison. The one before that, with gaming company CEO and money launderer, Nick Walker, had ended after her lover had rejected Natasha for another, less deadly woman. Both Nick and his new girlfriend were later found dead in Valletta's Grand Harbour.

The second Hakan had felt Natasha's eager lips meet his, his highly attuned instinct for self-preservation had kicked in and told him it was sensible to keep a distance between them. After all, he would not want his untimely demise to ruin this highly lucrative relationship!

That evening, Katia, the long-serving housekeeper, led him onto the castello's terrace, where he unbuttoned the jacket of his suit and took a seat. He casually crossed his legs and looked Natasha straight in the eye. It was the first time they had met in person since their kiss. They made a little small talk, until Katia brought Hakan a tray of tea and refreshed Natasha's wine glass. There was silence and a moment of unease between them after that. Hakan said nothing and Natasha watched, as he put one hand into the inside pocket of his jacket and produced a rectangular silver box, with embossed Turkish script. He slowly and deliberately slid it across the table towards her, never breaking eye contact.

Natasha looked at him, suspiciously.

"Hakan, you're not proposing to me, are you?"

He smiled and raised his eyebrows.

She took the box from the table and opened it. Inside she found a solid white gold bracelet, mounted with seven large diamonds, each accented with scarlet sapphires. Natasha was shocked and had no idea how to respond. She just looked at Hakan, who smiled back at her.

"It's amazing the bargains you can pick up in the Grand Bazaar these days. Anyway, this is a mark of my affection and respect for you."

"Wow! We should kiss more often, if this is what happens afterwards!"

His voice deepened and the smile vanished.

"Now, you must close the box. Literally and metaphorically."

Realising the fun was over, Natasha did so.

"So, can we talk about business?" he suggested.

Natasha sighed and shuffled around in her chair.

"OK, I get it. You know how to spoil a moment." She laid a hand on his arm and looked directly into his eyes. "Anyway, thank you for the gift. I've never been so thoughtfully rejected before. You're just too smooth, you know?"

They both laughed. The awkwardness had passed and easiness was restored. Now the air had been cleared, Natasha was curious to learn the reason for his visit.

"Go on then, what's on your mind?"

"Renewables. We have plenty of oil and gas, and supplies of both will be around for many years – but not forever. The climate, and the politics of climate change, will see to that. In fact, pressure to reduce the use of hydrocarbons will only become more intense. We need to make sure MalTech moves with public sentiment and stays ahead of the market."

"Agreed."

"How much do you know about what is going on in Catania?"

"You mean using Etna as a geothermal source?"

"Yes, and the hydrogen plant, and all the businesses that are springing up to take advantage of the cheap energy?"

"Some, not much."

Well, it is quite a story. Catania is set to become the first net carbon-neutral city. But there is a strong rumour the whole thing is owned, or under the control of, the 'Ndrangheta."

"I'd heard that too. The Southern Italians have a way of letting organised crime into every corner of life there."

"Well, there might be a way to change that. We could acquire our own net neutral-carbon city, as a show of MalTech's commitment to the future... and, at the same time gain a very interesting new profit centre.'"

Natasha took off her sunglasses and rubbed her eyes. On a clear day, you could, occasionally, make out the black shadow of the volcano from the terrace of the castello, but not today. She was interested in his proposal.

"Well, that's a fascinating idea, but there're two immediate problems. One, the volcano is a ticking time bomb, I can sometimes see the thing smoking from here, and secondly, pissing off the 'Ndrangheta is something the Family tries to avoid at any cost."

"Your first objection is debatable. The north side of the volcano is relatively stable and my sources say that the drilling and fracking might raise passions locally, but have little significant impact on a volcano the size of Etna. Second, the 'Ndrangheta have bitten off more than they can chew. Their public profile is becoming hot. They put the management of the plant in the hands of a 70-year-old winemaker, while their other associated cheap-energy businesses include a corrupt data centre that misuses personal information and a Bitcoin mining facility. I ask you, is that really how to profit from a copper-bottomed source of cheap energy? It makes a mockery of those in Rome and Brussels who gave them all that cheap money. Typical shortsighted behaviour. If this gets out, I guarantee you, Rome will have no choice but to put the anti-Mafia prosecutors onto them, if only to protect their own reputations. And that would be a shame, do you not think? I believe they could be persuaded to take a step back, if it is worth their while."

"You're talking about a partnership deal with them?"

"No, never a partnership. But we can buy them out, giving them a share of future profits and some other incentives. We cannot avoid them indefinitely. They are too big these days. We are all starting to fish in the same pond. If you like, you can leave this to me for now, Natasha, and I will see what I can do."

"OK Hakan, but be careful. These people don't play by the rules.

GEORGE AND LUCY approached the camp.

"You lead, Lucy. Tell them we're looking for Silvia. Say I'm a concerned uncle. No need to tell them I'm police. I get the feeling that won't help us much."

There were two men standing talking and smoking, who warily watched their approach. One had long dreadlocks, piled up under a knitted hat, and a multicoloured knitted jumper that reached down to his knees. The other was clean-shaven and wore a similar get up to Lucy – contemporary outdoor wear, made from lightweight, breathable, waterproof fabrics, aimed at walkers, climbers and skiers.

She confidently approached the pair.

"Hi, there. Have you got a minute? We're Lucy and George, friend and relative of Silvia Camilleri. We're worried about where she's got to and wondered if we could ask you guys some questions?"

The men looked at each other and the one with the dreads said: "Yeah, no problem, but we'd better bring in Monica. She was a good friend of Silvia's and is kind of the camp elder. Follow me. Who are you to her?"

"We're family. We're getting concerned, haven't heard anything for over two weeks."

"Yeah, it's a strange one all right. We're worried too."

They went 50 metres down the line of vehicles on the service road, to one of the old converted buses where smoke rose from a wood-burning stove through a short metal flue in the roof. All the windows along the side were draped with stiff fabric curtains, which were running with condensation. Dreads banged on the door and shouted, "Monica? There're people here looking for Silvia."

The bus's door opened. Monica was an attractive middle-aged woman, with striking green cat's eyes. She had a pointed jaw and greying curly hair, held back in a plaid headsquare. She stood on the step and looked them over. With a jerk of her head, she beckoned them in. At the back of the bus was a double bed. A young man with shoulder-length hair lay propped up in it, reading. The middle section contained a kitchen unit and a cubicle George assumed was a bathroom. Immediately behind the driver's seat was a banquette and a small table. Monica swivelled the driver's seat around to face them and pointed to an upholstered bench. She started to roll a cigarette.

"So, you're looking for Silvia?"

"Yeah, we are. She never came home." Lucy said. "There's been no contact for over two weeks. It's really not like her, there's definitely something wrong."

Monica focused on rolling the cigarette, eyes down.

"What do you want from me? Dates last seen and by whom, that sort of stuff? Or an opinion – my guess about what went on?"

Lucy craned forward.

"Anything really. Just tell us what you think's happened."

"OK. What we did here was non-violent, civil disobedience. We lay in front of the gates, disrupted the trucks and the people in expensive cars. At first, we chained ourselves to the railings –

all the usual stuff. We put our bodies on the line, because, as you know," she smiled ironically, *"there is an existential crisis for humanity."* She made quotation signs with her fingers. "Not that anyone here really gives a shit.

"Look around you. There's no PR smoothing things over, the company is not bothered about anything that happens. The police beat us up, the private security contractors beat us up, we've had our vehicles damaged. Women here have been physically and verbally assaulted. It's just anarchy. We can't fight them; we've lost every battle on every front. Then, on top of everything else, mind you, Silvia disappears!

"She was the one taking it to them, videoing their acts of brutality, so they grab her, push her around, take her camera and smash it in front of her. She resorts to filming on her phone. Then, they punch her and when she goes down, kick her, good and hard. Really hurt her. Two of our guys try to drag her back and they get beaten up."

Lucy fought back the tears she felt welling up inside. It was hard to listen to Monica recount Silvia getting a beating. Monica continued: "So, then we're left with three of them, beaten and lying injured on the tarmac. They need stitches and Jean-Paul, a cast on his wrist. We make a complaint to the police… nothing doing, complete waste of time. So, Silvia sends out a press release to the international journos, inviting them to a press conference outside the gates of the plant. We get ten responses, mainly left-wing Italian journalists, but some people from the UK *Guardian* and the BBC's guy from Rome, who's doing a piece about green politics in Italy. They all sign up to attend. We're in business.

"Next morning, we wake up – no Silvia. She's gone. Disappeared. She had her own tent, went to bed about ten, and that was the last we saw of her. Her tent's still there, her stuff is still there. You tell me, is that the story of a quitter?"

Lucy was biting her bottom lip and George saw the tears in

her eyes. He asked Monica: "So, what do you think happened to her?"

"We think she was kidnapped, so she couldn't do the press call and cause any more trouble."

"By the company?"

"The company, the contractors, their goons... somebody who could creep in here at night undetected, unzip her tent, silence her, whisk her away without a sound. Not as easy as it sounds, you hear everything on a camp site. Plus, Silvia could handle herself. But there's no other answer."

George could not resist making absolutely certain they had all the information.

"And nobody saw or heard anything at all? Obviously, you asked around the camp?"

"Of course, we did. Nobody saw or heard a thing. The under-growth was trampled, leading from her tent to the road, which is about 70 metres down the hill, so we guess she was taken down to a waiting car or van."

"And you told this to the police in Catania?"

"Told them all about it. We went down and saw the vice questora herself. Capozzi. *Che stronza!*"

Monica looked at Lucy, narrowing her green almond-shaped eyes slightly.

"And I guess you're not really relatives. You're the Maltese partner who lives with her in Rome, yes? And *you* haven't heard from her, either?"

"That's right."

"Well, there you go. If she hasn't contacted you, she's not able to contact anybody. And you?" Monica asked George. "Where are you from?"

"I'm with the Maltese Pulizija. Sorry for the deceit, we didn't want you to clam up. But I'm here in a private capacity, repre-senting her mother and uncle, that much is true. So, this was all reported to the Polizia di Stato?"

"Of course, I just said so. We filed a missing persons report, only for them to wipe their arses with it. Don't you waste my time as well." Monica was angry.

Lucy pulled herself together.

"Your report is not in Silvia's file at the Questura. The only report there was the one I filed. What will happen here now?"

"They've broken us. We're leaving. After we've gone, we hope Silvia will turn up in a nearby village somewhere. It's all we can do to get her released from wherever she's being held. Nobody else seems interested in helping. They've won, no need for them to keep her. We go tomorrow."

George asked: "What about security and people in the plant? What are they like?"

"There's a head of security, Roberto something. He's the worst. A molester, always grabbing the women and feeling them up. He carries a retractable baton and is happy to lash out with it. He's got a dozen or so guards, who take their lead from him. None of them are scared to mix it up. I'm an old hand at this stuff, but it's just too dangerous here. They do as they like. That's why we're off."

The visitors got up to go and stood at the door of Monica's bus, saying their farewells. George left his number for her to contact him if anything else turned up. She told him not to hold his breath. The camp was breaking up the next day and they had other battles to fight, where the odds were more in their favour. From the step, George looked over towards the main gate. He could see a short rotund figure talking to the security guards there. Then, to George's surprise, he disappeared under the barrier and went inside the gatehouse.

He and Lucy followed Dreads to Silvia's tent, where Lucy grimly went about collecting Silvia's possessions, bagging them in several large black bin liners. George walked to the rear of the tent and poked about, along the seams, until he noticed the rear of the tent, where the thicker impermeable groundsheet joined the inner liner. That seam had been neatly sliced all along the base, probably with a razor.

So that was how they had entered. He surmised Silvia's head would have been at the top of the tent, so her assailants would have had to cut the fabric, reach in, grab her head first and sedate her, all achievable without too much risk to themselves. He brought out his police notebook and made a careful sketch of the location and of the tent itself, showing measurements and exactly where the cut in the fabric had been made. He then took out his phone and carefully took pictures of the tent and especially the cut along the seam.

George turned around and looked down the hill, through the woods that were mainly of pine and Etna broom. The pines were interspersed with small groups of birch and the floor of the forest was covered with low shrubs and ferns. It had been over two weeks since Silvia's disappearance and George was no forensic examiner, but he could still see a faint trail of broken branches and trampled ferns, leading down from the tent through the trees. He followed it, taking photographs as he went, until he came to one of the hairpin bends on the road up to the plant. There, in the mud to one side of the tarmac, were definite tracks where a vehicle had been parked at some time or another. When they had been made, who could tell? Nevertheless, he photographed them and resolved to take the pictures back to the Questura, for all the good it would do.

Just at that moment, there was a tremendous crashing through the bushes behind him. George spun around in a rush of panic, images of ravenous wolves and charging wild boars racing through his mind. To his annoyance, he saw Diego barrelling down the mountainside, his short legs slipping and sliding on the loose vegetation and undergrowth, ripping up whatever evidence was left of Silvia's abduction.

"George, George, phew! I'm all out of breath. Wait till you hear what I've got!"

The young officer bent double, hands on his knees, breathing hard. George waited a moment for the boy's heart rate to slow, then said to him: "You wait here. I'll walk up and get Lucy, while trying not to destroy what evidence remains! Then, whatever it is, you can tell both of us."

"Hey, don't you want to hear?"

"Give me ten minutes – or don't wait at all and start walking down!"

George climbed back up the hill to the car, then collected Lucy who was standing with Dreads at the side of the service road, Silvia's backpack and four bin bags on the ground in front of them. They were not talking and Lucy was walking in slow circles, pushing aside the rough roadside grass with her feet. They loaded the car in silence and Lucy climbed into the back. George caught Dreads's eye and gave him a nod of thanks.

Once they had driven off, George said: "I'm sorry. This must be hard for you. I didn't really think about that."

"It's OK, I wasn't expecting to have to do this, either. But I'm glad I got her stuff."

At that moment, they rounded a hairpin bend and there, in the middle of the road, arms waving, bouncing up and down on his short legs, was Diego. He ducked into the car head first, huffing and puffing with the effort of wrestling himself into the seatbelt.

"Well, the plan didn't exactly work out. I was imagining a big crowd at the gate, so I could go and schmooze, you know? There was nobody there. It's a pretty rubbish protest, isn't it? Really quiet."

He leaned back between the two front seats, as far the belt would allow, and said to Lucy: "Did you have any luck?

But George asked him tersely, "What were you doing anyway, going into the gatehouse?"

"Oh, yeah, sorry! That's the juicy bit. I knew the guy on the gate, he's called Natalino Lelli. He's ex-police from Milo, got hurt in an RTA. Well, he was drunk and crashed one of the police Alfas actually, but they let him retire, rather than fire him. Anyway, he got a job up here doing security. He recognised me and asked me what I was doing. So, I told the truth, more or less. Said I was driving you two around, trying to find out more about the missing protester. He just laughed."

"He laughed?"

"Yeah, he said she was the main troublemaker and *they* got fed up with her. Then he told me, the protesters and my mates could search all they like, but they would never find her.'"

George said, "Who's *they*?"

"Sorry?"

"You said, *they* got fed up with her. So, who's *they*?"

"OK, yeah, sure. Um, I didn't ask."

George pulled the car over. There was a brief charged silence while Diego gawped at the pair of them.

Lucy turned to George.

"*They* can only mean the management at the plant, can't it?"

CHAPTER 13

VICE QUESTORA CRISTINA CAPOZZI

ETNA CALDERA

CRISTINA CAPOZZI GOT the call at about midday, just as she was thinking about what to have for lunch. She had some shopping to do; her nine-year-old had grown so much recently that some of her dresses were starting to look a bit ridiculous, with the poor girl's waistbands being nearer to her chest than her hips. The market would still be going strong. Perhaps she could buy some *arancini* from Aldo's and get a couple of cheap dresses, just to get them through, until they could manage a proper shopping trip one weekend.

The call put an end to those thoughts. She spoke to the Carabinieri at Nicolosi, who had received a report from the excursion centre at Rifugio Sapienza that a guide taking a party across the caldera had seen a body, halfway down the inside of the South Eastern Crater. They had notified the Corpo Nazionale Soccorso Alpino e Speleologico (National Alpine Cliff and Cave Rescue Corps (CNSAS)), who had sent a team to investigate. The CNSAS was a team of heroic local volunteers who specialised in rescuing tourists and adventurers from falls into cracks and craters, as well as those who got stuck or lost in the many caverns and tunnels under the volcano.

She knew that the CNSAS would not retrieve a body, if that was what it turned out to be, until the police had examined it first. The Carabinieri at Nicolosi were hopeless and would avoid a trip up to the summit of the crater on any pretext: too busy, too many absences, no certified rescue officers, too wet, too hot, any excuse they could think of.

Entering the crater was immensely dangerous, due to the risk of a vent suddenly blasting out steam, gas or worse. The CNSAS had a supply of heavy protective boots and clothing, together with face masks and breathing cylinders. The gases in the crater were toxic and the police insisted that officers received special training, before descending the loose slippery slopes. And, even then, any descent had to be done under the supervision of the CNSAS. Cristina had been trained in the necessary skills, but had never ventured over the lip of the summit and the thought of doing so now made her heartbeat quicken and her palms start to sweat.

She carefully selected two younger, athletic-looking colleagues to accompany her. They loaded the car and did the 45-minute drive up to the Rifugio Sapienza, at an altitude of 2,000 metres. On the journey up, she made a great show of her shock that neither of the able-bodied young men she had instructed to join her had passed the training course to allow them to enter the crater. Although the thought of descending into it terrified her, it had been made clear to her what needed to be done and there was no question that she had to be the one to do it. The Rifugio was a rough and ready affair. Despite the thousands of visitors who passed through each year, the buildings were crudely functional. From the car parks, the visitors rode the chairlift up to 2,500 metres, then transferred into one of the rugged off-road, six-wheel drive Unimog buses that were used for the tours of the upper slopes of the volcano.

Cristina always felt that civilisation stopped at Rifugio Sapienza. It was an unattractive site, a bit like a 1960s Alpine ski station, which was exactly what it had once been. The chairlift from the Rifugio itself led up to the crater area, where the absence of any vegetation from the bleak cinder-grey landscape made it look more like a giant abandoned slag heap than a tourist destination. The chairlift wheel would spin like the winding mechanism from an old coal mine. The tourist buses bore the scars of hours spent driving on loose, gravel-surfaced roads. Their paintwork was stripped away and all of them were covered with a fine black dust. Then, there was the all-pervading smell of sulphur that leaked out of cracks and fissures every-where. Cristina thought that were she ever to find herself on Mars, this was how it would be.

They had transferred into one of the Unimogs to be taken up to the rim of the crater. The vehicle eventually jolted to a halt, alongside the CNSAS Land Rover and a 4x4 Toyota ambulance. There was a small group waiting for them, including the *Capos-tazione*, the station master, from the CNSAS, in his orange jacket and yellow helmet. Mario Verraci helped her lug her gear the last few metres uphill to the rim of the crater. Cristina was gasping for all she was worth, not just from the effort of the climb, but the thinness of the air. Given they were at an altitude of 3,300 metres, it would be hard going for anyone. She felt the cold air on her cheeks and regretted not bringing gloves with her.

The circumference of Etna, at its base, is 150 kilometres, but the circumference of the South Eastern Crater is under two kilo-metres. There is a well-worn track around it. In between erup-tions, thousands of feet had trampled over ash and other glassy material to form a rudimentary path. Cristina noticed the CNSAS had closed the area with yellow police tape and diverted high-altitude walkers away from the summit.

They reached a certain way along the path, at which point Mario pulled a monocular from his pocket and offered it to her. He pointed to the opposite side of the crater, a spot about 100 metres below. Cristina was rocked by a gust of wind and, for a moment, was fearful she might be caught in a flurry, lifted high into the air and dumped into the infernal ash pit. Sulphurous smoke drifted up, obscuring the view but, on steadying herself and putting the instrument to her eye, she could see the outline of what had once been a human being. The hair seemed to have been burned away from the scalp, leaving the dome of a blackened head. The clothing was charred and in rags. It looked as though one leg had somehow become disconnected from the body, though Cristina could not be sure. She could not be one hundred percent sure, but she thought the corpse had been female. What was certain, was that all life had left it.

She handed the monocular back to Mario, who stood grimly at her side, looking over at the corpse.

"Are you going to go down and check it out, or should we just get on with it?"

"He or she's dead, but I suppose I should have a look at the site and see if there's anything there to recover. Then, you can do your stuff."

They all walked around to the other side of the crater and Mario wondered what on earth she, a Vice Questora, was doing suspending herself over the side of an active volcano. He passed the harness over her legs and secured the straps around her waist. He attached a self-braking descender to the working line, so she could regulate the speed of her descent and, just as importantly, be assisted in getting back up. She borrowed some gloves and decided against using the tanks of breathable air. Although the smell of the gas was strong, Mario told her she would not be descending far enough down for there to be a risk of her being overcome by the fumes.

Cristina leaned back and let the rope take her weight. Her pulse hammered in her ears. Once she got into the rhythm, she found she could slide down relatively quickly. In her heavy protective boots and clothing, the heat soon started to build up and the sweat steamed up her protective goggles. Before she knew it, she had reached the semi-desiccated corpse. Reluctantly, she kneeled forwards, into the rock, and let go of the working line, but felt the harness tighten around her, as the safety rope was pulled taut from above.

She looked around the area and slid two fingers into was left of the body's trouser pockets, finding nothing. She then pulled a small automatic camera from her voluminous jacket. Gritting her teeth, she took some shaky pictures of the corpse, which she could now see was definitely female. Its facial flesh was charred and blistered and seemed loose against the skeleton. The flesh beneath the skin seemed to have deformed and softened. She looked at the hands for signs of rings, but the fingers had been burned away. There was nothing around the body that might help identify it.

The rope went tight and she pushed her back straight, and ostensibly starting to prepare for the walk back up the side of the volcano, but surreptitiously stood on the corpse, with enough force to dislodge it and send it slithering down the scree into the smoking pit of the crater. She turned to see the body gain momentum as its limbs flailed uselessly in mid-air. When she was sure the body was well and truly lost, she bent over and held her head in her hands, in a pantomime of self-reproach.

There were those who had already tried to dispose of this body and had never expected it to be found. They had told Capozzi to ensure the corpse slid to the bottom of the crater and was totally consumed by the fires and molten rock, as originally intended. That was why she had brought two officers with her who had no training in mountain safety or rescue procedures, so she would personally have to enter the crater and use the opportunity to give the body one last, unholy shove.

After pausing a few moments, to convince those above her that they had just witnessed a terrible accident, she gave the thumbs up and the rope was tensioned. With the lift from the rope and the ratchet on the descender, she pulled herself up the 70 degree slope.

Once at the top, she was exhausted. The cool wind dried the sweat that plastered her hair to her skull and ran down her body. She noticed the crowd at the top of the crater had grown and saw the rotund form of Claudia Nardi, a famously garrulous officer in the *Polizia Giudiziaria*, the section that conducted investigations on behalf of the Prosecutor. Italy is unique in not having a system of medical examiners or coroners, so post-mortem examinations can only be ordered by the prosecutors, who are part of the judicial system. Cristina guessed that Claudia had been there to decide whether to take the body for further examination, a decision that no longer needed to be made.

Cristina stripped off her heavy protective clothing, wiped her sweaty face on her sleeve and greedily gulped from a bottle of water. She walked across to thank Mario and his team. He nodded soberly.

"You, OK? What happened down there?"

She sank to her haunches.

"I'm sorry, I slipped and stood on her... him... So unprofessional. I'm so embarrassed."

"It's OK. At least you had enough guts to go down there and you saved us an unpleasant job. You got photos?"

"Yes."

"That's something."

She slowly headed over towards Claudia Nardi, who was describing, in detail, the gory crime scene of one of her murder investigations to a small group of CNSAS volunteers

"You're quick on the scene. You saw what happened? I'm sorry your time was wasted."

Claudia broke off from recounting her story.

"Oh, don't be. In fact, you've probably saved me time. Now, I can close the report, saying the body couldn't be recovered. You got any photographs? Yes. From here it looked like it'd been there for some time."

"There was a lot of damage."

"Interesting. When you write it up, can you give me as much detail about the corpse as possible? I need to try and guess a time of death. Tourists falling into the crater are bad for business! You're very brave, well done. Where's the young muscle anyway?"

Cristina laughed. Her two colleagues were standing 50 metres away, chatting and drinking coffee from a flask provided by the guys from the Rifugio.

"Don't worry, Claudia, I've got their number. This won't be forgotten. You think it was a tourist?"

"I'm hoping so. *Dio Santo!* Have you noticed, every time the volcano starts to become active, we get something like this? Someone in the office asked me if it might be a sacrificial thing. Can you believe it? People are so stupid. It just sets all sorts of rumours going. It's usually just the 'fire-chasers', looking for a thrill or messing around for a bet. Now the body's vanished into the flames, they'll take that as a sign of something or other!"

"What – you mean, some sort of cult thing? The Brothers of Etna?"

Claudia Nardi raised her finger to her lips.

"Shhh! For God's sake, don't start that one running! I don't know what I mean. I've probably been working on this stupid volcano for too long."

Cristina thought she might as well get the rumour going, as she had been asked to do. She knew that after a few words in the right places, word would soon spread around all of Catania. Claudia Nardi was as good a place as any to start; she was renowned for her loose tongue.

"It's odd you should say that," Cristina confided in her. "I'm going to say in the report, it looked as through the corpse was dressed in something like a priest's cassock."

Claudia's eyes widened in delight to be the first to hear this juicy piece of information.

"You can't be serious! Of course, I promise I won't tell anyone."

They both knew she would not be able to resist.

CHAPTER 14

SUPERINTENDENT GEORGE ZAMMIT

PRESTIPINO'S, CATANIA

GEORGE TOOK MARIANNA, Gina and Giorgio to the airport, together with their numerous bags. They had only brought one suitcase with them and George warned Marianna that, just because they could all carry three shopping bags in each hand, it did not mean the airline would accept they were only travelling with hand luggage. Marianna's approach to these things was always to assume everybody would see the world as she did.

"I'll tell the girls at the check-in, it's clothes for Gina's wedding. They'll understand, George. Who'd be so miserable to not let us on?"

"I'm sure they've got better things to do than look over our wedding outfits. But rules are rules, Marianna, they won't let you on. I'm telling you."

George foresaw exactly what would happen at the check-in and had earlier slipped out to the market and bought two very large, flimsy nylon holdalls, which were rolled up in his small backpack. When the inevitable argument kicked-off at the check-in desk and Marianna realised her mistake, he appeared behind her and paid the excess luggage fare, while Marianna sheepishly folded the clothes into the two bags and, with a gesture of defiance, threw them onto the scales.

George waved the family off and waited as their chatter disappeared up the departures escalator. He allowed himself a loud exhalation of relief, and found a small café where he ordered an espresso and two cannoli. One, was not quite enough.

After he had taken a sip of the sugary coffee and, eaten the first of the pastries, he steeled himself, dialled the number for Malta Pulizija HQ and asked for Assistant Commissioner Camilleri.

After a lengthy wait, the assistant commissioner picked up the phone.

"George, tell me, what do you know?"

"Sir, I thought you might like to hear where we are so far?"

"Very thoughtful of you, George. Proceed."

"Mela, you were right, the Questura has done nothing to investigate Silvia's disappearance. They have it down as some 30-year-old hippy who got bored with the camp and wandered off to find a new adventure. We've been to the site of the protest, talked to people in the camp and asked around. I strongly believe she's been abducted."

There was a moment's silence on the other end of the line.

"Abducted? What is your evidence?"

"The back of her tent was cut with a razor and the under-growth between the tent and the road below seems to have been well trampled. There're tyre tracks at the bottom of the trail. Now, all this is two weeks old, so of no real evidential value, but this place is 1,500 metres up a volcano, in the middle of nowhere. It's not exactly overrun with people. I'm sending photographs."

"Hmm. I see."

"There's more. She had arranged some high-profile press coverage and disappeared just before it was all due to happen. And we've been assigned a young officer from Catania Questura as a driver, who knew someone from the gatehouse at the plant – a former cop. They got chatting and someone inside let slip that... hang on, I'll get my notes... *she was the main troublemaker and they got fed up with her. They can search all they like, but they won't find her.'"*

Camilleri immediately asked the obvious question: "Who do you think *they* are? Who got fed up?"

"It's got to be someone higher up in the plant, hasn't it? It looks to me as if Silvia provoked the management at the plant and they organised her removal, abduction or worse."

"Worse?"

"Well, possibly, who knows? I mean, it is Sicily."

"Enough, George, do not let your imagination run away with you. I hear what you are saying. And this young policeman will swear to what he was told?"

"I'm certainly going to raise it with the vice questora and see what she can do about it. But this guard is a friend, or acquaintance at least, of our guy, so there'll be loyalties, you know? I'm not sure how strong memories of the conversation will be, if we ask them to make written statements."

"Yes. I understand."

"So, I can speak to the vice questora, get her fired up and then that's me done. I can come home?"

He held his breath.

"George, I never had you down as the quitting type. As I recall, you usually followed your adventures in Libya right through to the end. I was hoping it would be no different in the case of my niece. So, no George, you have made good progress so far, give it another week or so.

"And, before you go, I thought you should know, I had an interesting conversation yesterday with an old friend of yours."

George said nothing, waiting for Camilleri to spring whatever trap he was setting.

"Apparently, Maltech Energy are interested in the arrangements at Nuovi Modi and Her Ladyship was quite excited when I told her we had a man in Catania. I suspect, in due course, you will be asked to give her, or somebody working with her, an update on what is happening on the ground. Or rather, under-neath it."

George's heart missed a beat. The 'Her Ladyship', his boss, was talking about could only be Natasha Bonnici. The woman always meant trouble for George. She and MalTech Energy had their fingers in every lucrative energy scheme across the Mediter-ranean. It should not have come as any surprise that she should show an interest in the first geothermal plant and clean hydrogen project in Southern Europe. George was not exactly frightened of Natasha Bonnici, so much as wary of her. It did not help that her beauty and the aura she created around her, still made him blush in her presence.

At one point, Camilleri had been heavily involved with the Bonnicis and George had been dragged into her orbit on more than one occasion. He was well aware that she was ruthless, amoral and highly dangerous. But, over the years he had known her, part of him had fallen under her spell and he knew he was unable to resist her manipulative behaviour. The last time he had had any dealings with Natasha, she had sent him to Libya, to ensure his friend, Abdullah Belkacem, did her bidding and buried a stolen US nuclear missile deep in a mountain in the Nafusa hills, under hundreds of tonnes of concrete and rock. After that episode, when he and Abdullah had not parted as friends, George had vowed he would do his level best to avoid Natasha in the future. He only hoped he could find Silvia Camil-leri and be safely back in Malta before he became entangled with the boss of the Family again.

That afternoon, there was a serious earthquake in Catania. Buildings shook, car alarms went off and there were crowds in the street, as people fled their apartments and offices. The damage in the centre of the city was slight – some scaffolding collapsed outside a boutique on Via Etna – but a tower block in the Librino district, out near the airport, had collapsed, killing twenty people and leaving another thirty unaccounted for. Those who lived in the architecturally brutal 1960s and 1970s highrises went into their usual panic mode, which was justifiable, given construction incorporating earthquake design norms only became law in Sicily in 1981. A large proportion of the population of Catania, and, more particularly, Librino, lived in shoddily built, pre-1981 apartment blocks, highly vulnerable to seismic shocks.

A little before the quake struck in southern Catania, ash emissions were seen from the volcano. Three hours later, as if to signal its complicity, Etna violently spewed out a fountain of lava, known as a paroxysm, from its South East Crater. The exact same place where, the day before, Cristina Capozzi had lowered herself down into the depths. There followed several explosions of viscous basaltic lava from the throat of the volcano, each accompanied by dramatic booms, generating an ash plume that quickly rose 5,000 metres into the sky. Air traffic into Fontanarossa was briefly diverted to Palermo but, by the time evening fell, all was quiet again and the population of Catania put the events of the afternoon to the back of their minds and went about their business.

George had been driving back from the airport when these things unfolded and was horrified. He was in two minds about turning his car around and driving south to Pozzallo, where he could board the high-speed catamaran and be home in Malta in under two hours. But, instead, he telephoned Lucy Borg, who was sitting on the top terrace of the Giardini Bellini park with her binoculars, utterly absorbed by the show.

"Isn't it fabulous, George? You can feel the explosions vibrate right through you!"

"Mela, you're enjoying it – are you? You've got to be kidding! It's the worst thing I've ever experienced. I need to get off this island. We could all be dead soon! I don't understand these locals, they're just carrying on as if nothing is happening."

"Relax, George, it's just Mother releasing a bit of tension.

That's what the locals call the volcano, you know – Mother. I think it's quite sweet. Anyway, it's not the big one. Everything's fine for now!"

"Fine for now?", George was terrified.

"Don't worry, if the big one comes, we'll know about it well before it happens. Anyway, I've spoken to Del Bosco in Rome and told him what's going on. He's happy to have me here to take a secondment for a month with the Observatory. I'm doing my best to be invaluable to Ornella Mancini on the analysis front, so hopefully she'll get me my own desk in the office soon. So I'm not going anywhere until I find out what's happened to Silvia. We know there's a link between that geothermal plant and her kidnap. But, apart from that, we've hit a brick wall."

"True. We need to see Capozzi, but she's up to her eyes dealing with that collapsed apartment block. She's said she might be able to give us some time at the end of the day. Anyway, I've spoken to the assistant commissioner at home and he's told me to stick around and try to push on with getting some answers about Silvia's abduction."

Lucy noted the change in his language, from the hunt for a missing person to an abduction.

"So you're calling it that? An abduction – a kidnapping?"

"Well, suspected kidnapping would be more accurate. But, yes, I believe that's what's happened. I'll get hold of Diego. I want him to tell Capozzi about the conversation at the gate-house. For now, you get back to the Observatory. Find out what's going on with that volcano, for God's sake!"

As George continued his drive, northwards, through the clouds of fine grit and smoke, towards the forbidding black mound of Etna, he felt a deep sense of foreboding.

———

By 17:30, the plume of smoke and ash was just starting to dissipate. People ceased to nervously scrutinise the mountain above them. The entire city had been holding its breath throughout the afternoon and now it slowly exhaled *en masse*, gradually relaxing. The Catanesi were familiar with the behaviour of Etna – they had grown up with it, heard all the stories, but it loomed over them, never entirely forgotten, never taken for granted, always threatening the worst. That afternoon's display had been relatively modest, but the town was shocked by the death toll in the collapsed apartment block in Librino. That was not usual.

George was sitting in Prestipino's, nursing the last of successive coffees when a very subdued Diego entered. He sat down without saying a word, his eyes focused on the tabletop in front of him. Finally, he looked up at George.

"I'm sorry about the news."

George looked at him.

"What news, Diego? About the volcano?"

"No, George, the body."

George paused, the cup half way to his lips.

"Diego, what body! I don't know anything about this."

Diego, along with the whole of the Catania police, the Carabinieri, the Vigili del Fuoco, CNSAS, anyone who worked at the Rifugio Sapienza, the coach drivers from Catania who did the tourist runs and everybody else who was at the crater, or related to someone who was at the crater, knew that a body had been found halfway down it and the vice questora, no less, had gone in to retrieve it. But then, she had accidentally trodden on it, sending it sliding, right to the bottom, where it could never be recovered!

Diego's eyes lifted and he looked nervously at George. George asked: "Is it Silvia Camilleri? Is that what you're saying?"

"No! Well, if you don't know, that's good, isn't it? If they thought it was... well, if it was your friend, they'd have told you, wouldn't they? The fact they haven't means... well, it could be they haven't thought of it yet... but no, they're not that stupid, not all of them. So it's got to be good, I think."

George slammed down his cup.

"Come on then!"

"Where are we going?"

"I'm going to see Vice Questora Capozzi. You'd better go and get Lucy from the Observatory. Don't tell her anything. Just bring her to me at the Questura. Got it? I mean it, don't tell her anything!"

"Right. You can rely on me. I won't tell her anything."

"I hope so, Diego. Listen to me – you'd better not!"

CHAPTER 15
ASSISTANT COMMISSIONER GERALD CAMILLERI

CASTELLO BONNICI, MALTA

IT HAD BEEN some months since Assistant Commissioner Gerald Camilleri had been to Castello Bonnici. In truth, his relationship with Natasha had deteriorated over the past few years, due to her tendency to act impulsively, without his knowledge, and assume his forbearance towards even her most extreme acts. The assistant commissioner had enjoyed a long and mutually benefi-cial relationship with Marco, her father, based on trust, openness and respect on both sides. His daughter, however, had become disrespectful and, worse, capable of the most serious criminal behaviour, to which he was expected to turn a blind eye.

Finding the bodies of Nick Walker, Natasha's former lover, and his new girlfriend, floating dead in the Grand Harbour, had been infuriating enough, but he was certain she was also behind the fatal knife attack on Amy Halliday, the deputy editor of the *Malta Telegraph*. Halliday had published several articles accusing Natasha of underhand dealings in her wider business activities and, in return, she had pursued the journalist through the courts and finally had her slain on her own doorstep. Camilleri had put his suspicions to Natasha and she had dismissed them, with a wave of her hand, as not worthy of her consideration. He did not like unsolved murders – they upset the island's equilibrium and made it appear to others that he was not in control of events; a situation he found hard to tolerate.

Camilleri also knew she had murdered her way to the top of the Family, a fact that had caused her own father to disown her and retire to a more peaceful life in Serbia. As the head of the blue-blooded, ancient organisation, she now had access to enormous wealth and power. He feared she thought she had become untouchable. The worst thing was, she could well have been right.

When he arrived, it was early evening and a cold, north-easterly wind was blowing across St Paul's Bay and up into the hills where the castello stood. Katia gave him a warm, welcoming smile. Although she would never say as much to the assistant commissioner, the housekeeper also found working for Natasha more difficult than for her gentlemanly father. Katia ushered the assistant commissioner into the library, where the familiar smell of old leather, tobacco and wood smoke immediately reminded him of the pleasant winter evenings he had spent there with Marco, in what seemed a different age. Camilleri took in the atmosphere, briefly indulging himself in the thought that the place had hosted more worthy residents than the present occupant and, one day, he hoped, might do so again.

Natasha stood at a large mahogany reading desk, at the far end of the room, a sheaf of papers in hand. She looked as beautiful as ever, in black leggings and a knee-length grey cashmere dress. Her spectacles were perched on top of her head, pushing back her tumbling dark brown hair.

Gerald decided some gentlemanly compliments might work best to break the ice.

"Natasha, as glamorous as ever. You seem to look younger every time I see you."

Sha laughed.

"Gerald, don't bullshit me, I'm not a schoolgirl who needs humouring."

"That is quite true. So, with my feeble attempt at pleasantries out of the way, I will say good evening and ask what do you want from me?"

Natasha moved over to a large ancient leather armchair and sat in it, tucking her legs beneath her. She gestured Camilleri to another chair on the opposite side of the fireplace. Another vision flashed through his mind: this was always the chair Marco had favoured. He could see him now, at ease in it, sinking back into the soft hide, a pile of books stacked on the floor alongside him. He would stretch out his legs, crossing them at the ankles, wearing his rumpled cords. Regardless of the season, he usually wore checked cotton and wool shirts and finished the English look with his blood-red brogues. These were different times and Gerald Camilleri began to notice he had started to have nostalgic moments recently; he conceded it was probably due to his advanced years.

"Whisky, Gerald?"

Camilleri shook himself free from the past.

"Not for me, thank you."

She reached for a decanter on a side table and poured a small measure into a crystal glass, adding a drop of water from a glass flask. When she had finished, she asked: "How's your Italian history?"

"As sketchy as everyone else's, I would imagine."

"What do you know about the Kingdom of the Two Sicilies?"

"Ah! A little. The kingdom was formed when the Kingdom of Sicily merged with the Kingdom of Naples, which was officially also known as the Kingdom of Sicily. Confusing, no? Since both kingdoms were named Sicily, it became the Kingdom of the Two Sicilies, centred on Naples. It all happened in the early 1800s, if I am not mistaken? The new kingdom covered the whole of Southern Italy, what we now call the Mezzogiorno, and the island of Sicily, of course. It was swept away by Garibaldi, in

1860 something, during the Unification of Italy. Is that about right?"

"Perfect, full marks! So, a bonus point, if you can tell me who the current heir to the kingdom is?"

"Oh, dear! I am afraid you have me there."

"Francis II, last of the Bourbons of Naples, who died in 1894, was the King of the Two Sicilies from 1859 until he was deposed by Garibaldi. Apparently, his distant heir, Ferdinand III, known as the Count of Ragusa, lives on. He has a small estate in the interior of Sicily and sits there, lamenting his family's loss and brooding about seizing back his kingdom."

"Fascinating. What does Rome have to say about that?"

"Well, for one thing, they turned down his request for the return of the Royal Palace at Caserta. Asking for the largest royal palace in Europe as an opening gambit might've been over-reaching a bit, but he's still got ambitions and a following. And, as you know, the Neapolitans and those in the South have never been fans of being governed from elsewhere. So, if the time was right, I suspect he could certainly wring some concessions out of Rome!"

Camilleri was thoughtful.

"Just as the Lega Nord, or 'the Lega', would be happy to see the Northern states given greater fiscal freedom and regional autonomy. Are you suggesting the republic has to loosen its grip even further? The devolution of the nineties is not sufficient? The natives are getting restless?"

"Exactly. The problem is, good old Ferdinand is broke, and hasn't the resources to start a campaign or the nous to create a political movement. He's a bit of an eccentric apparently."

"Well, as I said, fascinating, but what has this got to do with me being dragged out on such a foul night?"

"We want to plant a seed, an idea. We want him to think about making the case for the South to be given more autonomy from Rome. Real autonomy – not, as you say, the failed federalism of the 1990s, where, what do they say, 'the North keeps the money and the South, the pain'. We can give the South something it has never had. Something that will make the North's eyes water. Something that will change the fortunes of the South forever. Bring wealth and prosperity, the like of which it has never seen, since the House of Savoy stole it a hundred and fifty years ago."

Camilleri narrowed his eyes.

"And who is 'we' in this context?"

"Let's just say I have my reasons for having someone in Naples who would be sympathetic to my interests and vision. As a city, it's a wonderfully anarchic place. It's rotten, corrupt, decadent and beautiful, all at the same time. The Neapolitans are a law unto themselves and have never truly accepted Unification. It's no coincidence that Cosa Nostra, the Camorra and the 'Ndrangheta all originated in the South. It's a different country. I think we can make it ours!"

Camilleri knew she was speaking on behalf of the Family. Such naked ambition shocked him to the core.

"Natasha, I am stunned. This is a stretch, even for a person of your talents and resources."

She looked at him, wondering if there was a barb or a hint of sarcasm in the comment. She put the thought out of her mind and continued.

"Contrary to what the school history books say, reunification did not rescue the 'poor South' from the greedy and lazy Bourbons. The South had wealth. Naples had culture back in the day, and the Milan-based House of Savoy in the North was bankrupt. Unification allowed the South to be pillaged, to pay off those debts. I know this because the Family was actually the biggest lender to the House of Savoy in the late 1800s. That's how we got our money back! So, you see, we can help the South right an infamous wrong."

Natasha smiled at Gerald. She held him with her gaze and

said: "You're still a somebody in the Sovereign Military Order of Malta, aren't you, Gerald?"

"Yes, I have that honour."

The Knights of Malta, to use their short title, were one of several religious orders of the Catholic Church, formed late in the eleventh century, at the time of the Crusades, to protect pilgrims on their way to Jerusalem. Strangely, the Order, based in Malta for centuries, has the status of a sovereign country and is recognised by the UN, maintaining diplomatic relations with over a hundred countries. In former times, membership was drawn from the ancient European aristocratic families, who took vows of obedience, poverty and chastity, but these days invitations are made to select Catholics whom the Order feels have the correct morality and, in their words, 'have acquired merit over the years'. Of course, Gerald Camilleri was just such a person.

Natasha had a game, set and match expression on her face. She clapped her hands and sprang to her feet.

"In that case, Gerald, you're just the person to mediate between the Family and old Ferdinand. The Count of Ragusa is a high-up member of your lot, with papal honours coming out of his ears. Ask him, as a good Catholic, if he can forgive a bunch of old Milanese money lenders who taxed his ancestors and, incidentally, if he's interested in stirring up some passions in the former Kingdom of the Two Sicilies."

Camilleri was shocked.

"Now you mention him, I recollect the good Count is actually a member of the Sovereign Military Order of Tripoli, not Malta. It's very different."

"How so? You're all the same, knights in a papal order and all that?"

"Well, no Natasha, that is not the case. When the Ottomans forced our order out of the island of Rhodes, the King of Sicily gave us the island of Malta and the port of Tripoli, in modern day Libya. Forgive the history lesson, but when the Ottomans were beaten back from their first attack on Malta in the 1530s, they sailed on and defeated those Knights who had remained in Tripoli. The Tripoli knights were mortified that their Maltese brothers did not come to their aid and petitioned the Pope to establish a separate order, the Knights of Tripoli. A few years later, they fled to Spain, as the Muslims gathered in strength. There, they gradually formed a more or less secret society that infiltrated the Spanish aristocracy and, particularly, the House of Bourbon. They were not a pleasant bunch and we strongly disassociate ourselves from them."

"Right, so our modern-day Count of Ragusa comes from a long line of aristocratic rogues and villains? Sounds like just our man."

"I suppose. What exactly do you want of him?"

"We've got a project to turn Naples into one of the richest cities in southern Europe. We want to restore Naples to a position where it is the rival of Milan, Rome, even Istanbul. We need a genuine Italian figurehead to seize the imagination of the south and help us with the politics of this transformation. Someone who the peasants of the south will respect and who the hooligans of the Mafia, the Camorra and 'Ndrangheta will accept. And someone who will work with us and who understands our ways!"

Camilleri slumped back in his chair.

"Well, I am shocked. How exactly do you expect me to do that?"

"Go and talk to him."

"And say what? I will need to know a lot more."

"All in good time, Gerald, all in good time. Just sound him out for now."

"This is hardly police business, Natasha."

"No, but it's Bonnici and Family business, Gerald. And that's much more important. And, as you know, it pays a lot better."

CHAPTER 16

ALBI BENEVENTI
BENEVENTI WINERY, MOUNT ETNA

In Sicily, there were two people everyone wanted to meet: Vito Amato, the dynamic young Mayor of Catania, who had created the possibility of the first net carbon-neutral city in the world before 2030! The other was the entrepreneur who worked with him, the legendary winemaker, Albi Beneventi, who had harnessed the power of a volcano to ensure the delivery of the cheap power and hydrogen that would fuel the city's long-term goals.

In the large tasting room at the winery, yet another group of 'fact-finders' had gathered, this time from the EU Commission in Brussels. Bastiano was running through their standard presentation while Albi tried to shut his eyes, if only for a minute, without being noticed. For some reason, he had found Etna's latest eruption particularly stressful and the sense of unease that had been building in him for several weeks was becoming more intense. In the background, Bastiano's nasal voice droned on.

"The first thing we did was decide where we wanted to play. We knew harnessing a geothermal energy source, so near a centre of population, gave us a great advantage. So, our decarbonisation strategy began with geothermal energy generation. Zero emissions. Achieved in 24 months.

"I won't go into all the details, but we raised capital from local sources and you guys, of course, and before long we could start on the second major strategy: decarbonising transport, electric cars and all public transport in the city, following a huge rollout of charging infrastructure. We provide the highest subsidies in the world for new electric car purchases, with low-interest finance available to residents through our own bank. The cost to the car owners is negligible if they charge at off-peak times. Once we had the cars on the way to being all-electric, we started on hydrogen fuel for heavier vehicles and shipping.

"We built the hydrogen plant to split a molecule of water into hydrogen and oxygen alongside the geothermal plant and haven't missed a day's production since. Thirty-six months, that's all it took! The city bought into the vision and Mayor Amato was crucial in getting this out there. You don't have to know all the details, but defining a vision is vital. You share it with the world to engage your stakeholders; it keeps you accountable and contributes to a change in societal norms.

"The spin-offs from cheap energy just keep coming. We supported the foundation of a tech park, with the hook being cheap electricity and a net zero-carbon environment. You remember the infamous Cara di Mineo refugee centre? It housed four thousand migrants at its peak and was effectively run by the Nigerian Mafia. It was a dreadful place. Mayor Amato closed it, we bought and repurposed it. In so far as we could, we reused all the existing materials, provided it with endless cheap power... and guess what? It's not pretty, it's not Silicon Valley, but it's net zero-carbon and now the biggest data centre in Europe. That took eighteen months. "

And on it went, until Albi got a firm nudge from Bastiano.

"OK, Dad, I've finished! You can wake up now."

Albi smiled and said: "I've heard it all before! Of course, while the new world was being built, I was doing nothing, just napping the afternoons away!"

There was polite laughter.

A voice from the back of the room piped up.

"A question. All this is possible because you use the geothermal energy of the volcano. We've seen today how volatile that can be. How safe is this project?"

Albi stirred himself and got to his feet. He looked at Bastiano, who eyed him suspiciously.

"I've got this one, son."

Albi put his hands behind his back and started to pace around the table, pretending to be deep in thought. In reality, this was a routine he had used any number of times to answer this particular question.

"We Sicilians have lived on and around the volcano for generations. Its soils are ground magma, spewed from the craters. Yet we farm them. The earth shifts beneath our feet, yet we build here. Now, the magma chamber floods under the city, yet we tap its heat to create a revolution in the world of energy.

"We have learned to watch, listen and adapt. The plant has an enormous protective wall and channel, on its uphill side, to divert any flow of magma. In 1669, we scrabbled onto the hillside above Nicolosi and dug trenches with our hands, to divert the lava. Nowadays, we can forecast its route, as well as the date and time of its arrival. The site, on the north-west flank, is the least active side of the volcano and, as far as I am aware, has never in living memory been affected by a lava flow.

"Look, there is always risk in any human activity. Remember what happened with the Deepwater Horizon rig off Louisiana? But still oilmen press for permits to drill in Alaska and Antarctica, for God's sake! Are we mad?"

"One last question, Albi, if I may?" It was the young, smartly suited German again, with the big hair and chiselled face.

"An operation like this must have cost millions – no, billions. Nuovi Modi has an impenetrable ownership structure. Why?"

"I think you know the answer to that, Signore. We are a

private company and our investors prefer to keep it that way. We have investors from all around the world – tech billionaires, Middle Eastern investors, even some Russian energy money. People brave enough to back radically new business plans, which, by the way, traditional conservative financiers shied away from. A project like this requires long-term commitment. We do not have time to nurse nervous investment managers, giving three-monthly presentations to fickle stockholders, humouring syndicates of banks, arguing with rating agencies. I want long-term relationships with real people, who are committed to last the course. Real people I can speak to, not faceless institutions. People who see what we do as the future. People who can act quickly. These people provide the capital and, the government in Rome and your good selves, have topped it up. We all recognise this is a climate emergency; we need to move fast. We have turned on the blue lights! That is what we have done – and it works."

———

Three hours later, Albi was at the wheel of a battered Land Rover Defender that was used around the estate. Several roads around the base of the volcano were closed, to head off the inevitable rush of volcano freaks up the mountain. In recent years it had become quite the thing for people, mainly young men, to try and get as close as possible to the lava creeping out of the fissures. Several years ago, three such 'freaks' were killed, when they found themselves in the way of a phreatomagmatic explosion. In these violent events, magma mixes with steam below the surface, building up immense pressure and then sending ash and rock skyward – in this case, together with the three Catanesi youths.

There were so many back roads and farm tracks around the base of the volcano that it was impossible for the police to close them all. Even when a road was closed, all that happened was a simple red-and-white-painted wooden barrier was dragged into place, barring access. Albi had driven round to the west side of the mountain, past the eerie blood-red glow from the cooling rivers of lava that had crept down the southern flank. The pillar of smoke had died down, but a thick, dark grey mass shrouded the volcano's peak. The townspeople and farmers were ready with blowers and brushes, to clear away the fine grey ash and black grit that had already started to fall.

He turned up a narrow road that wound steeply up over the lower slopes. He drove through the belt of citrus and olive groves, past a field of pistachios and walnut trees, for which the area was famous. He passed numerous small cottages and farms. It was dark and he was cheered by the homely glow of cheap, green electricity shining through farmhouse windows, creating little blocks of light on the hillside. Eventually, the road came to a dead end, like so many roads up on the mountain. After opening the gate in the fence and killing the headlights, he carefully drove across the rocky track that led to a wooded area, higher up the mountain. The smell of sulphur and the tangy, earthy aroma of burning forestry was noticeable, even inside the car. He lowered the window to feast on the magical scent and feel the sheer power of the forces around him.

He often felt the volcano was a living thing and he was one of many parasites that clung to its back. Mongibello, the old Sicilian name for the volcano, was to be feared, as it had proved earlier in the day. But it was also to be thanked for the largesse it bestowed on the people who lived around it. It had to be studied and understood, so its behaviours were no longer mysterious and secret. He saw it as a gift to the community, not a latent destroyer and taker of lives. In his mind, the mystical nature of the volcano loomed large. He had been born beneath its peak and would die there. It was the cycle of fire and renewal that captivated him.

The very rock was consumed by it, to be cast back into the world as lava, then degraded into soil, which in turn gave life, only to be reinterred by the next wave of lava. His life had been spent trying to accept this. He understood the cleansing power of fire, the wiping away of the old and the creation of the new. He felt he was part of that cycle, which made total sense to him. This acceptance was more important to him than almost anything else in his life.

His work with Nuovi Modi had revealed another part of the mystery – a gift from the volcano. Endless energy, given freely, a gesture from the natural world to help man stop his descent into climate chaos. He had tried to explain his feelings to Bastiano and Benedetta, but they did not experience the spiritual link to the Mother that Albi felt. His wife, Anna, was Dutch, so was, of course, totally devoid of any passion or spirituality. She thought Albi was slowly going crazy. As he searched more deeply within himself, to better understand his relationship to the volcano, she spent more time at their apartment in Milan.

He parked the Land Rover, just inside the cover of the forest's lower slopes. He noticed the ranks of other 4x4s and realised he had arrived only just in time. Reaching into a bag behind him, he pulled out a full-length grey, hooded robe and headed towards the small single-roomed chapel that nestled out of sight, in a small clearing amidst the pines.

CHAPTER 17
SUPERINTENDENT GEORGE ZAMMIT
QUESTURA DI CATANIA

GEORGE WAITED in Vice Questora Cristina Capozzi's office for over thirty minutes, before she arrived. Lucy had turned up a little after him, in tears, accompanied by Diego. He looked sheepish, as George tried to explain to Lucy that, yes, there was a body in the volcano, but no, it had neither been confirmed, nor suggested, that it was that of Silvia Camilleri. Diego had ineptly told Lucy the corpse of a young woman had been found in the volcano, all burned up, and they had to go to meet George, as he had some bad news for her. Understandably, she had feared the worst. George calmed her down, saying they knew nothing yet, and told Diego, in no uncertain terms, that he was an insensitive fool.

Capozzi entered, having just returned from dealing with the disaster in Librino, throwing her heavy, all-weather police jacket into a corner of the room. She stopped for a moment to take stock of the three visitors awaiting her, then collapsed into the chair behind her green metal desk. George realised she was a mess. The sort of mess that only comes from long hours spent under intense pressure, in difficult circumstances. She looked dirty, upset and exhausted.

He opened the conversation.

"Mela, we know what's been going on, and I can see what you're going through. I wouldn't bother you if it weren't important. So, I'm sorry, but it's quite simple really. We need to know if the body found in the volcano yesterday is Silvia Camilleri's. We deserve to know that much."

Cristina Capozzi did a double take. She looked from George to Lucy, and back again. She furrowed her brow, and the ash and dust on her face had the effect of deepening the creases that appeared there.

"Oh, I see! That's what this is about. How did you find out? "

George looked pointedly at Diego, who seemed to squirm in his seat.

"Er, everybody's been talking about it... well, up until the eruption, then there were other things... "

"So what are people saying, Diego?"

"Well, that it's a homicide, maybe. That the body was dumped in the volcano. The victim was a woman, dressed like a priest – I mean, that's shocking enough. You were lucky to find it yesterday. I mean – today, there would have been nothing left if it had been..."

"I can't believe it! That's all I need. Who told you this?"

"The guy at the petrol station, this morning."

"The petrol station! How did he know?"

Cristina Capozzi's mouth had dropped open and Diego looked as if he was just about to bolt from the room.

George butted in.

"Cristina, who told what and to whom is irrelevant just now. Is it Silvia? We need to know."

Lucy sat, knuckles of one hand in her mouth, eyes unblinking, staring at Cristina.

The vice questora took a deep breath.

"I don't think so. I couldn't even confirm it was a woman, but I'm pretty sure the body was the wrong height and build. And I'd say what hair was left on it, was fair, not dark, like your friend's. We couldn't recover the body, so we can't check DNA, dental records and all that stuff. But my best guess is, no, it's not her."

Lucy visibly slumped as the tension left her body. She put her head into hands and said: "OK, OK, I'll take that. My God, I didn't know you could feel like this, just sick inside, all the time."

"I'm sorry," said Cristina, "but news of this wasn't supposed to get out until we had more information. We've no idea who that person is."

George leaned forward.

"There's another thing. We believe Silvia Camilleri has been abducted."

The vice questora sat back and put her arms behind her head, to stretch her shoulders.

"Really? Abducted? Go on, tell me. My day really couldn't get any worse."

George outlined their visit to the camp, showed her his photographs of the tent and the trail, and then told Diego to recount his conversation at the gatehouse. As George had feared, Diego became a little more circumspect when having to put the finger on an old colleague in front of the vice questora.

George's patience with him was wearing thin.

"Diego, please stop dancing around and tell the vice questora what you told us or so help me…"

Capozzi stopped him.

"Superintendent Zammit! If anyone's going to threaten my officers, it'll be me. Agente Russo, give me a full and unchanged account of this conversation, otherwise your career in this force is over. Do you understand me?"

George smiled.

"Excellent! Couldn't have threatened him better myself."

Diego grumpily started again.

"You remember Natalino Lelli? He was based in Milo,

crashed an Alfa Romeo Volante on the coast road and there was the suggestion he might have had a drink?"

"Yes, I remember the whole thing. So he's now a guard at Nuovi Modi? He was absolutely plastered when he wrote off that car, but then was stupid enough to fall asleep in the wreck and be woken up by the paramedics, who thought he was dead."

"Well, yes, that's not exactly how he tells it. But, anyway, he said Silvia Camilleri was the main troublemaker, which the woman in the camp confirmed, and he said *they* – and we don't know who *they* are – got fed up with her. Natalino said, 'her friends can search all they like, but they won't find her.' That's it. I think he meant someone in the management had got rid of her."

Cristina sat stock still, her dark brown eyes boring into Diego.

"Right, go back to your desk, write up that statement, sign and date it, exactly as you've just told me. Then tomorrow, check Lelli's shifts and take whichever *sovrintendente* is on duty. Go up to the plant, with the sergeant, and pull Lelli in. If he refuses, arrest him for withholding information that might assist our inquiries. I want to know exactly what he meant. Don't let him go until you have an answer. If he won't play ball, let me know. We need to get to the bottom of this."

The three of them left the Questura, with Diego in a deep sulk. He turned to George, his face screwed up in consternation.

"You've made trouble for me here, you know. I don't know what it's like in Malta, but in Sicily you don't go around grassing on your friends like that."

George was not impressed.

"Well, it'll teach him to keep his mouth shut, won't it? And, hopefully, not to look the other way when someone gets kidnapped. He's ex-police, too. He should be ashamed. Lay it on him when you pick him up."

Diego grimaced and gave George a moody look.

CHAPTER 18
LUISA MARONGIU
PALAZZO DEL VIMINALE, ROME

THE MINISTER BREEZED into her well-appointed office and threw her handbag into the corner of the room before plumping her hair and kicking off her shoes. All in all, it had been a good day. Her speech, closing down several migrant camps in the South, had been well received, and she had averted a crisis in the Polizia di Stato, following some whistle blowing by a disgruntled young female officer in Poggibonsi. By calling for a far-reaching enquiry into institutional sexism in its ranks, she had kicked the subject into the long grass for years. By the time the findings eventually appeared, she would have left this miserable government and landed a few well-paid jobs on the boards of some leading European companies! She flicked through the pile of telephone messages, looking at the subject headings on the ministry's yellow forms. *Sexism, migrants, Etna, Etna, Sexism, Etna, migrants, Etna, Etna.*

She took off her tortoiseshell Gucci spectacles.

"Michele, what the hell's happening in Sicily?"

He was sitting in an armchair, working his way through a pile of the minister's briefing papers. He noticed her tone. It was as if everything that happened to disturb the smooth running of her life had to be his fault.

"Well, we've spoken about this. It's Mount Etna – there have been earthquakes and an eruption. It's not a problem you can just bury and forget about. Active volcanoes have a habit of making themselves known."

"Well, I signed a Legislative Decree for that good looking Mayor of Catania. He said he was happy to take charge, being the man on the ground and all that. What's gone wrong?"

"Well, maybe the volcano didn't get a copy?"

Luisa Marongiu retrieved her spectacles and pushed them into her mass of glossy, thick brown hair.

"Michele, sarcasm doesn't suit you."

He had worked with the minister for over a year and was fully aware of her reluctance to take responsibility for anything that went wrong.

"Well, there was an earthquake this afternoon and an apartment block in the Librino district in Catania has collapsed, killing thirty at least. I'm afraid you'll be expected to pay a visit. Probably tomorrow will work best. There's a draft statement on your desk. We can record it and send it out in time for the evening news."

"Oh, no! How terrible! But Sicily... really? Must we? Can't we talk about me closing the migrant camps instead? No one gives a damn about Sicily. It plays so much better to talk about closing the camps than a volcano we can do nothing about."

"Well, the INGV in Rome, whom you side-lined at the request of the good looking Mayor of Catania, you recall, feels rather differently about that. They say the possibility of a large-scale eruption has been known about for weeks. You remember our telephone conference with Del Bosco? They make the point that there's been a complete failure by the ministry to enact any of the civil-protection plans. They also say their recommendations that all pre-1981 residential apartment blocks in Catania, over five storeys high, should be retrofitted with additional support to enable them to withstand seismic shocks, have been repeatedly ignored by this office. Unfortunately, they're laying the blame for today's deaths at your feet."

Luisa felt as though she was going to faint.

"Del Bosco said *that*?"

She staggered back to her desk and slumped into her chair.

"Quickly, Michele, we need to act. First, it's only right and proper that I pay my respects to..." she pondered for a moment, then, speaking slowly and thoughtfully, said '... the victims of a previous administration's unenlightened health and safety policy in public housing.' Michele, make a note of that – I'll use it! And while I'm in Sicily, I'm going to visit the *direttrice* of the Observatory there – that Ornella somebody – and tell her to make a public rebuttal of Del Bosco's hysterical outbursts."

A tight smile spread across her face.

"That's the good thing about promoting women. Unlike men, they never forget who did them a favour."

CHAPTER 19

ALBI BENEVENTI
HOTEL SAN GIORGIO, TAORMINA, SICILY

The Hotel San Giorgio stood on the cliffs, on the promontory famous for its Grotta Azzura, overlooking Taormina Bay. From his seat next to the open window, Albi smelled the briny tang of the seashore below him and felt the light breeze ruffle his short white hair, brushed forward towards a peak in the middle of his brow. Years in the sun, wandering through the Beneventi vineyards, had deepened his skin tone to walnut-brown and left his thin face deeply lined.

Despite his appreciation of the finer things in life, Albi remained of slight build and had the agility and lightness of step of a much younger man. It was warm enough for him to wear his beige linen suit and white collarless cotton shirt. Albi always dressed plainly and had a restrained, yet highly cultivated style, uncommon in men of his age.

Unusually for an Italian, let alone a Sicilian, he was not prone to outbursts of emotion. His coolness towards others extended to his immediate family, where displays of affection were rare, if not unknown. Once the children had become teenagers and independent, their mother, who had become bored with life in the winery and their father's detachment, spent an increasing amount of

time away from Sicily. Her periods of absence in cosmopolitan
Milan had forced the siblings to adapt and to compensate for the
lack of parental attention by becoming ever closer. Even though
their respective apartments in the wing of the winery shared a
common dining room and lounge, their father would more often
than not be immersed in some report or article concerning the
wine trade, sustainable agriculture or developments in Green
politics. Conversation tended to be between Bastiano and
Benedetta, while their father was absorbed in other matters. They
had long since accepted that his remoteness was not hostility
directed towards them, but just the way he was, or preferred
to be.

While he waited for the others to arrive, Albi absently
watched the cable cars slide up and down the 200 metres from
the pebble beach below the town centre. The beach was covered
with blocks of *ombrelloni*, assembled in colour order, which were
rented out by the half day, at a cost few locals could afford. The
town, and the resort below, had an end-of-season feel to it, which
Albi always enjoyed. The worst of the heat was over, the summer
crowds had departed, and the staff had recovered some of their
manners. The dining room in the hotel was nearly empty and
their table had been carefully chosen, being screened from the
main part of the room by two pillars supporting large pots of
ferns.

Taormina was to the north of Etna, not that those few kilometres would save it, were Etna to slide into the sea, following the
monster eruption of Albi's nightmares. The town itself was only
a 50-minute drive from the port of Messina, where the crossing to
Reggio Calabria, on the mainland, took a mere 25 minutes. Vito
had driven north to collect their guest, a representative of their
principal investor. These meetings were always tense affairs,
which usually ended with Vito and Albi feeling as though they
had been physically assaulted.

Agostino Basso was not, as his name suggested, short, and the only time Albi had attempted to make a joke about it, he had been met with stony silence. Basso was an accountant by training, a good one, diligent in his appraisal of reports and accounts. But, unlike the archetypical accountant, he exuded menace and freely made threats which he was quite prepared to follow through on. Basso represented the investor group who had put several hundred million euros into Catania's green crusade.

What was not so widely known was that the same group had simultaneously bought the failing Beneventi Winery from Albi. The fact was unknown to Vito, Bastiano, Benedetta and the world at large. The price for saving the Beneventi fortune and its reputation, was that Albi and his family should become the acceptable public face of Nuovi Modi and their other related operations, reporting directly to Agostino Basso.

The identity of the investment group could be traced to a series of offshore investment funds and trusts, but nobody could put their finger on which specific individual or organisation was behind the ambitious and ground-breaking project. The investment group had claimed extensive experience in creating and managing renewable energy businesses. Several of their companies were behind the largest wind farms on Sicily. In the tomato-growing area of Pachino, in the south-east of the island, the group was Sicily's biggest provider of photovoltaic power, from hectares of solar panels.

Agostino Basso was aware that there was also a local 'supervisor', who reported back directly to the investment group. His or her job was to watch and listen to what was happening across the project and act as a check on Basso. He had no idea who this supervisor was and did not like the arrangement, but that had been the way of it for several years now and Basso was no nearer to uncovering the identity. He just had to live with it.

Albi rose to meet Agostino Basso and Vito as they made their way across the large white dining room, pushing their way to the table through the voiles at the windows, dancing in the breeze. The fish was a large turbot, firm on the fork and presented as good-sized steaks. Albi was pleased to see the wine menu featured Beneventi's finest and chose one of his own Carricantes. In other circumstances he could have wished for nothing better. However, this was business, not pleasure and like all of Basso's conversations, it took a while for him to get around to what it was he wanted to say.

"I understand the volcano is worrying you, Albi."

He looked up and nodded. Basso took a mouthful of fish and spent a few seconds chewing, before continuing.

"I accept Etna seems particularly active, but that is to be expected from time to time. Please note, we are not expecting any interruption to supply. Our plans until the end of the year would not allow for that."

Vito Amato glanced furtively across at Albi, as a mouthful of turbot disappeared from his fork. Albi noticed the look. Vito had obviously been stirring the pot.

"It's fine for you to say that, Agostino, but there's a lot happening here we don't understand. I don't want to bore you, but the volcanologists in Rome are saying some frightening things. We'd be foolish not to heed them."

"As I understand it, it is not the volcanologists in Rome we need to be concerned about. What do our own people in Catania say?"

"If I were to be unkind, I'd say – anything Vito tells them to say."

Albi had been waiting for this. Vito's move to bring the Etna Observatory under his control and woo the impressionable new director, Ornella Mancini, was masterful, but, in Albi's mind, it did not change a thing.

Vito clattered his cutlery onto the plate.

"Albi, that's out of order and you know it!"

Albi held up his palms in a gesture of capitulation.

"Let's just say, they haven't found their own voice yet."

Vito dabbed his mouth with a linen napkin. He swallowed and pompously said: "The current position is that the Catania Observatory feels the recent activity is nothing out of the ordinary and there's no need to be concerned. I receive a daily update from the director, Ornella Mancini."

Albi raised an eyebrow, but kept his eyes on the fish.

Agostino Basso looked at him.

"You accept that?"

"Frankly, no. Such data as we get from the Observatory, our own drilling experience and my own instinct tell me we're heading for trouble. If we have a blow out, drilling into a magma chamber or whatever, our people will be at serious risk. Heat, pressure and volumes of gas are increasing day by day. As you know, we tell the world we're pumping the same water and steam around in a circle, extracting the heat and sending it back down into the volcano. That's not fracking. But our explanation isn't quite true, is it, because we're also pumping water into an injection borehole. And that *is* fracking. It's my guess that this is causing local land subsidence and the recent swarms of quakes. My engineers recommend a short pause in the drilling, to see if the situation improves, and I agree."

Agostino Basso sat impassively, pushing small pieces of grilled courgette and aubergine around in the lemon-butter sauce. His intimidating gaze never left Albi's face.

At last, Basso dropped his gaze and skewered some vegetables. Without lifting his head, he said: "The director of the Observatory says we are not to worry, but your *guesses* and *instinct* say we should shut down the plant? I do not understand. That would mean huge disruption, a loss of confidence in geothermal power, a weapon for our competitors and the regulators to use against us. Catania would grind to a halt. Our financial forecast for the year would become undeliverable, our plans for the second and third plant would be compromised – all because you *guess* and *listen* to your instinct. Is this what you are telling me?"

Vito was looking on anxiously.

"I'm sure Albi doesn't mean he's going to close down the plant. You're just thinking of all the options, right?"

Albi refused to take the way out that Vito had offered.

"No, Vito, as the Chair of Nuovi Modi, I'm going to instruct the managing director to cease drilling operations from tomorrow, for one week, and we'll take stock after that. But the shutdown could be for longer. I don't know. I'm sorry, Agostino, it's the right thing to do."

Basso was still for a second, then violently pushed his plate away from him, sending his wine glass spinning onto the white tablecloth. He leaned forwards, getting as close to Albi as the table allowed. His voice was low and he spoke slowly and very clearly.

"Think again, Albi. Think who you are dealing with. Think of the money involved. And, when you have done that, think of how much you love your family." He paused, to ensure Albi had time to take in exactly what he had just said. "The plant keeps working."

With that, Basso rose from his seat and threw his linen napkin at Albi's chest. He looked at Vito for a few seconds and said: "Give me your car keys. Suddenly, I am in no mood for company. You will find the Maserati in the port car park at Messina." He looked at Vito and pointed to Albi, who cowered back in his chair. "Make sure he does as he is told."

As he left the table, he took one last shot.

"Albi, do not make us do this. If that plant stops working, you, your family, will regret it. I promise you."

As he walked back through the car park, Basso thought of the directors, the *Provincia* – sitting around with their cigarettes and cigars. They would not understand or care about the volcano, or the risks involved. Albi's concerns meant nothing to them. They just wanted the power on and to keep the money flowing. They did not appreciate how difficult his job was. For the millionth time, he wondered who this local 'supervisor' was and what he thought of the situation? If he could only find out a name, he could be a useful ally in dealing with the greedy, ignorant old men back over the water.

CHAPTER 20

GEORGE ZAMMIT

NUOVI MODI, PIRAO, MOUNT ETNA

THE NEXT MORNING the sky was a sharp, clear blue. Some of the pall of dust and ash had been blown south-west by a strong wind coming in across the Ionian Sea. In the greater Catania municipality, a clean-up operation was underway and thousands of shopkeepers, municipal street sweepers, caretakers and householders were busy clearing ash deposits from their front steps, the tops of cars, pavements and paths. Farmers, trying to protect the late harvest, were out before first light, using blowers, brushes and hoses to wash the destructive acidic deposits from the fruit trees and the vines. By lunchtime, signs of the previous day's catastrophe had all but disappeared.

Nervous eyes glanced upwards to the summit of the volcano, where there was still a steady plume of smoke and steam issuing from the vents on the southern flank. Occasionally, there was a boom from the main crater, causing citizens to turn quickly or look over their shoulders. Each explosion caused a puff of smoke, a small mushroom cloud, to rise up into the otherwise clear sky, as the eruptions continued to relieve the pressure within the magma chamber.

In Librino, engineers had deemed another two tower blocks unsafe and the police and Carabinieri were hastily evacuating them. It was to Sicily's shame that much of the construction of the 1960s and 1970s was undertaken by corrupt contractors and overseen by even worse public officials. The brutalist concrete blocks that replaced the historic baroque squares and villas across the country were often rich in sand and aggregate, not so much in more expensive cement. In Catania, as in most Sicilian cities, it was inevitable that these buildings would deteriorate and fail faster than they otherwise should have, a process not helped by the vigorous shaking they received every time the African and European tectonic plates rubbed up against each other.

By mid-morning, the Minister of the Interior had arrived in Librino, wearing a carefully chosen ensemble of black fake-fur coat, huge octagonal sunglasses, deep purple lipstick and mid-calf, soft leather Gucci boots. Holding the arm of her assistant, she picked her way through the wreckage of the collapsed apartment block and passed a few words with the exhausted Vigili del Fuoco coordinator, who had been working through the night, supervising the rescue operation. Her assistant brought her a small, dirty, tear-stained child to comfort and the Minister crouched down to wrap her arms around her, promising she would build the family a new house, not to worry, that she should pray to God and all would be well. Satisfied the moment, and the quote, had been captured by the surrounding press pack and, after some vague assurances of money to help in rebuilding the Librino estate, the minister dabbed her eyes and made ready to leave.

She brushed aside questions as to why the inter-agency emergency plan had not been put into operation, directing them to the Mayor of Catania, who had suddenly announced he was too busy dealing with the emergency to accompany her. A journalist's insistent voice bleated on about why Rome had not made funds available to strengthen vulnerable buildings, when the risks of collapse were widely known, but the Minister ignored the questions, turned on her expensive, but now scratched and muddy heels, to head back to the fleet of vehicles for the trip to Fontanarossa and the Air Force plane that would return her to Rome.

George watched the charade on the television in Prestipino's, as he waited for Lucy to arrive, joining in with the locals' derisive laughter. He saw her come into the café's side room, past the huge refrigerated displays of cake, cannoli and tarts, just in time to catch the last piece of TV coverage on the rolling news programme.

She stared at the screen for a few minutes, then joined him, saying: "Look at that Marongiu woman – mutton dressed as lamb! She doesn't give a damn, does she? She's the one who sold us down the river. Giving control of the Etna Observatory to Amato and making Mancini its director. Direttrice of the Etna Observatory... she was in PR! She's not even got a scientific background – it's a bloody disgrace."

George laughed.

"*Buongiorno* to you too! What news about Nuovi Modi?"

"Oh! Yes, I've some intel about the plant. I've got a friend in the Observatory and we chatted last night. Good news, really. There is a head of security, ex-carabiniere from Palermo, who's best avoided, but the day-to-day boss is the son of the Beneventi family, Bastiano. He's full of himself apparently, but supposedly OK to deal with. There's an army of technical directors and managers, but he deals with the press, investors, all the public-facing stuff. I thought we might try to have a word with him?"

George nodded, noticing that Lucy was still looking at the TV screen.

"Hang on! It's Ornella Mancini, she's making a statement."

The direttrice stood stiffly in the centre of the screen. Suddenly the minister herself entered the frame from the left, plumping her hair, licking lipstick from her teeth, and squeezed up against Ornella Mancini, pushing her to one side, ensuring she was in the centre of the shot.

After a lengthy explanation of the cause of the quakes, the direttrice of the Observatory concluded by saying: "The severity of the tremors was unprecedented and, I believe, couldn't have been reasonably foreseen by any of the authorities." Here, Luisa Marongiu nodded vigorously. "Certainly, we at the Observatory, didn't anticipate tremors on this scale. Personally, I'm not surprised these earthquakes, which were unfortunately centred on the area of Librino, caused such damage to buildings in the locality. It's my opinion, however, that the damage they caused was due to the severity of the event, and not the pre-existing condition of the buildings."

The minister looked on, concerned, and placed a sympathetic hand on the direttrice's shoulder.

Lucy laughed out loud and said: "Well, well! Nicely played, Ornella. That should keep you in post for a while. Doesn't it make you sick?"

It was the next afternoon by the time George, Diego and a reluctant Sardinian *sovrintendente*, or senior sergeant, Andrea Lamieri, arrived at the gate of Nuovi Modi for their appointment with Signor Bastiano Beneventi. They were greeted by an enraged Natalino Lelli, who charged out of the guard house and ignored George, going straight to the hire car's rear window and repeatedly thumping it with his fist. Diego sat in the back, wide-eyed and open-mouthed, uncertain what to do. The security guard leaned against the car, pressed his face to the window, and started shouting at him in Sicilian dialect, liberally spraying the glass with his saliva. George did not understand, but gathered from the look on Lelli's face that this was no welcome.

At the height of the commotion, George realised Sovrintendente Lamieri was sitting in the front passenger seat, studying his nails, eyes averted. He showed no intention of intervening, let alone acknowledging what was happening only a metre away from him. Finally, George flung open the car door and shouted at Lelli.

"Hey, you! I'm Superintendent Zammit, here to see Signor Beneventi. Now, shut up, will you, and lift the barrier."

At that moment, a short, athletic-looking man, with greasy, backcombed jet black hair, appeared from the gatehouse. He was wearing a white shirt with epaulette badges. As he drew closer, George noticed his eyes, so dark as to appear black.

"Lelli! Inside. Raise the barrier," he ordered.

The enraged guard snarled at Diego, flourished his fist one last time and retreated inside the building. The man with the epaulettes ignored George, who was now standing beside him, and went to the passenger-side window. Lamieri lowered it and the man with the epaulettes leaned calmly against the car door and addressed the sergeant.

"Lamieri, *come stai?*"

The sergeant shrugged and said nothing.

"Who're these types you've brought with you?"

The short man jerked his thumb towards the back seat, where Diego sat hunched, knees drawn up into his chest.

"This tub of lard's the *agente* who's caused all the trouble. And him, next to you, is some police type from Malta. Capozzi says to be of service."

They smiled at each other.

George decided it was time to assert himself. He was not a tall man, but he had learned to appear so by thrusting out his chest, stretching his spine and raising himself slightly on the balls of his feet.

"I am Superintendent George Zammit of the Maltese Pulizija. We have an appointment with Signor Bastiano Beneventi." He looked at the man in the uniform shirt. "I believe you've heard of him?"

Epaulettes gave a half smile.

"Not so quickly, Mr Maltese policeman, I'm Roberto Crisponi, *capo di sicurezza*, the head of security. There's paperwork to be completed. Follow me."

They left Lamieri back at the car and followed through the plant to the very contemporary office of Bastiano Beneventi. The slimline chrome-and-glass fittings were straight from a Milan design studio and the full-length window commanded a view of the forest behind the plant. Despite his Sicilian heritage, Bastiano was the epitome of Northern Italian style, in elaborately casual designer dress down. Unlike his father, he was short, but had the same lean figure as Albi. He had tightly curled light hair and a prominent nose, probably from long-ago North African ancestry. Heavy stubble was professionally shaped around his jaw, leaving his cheeks and neckline clean-shaven.

George immediately became conscious of his own ill-fitting suit from a chain store in the Tigne Point mall and hitched up his trousers under his paunch. Before the introductions were made, he noticed that Crisponi had casually taken a seat at the back of the room. George decided he would test the waters before the conversation proper started.

"Signor Beneventi, grateful though we are to Signor Crisponi for escorting us to your office, is it essential to have him in the room with us now? I'd rather speak with you alone. We may catch up with Signor Crisponi later."

"Roberto is my head of security and, as you wish to talk about a security matter, it seems to me to make perfect sense that he sits in with us."

George could only mutter: "As you wish." He caught a slight smile on Crisponi's face. Pressing on, he said: "As I mentioned in the message I left, Agente Russo and I are looking into the disappearance of one of the protesters from the camp outside, Silvia Camilleri."

George took a moment and rummaged in his portmanteau for a photograph that was passed around the room in silence.

"We believe she was abducted while at the camp."

As George had intended, there was an instant change in atmosphere in the room. Beneventi's face hardened. Crisponi scraped his chair against the grey tiles of the floor, as he shifted position.

Beneventi said, "That's a serious allegation. I hope it's not directed against anybody in this room?"

George maintained eye contact with Beneventi.

"As you might imagine, halfway up a mountain, there's a very small pool of possible suspects. Unless, of course, someone made their way up from the valley below. I'd like to take a look at the security footage from the night she disappeared, if that's possible? Interview the guards who were responsible for the perimeter that evening. Have a look around the facility."

Crisponi spoke from the back of the room.

"Forgive me, you're not police – on whose authority are you acting exactly?"

George looked pointedly at Diego, who started nervously glancing around the people in the room.

"Er, yes, right. I'm Agente Diego Russo, from Catania Questura, and, if it's OK, I'd like to look too."

"*Look too?*" Crisponi repeated. "What on earth does that mean, Agente? *Look too?*"

"Well, I'm investigating the abduction... well, the alleged, possible abduction maybe.... and given how busy the vice questora is with the tragedy at Librino, she's asked Superintendent Zammit to assist me. Help me out, sort of."

"It sounds like he's doing a lot more than *assisting*, Agente Russo?" Crisponi sneered.

Beneventi intervened, once Crisponi had made his point.

"Superintendent Zammit, our police must be under pressure, given the events of the last two days. We'll assist where we can, won't we, Roberto?"

Crisponi bowed his head slightly and said: "Of course, Signor Beneventi, but our files from our security cameras are regularly deleted, as they take up a lot of computer space. After all, who wants to watch hours of film of a perimeter fence?"

He shrugged to emphasise his point and said,

"And Signore Beneventi, the Catania Questura have already questioned Natalino Lelli about the evening the girl went missing and", he added with a smile, "I understand he told them everything he knew."

Beneventi then added: "I'm trying to understand your interest in all this Superintendent. This woman may have been, or still is, a Maltese citizen, but it's not every day an inquiry gets the *assistance* of a senior Maltese police officer."

George had been expecting the question.

"Silvia Camilleri is the niece of Assistant Commissioner Gerald Camilleri, head of the Organised and Financial Crimes Division in Malta. He's taking a special interest in the case, as you might expect."

Crisponi snorted.

"Hah! I get it, feather in your cap if you get it all sorted out, eh?"

George rounded on him.

"Mela!, tell me, who led the search around the plant for the missing woman? I understand you searched the area yourselves, when the protesters first raised the alarm?"

"Someone came and asked if we'd seen the big, bolshie woman. We said no but that we'd have a look around the perimeter, to make sure there hadn't been an accident or she had somehow managed to get inside."

"Did you check her tent?"

"Lelli went and had a look around the camp – just in case she was hiding or they were taking the piss, wasting our time or something."

George pressed on.

"And he didn't see her tent had been cut open from the rear, with a razor, and that there was a trail of broken branches and trampled grass going down to the approach road? Or tyre tracks at the roadside?"

Crisponi was silent.

"And the other thing I find strange is that her disappearance coincided with the press conference she'd arranged and a visit from a British newspaper and a TV crew. Why would she voluntarily leave the protest when she had just got the very publicity she wanted? Makes me wonder who might have benefited from that."

Crisponi said softly to George, "We're not the police, Superintendent, we manage security only inside the perimeter. We don't search for missing persons."

George opened his briefcase and pulled out a sheet of paper. It was headed with the crest of the Polizia di Stato and signed by Agente Diego Russo. It was his statement of what Lelli had said to him inside the gatehouse. George passed this to Beneventi, who took some glasses from a crocodile-skin case and read, frowning. As he finished, George passed him a copy of a second statement, made by Natalino Lelli the previous day.

It was made in the presence of Avvacato Enzo Pizzino, who grandly stated that his client relied on the rule *nemo tenetur se detegere*, 'no man is bound to accuse himself', and Article 6 of the European Convention on Human Rights, that conferred the protection of the right to silence. In the statement, Natalino Lelli refused to answer any question, other than to confirm his name.

George glared at Crisponi: "As your *capo di sicurezza* said a moment ago, your man was quite prepared to tell us 'everything he knew'."

Bastiano Beneventi looked aghast. He stood and walked

across the room to hand the statements to Crisponi, who quickly cast his eyes over the papers. When he had finished, he dropped them on the floor beside him and looked at Beneventi, shaking his head.

"I guess he didn't have anything to say."

George looked at Crisponi, shaking his head.

"Nothing at all to add, *capo di sicurezza*? Like, did you know about the press conference and the TV people's visit? Of course, you did! Signor Beneventi, there is something going on here and I need your help in finding out what it is."

Crisponi crossed his legs, turning his head to look out of the long window and watch the wind rustle the branches of the silver birch trees.

Bastiano Beneventi asked no one in particular: "Who is paying for Enzo Pizzino? It can't be Lelli, he charges a fortune."

Beneventi sat back down and looked at George and Diego.

"Gentlemen, you've caught me by surprise. You'll have to leave this with me. I need to make some inquiries and will get back to you then. I'm not happy that I'm unable to answer your questions. I apologise for that. In the meantime, Roberto will be as helpful as he can in supplying the CCTV and organising interviews. *Vero*, Roberto?"

"Of course, Signor Beneventi," he said over his shoulder, already leaving the room.

The *capo di sicurezza* led them back to the gatehouse without another word. George took off his high vis vest and dumped the protective glasses in a bin on the desk. Diego did the same, but his vest slid off the desk and onto the floor.

"Pick it up!" snapped Crisponi.

Diego swooped down and hastily retrieved and folded the vest, placing it on the desk.

George said to Crisponi: "We'll be back tomorrow to review the security footage. If you can have it ready, we'd appreciate it. And I'm sure Agente Russo will want to take your full statement and those of the rest of the squad. Please, no need to pay Enzo Pizzino any more fees. It just makes Agente Russo and me even more suspicious that there are things being held back."

Diego shuffled about, hands in his pockets, and examined what he could see of his feet. Feeling, rather than seeing, the intensity of Crisponi's black-eyed gaze upon him, Diego left the gatehouse as quickly as he could. As he entered the car park, he saw Natalino Lelli and Sovrintendente Lamieri, smoking and deep in conversation, leaning against the side of George's hire car.

Lelli noticed Diego approaching.

"*E tu, fottuto spione!* You – you fucking snitch! You know what happens to *pentiti*? Don't you?"

He walked right up to Diego, blocking his way.

The young man tried to summon the courage to respond.

"Hey, you can't go round threatening state police officers. I could arrest you for that – couldn't I, sovrintendente?"

Lamieri leaned against the car, his head tilted back, examining the incoming dark clouds, heavy with moisture, which had blocked out the morning's sunshine. As if inspired by what he was seeing above him, he blew out a jet of cigarette smoke that lingered around his head.

"Sorry, talking to me? Wasn't listening."

Diego started taking his notebook out of his pocket. Lelli laughed at him.

"What the hell are you doing?"

"Making a note of what you said to me. I'm going to send it to the prosecutor; she's pretty hot on police intimidation."

"Don't be so stupid, *ciccione!*"

"Don't call me Fatso, you know I don't like it."

George had followed Diego out of the gatehouse, eating a pastry he had taken from the hotel buffet for his mid-morning snack. He heard some of the words being exchanged between the two policemen. He brushed the crumbs off his mouth and took

Diego's hand, turning the notebook towards him, reading what was written. He smiled at Lelli.

"Yes, Agente Russo, I heard Natalino Lelli say exactly those words! I think you're right, there's just not enough respect shown to the police these days; the prosecutor has said so herself. So, how do we do this? Are we going to hear from you, Lelli, exactly what was said inside that gatehouse, or do we pull you in on a charge of threatening a police officer?"

George opened the car door and gestured Lelli to sit inside. He climbed into the passenger seat, slamming the door behind him, while Diego manoeuvred himself into the back, notebook at the ready.

George opened the driver's door to get in and looked up to see the expectant face of Sovrintendente Lamieri.

"Oh, I forgot about you, you were being so quiet. You can start walking down the hill. When we're finished here, we'll pick you up somewhere on the road. Perhaps."

CHAPTER 21

BENEDETTA BENEVENTI
BENEVENTI WINERY, MOUNT ETNA

BENEDETTA WAS A BIG WOMAN, with wide hips and heavy thighs, but that never seemed to slow her down as she bustled her way around the winery, clipboard or stacks of papers balanced in her heavily ringed hands. She had long straight blonde hair, carefully tended during a monthly visit to one of Catania's more expensive salons, where her nails were manicured, eyebrows threaded and any down removed from her top lip and cheeks. Catania was at least an hour and a half's drive around the volcano from Randazzo, but Benedetta considered the trip an essential luxury and had a standing two-hour appointment for the last Thursday of every month. She had her father's dark brown eyes, but her full mouth could suggest, unfairly, a sulky demeanour. But looks could deceive. Benedetta was an open, giving person, lacking the subtlety of her brother or the messianic zeal of her father. Her mother had always been an unapproachable and aloof figurehead in the winery, but the continued absence of the Signora had opened the way for Benedetta to carve out her own position in the business. She became the winery's sounding board, counsellor, shoulder-to-cry-on and den mother to the fifty staff who worked in the business.

She had also taken full advantage of the space created when

her father's and Bastiano's focus shifted to running the energy plant at Pirao. As children, teenagers, and now adults in their thirties, she and her brother had always been close. The emotional aloofness of their mother and their father's belief that his time was always his own, meant that, even when they were very young, they had spent many long hours in each other's company. Whether it was playing around in the vineyards, annoying the workers, or begging snacks and hugs from the staff in the kitchens, the winery was their playground.

As they grew up, both spent more time in the business. Bastiano had shadowed the viticulturists, who patrolled the company's several vineyards, working to enhance the yields and supervising the harvests. Benedetta was a born saleswoman, charming the buyers and local customers alike. Occasionally, as older teenagers, they would meet in the tasting rooms, where Albi would methodically coach them in an appreciation of the various wines and vintages held in their cellars. Their father would stick his expert nose into the glass and inhale deeply. Once the flavours developed, he would close his eyes and 'chew' the wine. Satisfied he had grasped its character, he would spit the liquid back out in an unapologetic burst, into a stainless-steel spittoon. Finally, he would open his eyes and say to the siblings: "Your turn!"

These sessions were one of the few times they had their father's full attention, so they took the lessons seriously and, in due course, had both gathered enough knowledge to guide experts and buyers through the winery's better vintages. Bastiano left home first, to study Viticulture and Enology at the Università Cattolica del Sacro Cuore in Piacenza. Benedetta followed two years later, studying marketing and business administration at the Università degli Studi di Palermo. She knew that, in time, Bastiano would assume the senior role in the running of the winery, it was the Sicilian way. He was the man, after all. She understood that and nursed no resentment.

It had been a shock when their father unexpectedly announced that he had come to an arrangement to allow a group of foreign investors to build the geothermal plant on some of their marginal land at Pirao, high up on the volcano. He had argued that the green energy it was going to produce would be a huge benefit not only to the city, but the whole metropolitan area.

Over the years, Albi had become more and more concerned about environmental issues connected to wine production. In response, he had developed an organic sub-brand from one of the vineyards on the south-eastern flank of the volcano, and had the viticulturists working on turning all the Beneventi vineyards organic within the next five years. The winery itself relied on energy from several hundred photovoltaic panels, arranged high up on the mountainside, and he had also erected several wind turbines to generate additional electricity. In winter, the winery was heated by hot water, flowing from an underground volcanic spring.

He had increased the biodiversity around the vineyards, encouraging the presence of birds, insects and other animals. He planted groves of olives and rewilded areas of marginal land that had formerly been mowed and strimmed. He had even changed the company strapline to read, 'Wines of character and conscience'.

It was this interest in sustainable production and geothermal energy, as well as the parlous state of his business, that had made him such a pushover when the investors came knocking. It was, therefore, no surprise to his children that Albi should become involved in something so unique, so radical, that it had never previously been attempted – a project to create the first net carbon-neutral city, decades before anywhere else. When approached to head it up, he could not refuse. But it was a shock to both Bastiano and Benedetta, when their father told Bastiano he would also assume a position in the new energy business. Albi had explained that, times being what they were, diversification was the way forward. It would ease his mind that the family were not totally dependent on the winery for their future, and that they could make such an important contribution to the well-being of the wider community.

Gradually, as building works progressed, Bastiano had ceased to be seen around the winery, unapologetically claiming his job at Nuovi Modi had become his priority. He became as enthusiastic about the project as his father was. One evening, he and his sister, as they often did, had sat in the smoking area behind the offices, which had the best view up the volcano. They had rolled a cigarette, sprinkled it with some hash, out of their father's sight, and enjoyed a bottle of chilled rosé with their smoke. It was a still evening and darkness was falling, casting the bulk of the volcano into silhouette, against the ink-blue sky. They had watched the last of the seasons migrating curlews and starlings, urgently heading south to winter in Africa. Somewhere in the distance was the faint hooting of an owl. Both had been quiet and Bastiano seemed unusually thoughtful.

He had put his arm around his sister and told her that, as far as he was concerned, she was now in charge of running the winery. He said he was certain she was more than capable of carrying out the job but, should she need his help, he had promised he would always be there for her. He had told her to change her job title from Marketing Director to Managing Director. He said he had agreed the change with their father. In truth, that had been the case for many months, but it comforted her to hear her brother expressly announce his faith in her. It was more than her father had ever done.

Over the next few months, Benedetta found herself alone and deep into the challenge of running the complex business of the Beneventi Estate, together with its restaurants, tours and hospitality activities. Usually, she had energy to burn, but even she often staggered back to her apartment, late in the evening, absolutely spent after the day's labours.

She had expected marriage, children and all the usual things that happened to young women in her position but, as time went on, none of that had materialised. She had earlier had the misfortune to spend two years with a local man, Marco, who had been the Sicilian buyer for an American wholesaler. They had met at a sales fair in Palermo, where she tasted love and he smelled money. Within six months, he had moved in with her into the family apartments and shortly thereafter, began assuming the privileges the Beneventi name conferred. After a year, he had ceased to treat Benedetta with any respect, let alone affection, and then gradually began to torment her, in all manner of subtle, underhand ways. Over the time they were together, his behaviour towards her had deteriorated to the point where it had become abusive.

A fist fight between Bastiano and Marco finally brought things to a head. Marco had commandeered one of the executive tasting rooms in the cellars and he, and some friends from the city, had broken the strict winery rule that historic vintages should never be opened without the approval of a second company director. Bastiano had come into the room while in the process of locking up the winery, to find a party in full swing, with half-drunk bottles of their best vintages, some over eighty years old, littering the tables. Marco was drunk and had become belligerent upon being called out in front of his friends. Words were exchanged and Marco struck the first blow.

Bastiano woke Benedetta to tell her what had happened and the two of them retreated to Bastiano's apartment, where they talked late into the night. Bastiano had suspected that his sister was unhappy with Marco but did not quite realise how serious things had become. They agreed she should leave first thing in the morning, to stay with their mother in the Milan apartment. Once the guests had left, white-hot with anger, Bastiano told a hungover and sheepish Marco that any permission he had to remain in the family accommodation was revoked and he had to leave that same day. Benedetta would write to him in due course, telling him of her intentions. Over dinner that night, Albi calmly listened to Bastiano as he recounted the episode. At the end of the tale, he spent a moment looking out of the window, up the mountainside, then asked Bastiano to make a list of the wine that had been consumed, so that stock records could be duly adjusted. It was his only comment.

After that, Benedetta found it hard to trust men or enter any new relationship. It was not long before she started asking herself questions about any new lover's underlying motives. The recent approaches from the odious Vito Amato were a case in point. She had seen the glamorous creatures who usually hung from his arm, as well as the contempt with which he treated them. His ridiculous attempts to woo Benedetta were laughable. She could clearly see the road down which he would take her. She knew he had no genuine feelings for her and expected her to be flattered by his attentions. Any relationship between them would only be so that he could have someone respectable and well-connected at his side, to enhance his own self-image. There was nothing in it for her. There never would be.

On the afternoon of the day after the earthquake had hit Librino, Benedetta had walked into the sitting room in the family wing of the winery and found Bastiano and Albi sitting in silence in chairs set either side of the large stone fireplace. Bastiano was twirling the ends of the ruby-red silk scarf he wore. The atmosphere was heavy with spent anger. Her father was reclining in his deeply padded armchair, drumming his fingers on the arms, studying the ashes in the grate. He barely glanced up when Benedetta entered.

She could tell something had happened between the two them. She turned to Bastiano and raised her eyebrows enquiringly.

"Dad's gone totally crazy," said her brother. "The volcano has finally claimed him!"

"Bastiano, enough!"

Her brother crossed one leg over his knee, showing an expanse of brightly coloured hooped sock. He folded his arms across his chest.

"Go on, tell her."

Albi looked at his daughter who stood, slack-jawed and wide-eyed, waiting to hear what disaster had unfolded.

"I've decided to close down the plant for a week, to see if stopping the fracking will calm the earth tremors."

"Dad's also worried about a magma blow out, something everybody says will never happen."

Albi sighed.

"Bastiano, I'm telling you, things are happening out there. Tuesday's quake was just the start of it."

Benedetta was confused.

"Well, what do they say at the Etna Observatory?"

"Dad doesn't trust the Observatory, now that it's run by the city, and not Rome."

Albi stood up and placed one hand on the cold slab of the stone fireplace. He gazed out of the window, looking at the forest, as it climbed up towards the shale and cinder volcanic desert, 2,000 metres above them. He spoke as if to himself.

"Sometimes you've got to go with what you can sense. I can smell sulphur in places I never could before. The surface temperature is warmer. I stuck my hand into some of the streams in the forest above Pirao that come from underground. You can feel the heat. Tuesday's earthquake was in the south-west of the city. There's never been trouble there before. I can't give you a scientific assessment, but I know there're significant things happening around the volcano. Something is telling me that I can't take the risk of continuing the work. It's just not responsible, or at least not until we know a little more. A week to fully review the site and the wells We need to work out if anything underneath them has changed. That's all I'm talking about. I don't see why everybody is getting worked up about it."

Bastiano looked at his father.

"What do the investors have to say?"

"They don't know I've done it yet. I told them I was thinking about it. They weren't happy."

"Jesus, Dad! You'd better tell them then and give them your reasons. They're not going to be pleased."

Bastiano and Benedetta exchanged a look. Bastiano had long-since realised that the money that had flooded into the whole Green Catania project was not from conventional banking or financial sources. He and Benedetta had wondered why their father had got himself involved with such people in the first place. Bastiano had tried to raise the subject of the investors on several occasions, but Albi had completely closed up. Bastiano had watched in frustration, as his father disappeared to attend mysterious meetings, often accompanied by Vito Amato, only to return visibly upset, and even more distant and uncommunicative.

If Albi thought withholding the truth about the relationship with the investors from his children would protect them, he could not have been more wrong. They, in turn realised the deceit being practised and became even more suspicious of their father's motives and behaviour. Bastiano had soon worked out who the investors were. It was not difficult, and the arrival of people like Crisponi only served to confirm his suspicions.

Albi approached his daughter.

"With the volcano being as it is, why don't you two go and spend the next week or so with your mother in Milan? Have a short break. She'd like that."

The siblings looked at each other in amazement.

Benedetta was first to respond.

"I can't just pack a bag and disappear. What's got into you?"

"Why?" Bastiano challenged their father. "What's going on?

What're you scared of? If the plant's going to shut, then the last place I should be is out of town! Or it looks as if I'm abandoning ship."

Albi slumped back into his chair.

"Please yourselves, but be careful. I'd hate for anything to happen to either of you."

Bastiano turned to his sister, who was shaking her head in disbelief.

"I told you – he's gone crazy! What does that even mean? Why would you say a thing like that?" Suddenly, it made a nasty kind of sense. "Have they threatened us?"

They took Benedetta the next day as she went to retrieve her car, having visited the salon in central Catania. The multistorey was in via Teocrito, near the market in Piazza Carlo Alberto, and Benedetta had found a space on the third floor. As she locked up her car and headed towards the lift, she was not aware of a black VW van, with tinted-glass windows, that slowly cruised past her and started manoeuvring into the space directly opposite hers.

On her return, her hair glossy and face glowing, she barely noticed when two men fell in behind her. One of them clamped a sweet-smelling rag over her lower face. The second scooped her legs from under her, just as the back doors of the van flew open. She fought, kicked and dug her nail extensions deep into the face of one of her assailants, pulling hard against the flesh. The van rocked a little with the tussle. Her efforts were rewarded with a stiff blow to the side of the head. She slumped to the floor of the van, dazed, and the fight went out of her. She could not resist. They bound and then injected her with ketamine, a sedative that would keep her quiet until she awoke, to find herself in the most total, sense-depriving darkness she could ever have imagined. Blacker than the grave, surrounded by the faint smell of sulphur and the drip, drip, drip of water. That was when she started screaming.

CHAPTER 22
SUPERINTENDENT GEORGE ZAMMIT
PRESTIPINO'S, CATANIA

It was the middle of the afternoon before George and Diego returned from the plant at Pirao to meet up with Lucy. She was an early riser and had already done a full day's work at the Observatory, so did not too feel guilty about taking a late lunch. It was still warm enough to sit outside, so they took a table in the piazza, facing the Duomo. The baroque cathedral was built on three levels, piled one on top of the other like a giant tiered wedding cake. The white and grey marble pillars supporting each layer contrasted with the dark lava blocks that formed the piazza. Small crowds of late-season tourists drifted around the square, posing before the Fontana dell'Elefante and standing in front of the Duomo, vainly hoping their phone cameras could capture the intricate details of the façade behind them.

The three of them sat outside in the piazza, under the soft afternoon sky, overawed by what Diego had ordered as a 'light lunch'. Their table was filled with a selection of spinach *arancini*, *cartocciate* and *pizzette*. The antipasto buffet also offered a range of *contorni* or side dishes and Diego had ordered a plateful of each.

George and Lucy admitted defeat, but Diego, conscious that he had been trusted to order, ploughed on, until most of the plates at least looked like they had been sampled. Once oil had been wiped from lips and fingers, crumbs brushed from shirts and the three coffees had arrived, George started talking about the morning's events.

"I don't know about you, Diego, but I actually think Bastiano Beneventi was shocked by what he was hearing. I genuinely don't think he knows anything about how security is managed up there. The really nasty piece of work is Roberto Crisponi. As *capo di sicurezza*, he seems to be able to do as he pleases. He certainly didn't seem frightened or even respectful towards Beneventi."

"Yeah, and that Natalino Lelli... well, I don't like him. And I don't think he likes me. Well, not now he doesn't. I don't like not being liked."

"Hmm." George pondered. "No, I doubt you're his favourite person."

Lucy put down her coffee cup.

"What happens now?"

George puffed out his cheeks and exhaled loudly.

"Mewl, from what we squeezed out of Lelli, we know that Crisponi knew about the press interest and was determined to stop it. We also know Crisponi hated Silvia and had targeted her as the most effective of the protesters. According to Lelli, Crisponi was alarmed by her knowledge of what was happening inside the plant, particularly the risks associated with the fracking and drilling; knowledge she almost certainly got from you, by the way. He refused to say Crisponi, or anybody else, had a hand in Silvia's disappearance, but confessed that Crisponi had said, 'that woman has to be stopped'. That could mean anything, of course, but I still think he's holding something back."

Lucy looked down into her empty coffee cup and swallowed hard.

"So, that was enough to get her kidnapped?"

"Quite possibly. Diego and I'll go back to the plant tomorrow to take statements from Crisponi and the other security guards. We'll have a look through the security videos for the night before the press were due. Then, we need to see Bastiano Beneventi again. Maybe he'll be ready to finish our conversation by then."

George felt a sudden wave of frustration wash over him. In truth, they were no further forward in finding Silvia and had no hard evidence she had actually been abducted. He didn't know where to look beyond the plant. The others must have had similar thoughts. The table lapsed into silence.

Not for the first time, he wondered what he was doing there. It had been nearly a week and he had not really achieved anything. This was not his problem to solve. He had no real authority in Sicily, no connections, no local support other than his 'team', if that's what you could call it.

George became aware of a short, slight figure, in the navy-blue uniform of the Polizia di Stato, walking quickly across the piazza towards them. She took short, rapid steps, hair bouncing with each movement. Vice Questora Capozzi headed straight for their table. George felt like a schoolboy who had been caught smoking in the village. Diego obviously felt the same. He leaped to his feet and deferentially offered his chair to the vice questora.

She sat down, looking disparagingly at the chaos on the table.

"Oh, you didn't let Diego order, did you?"

His laughter was a little too loud and sounded slightly manic.

"You were spotted here and I needed to get some air," she continued. "I've received some information that we think might help to identify the body found in the crater."

Capozzi saw that Lucy looked startled.

"Don't worry, it's definitely not Silvia. There's a suggestion it could be a kidnap victim who disappeared eighteen months ago. As far as I could tell, the body might fit the description of a girl called Simona Pappalardo. Her father is an industrialist from Gela, a supplier to the petrochemicals industry. He reported her missing and said he'd paid a ransom, some months back, but whoever kidnapped her never handed her over. There has to be a lot of bad blood there that we don't know about. We can't be certain it's her, but that's our best guess. Anyway, it's not Silvia."

George asked, "Does the father know?"

"Yes, he said he wasn't surprised. He'd been mourning her passing since Easter. I can't be any more certain than that of her identity. We've no body and, without it, there is no evidence of a crime. Claudia Nardi, the prosecutor, says without a body, she can't even open a file."

George considered the legalities.

"But you saw it?"

"Sure, I saw *a* body, but we can't definitely identify it, give a date or time of death and, most importantly, we can't give a cause of death."

Diego let out a low whistle.

"Tricky." He looked sidelong at his boss.

"So, with the cassock and all that, are we talking about the Brothers?"

"No, Diego we're *not* talking about the Brothers! You weren't listening to me. We don't know who took her and we can't dismiss the possibility of suicide or even an accident. We'll never know."

George heard the sharpness in Capozzi's voice, but he had to ask.

"Who are these Brothers?"

Diego was happy to explain.

"They're a bunch of local people and priests who worship the volcano and think that..."

Capozzi brought her hand down onto the steel tabletop, causing the cutlery to jump and come clattering down on the stacked plates.

"Diego, be quiet! George, they're a bunch of superstitious farmers. A cult that believes praying to the magical volcano will save their crops and livelihoods from damage. They might as well be praying for rain! They worship the divine, just not the Christian sort. There're some ignorant people around Catania," she continued, glaring at Diego, "who believe every strange occurrence or unsolved crime is the work of the Brothers! So, Diego, do something useful for once. Go and get me a coffee."

George stroked his chin.

"If it was a kidnap, how active are the Mafia and the 'Ndrangheta around Catania?"

"I haven't time for a lecture about organised crime in Sicily, but yes, the 'Ndrangheta forced the old Mafia families out years ago. The Cosa Nostra, remember them – the Godfather and all that? The heroin trade dropped off during the AIDs crisis, the Sicilians didn't like the risks of injecting, so coke became the new big thing. The 'Ndrangheta had all the South American connections. So goodbye Cosa Nostra, hello 'Ndrangheta. But you know this stuff, I'm sure."

"Mela, yes, I do."

"The other news I have, which might be relevant, I can't tell, is that Nuovi Modi has ceased operations for a week, as from this morning."

Lucy leaned forward in her seat.

"Really? Why?"

"Apparently, Albi Beneventi wants some additional geoseismic reports done, following on from Tuesday's quake, and has halted all activity around the boreholes, as a precaution. He was worried it wasn't safe to operate the plant."

Lucy chewed her bottom lip.

"Interesting. They've finally realised the dangers of what they're doing? Silvia would be pleased, if only she knew."

The table went quiet.

Capozzi said: "Don't worry. We'll find her, I'm sure of it."

She stood up to leave, glancing into the café where Diego was leaning over the counter, chatting animatedly to the pretty girl in a white sweater, working the gigantic Gaggia coffee machine. The girl had her back to him, ignoring whatever conversational gambit he was using. She turned and put the espresso in front of him. Capozzi watched Diego fumble in his pocket for some change, which he managed to drop onto the zinc countertop. In his attempt to seize the rolling coins, he swiped the espresso cup and saucer to one side, splattering thick black coffee across the front of the girl's white angora sweater. Her contorted face was a picture of shock and anger. Capozzi shook her head and quickly left, before the girl recovered enough to tell Diego what she thought of him.

He recovered his composure and sheepishly returned to the table, carrying a half-filled cup.

"Has she gone already? After I've brought her coffee. Well!"

He lowered himself into his seat, looking thoughtful, hands clasped in front of him. George and Lucy realised he had something to say and waited patiently for him to begin.

"You heard her shut me up about the Brothers? Well, it's all true. When you go up the volcano, most of the farmers and people living there believe all that stuff. Also, lots of the families were traditionally Mafia. I mean there's nothing really in that these days, it's just families or clans who work together, but you do still get bad ones. Call them 'Ndrangheta these days. They don't just do drugs and stuff. They're also big into kidnapping."

George and Lucy exchanged a glance.

"What're you saying, Diego?" George asked.

"Nothing."

"Yes, you are. Out with it."

"Well, there're stories about what goes on up the mountain. You know, about the kidnaps and stuff."

Lucy pressed him.

"What stories?"

"Stories about kidnappers holding hostages from Palermo,

even the mainland, in tunnels under the volcano. I can't imagine how scary that must be!"

Lucy thought for a moment.

"It's true, Diego. There are ways into the sides of the volcano. There're a dozen or so popular caverns tourists can visit – the Frost Cave, Snow Cave, Corruccio Cave, Serracozzo Cave, Three Level Cave – I could name a couple of dozen. They're all at around the 1,500-metre mark. But underneath these caves are extensive systems. People have guessed there must be over 100 kilometres of tunnels, but nobody knows for sure.

"From what I've heard, the quietest side for caves, and the least explored, is the west side. There's the Cave of Aci, but that's in Randazzo to the north. Some of these systems are accessed through cracks in the rock. Mind you, I don't think we should start exploring by ourselves, if that's what you were thinking?

She looked at George.

He said hastily: "That's the last thing I was thinking."

"Good, because these systems go deep. There're siphons and wells that drop steeply between levels. But it's an interesting thought."

Diego nodded.

"It's true. They're really dangerous. But they also say the Brothers have chapels in the caves, inside the volcano. It's kept secret and that's, like, what they're worshipping: the volcano. I suppose if you lived around the volcano, you could be a Brother, as well as a member of the 'Ndrangheta. You could be both."

George furrowed his brow. He was confused.

"Sorry, what're you talking about now?"

"Well, some of the Brothers are 'Ndrangheta, and the other way round. If that makes sense. I mean, they all live on the volcano, don't they? So, if you were a Brother and a kidnapper, you could use the tunnels to go to the chapels and to hide your victims. See?"

CHAPTER 23
THE BROTHERS OF ETNA
CHAPEL OF ST FLORIAN,
MOUNT ETNA

THE OLD PRIEST stooped to sweep away the layer of ash that had found its way onto the porch of the single-roomed, nineteenth-century chapel. He wore the full-length cowled grey habit of a monk, tied around the waist with a length of blue nylon twine. Beneath that, he wore a pair of walking boots, of Gortex and suede, with all-weather Vibram soles – a gift from a grateful member of the Brotherhood – so much better than the leaky leather boots he had worn for the last twenty years. A dozen or so of the faithful had gathered for the service today, not bad for a weekday afternoon, but the increased numbers were no doubt due to the recent earthquakes and activity around the various craters and vents on the volcano.

He put his brush to one side and opened the iron latch of the planked door that led into the chapel. The floor was covered with a thick bed of pine needles, gathered from the forest and spread liberally, to bring the congregation closer to the calming serenity of nature. Although the oils in the needles gave off a rich pine aroma for several days, they also lubricated the dark lava stone beneath, making the surface treacherously slippery to the unaware.

There was no electricity that high up on the volcano, so the chapel was lit by dozens of candles, hanging from crude wooden chandeliers or arranged in recesses and alcoves, casting an eerie, flickering glow over the whitewashed walls. Every niche or surface was coated with mounds of spent wax that rose in the form of miniature volcanoes, bathed in fiery candlelight. There were five rows of short pews to each side of the central aisle, long enough for four men to sit abreast.

At the small altar, made from two pillars of basalt and a single piece of polished black marble, two robed men were swinging dark-grey stone thuribles, made from drilled, pulverised lava rock, bravely plucked from the live flows of the volcano. The burning resin inside mingled with the aroma of pine, casting a pall of sweet-smelling smoke throughout the chapel. To the left of the altar was a Tenebrae hearse, a set of candles on an arrow-headed candelabra. To the right stood a model of the volcano in silver, studded with gems, copied from the original held in the crypt of Santa Maria del Carmelo, Nicolosi. In the middle of the altar was a silver Communion chalice for the sacramental wine and a covered silver goblet, the ciborium, for the Eucharist.

Behind the altar, the rear wall was completely covered by a mural of the volcano, as viewed from Catania, looking up at its south-eastern aspect. In the bottom right-hand corner, the brilliant white of the buildings and the child-like representation of the Cattedrale di Sant'Agata showed the centre of the city, bathed in bright summer light, going about its business without a care. The environs of Catania spread out into the distance until the colours and shading changed, darkening shadows cast over the red roofs of Nicolosi, 700 metres higher up the side of the volcano.

After that everything changed again. The lighter greens and pale yellows of the agricultural areas were shrouded by puffs of grey cloud, with tendrils of ash and tephra reaching down like long withered fingers. The forests above 1,500 metres were represented in dark and forbidding blackened green, flecked with orange and red, as fissures opened and vents started to spew the first flows of lava onto the lower slopes.

Above that, all subtlety was lost as the crater erupted with the full force of the artist's imagination. Blasts of white-blue fire roared from the crown, cooling to yellow flame and semi-solid rivers of pulsing black and orange rock. Fountains of lava were cast high into the sky, the lethal spray destined to land and ignite the pine, birch and oak forests below. A wall of liquid fire was rolling down the upper slopes, a terrible tsunami of molten rock, this time not to be diverted by a humble manmade trench. The top of the mural, up to where the wall joined the ceiling, was a mass of thick, tumbling grey and white cloud, so dense you could imagine walking across it. The cloud filled the top of the wall and spilled over onto the ceiling, just as in reality it would spread beyond the Sicilian sky and disperse the thousands of cubic kilometres of ash and volcanic material across far-flung continents.

To the left of the picture stood a half-sized painting of Saint Januarius, who protected people against volcanic eruptions, eyes looking down in pity at the plight of those whose prayers had gone unanswered. On the right-hand side, stood the figure of Empedocles, the scientist who followed Pythagoras and had promised eternal life and rebirth to those willingly surrendering themselves to the fire in the mountain.

The priest finished clearing the porch and entered the chapel, adjusting his cowl and keeping his back turned to the congregation of a dozen, similarly clad men. He started speaking in Latin, quietly at first, without too much inflection but, as he progressed, the words of the traditional Tridentine Mass started to flow. He had said these words many thousands of times, but the special sections and modifications he had included among them always thrilled him. In the secrecy of the chapel, the worshippers shared this special understanding, putting into words beliefs and emotions as profoundly held as those of any other faith.

This Mass was different, very different. Not only did it acknowledge the parallel practices of the Empedocleans, it confirmed their submission to a fiery cleansing and rebirth at the hands of the crater, as the mystical bowl into which life was received and renewed. The words of the Mass itself were altered to include the Mother as an addition to the Trinity; references to majesty, the dominations, the powers, the hosts, included additional mentions of the Gnostic and Hermetic traditions of antiquity. When the priest came to the Communion itself, not only did the congregation mingle their blood and body with that of Jesus Christ, but the lid of the small silver pyramid, representing the volcano, was lifted and the celebrant dipped his finger into the powdered grey ash within, and drew a triangle on every forehead, as a symbol of the pursuit of perfection the Mother required, to ensure the reward of eternal life.

Once the ceremony was over, the congregation gathered outside the dingy chapel, to chat in the sunshine. Cigarettes were lit and robes were neatly folded and placed in bags and cases, away from prying eyes.

A pair of older men stood talking earnestly in hushed tones. One was short and slightly bow-legged, a quarryman with a lifetime of back-breaking work behind him. His hands were in a permanently cupped shape; he was unable to straighten his fingers, but still quite capable of working a shovel or a sledgehammer. The other was thin and slightly taller, his pure white hair brushed forward to a peak. He looked to be some years older and had the same weathered walnut skin. The creases on his face came not from labouring breaking rock under the Sicilian sun, but a lifetime of tending vines.

The old priest came out of the chapel, saw the taller man break off the conversation and made his way across towards him.

"Father Greco, you've heard, no doubt?"

"Yes, Albi, about the woman in the crater?"

"They say she was dressed in a cassock."

"Yes, I heard. If it was a she."

"Well, what happened to her? Who was involved?"

"Albi, I do not know these things. Probably a nobody, of no concern to us. Do not believe the rumours. Whoever it was, they were put there by the hand of man, not on behalf of God. None of the Brothers would have been involved. This is other men's business."

Albi looked at Father Greco. He knew and watched everything that happened on Etna, from the scientific outposts measuring the gases and lava flows, the tourist expeditions around the summits of the craters, to the speleologists who squeezed thorough the lava tunnels and dived the watercourses. He also knew the families who used the terrain for more nefarious purposes. The smugglers and kidnappers, who still hid their bounty around, and under, the more desolate reaches of the mountain. They all co-existed, helping one another when necessary; the priest included. Nobody could afford not to, if they chose to live on the volcano.

Albi was curious.

"'Other men's business' you say? But who is she, the person in the crater? I suppose the police will never find out. Apparently that Capozzi woman kicked the corpse down into the fires. No chance of DNA or an identification now."

The old priest tugged on his white beard.

"I do not worry about these things. I repeat, they are not our business. You should not get yourself excited, Albi. Whoever she was, she has been claimed by the Mother. Who knows, maybe she found the perfection we all seek?" A benevolent smile crossed the priest's face and he laid an arm on Albi's shoulder. "I have been praying for her. Maybe you should too. "

CHAPTER 24

BASTIANO BENEVENTI
BENEVENTI WINERY, MOUNT ETNA

AT THE WINERY, mid-October was one of the busiest times of the year. As the vineyards were at altitude, high up the volcano and on the sheltered north side, the harvest was always late in the year. So, the grape-picking had just finished, with the fruit containing the essence of sun, earth and air now being pressed and processed. The large steel tanks were full of thousands of litres of deep purple juice, in the first stages of fermentation.

Normally, this was the time of year when the Beneventi family could relax or commiserate with each other, depending on how the harvest had gone. By this point, they knew what the year would yield, and the crop had to be accepted for what it was. The effects of a scorching summer, or early torrential rains, or a fall of volcanic ash at the wrong time, could ruin an entire harvest. From September onwards, the Beneventis spent a lot of time searching the clouds for any portent of peril. But by October, that anxious time was over.

One thing they did not forecast was that October would be the kidnap of Benedetta. It had taken a while before they actually noticed that she was missing. Sometimes the family dined together but, quite often, the three of them made their own arrangements.

It was Bastiano who realised his sister was gone. The previous evening, he had returned home late and registered the fact that her car was not in its usual place. Albi was already in bed, so Bastiano was not to know she had not been in for dinner. When the winery rang him at the plant, mid-morning the next day, telling him a group of German buyers was waiting to start their meeting with Benedetta, he realised something was very wrong. He immediately returned to the winery and tried to reconstruct her movements of the previous day. Her phone, bag and work diary were all missing; presumably she had taken them with her, wherever she was.

A colleague who worked with her in the tasting rooms told Bastiano his sister had said she was going to the hair salon in Catania. He discovered she had kept her appointment at Dimensione Eleonora. He knew, whenever she went into the city, she parked in the multistorey in via Teocrito, so he sent one of the sales team down to check for her car. When he received a call saying that the car had been found, safe and sound, on the third storey, Bastiano's heart lurched. He found Albi, who was entertaining the group of buyers over lunch, and dragged him aside.

His father was so shocked, Bastiano actually thought he was about to collapse and quickly ushered him towards a chair. He was muttering to himself, staring around, his eyes unfocused.

"No! It can't be. All my fault... My Benedetta... All my fault. Jesus! All my fault. I'm so sorry."

Albi started to beat his knees with his clenched fists.

Bastiano kneeled down in front of him.

"Stop it, Dad! Dad! What's your fault? What're you not telling me? What's your fault?"

"It's my fault they've taken her. Get Vito... bring Vito here. I'll kill them!"

"Dad, kill who? What're you talking about? Speak to me. Where is she? Do you think she's been kidnapped? Christ!"

Albi struggled to his feet and swayed a little. Bastiano

ushered him out of the tasting rooms, leaving the confused German buyers midway through their foie gras starter. Bastiano held his father by the arm and led him back to the apartments and upstairs to his bedroom, feeling the old man shaking, as if suffering from a fever. Bastiano felt helpless. The dread he felt was now several times worse than before. His father lay on the bed and turned his face towards the ceiling, disappearing into himself.

All he said was: "Bastiano, leave me and ring Vito now, please!"

He realised Albi knew more than he was saying. The speed with which he had accepted the gravity of Benedetta's disappearance, and his insistence that he was at fault, told Bastiano his father had had at least some foreknowledge of what might have happened. But why ask for Vito?

"Dad, forget Vito, I'm ringing the police. They're the ones who can help, not Vito Amato."

Albi leaped to his feet, his body rigid with a sudden burst of energy. His eyes blazed with a fury Bastiano had never seen in them before.

"No! No police! Get Vito, he's the only one who can help."

Bastiano recoiled in shock. He remembered his father's suggestion that his children should leave the winery and spend some time in Milan, with their mother. He suspected then that his father knew there was a good reason why they should leave. No use thinking about that now. What he had feared had come to pass: Benedetta had been kidnapped, and her brother was sure it had something to do with the shutdown of the Nuovi Modi plant.

CHAPTER 25

GEORGE ZAMMIT
HOTEL CELESTE, CATANIA, SICILY

GEORGE FELT as if he had hit a dead end. Capozzi was never available and, without her cooperation, his hands were tied. He understood the scale of the problems facing her: there was the aftermath of the earthquake and the investigation of the contractors on her desk, as well as the unidentified corpse from the crater. He could feel Silvia's case slipping down the list of priorities. George was supposed to be shadowing the Catania state police investigation. How could he shadow something that was not happening?

Then, the closure of the Nuovi Modi plant had thrown that element of his investigation up in the air and provided Crisponi with the perfect excuse to cancel their appointments. George had no official standing in Catania and was in no position to insist people give him their time. Even Diego, who had added an element of legitimacy to his inquiries at the plant, had been transferred from his minder duties to working with the team on the collapsed apartment block in Librino.

Lying on the bed in his hotel room, George conceded defeat. He rang Camilleri to plead his case to come home.

"I'm getting nowhere here. I've got no resources, no powers

to investigate, all hell is breaking loose and nobody is interested in a missing person's case."

There was a brief silence, before Camilleri replied.

"Do you still believe my niece was abducted?

"I do. But all I've got is circumstantial evidence, at best. Unless something drops out of the sky into my lap, I can't see how I can take this any further forward."

"George, this is a member of my family we are talking about. You say she has been abducted and I have to believe you, which means she is in some hellhole and probably in danger. I cannot accept you just want to give up and come home!"

"But there's nothing more I can do. We're all out of ideas!"

"Give it a few more days. If things are as hopeless as you say they are, we will think again then. For now, do your best, *Acting* Superintendent."

Something had caught George's attention. One little word.

"Acting?"

"Yes, of course, *Acting*. If a superintendent's job becomes available, it's yours. If not, well…"

"But you said…"

"Stick with it, George. I am sure you will come up trumps! And listen, since you are feeling stuck, I have to come to Sicily on business in a day or so. I was going to take a military plane and have it fly me to Cosimo, but I suppose I could come scheduled, direct into Catania, and then we can meet up and see if I can add anything to the situation. As you know, I am always on for a bit of teamwork and morale-boosting. So, that sounds like a plan, do you agree? I will be in touch."

"Right, I'll wait to hear from you." George cut the call.

He was shocked. Firstly, that Camilleri was threatening to rescind the promotion, and secondly, at the prospect of having to spend time with his boss. Just the two of them. For how long?

Feeling agitated, George decided the best solution was to go to Prestipino's for a coffee and one, or maybe two, of those cream pastries he had become so fond of. As he ambled down the road towards the Piazza dell'Elefante, his thoughts were suddenly interrupted by a mighty thunderous boom that resonated across the city. It rattled the glass in the shop windows and sent a flock of pigeons fluttering up from the small square ahead. Somewhere, a car alarm was activated. The city held its breath as a strange silence fell over the streets. But that was all, for now. The volcano pumped out a ribbon of gas and steam that spread into a giant mushroom shape as it gained altitude. And that was the end of the episode. The moment had passed. The eerie silence continued for over a minute, then cars started moving, voices called out across the street, life continued as usual.

George looked around awkwardly, feeling his heart beating a fast, incessant rhythm in his chest.

CHAPTER 26

BENEDETTA BENEVENTI

IN CAPTIVITY, MOUNT ETNA

WHEN THE SCREAMING and hyperventilation stopped, she was left with the sobbing. She shivered and shook. Even after what had seemed like an hour, her surroundings were still as intensely dark as they had been when she had first regained consciousness. It was as though some mighty force had sucked the light out of the world and left her blinded and buried in the dampness and cold. Shaking and whimpering, she searched around her, by touch. Her fingertips discovered she was lying on a low bed of rough wooden pallets, with a plastic-covered mattress. At the foot were two folded blankets and there was also a heavy-duty shopping bag that contained some items of clothing. A quilted jacket, a woollen beanie hat, thick socks and some large plastic sandals.

Nearby, she was aware of the sound of running water, a gentle but persistent babble. The sound evoked a small brook, with overhanging willows, reeds and adjacent green meadows. It provided some comfort. At the head of the bed, at about a metre off the floor, was a substantial rope, held taut by some arrangement she could not discern. She slowly clasped the rope with both hands and moved across the wet jagged rock beneath her feet, heading towards the water. Conscious that she had no idea of the height of the cave, she reached above her head, with every pace she took and soon concluded she must be in a cavern of unknown height.

Eventually, she reached the end of the rope, which was attached to a smooth metal stake, somehow driven into the rock. The rope travelled through an eyelet and was spliced back into itself and bound tight, with some sort of wire sheath. There was no chance of untying it.

She could now almost feel the water next to her. It gurgled somewhere beneath the level of her feet. She squatted down and placed her hand into the flow, feeling the cool water moving past her fingers. The stream was only a few centimetres deep and ran over a bed of loose pebbles. The course was not wide, she could easily straddle it, safely placing a foot onto the smooth rock on the other side. It was then that she realised the significance of the rope. This was to be her toilet. The tears began again.

She made her way back to her pallet. Feeling around at the base of the bed, she located the shopping bag and pulled out the additional clothing. It had not seemed cold at first, she was probably too shocked to register much but, after the first hour, she started to realise how the lack of heat and the damp would, from now on, become her enemies. Ticking off the basics of existence, she accepted she had a bed, some warm clothing, a process for relieving herself, but how was she going to eat? The thought of food made her stomach churn; she would rather start starving herself to death now, than spend weeks enduring an existence in total darkness. She had heard of people being held captive in caves and did not know how they had not killed themselves, in sheer despair or madness.

Yes, despair. That was what she felt. No clue what was happening to her, or why, or how long it might go on. For a moment, she wondered if whoever it was had taken the wrong person. They could not have had more than a glance at her, before she was bundled into the van. The four fingers of her right hand stung, where she had ripped off her nail extensions, tearing the face of one of the attackers. There was at least some grim satisfaction at that thought.

But she was part of the Beneventi family. The estate was famous all over the world. Suddenly a terrible fear gripped her. They did not have the sort of money people assumed they did. In fact, money had been an ongoing problem, ever since the quake of 2015. In the last two years their bank balance had begun to improve, but was not healthy enough to satisfy a group of rapacious kidnappers.

She lay on the bed and wondered how she would ever be able to remain sane in the days, weeks – she could not contemplate months – that might follow. She snivelled and moaned softly. It was the not knowing; not knowing anything. They would find her car, but what then? There would be a demand for a ransom. How long would that take? What would they ask for? Could her father and brother pay it, even if they wanted to?

It was then that she thought she heard the distant rattle of stones, high above her. A tinkling almost. She strained to hear more, her hearing now more acute in the darkness. At first, she thought it might just be a random slide of loose debris, brought down by the action of a watercourse. But no, the darkness was not as absolute as before; a faint white glow had appeared, not yet strong enough for her to see anything, but sufficient for her to make out shapes and angles on the roof of the cavern, at least 20 metres above her. Halfway up, there was a ledge and the light was coming from there.

She called out: "Hello! Who's there? Hello?"

There was no answer. Whoever was above her shuffled around, until she saw the light get brighter and suddenly, for a moment, blaze directly upon her, forcing her to shield her eyes. The shadows returned as the light source retreated from the edge of the overhang. Then, a plastic shopping bag appeared on the end of a line. This was gently lowered until it reached the floor of the cave.

"Hello? I need to speak to you. What do you want? Help me, please!"

Intense white light from a torch appeared, six or seven metres above her. She saw the silhouetted outline of a domed head, with bat ears.

A man's voice said in thick Sicilian dialect: "I'm only speaking to you once. After today, no more speaking. Take the bag. I come every day, but no speaking. Eat the food and drink water. Put the waste in the bag. I take it tomorrow. Use the water in the stream to keep clean. There's soap in the bag. If you make yourself dirty, like the other one, I'll not come again. You stay here for some time as punishment."

"Punishment?" She nearly laughed. "What've I done?"

"You hurt one man's face and his eye. He can't see good. He's very angry. That's why they keep you in darkness. Like him, he says."

She shouted: "Good, I wish I'd put both his eyes out. I hope he's blind!"

Benedetta felt her way across to the wall of the cavern and groped for the rope that was attached to the bag, frightened it might vanish back up into the darkness, before she had a chance to empty it. She took out a large plastic bottle of water, a stick of bread, one square plastic packet of something or other and a piece of fruit, which felt like an apple. As the figure started to shuffle around again, and the light faded, she started calling to him.

"Why am I here? What do you want? I can't help, if I don't know that."

She saw the empty bag jolt upwards, disappearing into the shadow of the overhang and then being pulled over the ledge.

The white light started to recede and darkness descended. The footsteps became a little fainter and the rattle of rock less distinct. Solitude and emptiness started to reclaim her. Enduring night fell.

She screamed, giving way to the hysteria she felt rising from her stomach.

"No! Don't go, please! Tell me what you want. I can help! Please!"

She collapsed in a fit of huge gulping sobs, beating her fists against the softwood pallet, her cries echoing around the pitch-dark cavern. Then, a phrase caught her attention. Which *other one*? It hit her like a punch in the stomach. There had been someone else here before her. Another person who had wailed, sobbed and smashed her own fists against her head in frustration. A 'her'? Yes, it felt like a her. What did he say? '*... if you make yourself dirty, like the other one...*'

She had smelled it. Faintly in places, more strongly in others. She had thought it was the natural decomposition of the cave, the damp and the rot, and her mind had been locked in terror and slow to process such details. But no, now she had been told, she could smell it everywhere. How long could the smell of human excrement last? Days... weeks? Surely not longer? This was recent. The last visitor was not long gone.

CHAPTER 27

VITO AMATO

CARA DI MINEO KNOWLEDGE PARK

VITO AMATO WAS SITTING in his black Maserati. A light drizzle was falling and he was considering whether the acid rain, from the sulphur gases discharged during the latest eruption, might damage the paintwork. He watched intently as raindrops pooled on the bonnet, imagining each one eating its way through the lacquer, to rot the metallic paint and leave a mottled finish of bare metal.

Out of the corner of his eye, he saw a minibus full of bubbly, business types decanting on the other side of the car park of the CatTech Data Centre. The facility was part of the new business park on what had once been the Cara di Mineo migrant reception centre. The new arrivals, from a German regional bank, stretched their limbs, donned their suit jackets and turned to the northeast, to take in the view. They were 50 kilometres south-west of Catania and about eighty from the summit of Etna, which rose majestically in the mid-distance, a lazy thread of smoke rising vertically from the crater into the still morning air.

The site had originally been a residential complex for US military personnel, stationed at the nearby Sigonella air base, until its closure in 2011. The park lay amid acres of orange and lemon groves, in the middle of nowhere, at the end of a long and winding country road. The politicians in Rome had thought it a convenient piece of wasteland to fill with 4,000 North African migrants, often hanging around for years, waiting for Italian bureaucracy to process their asylum cases. When it was discovered that putting this number of disillusioned, desperate, bored young men together could have undesirable outcomes, such as violence, intimidation, mental illness and a flourishing culture of organised crime, it too was closed and the occupants were dispersed.

Vito, as Mayor of the metropolitan district of Catania in which Mineo fell, had fast-tracked planning consent and ordered the demolition of the housing units and the recycling of as much material as possible, in order to build the new technology park. In exchange for almost zero-cost power and negligible rents, the council in Catania had found a willing partner in Agostino Basso's investment group for the redevelopment and financing of the site. The enormous CatTech Data Centre, with its hundreds of thousands of servers, had opened eighteen months after the first ceremonial tree was planted, operating on a zero-carbon basis. In the world of big business, it was an opportunity for companies to build their green credentials, without compromising profit. It had been a huge success. CatTech had particularly targeted its data-management services at insurance companies, health providers, banks and wider financial services, offering an efficient, attractively priced service, in a zero-carbon environment.

Alongside it sat ReachAd, which was another company owned by Basso's investment group. ReachAd gathered huge volumes of personal information and created databases of suitable targets for the growing industry of online advertising. Every time a webpage was opened and an advert appeared, it was likely to have been selected by ReachAd, based on the personal data it had harvested from the person innocently browsing the web. When an ad appeared on a Facebook page, a web browser, or in an email account, the chances were that a file of personal information had fed ReachAd's algorithms and that advertisement had been selected for that custom audience, making ReachAd one of the most successful companies in the multi-billion-dollar online advertising industry.

Quite simply, it had rapidly become one of the biggest and most effective global players, achieving better-placed ads and enjoying a better return on investment for its clients than any of its competitors. ReachAd claimed its success was due to the design and programming of its algorithms and the expertise of its management. Like most others in the industry, the company collected all the usual customer data from millions of users, such as dates of birth, gender, browsing history, purchase histories, locations visited, advertisements clicked – but what was not generally known was that CatTech also secretly transferred the personal details of the millions of customers, held by its health, banking and financial services clients, to ReachAd, illegally enriching its database with a vast range of confidential, but invaluable, financial and health information, not available to anybody else in the data-collection market. The investor group was delighted with the overall arrangement, but not with Albi's decision to cut the flow of power from the Nuovi Modi plant.

As the shower turned into a squall, Vito saw the trim, navy-suited figure of Agostino Basso leave the entrance of ReachAd to walk across the car park towards him. Abandoning the cover of the reception portico, he hunched his shoulders and quickened his pace as the rain, bounced off the tarmac around him. Vito leaned across and opened the passenger door. Agostino quickly slid inside.

"*Porca miseria!* This weather. One minute sun, the next rain! I swear, in Calabria it is different!"

Vito said: "In Calabria, you don't live under a 3,000-metre volcano."

"True." Basso ran his hand through his short brown hair and

then rubbed it over his heavy features, to rid them of any drops of moisture. "Have you seen or heard from Albi or Bastiano?"

"Yes, I was there yesterday. They're sick with worry about the kidnap. You've got her, I assume?"

Vito had gone through a range of emotions about his relations with Basso and his compatriots. When he had first been approached, four years ago now, he was wooed and courted. There were smiles, dinners, gifts... even women. He was the man everyone wanted to meet. A series of mysterious elders, some unnamed, from all walks of life, spoke of a future for Catania in terms that amazed him. Their vision for the city was incredible. A green revolution, using the volcano's unlimited geothermal power and free green hydrogen. They dangled the promise of the investment they would make in local businesses on the back of it, guaranteeing jobs and wealth for the city.

Vito also knew it would secure him further mayoral terms and even make his legacy. The fame and international acclamation that would inevitably follow were his to enjoy, these people wanted no part of the public profile. Had he thought of national politics? There were introductions to contacts in Rome, who promised to be of help. His re-election campaign was taken care of, funds cleverly routed through a whole series of people and businesses that Vito did not know. There was no end to what they could achieve for him, or the rewards they would pay.

But then, he had to deliver and not at his pace. No allowance was made for the speed at which the council moved, no chance for him to bring colleagues with him; everything had to be done at once, as if all he had to do was pull a switch and things would miraculously happen. He soon lost control of the agenda. Huge decisions had to be simply steamrollered through. Colleagues complained and challenged him. Many times, he had signed papers he had no authority to sign, granted consents and permits that were not his to grant. His reputation tumbled and the rumours started. Whose pocket was he in? What was he getting out of it? But all the time, in his ear, to his face, behind his back, the pressure was on to, 'Get it done.' 'Fix it.' 'Get on with it.' He had to style himself a man of action, a man certain of the rightness of his course, sweeping process aside, to deliver the glittering future of Catania. His wide smile and new veneers made light of the bureaucratic impediments. The radical Mayor of Catania brushed aside all complaints, to deliver the dream of the first net zero-carbon city. Many believed it was his essential nature, bold and brash. But the persona he put on was not easy to keep up because, by then, Vito was actually frightened.

He had seen their hard side. First, the contractor who cheated on his project, gunned down on site, in front of his brothers and workers, none of whom would say a word about what happened. Then, the stubborn old farmer who refused consent for the water pipes for the Nuovi Modi fracking wells to cross his land. Crippled now, with one hand crushed in his own woodworking vice. A colleague on the council who became difficult, too vocal in his criticism of drilling into the volcano, would nevertheless appear at Vito's side, terrified by the threats made against his daughters. As the pace of change increased, so did the instances of coercion.

The violence did not go unnoticed. Vito had spoken several times to two journalists from the Catania daily, La Sicilia, who had started to ask questions. They were looking behind the ambitious projects and were well acquainted with the ways of organised crime. Their focus was the less savoury aspects of the miracle that was Catania's green story. Vito voiced his frustration at the time spent fielding their enquiries and, within a month, the two journalists ceased to worry him. One left, with his young family, to work in the North; the second inexplicably retired, dropping out of public life entirely.

Then there was the kidnapping of the activist, who had been an annoyance, but whose disappearance had caused more problems than it had solved. And now, Benedetta! Poor, put upon, hard-working Benedetta! She did not deserve that. He felt sincerely sorry for her. He even found himself thinking fondly of her. He would make a point of taking her out, he decided, if they ever released her. Possibly, Villa Bianca, in the old town. He had heard it was good, and not too expensive.

Basso exploded into his chain of thought.

"Of course, we have her!" Basso said impatiently. "You were there, at the lunch. I told the old man what to expect, or as good as. It was only last week. I tried to be clear... maybe I was not clear enough? What is the fool doing? I do not want to get into all of this with him directly. So, I want you to talk to him. Today. Put it straight – get those generators on immediately. If he does not act, he knows what we will do to his daughter. She fought like a cat, blinded one of my men. She took his eye, with her stupid nails. He would happily finish her – no problem. We are serious, Vito. Then, tell him, we will come for him, which will leave Bastiano in charge. Our bet is, unlike his father, he will see reason."

"Agostino, come on! There's got to be another way. Why is it always the fucking nuclear option with you people?"

"Because that way, there is no bullshit! That is what it always comes down to. Either people do what they have to or... they do not. And if they do not, they know what happens next. I think that is fair. Everybody knows where they stand. Yeah? I am a simple man, I like to make things easy for people."

Basso ran his hand through his wet hair, which was sticking to his scalp again. Twisting the rearview mirror towards him, he checked his appearance, adjusting his plain navy tie.

"Now, can you take that very simple message back to Albi and tell him how it is? Just as I have told you. There is no discussion to be had. It is a binary position. Either he does it or he does not do it. It is up to him. But he knows the outcome. Our power will go back on, with or without him. Make it clear we will kill his daughter, then him, then I will personally turn the lights on."

Agostino twisted his lips in an unpleasant smile.

"Do you understand, Vito?"

"You couldn't be clearer."

"Good. Off you go! You have to shake hands with some German bankers. One more customer for CatTech, seven million more data sets for us."

CHAPTER 28

LUISA MARONGIU
PALAZZO DEL VIMINALE, ROME

HAKAN TOPRAK HAD ORGANISED a car to meet him at Rome's Fiumicino Airport. He liked having the security of a professional driver, who could negotiate the traffic in a calm and relaxed manner. It took the stress out of any journey. In every city in the world, he found local taxi drivers were impatient, hot-headed, and quite happy to risk their fare's life and limb, with erratic, high-speed driving. It was particularly the case with Italian taxi drivers.

As he entered Rome from the south-west, Hakan was struck by the differences between this city and his home, Istanbul. As the former Constantinople, Istanbul had once been the capital of the eastern Roman Empire. Following the split from Rome, it had flourished as the Byzantine Empire. Later, the Ottomans had, for 600 years, ruled one of the greatest trading empires the world had ever seen from Istanbul, until they threw it all away on the battlefields of World War One. But still, Istanbul remained one of the great commercial cities of the world.

Rome, on the other hand, after the split between the two imperial cities, became the capital of the Papal States, and its influence had waned. Hakan thought modern Rome had taken the jewels of antiquity and the Renaissance – the extravagant churches, bridges, town squares and public spaces – and turned itself into a living museum. So it seemed appropriate, when the driver pulled up outside the Viminale Palace, the five-storey, classically styled, hundred-roomed *palazzo*, and announced that they had arrived at the Ministry of the Interior.

Hakan had met Luisa Marongiu on several occasions previously and thought she was politically sharp and ambitious, but a ridiculous flirt. However, as she was responsible for Italian internal security, and the protection of constitutional order, he considered she would be a good starting point to begin sowing the seeds of doubt about what was happening in Catania.

Luisa Marongiu, on the other hand, thought Hakan Toprak was a prince amongst men. She considered him exotic, handsome, impeccably well-mannered and sophisticated. His sense of calm, self-assurance and poise made him...well, just so damn' sexy. Seeing his name in her diary that morning had caused a flutter in her stomach and, conscious of the forthcoming meeting, she had dressed with extra care. She favoured a fitted black Fendi jacket and a matching pleated skirt, finishing a little above the knee. Her black patent Gucci heels, that were reserved for special occasions, were carefully removed from their box and she squeezed her feet into them. Rather daringly, she failed to fasten the second button on the scarlet silk Moschino blouse, revealing a hint of décolletage and a centimetre of black lace underwear. She looked at herself in her dressing room's full-length mirror, patted her long brown hair and nodded her approval.

Her private secretary, Michele, looked her up and down as she entered the office, noting the difference in her appearance. He glanced down at the diary and mentally drew a circle around the 11:00 slot allocated to Hakan Toprak. It was going to be one of those days.

Hakan had arrived early. He and Michele stood in the minister's grand office looking out of the full-length window at the traffic on Via Agostino Depretis. Michele tried to gently explore what might be the purpose of his visit, and Hakan, being the assured politician he was, knew that a minister's aide was often as key to achieving his objective as the politicians themselves.

"Well, Michele, it is sensitive, but you know our sovereign wealth fund has interests in energy and we are now involved with the Maltese in exploiting marine resources in the Eastern Mediterrean?"

"Yes, the Greeks never stop going on about it."

"Well, yes. In this world there are winners and losers. And the Greeks are poor losers. Always have been. Anyway, we are alert to new developments in the energy sectors. Being where we are geographically places us right on the heroin route from Afghanistan through Iran, so our security forces take an interest in the activities of organised crime, often far beyond our borders."

Michele did not see the connection to any of his own concerns here.

"I'm sorry, Hakan, I'm not sure I follow?"

"Well, to be blunt, Michele, the whole green operation in Catania is funded, run and accountable to the 'Ndrangheta. Ownership of Nuovi Modi is fronted by a proxy and all this pretence about European billionaires and sovereign funds, covertly investing to solve the climate emergency is, frankly, nonsense. It is going to blow up, no pun intended, and then your minister will be damaged in the fall-out. I thought I should give you the heads up."

"I see." Michele went to the phone and made an internal call. "Marco, is the minister still with Guido?... Yes? Good. Do me a favour: make sure you keep her there for the next ten minutes, please.

"Talk to me, Hakan," he said, when he was able to give the visitor his undivided attention.

"The basics of what they have done work. As a model for a net zero-carbon city, that should be celebrated. However, they are a bunch of criminals and I worry that, sooner or later, that will come out, to Rome's embarrassment. While your ministers are travelling the world, boasting about the miracle of Catania's success, organised crime is profiting behind your back."

"You know all this for certain?"

"Yes. Definitely. As an example, their operation at the Mineo data centre is a front to steal and trade personal data, and, behind that, they have the world's biggest crypto-currency mining set-up. That is how they use the cheap energy you so thoughtfully gave them. That is their mindset. The entire city has been rigged for their profit. My sources tell me Vito Amato sits alongside them."

"The mayor?"

"Of course. Think about it. It could not happen without him, could it?"

Michele was thoughtful.

"Well, if you're right, the data centre's an issue, but the Bitcoin thing?... What's wrong with that?"

"Ah! I see you're becoming out of touch. Happens to us all. Well, what is wrong is that the EU and Rome gave the city and Nuovi Modi millions of euros to help build a geothermal power plant, to generate green electricity. They divert ten per cent of that power output into solving complex mathematical problems, to verify cryptocurrency transactions and are rewarded with new crypto-coins for doing so. These set-ups use huge amounts of electricity. In this case, *free* electricity, paid for by you and the EU. The 'Ndrangheta are raking in huge amounts of cash at absolutely no cost to themselves. Embarrassing, wouldn't you say?"

Michele was shocked. He slumped into a chair at the conference table.

"Sit, Hakan. Listen, thanks for the information. We are indebted to you." He looked at the Turk, who joined him at the table and sat in silence, waiting. Michele studied his inscrutable expression and unwavering gaze. "Well, what do you propose? You obviously have a play in mind or you wouldn't be here?"

"I have an idea the minister might like to consider. Your EU partners in Malta have an interest in MalTech Energy, as do we, the Turkish Sovereign wealth fund. We would all be very interested in understanding more about the geothermal technologies used by Nuovi Modi on Etna. They have suggested that if that technology and expertise could be acquired, we would continue the operation in Catania, the good bits of it, and apply the learning to transform other cities, elsewhere in the country."

Michele met Hakan's gaze, his large, dark brown unblinking eyes giving nothing away. Silence stretched between them. Hakan was always comfortable with silence. It meant the other party was thinking. Eventually he continued.

"You have heard of the Campi Flegrei, or the Phlegraean Fields? It's a huge calderic system to the north of Naples, manifesting as the volcanoes Vesuvius, Ischia and Campi Flegrei itself. There is the possibility of extending what has been achieved in Catania to Naples, and turning that too, into a net zero-carbon city. I suspect it would make Italy the world leader in addressing climate change."

Hakan smiled.

Michele immediately realised this was an idea that would be well received by the Council of Ministers in the Palazzo Chigi. On the other hand, the revelation that Catania was being run, at a profit, by organised crime would be shocking. It would undo the years of good policework leading to the super trials that finally loosened the Mafia's grip on the country. It would reinforce the old image of Italy being in the thrall of criminal enterprise, would certainly be a humiliation for the current government and would most definitely mean the end of this minister of the interior, who was responsible for internal security.

Michele set aside his personal reaction to this prospect.

"So, you want to displace the current ownership at Nuovi

Modi and take the learning to Naples?"

"Yes, that is about the size of it."

"And you can do that? Push out the 'Ndrangheta?"

"Oh, I think so. With a little help."

"Help?"

"A specialist anti-Mafia prosecutor or two, acting discreetly, to pick up some low-level types. I can provide some names. It will let them know you are on to them. The mayor's office would be a good place to start. Have a look at his sources of election funding. Let them feel the heat, give them something to think about and provide me with some leverage."

"Then you swoop in and let them off the hook?"

"Something like that. Then, obviously, we will need financial support if we are going to turn a city like Naples upside down."

At that moment, Luisa Marongiu flung open the high wooden doors and burst into the room. She held out her arms in an extravagant gesture of welcome. She cackled her high-pitched laugh, that she always used when she was nervous, and ignored Hakan's outstretched hand, advancing to smother him in an embrace, dowsing his shoulder in floral Lalique scent.

Michele gathered some papers and made to leave the office.

"Minister, Toprak *bey* and I have had a very interesting conversation, which I can fill you in on later. If you like, I can leave you two to chat, shall I?"

"Yes, that's fine, Michele, thank you."

Michele nodded to Hakan and raised an eyebrow meaning-fully, as he closed the door behind him. Luisa leaned back against the conference table, stretching out one leg, her skirt rucking up slightly to reveal a little of her lower thigh. Tucking her rich brown hair behind her ears, she sat back a little further, so that her satin shirt strained across her breasts.

"Now, Hakan, remind me. When was it we last saw each other? Was it Geneva? Tell me, you awful man, what've you been up to?"

CHAPTER 29

BENEDETTA BENEVENTI
IN CAPTIVITY, MOUNT ETNA

BENEDETTA LAY BACK on the rough wooden pallet and peered into the void above her. She closed her eyes and tried to engage her other senses. She needed to think, to control the shaking and breathlessness brought on by her moments of panic. If she was going to get out of there, she had to try and think clearly. Moments of clarity came and went, interspersed with bouts of tears and despair. One thing was clear. She had no intention of lying on the pallet and covering herself in her own shit, as she assumed the previous captive must have done.

There was still some fight left in her. She had always had to battle for what she wanted. Bastiano was the family favourite. A boy; a nice boy. Expectations of her were different. When it was clear, in her teens, that she would never be a beauty, her mother had put distance between them. Not deliberately, she just lost interest and found something more to her liking in the salons of Milan. But Benedetta had devoted herself to work and achieved more than Bastiano was ever capable of doing. It was enough to win her back her self-respect, but never enough to earn her the prize she most wanted – Albi's acknowledgement and respect.

After the embarrassment that followed Marco's departure, she never introduced another man into the family again. There were men, her name alone assured her of masculine attention, but she was wiser now. She felt the experience had diminished her, a humiliation from which she would never recover. Or, at least, not in her mother's eyes. But Benedetta had dug deep and lived one day at a time. Until now. This was different. Cast on her own, with only her own resources, in the cavern, it was purely about survival. She saw herself as a fighter, someone used to emotional adversity. She could cope, she would prove it.

She considered the strange man who appeared occasionally, she supposed it must be daily, although here there was no night and no day, just unending absolute darkness, so thick you could reach out and rub it with your fingers. Her first thought was to use the rope as a means of escape. Wait for it to be lowered, then grab it and try to climb the face of the rough, slimy rock. But she had no idea whether the rope was secured or if the man just held it. If so, he could drop it, leaving her to fall straight back, hopelessly marooned again. Or, if it took the strain, and she somehow got some purchase on the rock face, the rope could be unsecured or cut. That would see her tumbling backwards, from a height, onto the cavern floor, potentially injuring herself badly in a place where there was no guarantee medical help would ever arrive. She imagined herself just as she was now, but suffering the pain of an untreated fracture. It was more than she could bear.

The second option was to explore the cave. The supply of running water came from somewhere and must flow to somewhere else. There was the rope that led towards it. She could follow its course upstream or down, then retrace her steps back to the safety of the pallet. That had to be her first challenge. In a flurry of resolve, she took off her jeans, the quilted jacket and the thick woollen socks, but slipped on the plastic sandals from the carrier bag. She wanted to keep as much clothing dry as possible, to avoid the risk of hypothermia on her return. She only had to feel the slippery, wet rock around her to know that clothes would never dry, down here in the cavern.

Slowly, she followed the rope towards the gurgling water. Once she let go of it, things immediately became more difficult. She felt somewhat unbalanced. She lowered herself forwards, crouching down with hands in front of her, feeling the way ahead. One metre became two... two became three. Slowly, she made progress, descending as she followed the course of the stream. The counting was to give her some idea of the distance of her return journey, to ensure she did not crawl past the rope and become hopelessly stranded in the darkness.

After 26 metres of tortuous crawling along the side of the watercourse, hand over hand, foot over foot, the walls of the cave started to narrow around her. The only choice left was to enter the water itself. Reluctantly, she put her feet into the stream and instantly the ice-cold water chilled her feet. She was grateful that, back on the pallet, there were at least dry socks and her high boots. She pressed forwards, searching under the water for hand-holds and walking her feet crab-like behind her. Suddenly, her head struck the roof of the cavern. The sharp rock drew blood and she rubbed the gash on her brow, licking the warm liquid from her fingers. She bathed the wound in the iced water and dropped to her knees in the freezing flow.

The next minutes were terrifying. The sound of the water intensified and the depth increased. Soon water rose above her elbows and the lower half of her crawling body was submerged. Not only did she have to feel forwards to find the underwater path, she had to reach above her head and check the clearance in front of her. If anything, the absolute blackness had intensified. The dark had become more dense, more absolute. The channel narrowed further and the pressure of the water around her was becoming forceful, as the passage became more and more constricted. She realised there was now not enough room for her to turn around. If she chose to go back, she would have to scuttle against the flow of the water. For the first time, she realised her strength was ebbing. It occurred to her, she might not be able to make it back to the safety of the pallet.

The cold had eaten its way into her. Her long hair was hanging in sodden clumps and her woollen rollneck sweater was hanging loose, saturated and useless. It was then that she decided she had to press on, no matter what. To give up now was not possible; she had come too far. But the roof seemed to be closing in around her and the level of the water was nearly up to her shoulders. Instinctively, she lifted her head higher, to keep her face above the water, but only succeeded in taking another wound to her scalp from the jagged rocks above. Reluctantly, she lowered her face and let the water run over her shoulders and down her back. She continued to move forwards. Seventy-three metres from the rope. It might as well have been 73 kilometres. The prospect of a return journey was unthinkable. The cold had sapped her of strength and any sense of focus. She did not have the will to turn back.

The hand in front of her now felt rock, all the way down to the water level, barring the way ahead. The gushing water could flow underneath the rock, but she was at a dead end. She reached to left and right, but the rocky barrier extended beneath the surface of the water, which was now up over her shoulders. In a way, she had found the last 15 metres easier, as the water had supported her body and she had floated along, rather than carrying her weight on her hands and knees. But the cold had her now. She was shivering and shaking. In a last flicker of hope, she ducked her head under the torrent and stretched her hand ahead into the racing water. Passing it under the rock in front of her. Then, reaching up, it seemed her hand had become warmer, as though it had passed out of the icy stream and into a different temperature zone.

There was no choice really. Benedetta took a deep breath, submerged her head and wriggled forward underwater, her head banging, banging, against the submerged roof of the watercourse. She kicked and pushed with her feet, hands grasping at rocks on the bed of the stream, propelling herself forward. Her panic, the piercing cold and the sheer effort of moving underwater, consumed her supply of oxygen within seconds. Then, there was an unbearable pain in her chest and she felt her head starting to spin and peace descend upon her. But, finding a will to live she never knew she had, she made one last effort, kicking and hurling herself forwards, until her last reserves of oxygen were entirely spent and all her muscles started to slacken.

CHAPTER 30

BASTIANO BENEVENTI
BENEVENTI WINERY, MOUNT ETNA

VITO ARRIVED at the winery in the early afternoon and was greeted by Bastiano, waiting in the car park. Bastiano's hair was unkempt and his face pale and drawn. He walked swiftly across the courtyard to confront the new arrival as he climbed out of his car.

"Where've you been? He's desperate to see you and I need to know what the hell is going on here. Let's walk."

They set off towards the main entrance to the winery at speed. Vito was lagging behind and pulled at Bastiano's arm to slow him down.

"Look, I can't say much, this is for your father to explain. All I can tell you is to get the plant running immediately, this afternoon if you can, and then it'll be OK. You've got to do it!"

Bastiano was confused.

"What has the plant shutdown got to do with my sister disappearing?"

"Everything! Let's go and see Albi. He's got to explain it to you."

The pair of them walked through the shop and offices, turning the heads of the sales and accounts teams, before making their way to the family apartments. They went into the large, sumptuous lounge where full-length picture windows gave a view onto the mountain. Two or three new fissures, a little below the crater, were smoking away, making large cotton wool-like clouds that the wind was blowing westwards. Albi was sat in a large red velvet-upholstered armchair, shrinking into it, legs outstretched in front of him. On seeing Vito, he pulled himself up expectantly, grasping the arms of the chair.

"Well, have you spoken to him?"

Vito looked at the broken man in front of him. Overnight, Albi had aged. His red-rimmed eyes had sunk into his head and the lines on his face seemed to have deepened. Even Vito's arrival could not lift the slump in his shoulders or raise the timbre of his voice.

"I met him this morning at Cara di Mineo. He's not happy," Vito began.

He looked at Bastiano and then at Albi.

"Are we talking freely? How much does he know?"

Bastiano nearly exploded with rage. He stalked across the room and stood face to face with Vito.

"How much do I know? Enough! I know my sister has been kidnapped and that you two are to blame! What I don't know is the why or the how, but I know shutting down the plant has pissed off the so-called 'investors'. Yes, let's call them that, rather than what they really are. A bunch of gangsters. So, you can take it I know enough. Is that right, Dad? Are you going to be straight with me now?"

Bastiano looked accusingly at his father.

Albi had slumped back in his chair, head cradled in his left hand.

"It doesn't matter now. Nothing matters. We just need Benedetta back. I've made a terrible mistake."

Bastiano rounded on his father.

"You see, this is where you're selfish, arrogant attitude gets you. You always assume you're right. Nobody else matters. You just carry on as if we're not important. You guessed straight away what had happened, didn't you? Did they threaten you and you then ignored them? Is that what happened?"

Vito put an arm around Bastiano, who violently flung it away.

"Don't touch me, Vito. You're as bad as he is. The two of you are in this way over your heads and Benedetta is paying the price."

Vito said, "Look, there's something we can do. Start the plant, get it running and she'll be back. You're right Bastiano, you can't mess these people around. It's a message, Albi. Just do it. They'll bring her straight back, I know they will."

Albi glared at him but said nothing. Getting no reaction there, Vito spoke directly to Bastiano.

"He's got to restart Nuovi Modi, that's what he's got to do; otherwise, this situation is going to get a whole lot worse."

Bastiano saw the look in Vito's eyes. Basso had told Vito to scare the hell out of the Beneventis. That was what he was trying to do.

"Albi, if you don't get the plant back on, they'll kill her. Then they'll kill you. That's the message. OK? That's what he said."

Bastiano could not believe what he was hearing. He asked: "Who said that? What've you two got us into?"

He looked at Albi, then at Vito. Both of them remained silent. Bastiano took his mobile from the pocket of his trousers and waved it. Time to let his father know that he had worked things out.

"Right, given that we all know who we're really talking about here and exactly what they're capable of, I'm going to ring the plant and start it up. That's what this is all about, isn't it?"

Vito nodded.

"If that's the case then you call the investors, tell them what we're doing and that I want my sister back here, tonight."

Albi was tearful, rocking back and forth in the armchair, fists gently beating the padded velvet arms.

"I'm sorry, I should never have dragged you all into this mess. But it was the only way out. If I hadn't done it, we would've lost the winery. My life's work, your futures, gone. Generations of the family have run this place, I couldn't be the one to lose it. I couldn't face that. After the earthquake and the eruptions we were ruined. We couldn't survive after two lost years."

Bastiano turned to face his father. He said, more gently: "You mean, you borrowed money from them?"

"No, worse. I sold the land and the business to them, with a buy-back clause. If I do what they say and keep them happy, I can buy it back in five years, for what they paid for it."

"Madonna Santa! Then they've got you. You have mortgaged the future to them. Our future!"

"I had no choice."

"Yes, you did. Banks, other investors. Our brand is world-famous, you didn't need to put us at the mercy of criminals! "

"I didn't want anybody to know."

"Your stupid pride! I can't believe it. So we don't own the winery anymore and you were prepared to gamble Benedetta's life to save your pride? What sort of person are you? You let those people into our lives. Do you really think they're going to let you buy back the winery and everything will be all right?"

Vito kept his eyes down, looking at the floor.

Bastiano shook his head. He turned to Vito.

"I know what you got out of it. The office of mayor. You're a corrupt puppet, nothing more. A slave to those murdering bastards. Jesus! The pair of you disgust me. I'll make my call. Vito, you go and make yours."

CHAPTER 31

LUCY BORG

ETNA OBSERVATORY, INGV,
CATANIA

BACK IN THE NINETEENTH CENTURY, it was decided to build a volcanological observatory high up on Etna but, in one of those inexplicable cases that sometimes happen, what was constructed was an astronomical rather than a volcanological observatory. The large domed building, with stone walls a metre thick, allowed a huge Metz refracting telescope with a 34-centimetre lens, to provide views of the heavens from 3,000 metres above sea level. But by placing a precision optical instrument so close to the craters and fissures of an active volcano, the corrosive effect of the gases and unpredictable weather soon rendered both the beautiful German-engineered instrument and the astronomical observatory useless. The building then settled down to its original purpose as a volcanological observatory, until it, too, was abandoned in the early 1970s, when the volcano opened new fissures that threatened to swallow it whole.

The new, classically grand, Etna Observatory was rehoused in a former villa in central Catania, facing the formal gardens of Piazza Roma, safe from the unpredictable tantrums of the volcano, 30 kilometres away. The once stylish villa had been enthusiastically tagged by graffiti artists and the once grand square itself was awaiting the start of a significant regeneration project, but none of this affected Lucy, who was reflecting on how sharply her fortunes had changed. A week ago, she had nearly been thrown out of this building, today the director was her new best friend, asking her opinion on the reams of data coming in from the instruments scattered across the volcano.

Ornella Mancini guided Lucy to the conference room, making small talk and praising her contribution to the findings coming from the analysis and evaluation team. On entering the room, they were immediately confronted by a conference table large enough for at least twenty people. Lucy immediately recognised several senior managers within the Observatory, perched behind laptops. The atmosphere was sombre and only a few raised a smile as she walked in.

Ornella Mancini asked Tonino Gentile, the technical director, to provide an update. He summarised the recent seismic disturbances, the deformation of the southern flank in particular, the appearance of several new fissures, the temperature readings in a sample of the craters, the larger fissures and the latest sulphur-dioxide levels. As Lucy had expected, all had increased to predictable levels. He also explained that the pressure within the magma chamber was growing and the volume of molten magma was increasing. It seemed inevitable that a significant eruption was imminent.

Gentile presented the detailed figures, then pushed his chair back and clasped his hands behind his head. Lucy was familiar with the readings, but the most recent figures provided little comfort. Gentile looked exhausted.

"If this blows, it will be…"

Lucy interjected.

"We all know the possible consequences. What we also know is that they've stopped fracking at Nuovi Modi. They've asked us for an impact survey. I'm of the view it's a complete red herring and has nothing to do with the big picture."

"It might have created some additional local seismic stress, but you're right, it's irrelevant to what's happening here. All I would say is that they'd better be careful. The substructure of the volcano is changing rapidly, so if they keep drilling there's always the risk of a blowout."

Lucy pushed back her chair and thanked him for the update.

She turned to Ornella.

"If you agree, I'll get a view from Del Bosco, but I think we should tell Nuovi Modi that we don't need a full impact survey to advise that they can reopen the plant and continue to tap the volcano, while exercising extreme caution."

She shuddered to think what Silvia would have said had she heard Lucy say that. But, as a scientist, she was sure that, in the context of what was happening with the volcano, some pin-pricks on the relatively stable north side were incidental.

On the way out, Lucy took the opportunity to ask Ornella: "How do things stand with the mayor's office at the moment? Do they know about our new arrangement, co-operating with Rome?"

"Frankly, I don't know and don't care. For Vito Amato, it seems to be all about the site at Nuovi Modi. So long as that keeps running and his Green Catania remains unaffected, I honestly don't think he gives a damn. He doesn't get how big the problem is. Did you know, he's one of those Catholic Brothers who worship the volcano? Lunatics."

"No, I didn't."

"He says he just does it for the votes, but I know the man too well, I'm afraid, and I'm not so sure. He goes to their chapels and processions. When he was a boy, he was very close to the priest who revived all this stuff. Father Greco helped bring him up, got him into school and his first job. The Brothers' beliefs are all mumbo-jumbo, but there're still powerful social ties at work. Anyway, we argued about it and that's when I decided to ring Gianni again. Who wouldn't be scared by what's going on with

Etna? This isn't just a local matter anymore. A significant volcanic event could affect the whole earth. Meanwhile, if a few crackpots want to go and wave incense around in the woods, good luck to them."

CHAPTER 32
ASSISTANT COMMISSIONER GERALD CAMILLERI

CATANIA, SICILY

THE ASSISTANT COMMISSIONER arrived in Catania around midday, on a budget flight from Malta. The minute he stepped out of the plane he was aware of the pungent, sulphurous smell from the volcano gases, as familiar as the smell of a just-struck match. For a moment, he raised his clean white handkerchief to his face. He realised he would have to get used to the smell and replaced the handkerchief in his pocket, wrinkling his nose as he did so.

George was waiting in the arrivals hall, looking relaxed and slightly shambolic, his checked shirt hanging loose over some maroon slacks that Marianna had picked up for him in the retail parks of Catania. For the first time in their ten-year relationship, the assistant commissioner held out his hand in greeting, offering George a limp handshake. He took the long, cool hand with a degree of misgiving.

They did not speak until they were both sitting in George's hire car and driving back towards the city centre.

"So, fill me in. Where are we now?" Camilleri began.

George went back over the circumstances of Silvia's kidnap. He then talked about the mysterious Brothers and the strange cult of the volcano, which Camilleri dismissed as 'the patent nonsense that always exists around natural phenomena'.

Ignoring Camilleri's comment, George pressed on, mentioning organised crime in the area and a possible link to the mystical Brothers, who worshipped the cult of the volcano.

Camilleri said dismissively: "Interesting piece of local colour. Thank you, George. But I am more interested in solid policework."

As they drove north, into the city and towards the smoking volcano, George could feel Camilleri start to tense and saw his neck craning, so he could get a better view of the smoking mountain ahead. George realised just how awesome it must be to see the monstrous volcano for the first time and experience the true existential threat it posed. He smiled to himself.

"Mela, assistant Commissioner, it's a sight to behold, isn't it?"

"My word! It is quite alarming. And, as we are not strictly speaking on duty, please call me Gerald."

"Really? Yes, sir. Sorry... Gerald."

George than gave a potted version of what was happening with the volcano, gleaned from his conversations with Lucy. Camilleri was no less alarmed when George had finished.

They sat in silence for a few moments, before George suggested a plan of action.

"I think we need to get the Beneventi family onside. You can help there, sir... sorry, Gerald... as we've got no jurisdiction here. Lend a bit of seniority. If we both turn up and talk to them, we'll have a better chance of getting somewhere. But after that, I don't know what more we can do, except wait."

Camilleri nodded.

"All right, George. I will follow your lead. Anything to help. I shall stay for two nights, then I have an appointment in Ragusa. I trust you will be available to drive me?"

"Of course, Gerald." George already knew he would never get used to calling him that.

Later on, George was lying in bed, dreaming he and his Libyan friend Abdullah were racing across the southern Libyan desert in a Toyota pick-up, a warm wind blowing the earthy desert scent through the lowered windows and traditional Berber folk music blaring from the CD player. Out of nowhere, it felt as though the truck was hit by a mighty explosion. It was too big and sonorous to be a grenade or even a mortar. He felt the vibrations and shock wave hit him. It must be an airstrike.

He woke and looked up at the ceiling, taking stock of his surroundings. Gradually, images of the desert and the upturned Toyota faded from his mind when he saw the dangling pendant light of his hotel bedroom, swinging lazily back and forth. The cupboard doors had swung open and there was an eerie light behind the thin floral-patterned curtains. Outside, car alarms blared and there was the sound of raised voices in the street.

George got out of bed and slipped his feet into sandals. At the window, he pulled the curtains aside, displaying himself to those below, in his white singlet and baggy Y-fronts. His room faced across the public area of Giardino Bellini, giving him a clear view over the rooftops and up towards the volcano. Fortunately for George's modesty, the people in the street were all facing northwards where the night-time sky was alive with fountains of lava, jetting over a kilometre up into the heavens. The volcano's South East Crater was erupting in the most spectacular fashion. The crater itself was lit deep orange, with the sky above it glowing in shades from claret to crimson. The jets of lava eventually changed direction and rained down out of the sky, in orange and white cascades. On both sides of the crater, numerous fissures were also spouting lava like Roman Candles, and threads of it wound down to join the red and white-hot column of molten rock advancing slowly down the southern flank.

George was so in awe of the sight of the mountain, in its true, terrible, magnificence, he did not hear the banging on his door. Suddenly, the noise caught his attention. Lucy was standing outside in the corridor, eyes wide with excitement. She had not stopped to dress but thrown on a jumper over her pyjamas.

"Sorry, George, can I come in? I haven't got a view from my room. Can you see it?"

He opened the door a little further and Lucy brushed past him and went straight to the window, oblivious to the sight of him in his roomy Y-fronts.

"Wow! Look at that, it's incredible! Look at it, it's blowing through the South East Crater, the Voragine, and the Bocca Nuova, all at the same time. It's even making new fissures in the side of the cone. That lava flow is moving fast, which isn't usual." She paused and spoke, as though to herself. "Etna's magma is usually viscous and so it moves slowly. This lava is free-flowing, meaning the chambers are full of melt. I need to get to the Observatory. You stay here, George. Watch that column of lava. If it gets to Nicolosi, and hasn't cooled and slowed, think about getting in the car and going south."

"You're kidding? Do you really think so?"

"I do."

At that moment the room telephone rang. Transfixed by what was happening on the mountain, George answered it, without taking his eyes off the spectacle in front of him.

"George? It's Gerald. Are you looking out of the window? Is this quite usual?"

George could not help but laugh. With his hand over the mouthpiece, he whispered to Lucy: "The assistant commissioner wants to know if this is 'quite usual?'"

Lucy sniggered, just loud enough for Camilleri to hear.

"George, have you got a woman in your room?" he demanded.

George blanched, just as a tremendous flash lit the room, transforming the sight of Lucy at the window into an eerie photographic negative. Then, a fraction of a second later, the loudest sound he had ever heard sent him diving for the floor.

Lucy was thrilled.

"My God, volcanic lightning… It's the earthing of the positive charge of the fresh ejecta. Incredible! Right, I've got to go. Stay safe."

With that, she was gone. George decided there would be no more sleep for him that night, so he assured Gerald there was no woman in his room and told him, if there was word from the Observatory that the city was at risk, he would call him immediately. He then went to the window, pulled up a chair and rested his chin on his arms, slumping onto the cool marble sill. He watched, fascinated, as the blue-white arrows of lightning shot clear of the immense plumes of debris, blasting the volcano's flanks. Meanwhile, around the summit, flames rose higher by the hour and there seemed to be no end to the lava boiling out of the South East Crater and progressing down the mountain.

As dawn arrived, the scene lost the vibrancy of its night-time colours and the huge cloud of stormy gas and tephra mushroomed high into the stratosphere, kilometres above the summit. The whole city was now covered in a thick layer of black ash that lay heavily on roofs and blocked the gutters. The lava continued to flow, glowing rust-red and basketball orange, but the edges were cooling, black and dirty as old snow, while fresh basaltic rock formed new inclines on the cone. George thought the lava was moving more slowly, but it was still creeping inexorably towards the green forested regions of the mid-slopes, a giant scorching glacier, carving its way through the landscape.

He felt the coming of the cool dawn relieve him of the worst of his fears. It soothed him like a cold compress on his brow and, within minutes of sitting back in the poorly padded armchair in a corner of the room, he had fallen into a short but, deep and dreamless sleep.

CHAPTER 33

SUPERINTENDENT GEORGE ZAMMIT
BENEVENTI WINERY, MOUNT ETNA

THE NEXT MORNING, George and Camilleri picked their way through the aftermath of the previous night's eruptions and, to Gerald's consternation, drove up the northern flank of the still-smoking volcano, to the Beneventi Winery.

George had arranged to meet Bastiano there. On the phone, he had seemed more chastened than when they had previously met. George mentioned that an assistant commissioner of the Maltese Pulizija would be accompanying him, but in the capacity of a family member.

He parked where the tourist coaches and visitors' cars normally lined up. Today the immaculately maintained reception area was empty. Police roadblocks had isolated the upper reaches of the volcano, until the risk of injury from jettisoned rocks or streaming lava was deemed to have passed. George and Camilleri only managed to negotiate the roadblocks by showing their police identification and mentioning the name of Vice Questora Capozzi.

While waiting in reception, George perused photographs of past generations of the Beneventi family, hanging proudly on the native oak panelling. Moustached men of varying ages were dressed in suits and boaters, white woollen jackets, shirts with detachable collars and bow ties. Women accompanied them, in dark two-pieces with ankle-length skirts, carrying parasols or sheltering from the sun under elaborate hats. Children stood stiffly alongside their parents, seemingly at ease in the drab, heavy clothes they wore, dressed as miniature versions of the adults. They were all captured in and amongst the vines, surveying line after line of plantings. Dressed up in their finery, they were inspecting bunches of full ripe grapes, placing the timing of the pictures immediately before the harvest, in the heat of late summer. George wondered how they had survived the Sicilian temperatures dressed in those clothes.

Somewhere, in every picture, the photographer had felt it necessary to capture the ash grey summit of the volcano in the background, as if to fix the location of the shot. In some, the bare, cinder pyramid seemed merely a distant detail, the focus relegating it to the back of the photograph. In others, it loomed ominously close, dominant, making the overdressed Beneventis look insignificant and ridiculous by the sheer power of its presence.

When Bastiano appeared, George was surprised by his appearance. In contrast to the formal images of his ancestors and his smart casual clothes of before, he was wearing jogging bottoms, trainers and a baggy hooded sweatshirt. He saw George's surprised reaction and immediately apologised for his appearance.

"I'm sorry for the informality, things are a little fraught around here at the moment."

George introduced Gerald Camilleri as an assistant police commissioner in Malta and also a close relative of the missing woman, Silvia Camilleri. Bastiano nodded respectfully and gestured for them to follow him up to the private apartments.

It was not only Bastiano's informal dress that caught George's eye, it was also the tension written across his face and the bags under his eyes.

Once they reached the lounge, George noticed a thin elderly man, standing with the well-balanced poise of a regular yoga or Pilates practitioner, staring vacantly out of the picture window and up at the volcano. As they entered, he slowly turned and raised his eyebrows in surprise.

"Father, this is Superintendent Zammit from the Maltese Police, whom I mentioned to you the other day. We spoke about the disappearance of the protester at the plant. Also, Assistant Commissioner Camilleri of the Maltese force, who is the uncle of the missing girl."

Albi said nothing but looked them over with a faint smile on his face, then slowly walked to an armchair by the fireside and sat down.

Bastiano said: "Er, Dad, I brought them up here for a private chat. Away from prying eyes and ears downstairs. You do not need to stay."

Albi looked on, the half-smile still on his lips.

"I think I'll stay, if that's OK? I've got nothing better to do. It'll take my mind off things."

Camilleri took a seat on the sofa and watched Albi for a moment, in case he had anything further to add. Seeing that the comment was to be left unexplained, he started talking.

"Mr Beneventi, I am Silvia's uncle, but more than that – I have taken the place of the father she never knew. I raised the girl, together with my sister, and love her as my own child."

George studied the rug under his feet. He had never heard Camilleri talk so unguardedly before.

His boss continued. "Silvia is an intelligent girl, a doctor of science and committed to all the green causes you might expect. I am sorry if that has brought her into conflict with your organisation. All I hope is that we can look beyond that, to the pain her absence is causing her mother, and of course myself. We do not know where to turn next. My friend and colleague, George Zammit, has followed the Polizia di Stato inquiry and it is going nowhere. He discovered that, without a doubt, she was taken less than 100 metres away from the gates of the Nuovi Modi plant at Pirao.

"He believes your head of security, Roberto Crisponi, might be of help to us with CCTV footage, access to the security staff on duty that night, all that sort of thing. I humbly ask you for your assistance."

George could not believe it. Camilleri was all but pleading for help.

Bastiano nodded, recognising how things between George and him had been left. He replied to Camilleri.

"There's still no news, I'm afraid, even though the protesters have left our site. Which is..." he searched for the appropriate word "... disappointing. I was hoping that if she had been taken against her will, the breaking up of the camp would be enough to prompt her release."

Camilleri looked at Bastiano through narrowed eyes.

"Well, George assures me there is enough evidence to suggest she *was* taken against her will, and you imply that you accept the motive for her kidnap was her involvement in the protest?"

Bastiano shrugged and glanced at his father. Albi went over to the window and opened the catch so he could slide one large pane aside. The wind was blowing down the mountain and the air smelled strongly of sulphur, causing him to wrinkle his nose. He turned back to face them.

"Yes, it's a strong odour today, isn't it? The grapes will have a faintly smoky tinge this year. Hopefully it will flash off during fermentation, but no doubt the critics will pick it up."

He closed the window and walked back to his seat. Leaning forward with his elbows on his knees, he said: "How long has she been missing?"

George answered him.

"Nearly three weeks."

It had been several days since the plant recommenced operations, but there was still no sign of Benedetta. Vito had spoken to Basso several times, and he would only say, "Soon, it will happen soon." It had not. Albi feared the worst. They had not released her either because they wanted to ensure he did not shut the plant again or because she was dead. He hardly dared contemplate the latter possibility.

Camilleri sensed Albi was engaging with them.

"Signor Beneventi, we are worried sick. You cannot appreciate how it is for us. Neither my sister nor I can eat, sleep or work. I can think of little else. Love for a child is a powerful thing, and for a missing child.... I do not suppose you have ever experienced such a loss. I cannot begin to describe it to you."

Albi looked at Camilleri with tired eyes.

"Assistant commissioner, if only you knew how wrong you are."

There was a moment's silence as the sentence hung in the air. Bastiano studied his feet, George and Camilleri exchanged a glance. Camilleri broke it, saying: "I am sorry, Signor Beneventi, I do not understand. Are you saying you have experienced such a loss?"

Albi said nothing but avoided eye contact with everybody in the room. The silence spoke of his pain – the broken sleep, then waking to face the same emptiness, the same doubt, over and over, every long, dreary day.

Bastiano turned to his father and said softly: "Dad, are you going to help them, or shall I?"

Albi shifted in his seat. Staring at the floor in front of him, he said: "I'll try to help. Before I go any further, though, I want your word that you'll not report anything I might say here to the Italian police or the Carabinieri? Anything we say to the Polizia is to be agreed in advance between us. Two girls' lives are at stake here; it's serious."

Camilleri nodded, wondering why another girl had been mentioned.

Albi took a deep breath and said: "My daughter, too, has been kidnapped. By the 'Ndrangheta."

He spat out the word. What he had said could never be unsaid. He was now committed to answering all their questions.

Camilleri fixed him with a hard look.

"Your daughter has been kidnapped?" He paused. This was not what he had expected to hear. "But why would they take your child?"

"You must understand, the 'Ndrangheta own the geothermal plant we run, as well as half of Catania. All their new green businesses rely on cheap power from the plant. Nothing works without it. The council are involved, the Polizia, the Carabinieri, the Sicilian Parliament... they're all in on it, at least, I think they must be! Making Catania the green city, net-zero, cutting-edge technology, the envy of the world... what a joke!" Albi laughed. "They own this winery, they own *me*. I took a stand against them on fracking, so they stole my daughter."

George was all but speechless. One girl dead in the volcano, two others missing? Albi could not make eye contact with any of them. He continued to speak, staring down at his Japanese straw sandals. "At best, I think they're holding her to make it plain who the boss is; at worst, they've killed her. Either way, they're torturing me, just as they are torturing you, assistant commissioner."

"So you have not spoken about this to the police?"

Albi smiled.

"Why would I? I know who's got her and I know why. The police are in their pockets; have been for years. They do what they're told, just like the rest of us do. This is Sicily, assistant commissioner. It's different where you come from. But I think I can find both girls. You see, I know who to ask."

Bastiano laid an arm across his father's shoulders.

"That's more like it, Dad!"

CHAPTER 34

PIETRO POMODORO

PORT OF AUGUSTA,
METROPOLITAN DISTRICT OF
CATANIA

PIETRO POMODORO WAS a senior man in the southern Sicilian 'Ndrangheta clan. Pietro 'Tomato' was so-called not only due to the huge profits he made from his tomato farms, based around Pachino, but also for his florid complexion, which was the colour of passata and an indication of his red-hot temper. He had heard about the female hostages currently being held and, to him, something did not seem quite right about the story.

He had called Crisponi wanting to know what was happening to the eco-girl from the camp. He was worried that the Maltese policeman was still sniffing around, asking questions that could lead to problems. Pietro had various businesses in Catania and kept a cache of arms, as well as a large stock of smuggled cigarettes and drugs, tucked away in tunnels on the north-west side of the volcano, not far from where his associates kept their kidnap victims. They were so near to one another, they actually shared a common power supply, from the small hydro-electric generator powered by one of the underground streams. The local Polizia and Carabinieri were onside, naturally, and would never dare go near their tunnels, but foreign police, poking around on the mountain, was not good news.

He was sitting in the car park of the Augusta docks,

observing the loading of several containers of refrigerated tomatoes bound for the UAE, together with several hundred kilos of Bolivian cocaine, concealed within the insulated lining of the container walls. All was going smoothly. He had the phone to his ear and a plastic cup of machine coffee in his hand. He could not tell which was annoying him the most, the disgusting coffee or the phone conversation.

"So, I don't get it. Where's the *guerriera ecologica,* eh? All the other protesters have gone, disappeared. The camp's clear. But still no sign of her. The Maltese *sbirro* is still in town, sticking his nose in where it doesn't belong. And now I hear there're two women missing! Tomorrow how many will it be? Three… four? You were told to let the woman from the camp go! So, what's happening?"

"Look, Pietro," said Crisponi, "the eco-girl was released two weeks ago, given her air fare and dropped off near the airport. If she's chosen to lie low ever since, that's her affair. You're right, all the other eco-types have left – I get it, it wouldn't make any sense for her to hang around here."

A red flush was spreading up Pietro Pomodoro's neck – a clear sign that his temper was rising.

"You don't get it, *stupido!* If that's happened, then the Maltese policeman would've gone home. But he hasn't!" Pietro screamed. "Instead, he's brought a friend in! Now there's two of them! You were told to let her go, but you haven't, or else you've finished her, or lost her. But you *haven't let her go*! It's jeopardising my business and I won't have that."

Pietro Pomodoro was the first person ever to call out Crisponi as a liar, but he did not believe a word of his story about leaving the girl at the airport.

"So, tell me again… you drove her to Palermo and gave her three hundred euros?"

"Sure, so she could take a flight back to Malta and get out of our hair."

"Did you buy her a coffee, too? Give her some money for a glass of wine on the plane?"

"I'm telling you, we dropped her in Palermo."

"Where?"

"Near Vucciria market."

"Bullshit! You can't get near that place in a car, and it's always so full of people. I don't believe you. Why not drop her locally, on the roadside after dark, like we usually do? What's the matter with you? *Che ti sei impazzito?* You're mad! If you released her in Palermo, why has nothing been heard of her? And why is the *poliziotto Maltese* still in Catania, asking questions? If we find out you're lying to us, I'll slit your throat myself!"

"Pietro, why're you disrespecting me like this? I don't know why there's a problem. Trust me, it'll all come good. You'll never hear from her again."

"You see, Roberto, you don't get it! We said release her but now she's disappeared. We wanted you to solve a problem for us and instead you've caused us more trouble. Let's hope, for your sake, nothing bad comes of this. *Capisci?* Do you understand me?"

"Sure, sure. I swear to you, she's alive and well. We probably taught her a lesson and she's gone back to Malta to lie low for a while. Yes? *Nessun problema* – on my mother's life."

"You're a lying piece of shit, Crisponi."

THE AIR HUNG close and humid, filled with the acrid smell of burned wood from the fires on the mountainside, and eggy sulphur from the noxious gases expelled by the belching mountain. The city was in a perpetual twilight, cars flooding the streets with yellow light even at midday in early October. In the distance, the continuous rumble of the volcano jarred everyone's nerves, as it prepared for another roaring paroxysm.

George had asked Diego to meet him at Prestipino's. Lucy had been at work since the early hours when she had left George's room. She had spent the rest of the night having conversations with Del Bosco, sending him real-time information from the Observatory and her own assessment of what was happening with the volcano. She had finally returned to the Hotel Celeste to grab some well-earned rest.

When a continuous rain of ash started to fall, tourists beat a hasty retreat from Catania. They realised that the awesome beauty of the paroxysmal eruptions and distant pyroclastic lava flows were one thing, but the unpleasantness of the suffocating deposits coating their clothes, getting in their hair and clogging their airways, was something else altogether.

George sat at a small table, under the shelter of the large

umbrellas, waiting for Diego. A few minutes later, he saw the young policeman come plodding towards him, sheltering from the falling grit under a short-handled, multi-coloured umbrella. Diego seemed very relaxed in the circumstances.

"Hi, some morning, eh? Never mind, yeah? It'll settle down soon. It always does."

George was doubtful.

"Is that what you really think?"

Diego smiled and shrugged.

"Well, no. But I mean, you've got to be positive, so, yeah, it's all good. Anyway, I've got something for you."

Diego looked smug. He waved a small computer memory stick at George.

George was amused.

"Well, you seem pleased with yourself. What is it?"

"It's the CCTV from the multistorey in via Teocrito, where Benedetta left her car. And it's very interesting."

"Oh, I'm impressed. Well done, Diego. We might make a policeman of you yet. How did you get it?"

"I told the attendant there were some kids messing about on the sixth floor and he asked me to mind his booth. I did, and downloaded the file onto this, at the same time."

He smiled proudly. George looked at him disapprovingly.

"So you stole it?"

The young man laughed, nervously.

"Well, not really. I mean, the guy didn't give it to me, but it's only a copy – can you steal a copy?"

"I don't know, Diego, but if you took it without his consent and entered his office without permission, I do know it's of no evidential value."

Diego looked downcast.

"No, really? Bummer. I was only trying to help."

———

George planned to go and see if he could learn anything further from Roberto Crisponi. Rather than face him at the plant, he had decided to follow him and try to talk to him at home. He hoped Crisponi would be less confrontational and more relaxed in his own surroundings. He had learned from Bastiano that Crisponi rented a place on the outskirts Randazzo and tended to leave the plant around 18:00 each evening, driving a dark green SUV. So, George found a spot at the bottom of the road that led down from Pirao and waited for Crisponi's car to pass him. He had been there for forty minutes and had just woken, with a start, from a brief but very restorative nap. The remnants of a *pizzette* lay on the passenger seat beside him. He hastily stuffed it into his jacket pocket, for later consumption. For a moment, he thought he might have missed his quarry but, just as he was about to berate himself for his lack of attention, Crisponi's vehicle swept by and the chase was on.

As he had learned at Malta's Academy for Disciplined Forces at Siġġiewi, George counted to thirty then slowly set off after Crisponi. He presumed Crisponi would be heading for Randazzo, so George did not need to close the gap until they got within sight of the town. To his satisfaction, he timed the approach perfectly and was just in time to see Crisponi enter a series of narrow back streets and pull up outside a four-storey apartment block. George waited until he saw a light go on in a room on the left-hand side of the second floor. He left the car and entered the block. His heart rate increased, as he climbed the stairs. He wasn't sure whether it was the exertion of climbing them or nervousness at what might lie ahead that had tightened his chest.

On ringing the bell, he stepped back and braced himself for Crisponi's dead-looking coal-black eyes to widen in surprise, on seeing a policeman standing on his threshold. In fact, it was a crop-haired, petite woman in short shorts and too much deep red lipstick who opened the door. She cast a disparaging eye over George and said gruffly: "He's inside."

She held the door open and ushered him in. Crisponi was standing at a breakfast bar at the far end of the apartment, looking at his phone, when George entered. George was feeling distinctly uncomfortable. Crisponi looked at him and took a moment to work out who he was and what he might be doing there. George was relieved when the other man took the lead, saying: "Ah! Superintendent, good of you to come round. I'm going to smoke. Let's go out onto the balcony. Andrea hates the smell inside the house, don't you, *amore*?"

Andrea shook her head and wafted one hand in front of her face. "Disgusting habit."

They stepped out onto the narrow balcony and Crisponi slid the glass door shut. With a glance inside, to ensure all was well, he quickly came right up to George and pushed his face close to the policeman.

"What the fuck are you doing in my house?"

"I wanted a word. Away from the plant. Your wife let me in."

"She's not my wife and I've got nothing to say to you."

George's heart was pounding and his mouth felt dry. He hoped he could get his words out.

"Well, that might be what you think, but I know you work with the 'Ndrangheta and I believe you've kidnapped Silvia Camilleri. I want her released."

Crisponi paused and shook his head in disbelief.

"My God! You stupid, stupid man. Even saying that is enough to get you killed. You've got no idea where you are or what you're getting involved in, do you?"

George swallowed hard.

"Mela! That may be so, but neither does Silvia Camilleri. Let her go and we want nothing more than to be on a plane back to Malta. You can carry on doing whatever it is you're doing here. I don't care, we're not after you, I promise, just release Silvia. The protest is over, why're you keeping her?"

Crisponi was thoughtful. His reticence in releasing Silvia was due to the fact that he was convinced she had woken briefly from her drugged stupor and seen him leaning over her as she lay in the boot of his SUV. If she had recognised him, there was no way he could release her. He was trying to bring himself to get rid of the problem posed by the girl, but could not imagine himself murdering her in cold blood. He had pulled a trigger of a gun, with lethal consequences before, but that had been in different circumstances and in a kill or be killed situation. This was not the same and he was becoming seriously rattled by the pressure being applied by Pietro Pomodoro.

He took a drag on his cigarette and blew a jet of smoke above George's head. If he did release Silvia and give her to this man, he might be able to score a few euros and make a quick exit from the island, relying on their promise not to identify him and Lelli. The girl's reappearance in Malta would get Pietro Pomodoro off his back and also rid them of this meddling Maltese policeman.

Finally, Crisponi snapped at George "What we're doing is our business. You don't tell me what is or is not going to happen here. I tell you! She's fine. That's all I'm saying. If anyone asks me about this conversation, I'll deny it. Got it? Now go. You're in danger, just being here. You're lucky you're walking out. If you mess with me, you'll never get her back. *Capisci*? I'll be in touch when I'm ready. Approach me again and that's it, over."

George left and quickly made his way back to the car, with several glances over his shoulder. So, not an entirely wasted trip, he thought. He knew Silvia was alive, held somewhere by Crisponi and his crew. At least he had something positive to tell Camilleri. What he still did not know was why she was being held or what they needed to do to secure her release.

CHAPTER 36

SILVIA CAMILLERI
IN CAPTIVITY, MOUNT ETNA

SILVIA WAS with Lucy in Trastevere. They had just stumbled out of Cosmo, their favourite club. It was a promo night and the floor was packed with hot, sweaty dancers. Silvia and Lucy had danced for the last forty minutes solid and were overheated. Silvia wiped beads of sweat from Lucy's temples with her forefinger and suggested it was time for them to go. They said their farewells to their friends and made their way out of the basement club. The fresh air hit them and their hot bodies started to steam, as wispy clouds of perspiration condensed around them. They threw their arms around each other's shoulders and made the short walk home. That was the joy of living in Trastevere, everything was on their doorstep. In the stairwell of their flat, Silvia drew Lucy towards her. They embraced and kissed eagerly. Silvia urged Lucy up the stairs towards their bedroom. The windows were open and, despite the hour, there was music from the flat across the street. Silvia did not bother to pull the blinds down, pushing Lucy onto the unmade bed. She lay beside her, kissing her and hastily loosening her clothing.

Silvia turned over and the feel of the damp, cold mattress woke her, causing the images and heat of Lucy's body to fade rapidly and be replaced by the dank and musty atmosphere of the cave. She groaned, as much in frustration as despair. She was lying on the bed, with a thick coarse blanket thrown over her. Above her was rock. Black rock. There was a light, an unshielded bulb, hanging by its cable from a hook driven into the roof of the cavern.

She had been there for nearly three weeks. Her only contact was with a short, sturdy Sicilian, in his later years, with slightly bowed legs and a barrel chest. He wore the clothes of a farmer or manual worker who spent his time outdoors. He came every day, letting her out through the stout wooden door of her cell into a rock tunnel, where she emptied the stinking slop bucket down a sluice in the rock. Next to that was a large, blue waist-high plastic drum, which was topped up by a yellow hosepipe that led to somewhere out of sight. The old man would rinse the sluice with a second bucket of water, then hand her a towel and some soap. She was allowed to re-fill the bucket and wash herself. She had quickly overcome her revulsion at using one bucket for all her bodily needs.

He always turned his back and walked a little way down the tunnel to wait out of sight. Gradually, Silvia became confident that he would let her have her privacy. She would strip to her underwear and, despite the cold and damp of the tunnel, use the soap and icy water to rinse herself. It invigorated her and she came to look forward to her chilling tunnel-baths.

When she had finished, she would call and he would return. He brought food – bread, packets of meat or cheese, one piece of fruit and two litres of water. At first, it was never enough and Silvia was permanently hungry, but soon, as the days passed, she became accustomed to the meagre diet. For a time, she thought about escape. Trying to arrive at a plan that would take her back to the light, away from the gloom and the dank air that lay heavily on her chest. She was a tall, strong woman, a match for many a man, so she had little to fear from an old Sicilian, even though he was no doubt hardened by years of labour.

She thought about finding a rock to strike him down with. Before the time of his arrival and after he had put her back in her prison, Silvia would press one ear against the door, listening for any sound. She guessed the entrance to the tunnel lay just a few metres away, around the corner, but she did not believe it would be left open and unprotected. If there was a key, would the old man carry it on him? Quite possibly. If so, the plan to attack him had legs. Find a rock, wait till he passed her at the water tub, then strike him from behind and keep hitting him. Search his pockets, find the key.

The only thing that stopped her was the genuine belief that she would be freed before too long. Silvia had reasoned her captivity was due to her actions at the plant and, in particular, the media attention she had started to generate. She knew her kidnap would be a big story and the press would become even more interested in the reasons for the protest at the Nuovi Modi. She saw her imprisonment as a price she was prepared to pay to further the cause. If she had known that, following her abduction, morale had collapsed and the protest abandoned, her mental state would have been very different.

She had tried to speak to her captor. Every day, she would address him as Signore and ask why she was being held. When she might be released? What conditions were attached to her release? Whether they were negotiating a ransom? She urged him to call her Silvia. 'That's my name', she would tell him.

But he only ever replied: "No questions. I have no answers, so no speaking."

She had long since lost all track of time; the days and nights came and went, indistinguishable. The small Sicilian still appeared, left food and water, then departed, always maintaining his silence.

But, as more days passed, she became conscious of things happening around her. The solidity of the cavern became something she could no longer take for granted. Visions of collapsed roofs, blocked, dusty tunnels and caverns filling with rising water began to eat away at her. There were regular distant rumblings, almost like an underground train passing in a faraway tunnel. Occasionally, there were vibrations, causing the pendant lamp to swing back and forth. Then she realised she had cast off the coat and discarded the hat she had been given. It was getting warmer. How could she have been so stupid as to not notice before now?

One morning, when the Sicilian was letting her out, there was a distinct and loud boom and the light swung madly back and forth. The reverberations threw Silvia against the door pillar, where she crouched, hands firmly grasping the frame, while small, loose stones and dust rattled down from the cave roof.

The Sicilian looked around, instinctively glancing to the roof of the cave. Silvia started screaming.

"You can't leave me in here! What's happening? It's getting hotter. What's going on?"

The Sicilian looked at her and shook his head.

After she had washed and been returned to the cell, he pointed to the bed. It was an unusual instruction but Silvia obeyed and sat down, knees drawn up in front of her. She had noticed a series of metal struts, stacked outside the door, together with a rectangular frame covered in springs. Without saying a word, he brought the pieces into the cell and began to assemble a second bed.

"So, am I getting company? It wouldn't hurt to tell me. Come on, you bastard – say something. Anything."

Once the bolts were fixed, he disappeared and returned with a thin black-and-white striped mattress and a stack of blankets. On top of the pile was a yellow bucket, which he carefully placed next to Silvia's.

"No way! You can't expect us to do that in front of each other?"

Then she had a terrible thought. What if it was a man?

Terror gripped her.

"Tell me it's a woman, at least! Please, just nod... anything!"

She screamed: *"Giurami che non è un uomo! Dimmelo! Tell me!"*

He replied: *"Calmati, è una donna."*

When the bed was assembled and Silvia had carefully inspected the bedding left for the new guest and swapped several superior items with her own, she settled down to wait. After what seemed like an age, she heard the sounds of footsteps and muffled voices. The key turned in the door to her cell and she stood expectantly by her bed. The Sicilian was accompanied by a small woman with short, thinning grey hair, an apron over her thick woollen jumper and stretch nylon trousers. Between them was a much larger, wide-hipped woman, with a turban of bandages around her head. She was possibly in her early thirties. She had her arms slung over their shoulders and was struggling to walk. Silvia thought she was either terribly ill or drugged.

Her face was a mass of deep cuts and abrasions, some partially healed, others bloody and weeping. She obviously needed medical attention. The white turban was heavily stained with dark brown patches where blood had seeped through the bandages and congealed. Similarly, her hands were grazed and hung like limp squid from the sleeves of a ragged fleece jacket. Whether she was sedated or otherwise, she was barely conscious. Whoever had patched her up had not been a professional. Silvia looked at the Sicilian's wife; they exchanged glances. Silvia was appalled by the condition of the new arrival and so too was the old lady, who was keen to dump her charge and get out of the cave.

The wife laid the wounded woman on the mattress and lifted her feet up onto the bed. Silvia saw the stricken woman visibly relax and some of the tension eased out of her. The wife arranged the bedding, then squinted unpleasantly at Silvia, the creases around her eyes deepening and her cheeks hollowing. She fished around in her trouser pocket and produced several orange plastic cylinders of tablets. She handed the first to Silvia.

"*Due, tre volte al giorno. Sì? Parli italiano?*"

"*Sì.*"

She waved two fingers, then three, in front of Silvia's face.

"*Sì, sì. Capisco.*"

To Silvia, these looked like strong painkillers. The second were antibiotic capsules and the third, touchingly, the tablets all Italians take to protect their stomachs when on a course of antibiotics. Satisfied the responsibility for the injured woman had been passed over, the wife glanced at her compliant husband and said: "*Andiamo.*"

With that they were gone, leaving Silvia with a half-dead woman, both of them stuck in the middle of an erupting volcano. She watched the other captive's chest rise and fall with every breath. If she was sedated, it had to be because she was badly injured. Silvia approached her and rolled the blankets back. She risked lifting the fleece to have a look at the woman's torso, and winced, as she studied the deep yellow and green bruising down the side of her chest, as well as the the cuts and punctures on her breasts and abdomen. Silvia was at a loss as to what might have caused the injuries. She adjusted the woman's clothing and replaced the blankets. There was nothing for it but to wait for her to come round, then try and find out what her story was.

Silvia was asleep when she became conscious of a loud squeaking in the cell. She was so attuned to the noises of the cave, the dripping of water that leached through the fissures in the roof, the alarming booms and the cracking of faraway rocks, that when there was the sound of a metallic creak it might as well have been an old tin-cased alarm clock ringing. Silvia raised herself to lean on one elbow. The new arrival was sitting on the side of her bed, the springs groaning with every movement she made. Her head hung limply and her shoulders were slumped. She gingerly raised one arm above her shoulder and immediately grimaced.

Silvia said, "Ribs?"

The woman slowly turned towards her and seemed to see her for the first time. She did not speak. Without a word, she lay back on the cot and, with a whimper, lifted her legs so she was flat again. She shut her eyes and muttered "I don't know what they've given me, but I feel terrible," she said.

"You're in a bit of a mess, to be fair. Can you tell me what happened and why you're here?"

Her answer sounded as if it came from faraway. Vague, weak and uncertain.

"I don't really know. I tried to escape down a watercourse but was swept away into an underground tunnel. I drowned. I was actually dead, it seems. That's where the cuts and bruising are from. I don't think anything is broken."

"You were *dead*?"

"Yeah, or that's what the priest said. But I don't know what's real and what isn't here. I'm so tired. Is the priest with us?" She raised her voice. "Father? Father, are you here? No?"

Silvia thought that, in her delirium, the woman must have mistaken the Sicilian for a priest. It was possible.

With that, she disappeared back into unconsciousness, leaving her fear and pain behind. Silvia felt mildly jealous. For a moment, it crossed her mind to take a second look at the painkillers and maybe find her own oblivion. She told herself to get a grip. Her first job was to wean this woman off the painkillers and find out what she knew and where had she been held. Silvia wanted to know where the Sicilian and his wife had brought her from and whether there really was a life-saving priest roaming the tunnels. Or, was the idea of the priest just a figment of the woman's exhausted, confused and drug-addled imagination?

Escape. They had to escape. With two of them, the odds had just improved dramatically. But first, Silvia had to get this woman on her feet and functioning. Then, they could work something out. She could not stand much longer in captivity and they had to get out of the volcano.

CHAPTER 37
ASSISTANT COMMISSIONER GERALD CAMILLERI

PALAZZO DI LAREDO, RAGUSA IBLA, SICILY

GEORGE WAS LOOKING FORWARD to taking Camilleri to his meeting, one and a half hour's drive away, to the hilltop town of Ragusa. As he drove south, he felt the pressure and anxiety of the past few days starting to ease, as Mount Etna disappeared from his rearview mirror. He had not realised how tense he had become over the past week.

George tried to make conversation with Camilleri, but the assistant commissioner seemed to prefer to make the journey in silence and spent much of the time with his head back and his eyes half closed. George noticed he was wearing a strange lapel pin on his usual grey pinstripe suit and asked what it was. His boss sighed and shifted in his seat, reconciling himself to conversation.

"You have heard of the Knights of Malta, of course?"

Of course, George had heard of the Knights of Malta. The story and works of the Knights were at the heart of Malta's history and culture. Against the odds, the massively outnumbered Knights had defeated the Ottomans in 1565, at the Great Siege, and preserved the Christian faith in southern Europe. Their forts, defences and auberges, where they had once lived, were all within the walled city of Valletta and the Three Cities to the south of the Grand Harbour. George knew the order still existed, and every Maltese schoolchild knew the order was sovereign under the law. He did not really understand what that meant, but he knew the Knights issued their own passports, had their own coins and postage stamps, as well as having their own embassies in other countries.

"Of course I have, but I've never met a real Knight. I don't move in those circles."

"Well, you have met one now."

George looked at Camilleri, only averting his gaze when the car veered across to the wrong side of the road.

"You're a Knight?" He was aghast.

"Yes, and today we are abroad on the business of the Sovereign Military Order of Malta! Sounds exciting, does it not?"

"Mela, yes it does. What're we doing, exactly?"

"You are driving and I am going to talk to another Knight, although the one we are going to visit is not of the Sovereign Order of Malta. He is from a reject sub-order, if I can put it like that." Camilleri smiled. He had woken up, and seemed to be enjoying himself.

George had a million questions and, for once, his boss seemed happy to answer all but the most ludicrous of them. George learned that the Order had spread across the world and now had over 13,000 so-called associate members, who used the Knights of Malta name in their charitable works. These members had little connection to the true Order, now headquartered in Rome. In reality, there were only a handful of real Knights still alive.

"So, I thought to be a Knight you had to be from a royal family, nobility or something?"

"Not quite, George. It is true, until recently, you had to be of noble descent, but these days even sons of a humble policeman, such as myself, are eligible to receive an invitation."

Camilleri went on to describe how the Order had a very structured hierarchy, which demanded each class of member wore different insignia and formal costumes.

George was fascinated.

"Mela, what level are you then?"

"I'm a Knight in Obedience, which is the second-highest rank. It means I promise to 'strive for the perfection of Christian life in conformity with the obligation of my state, in the spirit of the Order'. How do you think I am doing?"

He laughed again, his face suffused with genuine warmth.

George was not quite sure what to say.

"Well, I suppose you're still a member, so they must think you're doing OK."

"Well, we shall see what this particular Knight thinks of me. I have got a feeling he might not be so gracious in his judgement as you. The Knights of Tripoli disappeared from public view over 500 years ago and have been a self-serving, clandestine band who have caused a lot of trouble at various times. The man we are going to see comes from a branch of the Spanish Bourbon family and claims to be the heir to the Kingdom of the Two Sicilies. Natasha Bonnici thinks she can help restore to him an element of power and influence that was lost when Italy was unified in 1861."

"Can she?"

"I am not sure. You know her as well as anybody. She is capable of anything. But I have told her, she is playing with fire tangling with the Knights of Tripoli. They do not have a reputation for being very collaborative and they have held a grudge against the Knights of Malta since we cast them to the infidels in 1530."

"Oh! Who is this… Knight of Tripoli?"

"Do not be shocked, but he's the Count of Ragusa. He says he is the last living ancestor of Francis II, last of the Bourbon kings of Naples. Be warned, just because he says it, does not mean it is true. Some people contest his claim. However, if that is true, he is a man with a claim to be King of the Mezzogiorno, the South of Italy and Sicily.

"Why on earth are you going to see him?"

"Apparently, Natasha Bonnici wants to turn Naples into the new Catania, I do not know the details. She believes a figurehead like the Count would help rally the citizenry of the south to her cause. It is all very vague, but you know Natasha, you never get the whole story."

Camilleri turned to meet George's shocked gaze and raised his eyebrows.

"Yes, I am afraid I still run errands for Her Ladyship up on the hill."

George said nothing, but shook his head. He continued to drive. Camilleri turned away and resumed gazing out of the window. As they approached Ragusa, they followed the signs for Ragusa Ibla, the old town, across the narrow bridge over a deeply incised ravine. Camilleri had a sheet of paper with a map and directed George up narrow cobbled streets, with snaking corners, through small piazzas and down steep, slippery inclines. George wondered where they would park as the sides of the car already seemed to graze the walls of the narrow, ancient stone buildings, which all seemed to be piled on top of one another. Eventually, on the crest of the hill, overlooking the jumble of ancient buildings below them and the rear of Duomo di San Giorgio, they arrived alongside an imposing stone building. The only opening from the narrow, stone-paved street was an arched entrance, with huge, wooden double doors and an engraved brass plate reading *Palazzo di Laredo*.

Camilleri got out of the car and pressed an intercom on the wall. The black wooden doors slowly swung open, creaking and groaning on their hinges. Camilleri told George to bring the car inside and park in the courtyard.

"And, if you do not mind, would you please stay here with it? Some of the older members of these orders can be a bit prickly about protocol. I am sure you understand."

He did not understand at all, but was only too happy to sit in the car and wait for Camilleri's return. George got the sense this was a business meeting he was better off knowing nothing about.

———

At the far end of the courtyard a door opened and a black-suited footman appeared and waited for Camilleri's approach. Without a word being spoken, the man led him through cold stone corridors and up polished marble stairs to a dimly lit study.

The Count was in his late fifties, dressed in a plain grey suit, beneath it an old-fashioned ruby-red, double-breasted silk waistcoat complete with a gold chain stretching from one buttonhole to his waistcoat pocket. He had the plumpness of middle age and his thinning hair was slicked close to his skull. He sat behind an ornate desk and did not stand when Camilleri entered.

To his right, under a mullioned window, a small man swathed in a black cloak sat on a wooden stool before a low, plain wooden desk, working on an old leather-bound ledger. On the left breast of the cloak was a large cross. Around his neck was a silver chain, with another large silver cross. Together, they indicated he was a high-ranking knight in the Order of Tripoli who, Camilleri guessed, had taken vows of obedience, poverty and chastity. The small man lifted his head from his work and laid his pen down. His weasel face still held the screwed-up expression of someone who had been trying to read and write in the dimmest of light.

Finally, the man behind the desk raised himself and walked round to stand in front of Camilleri, still without offering his hand or a word of introduction. Camilleri was not intimidated by the theatrics. In his line of work, he had met all kinds of people, many of whom felt they had good reason to be hostile towards him. The small man under the window shuffled on his stool. Camilleri studied the pin in the lapel of the Count's suit. It identified him as a senior member of the Knights of Tripoli.

The other man caught him looking at the pin.

"Don't be fooled by this. I'm a member of several religious chivalric orders. The ones I take most seriously still require one to be of noble birth, not the son of a policeman." A nasty smile spread across his face. "I'm afraid you wouldn't qualify." He went on, "I mean, look at Fra Fattorini here." He indicated the man sitting in the corner, who grimaced back at them. "He's one of the highest-ranking knights in my order. A knight, first-class no less, a man who's taken religious vows and has noble blood running through his veins. I treat him like a dog." He paused. "You can imagine what I think of you."

Camilleri struggled to find a suitable response, other than to remain perfectly still and hold a neutral expression.

"I know you, Camilleri. Or rather, should I say, I know who you represent: those Savoyard moneylenders of Milan."

Camilleri raised an eyebrow.

The Count had not yet finished.

"Oh, yes. I know how to carry a grudge. Forget about your order's treachery in the sixteenth century, I'm a reasonable man and can put that to one side. But, your usurer friends in Milan funded the Unification of Italy. Their money armed Garibaldi's Redcoats and your friend Victor Emmanuel took our family's crown. You cost my family, and me, the Kingdom of the Two Sicilies."

Camilleri had been warned by Natasha this was all true. The Family, back in the 1860s, operated as a financial guild, lending money to royalty, the church and aristocrats. It had benefited hugely from the financial support given to Garibaldi, to allow him to bring the various kingdoms and provinces of the country together and form the modern Italy. This had meant the end of the Bourbons, a dynasty which had ruled from its seat in Naples since 1734 and, to the Count of Ragusa, the loss of royal lineage.

Camilleri tried to rationalise the depth of resentment the count still harboured.

"So, I do not suppose you are interested in a suggestion that you might be able to recover some of your influence in the Mezzogiorno?"

The Count looked at him contemptuously. The little man in the corner sniggered. Camilleri glanced his way and saw that he had resumed his crouched position, over his little schoolboy's desk, and was scribbling away, his head bowed, centimetres away from the ledger.

"You've no idea who I am, have you? I'm glad to see that murderous Bonnici woman doesn't know everything. Before I throw you out, Sir Knight, be aware, I'm going to send a message to your mistress, not to meddle in things that don't concern her. She made a mistake sending you here. So be warned. I've got nothing more to say to you. I'll show her in no uncertain terms why she has to stay away from Naples. I've no idea what she's got in mind, but there's nothing she can give me that I want or need. She may not know it, but I already have all the influence I'll ever require."

The Count turned to resume his seat at his desk.

Camilleri knew when to make a tactical withdrawal and could not get out of the Palazzo di Laredo fast enough. The black-suited footman waited by the door to the courtyard and, with a supercilious smile, deliberately slammed it shut, nearly knocking Camilleri off his feet. He found himself practically running to get back in the car.

George was listening to the radio when his white-faced superior climbed hastily into the passenger seat.

George said with a smile, "That was quick. All good?"

Camilleri cast a glance back to the footman standing at the door, watching them leave.

"I think the count is quite insane."

CHURCH OF SANTA MARIA DEL CARMELO, NICOLOSI, MOUNT ETNA

HAKAN WAS STANDING in the shadows, pressed tight against the wall, as the procession made its way past him. It was nearly midnight. First came the brass band, dressed in black trousers, white shirts and peaked caps, their music solemn, but not funereal. A large group of monks followed the band, dressed in plain grey robes, their heads bowed. Each held a candle in front of him, in a closed lantern suspended from a thin chain. A few of the 'monks' had worn the traditional priest's vestments earlier that day, but most of them had never taken holy orders nor set foot inside a monastery.

Behind the Brothers came the parish priest from Santa Maria del Carmelo. He held a metre-high wooden cross in front of him. It was unadorned apart from the crossbar, which was studded with a row of flame-red rubies that flashed in the intermittent street lighting. Behind the cross came the Icon of the Mother, its jewels sparkling and glinting. The body of the Icon was cast mostly in shadow, as it passed through the poorly lit streets. Together with the solid wooden stretcher, the ensemble weighed nearly half a tonne and the sixteen men carrying it laboured through the streets, up and down the steps of the piazzas and through the narrow alleys. They swayed in step, left to right, as they coordinated their movements, the precious load balanced on their shoulders. The man at the front of the litter was the one Hakan had come to see, the Mayor of Catania, Vito Amato. He set the rhythm and the pace for the rest of the bearers. His focus on the task was total. He seemed oblivious to everything except the movement of the litter. There was no eye contact with any of the crowd around him – it was as though he had undergone some form of beatific transformation.

Bringing up the rear of the parade were people from all the villages around the volcano, Nicolosi, Adrano, Bronte, Zafferena, Milo and many others. Everybody who lived in the shadow of the Mother seemed to be in Nicolosi that night, to join together in prayer to whichever god they thought was listening. This parade and the prayers were a special occasion, arranged by the Brothers because of the extreme events of the past weeks. To bring out the Icon, other than for the July parade, was unknown and a reflection of the deep unease felt amongst those who lived in the shadow of Etna.

The volcano showed no signs of quietening. Behind the town, Hakan had a view up the mountain, a dark and ominous presence above him. He could see the deep red gashes, wounds in the side of the volcano, where viscous lava slowly oozed down towards the town in which he stood. A huge tumbling plume of dark grey smoke, steam and gas was visible, as a shadowy mass against the moonless sky. The volcano had continuously rumbled throughout the evening and, on several occasions, blasted rock and debris high into the darkness above it. This then fell as a black solid hail onto the parading population, causing them to press themselves against walls in the narrow streets for shelter.

Hakan's feet crunched on the volcanic grit that covered the stone cobbles; the smell of volcanic gases filling his nostrils. He was standing on a 3,000-metre high, pulsing mound of fire. A few kilometres beneath him was a lake of molten rock, bubbling and churning, forcing its way towards the surface on which he stood. He was in awe of the raw, naked power of this place. To be able to harness that energy, to tap the might of the volcano and transform it into electricity and hydrogen, was an amazing thing and certainly not one that could be left in untrustworthy hands. He was excited by the prospect of taming it.

Hakan had asked the University of Washington, Earth and Space Sciences Department, in Seattle, to prepare a report on the status of Etna, based on currently available data. Their conclusions differed from Del Bosco's, who they thought was too emotionally involved to be objective and 'too big on the downside'. They had said, on balance, they believed the African and European tectonic plates would eventually stabilise and, once the pressure in Etna's magma chambers had been released, through continual small eruptions, the magma would cool and the crisis would subside. They put the chances of a major eruption as 'slight'. Somehow, on this particular evening, halfway up the flank of the turbulent volcano, Hakan struggled to be totally reassured by their findings.

Despite being a Muslim, he squeezed into the back of the packed church to watch the service. He was surprised to hear the Catholic Ordinary Mass being said in Latin and noted that almost all the congregation knew the correct responses. The Icon had been placed on the floor in front of the altar and two Brothers stood alongside it, gently swinging thuribles, suspended from chains, to fill the church with the scent of burning incense. The elder of the two Brothers was Albi Beneventi, who, eyes closed, mumbled the prayers and responses above the pall of scented smoke that had collected over the Icon.

When it was time for the sermon, Hakan realised something special was happening. He noticed shuffling in the pews and the congregation turning to each other, speaking urgently, wide excited smiles on their faces. Looking around, he realised the entire church was in a state of agitation. An old monk had emerged from the sacristy to the rear of the church and was slowly making his way towards the pulpit. He was short and stooped with sparse hair and a long beard of pure white. His thin body barely filled the grey robes in which he was dressed. Slowly, he climbed the few stairs of the pulpit. All around, the congregation were falling to their knees and crossing themselves; the general hubbub rising to a clamour.

As the old man raised his hands for silence, Hakan whispered to the woman next to him: "Who is he?"

"He's Father Greco... hasn't been seen here in town for years. Some said he'd died, some that he'd gone to live in the caves and tunnels under the volcano itself. Now, he's come back to preach to us!"

She clasped her hands in front of her, as the old man began to speak. The atmosphere in the church was rapt. People craned forward to hear him. He spoke vernacular Sicilian, which is not a dialect of Italian, but a separate language, incorporating Greek, Arabic, French, Catalan and Spanish. Hakan did not understand a word he said.

At the end of the service, the Turk set about making himself known to Vito Amato. He left the church and took the stairs down onto the main floor of the piazza. He spotted the black Maserati, with its driver and blue pennant, parked in the middle of the square. He settled down in the shadow of a café doorway to wait. It was well after two in the morning by the time the crowd had all streamed out of the church and gathered excitedly around the doorway. Some sprinted round to the rear entrance, to catch the mysterious priest leaving via the sacristy, but word soon spread that Father Greco had vanished as magically as he had appeared. Eventually, Vito Amato said farewell to those who had surrounded him on the church steps and crossed the piazza towards his car.

Hakan came out of the café doorway and walked purposefully towards him. Vito tracked his approach across the piazza. He stood at the open door of his car, wondering who this well-dressed, foreign-looking character might be. The stranger had fixed him with an unwavering stare, coming to a halt a metre away.

"Sorry to accost you in the street so late in the evening, but I have good news for you."

"I'm sorry, who're you?"

"I am here to get the 'Ndrangheta off your back, legitimise their businesses and allow you to keep making money to further your political ambitions. All this can be accomplished nice and peacefully, amongst friends."

Vito recoiled in shock.

"Get away from me! What the hell are you talking about?"

Hakan maintained his calm, neutral tone.

"If you do not listen to me now, I promise you, you will regret it. You will spend the next twenty years in prison, your green city ruined by a bunch of incompetent bureaucrats, and quite probably some thug will be sent to kill you, to ensure your silence. If you listen to me, that need not happen. So which is it to be?"

"You're talking rubbish. Go to hell."

"Really? Did you know that a team of anti-Mafia specialist prosecutors is arriving next week? And they are very interested in the political donations you have received over the last few years. But I can arrange it so they are not a problem."

Vito said nothing, but fixed the stranger with a cold stare. The man smiled back at him from beneath the bristles of his luxuriant moustache.

"No, you didn't know that, did you? Have a think and then contact me at the Catania Palace Hotel. Be at the rooftop bar, tomorrow evening, six p.m."

"Who *are* you?"

"I will tell you more tomorrow at six. And, by the way, I

would not say anything about this conversation to anyone else, for my sake and for yours. If they get a hint that you have even spoken to me, I suspect there will be only one outcome. They are a suspicious lot, as you know."

CHAPTER 39
SUPERINTENDENT GEORGE ZAMMIT

RAGUSA, SICILY

CAMILLERI SAT rigid in the passenger seat, staring straight ahead and clearly wishing to be out of that place, as soon as it could be managed. George risked a glance or two at him, while weaving his way down the narrow streets to exit the hilltop town. He crossed the gorge and picked up the state road to Modica, which led to the coastal motorway back to Catania. He sensed Camilleri was not in the mood for the nice scenic route back that George had planned to take, nor would there be the stop for lunch along the way he had also hoped for.

As they left the town behind them, they followed the road along the contour of the gorge that deepened and widened beneath them. Gradually, Camilleri seemed to recover himself. He shifted in his seat and lowered the window slightly.

George ventured a question.

"You seem a little distracted. How did it go?"

Camilleri let out a long breath and turned to face him.

"Very rarely am I blindsided, but I am afraid Natasha Bonnici seriously misjudged this situation. She has made a profound error of judgement." He considered this in silence for a moment, then shook his head as if to clear it. "Most unpleasant. I shall be having words with her."

They drove in silence, looking at the dramatic landscape. They crossed the Catania to Ragusa railway line and started to climb the side of the spectacular gorge. George felt the car struggle and went down the gears to keep up the revs. Gradually, they left the railway far beneath them and the road twisted and turned around the side of a limestone canyon. After Malta's congested and urban traffic, George enjoyed the freedom of driving on the wide, open roads of Sicily. He noted the total absence of other cars, apart from a black SUV a kilometre or so behind them. He kept catching glimpses of the vehicle in the mirror, as the road doubled back on itself.

Suddenly, George was aware of the black car closing in from behind, at speed. He veered as far right as he dared, to leave room for the SUV to overtake, but there were no barriers on the roadside to prevent a careless driver dropping hundreds of metres into the canyon below. George held his line and indicated right, to tell the driver he was prepared to be overtaken. The car closed still tighter to them, so their bumpers were nearly touching.

"Mela! What's he playing at?" George complained.

Camilleri turned around in his seat to see what was going on behind.

"George, drive," he ordered. "Just drive, as fast as you can. Foot down *now!*"

George glanced sideways and opened his mouth to protest.

"Do not look at *me*, for God's sake! Just put your foot down!"

Despite the dark glasses, Camilleri could see that the driver of the car behind was the footman from the Palazzo di Laredo. He was smiling broadly, as he urged the SUV forwards, to nudge George's hire car.

George wrestled with the steering and managed to correct the trajectory. The two vehicles were almost locked together. He could not shake off the SUV, which now accelerated and hit their car with a massive thud. In the driver's mirror, George saw the plastic trim of his bumper fly off and somersault down into the depths of the gorge. He was now travelling at a speed way above his comfort zone and way beyond what was safe, given the winding nature of the road. Camilleri had one hand on the dashboard and another clutching the strap hanging above the passenger door. He kept looking behind.

"Here he comes again, George! You *have* to do something!"

At that moment, a tight left-hand bend loomed ahead and George was doing 120 kilometres per hour. He realised he had no chance of making the corner, as soon as he started to turn the wheel. The gorge was to their right, so the car crossed the carriageway, heading away from the sheer drop, flew over a deep drainage ditch and careered onto roadside scrub, bouncing over the rocks and uneven ground. It seemed to leave the surface for several seconds and fly, before hitting the scrub at such an angle that the road now reappeared at right angles to them.

Camilleri saw that, if they made it back onto tarmac, their accumulated speed would carry them straight across it, over the opposite verge and down into the canyon.

"Brake, George! Brake!" he screamed.

George had his eyes shut and was practically pushing the brake pedal through the floor in his efforts to take some speed off, but it was not enough to stop the car bouncing back over the drainage ditch and onto the road – at the very same moment as the black SUV came hurtling around the corner. The hire car hit it full force, side on, and the airbags exploded in their faces. He still had his feet jammed on the brake pedal, as both he and Camilleri were rocked by the collision.

After a minute or so, they realised they were shaken, but still alive and uninjured. They dragged themselves free from the airbags and gingerly climbed out of the car. It was in the middle of the road, back on track for Modica. George shielded his eyes from the sun and scoured the road that dwindled into the distance in both directions, hugging the side of the canyon. He could see no trace of the black SUV.

Camilleri, however, had crossed the road and was peering down into the gorge. He turned and beckoned George over.

"Can you see that?"

Hundreds of metres below them, a glint of metal and a black patch contrasted with the honey-coloured limestone.

"Oh! My word, that looks like it, doesn't it? What do you think? Should we go down and see if he's alright?"

They peered down into the chasm. Camilleri had a thin smile on his lips.

"I do not think so. Best to put this little episode out of our minds entirely. But first, I must say, George, that was incredible driving! Where on earth did you learn to handle a car like that? I really thought for a moment you had completely lost control. Well done! Remarkable skill."

They climbed back into the hire car that was badly battered but, to their surprise, still driveable. Camilleri looked at his phone.

"Keep going for now. When I have got a signal, we'll, stop. I need to make two calls. One to the Palazzo di Laredo, telling them they should advertise for a new footman, and the other to Signorina Bonnici. I will not tell you exactly what I am going to say to her, but I do not mind admitting to you I am very disappointed in her."

CHAPTER 40

SUPERINTENDENT GEORGE ZAMMIT
QUESTURA DI CATANIA

THE NEXT MORNING, George slid into the Questura with two takeout coffees and a bulging bag of pastries from Prestipino's. He felt a little guilty that he was straying well beyond his role as observer to the inquiry into Silvia's disappearance, but it seemed nobody there was in the least bothered about his presence or his activities. He walked up to the door behind the reception counter and, with a *buongiorno*, the desk sergeant buzzed him through into the offices. He quickly descended the stone staircase to basement level and found his way to the broom cupboard that Vice Questora Capozzi had allocated them.

Diego was sitting there, in front of a laptop, watching the highlights of a football match. He hastily tried to close the lid.

"Oh! Sorry! I didn't know who that was."

George pushed a cup of coffee in front of him and offered him a *sfogliatella*, a shell shaped pastry, with a sweet custard filling made with semolina and ricotta.

Diego said: "Oh yeah!" taking a pastry.

"Right, put it down for a minute and let's see this stolen security camera footage of yours"

Reluctantly, Diego placed the pastry on the table and the two of them peered down at the laptop. The images were divided between a grid of four frames, each date and time stamped.

"Look at this one, up here." Diego pointed with a chubby finger. "That's Benedetta's BMW arriving, we know the reg. The time is 14:51. Her appointment at the hairdresser's was for three. Keep watching."

Benedetta got out of the car and slipped on a long blue raincoat, shouldered her bag and disappeared from the frame. Within seconds, George saw a black VW Transporter pull into the space opposite the BMW, cab first. He noticed nobody got out. Diego clicked the cursor over the fast-forward control.

"OK, I'll run this forward to 16:17."

"No one gets out of the van?"

"No, unless I've missed it. It gets a bit boring, all this watching, you know! Sometimes they wind down the window to get rid of cigarettes, but they stay inside. Now... this bit is good."

In the foreground of the frame, Benedetta appeared in her long, belted raincoat, newly coiffed hair under a plain, sky blue headscarf. She stopped for a moment to look in her bag for her keys, then the side doors of the van swung open and two men in balaclavas jumped out and ran the three or four paces towards her. As they grabbed her, the rear doors of the van swung open and a third man, also in a balaclava, stepped out. Benedetta was carried, arms and legs thrashing widely, to the van and quickly bundled through the rear doors, which were shut behind her.

Diego watched the grab and said: "There we are. That's the good bit. The rest's rubbish."

George was confused. "You mean, you watched more?"

"Yeah, hours of it. Nothing else happens."

"Mela... , nothing? Play back the 'good bit', will you."

They ran the clip back and forth, several times, trying to recognise the men from the van. Finally, George said: "It could be Lelli and Crisponi but, then again, it could be anybody. There's no conclusive ID to be had from these pictures. What about the van? We've got a clear view of the registration."

"Yeah, I looked into it. The van's a rental, but on the date and time they took her, it wasn't booked out."

"Right," said George. "You go and pay a visit to the van company. Get a list of employees, find out who could have taken it. Check out any security cameras. I bet if there's a fenced yard for the vehicles, there'll be cameras. Maybe we'll get something from that."

"OK, right, I'm on it."

As Diego opened the door to leave the room, Vice Questora Capozzi entered. The pair collided, her head striking his sternum.

"Whoa, I'm sorry!" Diego backed into the room.

Capozzi stood in the doorway, taking stock of what was before her.

"Well, look at this cosy scene! I didn't realise you were still with us, Superintendent. Where are you off to, Agente Russo?"

"Me? I'm checking out the van that was used to kidnap…"

George immediately jumped in, before Diego could utter another indiscreet word.

"Er, it's just part of the thing we've got on."

"The *thing*?"

"You know, our inquiries into Silvia Camilleri's abduction. I asked Diego to get some security camera footage. We thought there was a vehicle that might be of interest, but there's nothing that helps us."

"Abduction? Last time we talked, you didn't have any proof Silvia Camilleri was abducted."

George looked shifty.

Capozzi was not impressed.

"Also, what authority do you have to be taking security camera files?"

She turned to Diego, pointing at the laptop.

"Did you do this, Agente?"

"I did, yes, I thought…"

"Superintendent, you've grossly overstepped the mark and I think your time 'observing' our inquiries has just come to an end. I don't like what I see. I'm instructing the *sovrintendente capo* on the front desk that, as from tonight, your access privileges have expired."

Diego was flustered.

"Does that mean me as well?"

Capozzi looked at him scornfully.

"I'll deal with you later."

She remained in the doorway, daring anyone to raise any objection, while the sheepish men gathered their belongings and made ready to leave. Diego started to close down the laptop, but the vice questora said: "Leave that. I'll come down and have a look at it when I've got a moment."

They shuffled past Capozzi, who stood holding the door open for them. Once they were in the corridor, she produced a bunch of keys from her jacket pocket, locked the door to what had been their office and walked away without looking back. After she had climbed the stairs back up to the ground floor, Diego spoke.

"Wow, that was bad. Looks like I'm in trouble, again."

George sighed.

"Well, I can't blame her. She's the boss here. I've had a message from Bastiano Beneventi, asking me to meet him. I can tell him what we've found, then check out this rental place. Actually, Diego, if you've been reassigned back to wherever you came from, it's probably best if we call it a day. You've done enough to help me. You don't want to get on the wrong side of the boss, do you?"

"Yes, er, no. But I want to see this through. On my own time even. Let me know what's going on, will you?"

"Diego, I will, but please send me a copy of the security

camera footage that shows the abduction. I need to show it to the Beneventis."

"Well, yeah, sure – but it's sort of locked in there." He pointed to the door of their former office.

George sighed.

"Yes, that's true. Listen, I've one last favour. I need to pick up a new hire car – the last one sort of… well, got a few scrapes on it! So, could you take my boss, the assistant commissioner back to the airport later on?"

"Me? Take the assistant commissioner? By myself? Just the two of us? Wow! I mean, yeah, sure, great! Can I talk to him?"

CHAPTER 41

SILVIA CAMILLERI
IN CAPTIVITY, MOUNT ETNA

IT TOOK 24 hours before Benedetta recovered sufficiently to speak. Silvia had pushed her bed next to the new prisoner's and the pair of them huddled as close together as they could, to preserve warmth. It was a tricky exercise, as Benedetta's injuries made any physical contact painful. Silvia had lain for hours listening to her cellmate's soft breathing, as she slept deeply. Whenever she moved, she would moan.

When Benedetta did wake, Silvia would urge her to take half a painkiller and sip water. On one awful occasion, only half-conscious, she had said she needed to pee and Silvia had helped her ease her battered body off the bed and introduced her to the yellow bucket, holding her while she relieved herself. Eventually, Benedetta's spells of wakefulness became longer and she was lucid enough to be able to talk.

They soon realised they had several things in common. Neither had a clue why they were being held, nor could they guess what circumstances would lead to their release. When Silvia discovered who Benedetta's family was, she even managed to laugh out loud at the irony.

"My God, I thought it was your family who were holding me here! Don't you see how ridiculous that seems now? God, I'm really confused. The reason I'm here is because of that protest up at Nuovi Modi. Protesting against your family's business!"

Benedetta turned onto her side, with a grimace.

"This has nothing to do with my family. They would never sink so low or ask anybody else to act for them. I'm not saying... I don't know. There're some people involved with them who I don't like. Maybe there's been a falling out. Maybe Dad shut the plant down. I've always just worked in the winery, but now I'm here with you! It can't be my family, don't you see?"

"Wait... The plant was shut down? You're kidding?"

"Yeah. Dad was nervous with all the recent tremors and eruptions and stuff. He didn't trust the messages coming from the INGV in Catania. So, he closed it down."

"And the protesters?"

"Oh, they all left. Even before it was shut down. My brother said they'd had enough and were getting nowhere."

After that, Silvia had lain very quietly and looked at the roof for a long time. She had no reason to doubt Benedetta, but could not understand why they would just pack up and go. If that was right, why was she still being held captive? it did not make any sense.

Benedetta then asked Silvia how she had been taken.

"The first thing I remember is the sound of a mosquito buzzing in my ear. I hate mosquitoes and I'm always careful to zip the tent, so I thought it was strange. But it wasn't a mozzie, it was someone trying to get into the tent. They cut a way in through the back and grabbed me. I fought for a bit, but they held a cloth over my face and I couldn't scream. I felt I was going to suffocate. Then, they stuck a needle into me. I felt that – in my arm. I fought for a bit more, and then, I suppose, whatever it was took hold of me and that was that. I've got some memory of waking up in a van. I smelled oranges. Then this bloke was leaning over me, saying, 'I think she's awake. She's blinking,' or something, I never saw his face. A second guy – there were definitely two of them said something like, 'She's seen your face, you idiot! Give her some more, you need to keep dosing her.' I mean, I hadn't at all – seen either of them. The next thing I knew, I woke up here, on this bed, with a smelly blanket over me."

Benedetta asked: "How long have you been here?"

Silvia did not have a clue.

"I think, forever, no, maybe a few weeks, I can't really say. No days or nights in here, just the eternal light bulb. It's torture. I used to count the man's visits, but stopped at eleven, because I thought it might drive me mad. I didn't want to know. And you, how long?"

Benedetta thought.

"It was only a day or two in that wet hole. The old man said it was a punishment for scratching the eyes of one of the guys who grabbed me. Can you believe it? Then I went down the tunnel. But they kept me in total darkness, so I can't say for sure. I couldn't stand it. I cried and cried. I was hysterical."

She told Silvia about her attempted escape and how she had ended up in the tunnel, underwater.

"You did that? God! That's pretty brave."

"Not really, just pretty stupid. I should be dead. But, after a while, I just felt I had no choice. I wanted to go back, but I just couldn't, the flow was too strong. I was weak and I remember struggling under the water, hitting my head, my back, and swallowing water. My chest got really tight. I was being tumbled over and over – and that was that."

"No, Benedetta, it sounds horrible!"

"Yeah, it was. I never want to drown again."

Benedetta started to sob softly. Then, they lay quietly, both reliving their experiences. Silvia asked: "What was this priest thing about? When they brought you in, you were calling for 'father'. You didn't mean your dad, I'm sure of that."

"Oh, was I? A priest? Oh, yeah… he was there, I'm sure of it. An old man with a white beard and in a priest's robe. He was the one who said I'd died and been brought back. He said it was a miracle. I believe it, as well. Well, maybe a near-death experience – you know, a light at the end of a tunnel? He said he'd found me in the water and must've brought me round somehow. My ribs do feel as though they've been pounded."

She gingerly felt her chest and grimaced, before continuing.

"We were in a cave. There was light and a bed. He sat at a desk. I can't be sure what exactly I saw." She lay quietly, casting back for more details. "There were even figures… full-size statues, like you see in churches. An underground church, maybe? But smaller. That's all I remember. I don't know how I got here. Maybe it was him who bandaged my head?"

"The old man and his wife brought you here. Is that where they brought you from, do you suppose?"

"I don't know."

As they spoke, the ground suddenly trembled and started to shake. There was a low reverberation that grew in intensity. Benedetta instinctively grabbed hold of Silvia. The shaking abated, as suddenly as it had started. Benedetta had been oblivious to the volcano's agitation and only now realised the implications.

"We're in the volcano, aren't we?"

Silvia looked up at the roof of the cell, biting her lower lip.

"Yeah; we are. It's been like this for days. The volcano is really active – it's like being at the end of a runway and a jet flying overhead. But the quakes are also shaking things around here. These tunnels could become unstable and the temperature is rising daily, you'll notice that too. I'm really scared. Listen, I know you're hurting, but we need to get out of here, as soon as we can. We have to find a way."

"I'm not going back into the water."

"God no! That's not what I have in mind."

At that moment, the next paroxysmal eruption from the South Eastern Crater blew thousands of tonnes of debris high into the sky and a fountain of molten lava spurted into the air, cascading down like a mighty firework.

Above ground, it was late evening, and those in Catania were treated to another awesome display of the power of the volcano. The villages above Zafferana Etnea had already been evacuated, but those left in the town, from its usual population of 10,000, knew now was the time to flee. The enormous explosion had destroyed the southern rim of the South East Crater and a huge mass had collapsed back down into the crater itself. This left the way free for thousands of tonnes of material to be swept along by the lava and roll down the Valle del Bove, to the very doorstep of the town of Zafferana Etnea.

It was as if the volcano had heard their conversation and was angered by talk of escape. In response, it exploded with the biggest eruption yet. In their cell, the women screamed, as a shower of dust and rock particles fell from the roof. They clung to each other. In her terror, Benedetta was oblivious to the pain caused by Silvia burrowing into her bruised ribs. Shadows danced madly on the walls of the cave, as tremors swung the single light bulb around and around. For several minutes there was a deep and sustained roar, as the fabric of the mountain tore open. Magma spewed upwards from kilometres beneath the surface, spurting out of the volcano in a rush of energy. Once the worst of the violence and the noise had subsided, Silvia noticed one minor consequence. The violence of the tremor had heaved the rock that formed their cell and splintered the frame around the door. Silvia peered through a cloud of dust. Both door and frame had separated from the wall and were leaning outwards, into the tunnel beyond. One push and they could walk out of their cell.

CHAPTER 42
SUPERINTENDENT
GEORGE ZAMMIT

BENEVENTI WINERY, MOUNT ETNA

LATER THAT DAY, George and Camilleri were impatiently waiting outside the Hotel Celeste for Diego to arrive, to drive Camilleri to the airport. Fifteen minutes later than the agreed time the young man arrived in the Fiat to collect him. The assistant commissioner was not impressed when he saw the vehicle.

"George, what on earth…?"

Diego leaped out and nearly threw himself at Camilleri's feet.

Sir, good morning, I'm Agente Diego Russo – named after the footballer!" His round face was red with the pleasure of being able to speak to such a high-ranking officer.

Camilleri was puzzled.

"I don't recall a footballer named Russo?"

Diego pulled a face.

"No, you've got it wrong…"

George butted in.

"Diego, enough. Just drive the assistant commissioner to the airport."

But Diego was not finished trying to ingratiate himself.

"Well, sir… assistant commissioner, sir… we've got some time, well, we have if I step on it, so would you like a little trip around the city, as we pass through? I've lived here all my life and..."

George barked, "Diego, the assistant commissioner is not a tourist! Just drive him please. And be quiet!"

"Yes, sir, sirs, yeah, I will."

Unusually for him, Camilleri took pity on the young man.

"I have seen the city on many occasions, thank you, so no need for a tour. I understand from Superintendent Zammit that you have been most helpful. The Maltese Pulizija is in your debt so, if there is anything we can do for you in the future, you only have to ask."

Diego's chest swelled with pride and he beamed at them.

George could not help but smile back. He nodded in the direction of the car and Diego took his cue and marched around to the driver's door.

———

After taking possession of the new hire car, George drove back up the familiar road to the winery. The autostrada was eerily quiet as those in the coastal towns were busy cleaning the grit and ash from their streets and properties. The whole mountain seemed to be holding its breath, waiting for something. Up above him, he could see Zafferana Etnea and make out the spires and domes of its baroque churches, rising from the red tiled roofs. The Valle del Bove, above Zafferana Etnea, was a huge basin on the side of the volcano, formed some 60,000 years ago, when Etna was twice the size it was today and a huge eruption had collapsed its eastern side into the sea. The basin had long protected the eastern towns, its deep lip halting lava flows and pyroclastic rushes. Here, the ancient, barren lava fields extended far down the volcano to the very doors of the eastern villages. A further reminder of what the volcano was capable of, lest anyone should forget.

On arriving at the winery, George found Bastiano and Albi in their communal lounge, with a log fire crackling away in the hearth. The pair seemed more alert than the last time George had seen them. Excited even.

George started by describing his visit to Crisponi's flat the previous evening.

"He all but admitted he had Silvia. What about Benedetta? What's been said about her?"

Albi straightened himself in his armchair, his eyes brighter and his movements more decisive than previously.

"I've spoken to the man who can make things happen and told him I've made a mistake and will learn from it. They made me repeat that I'd learned my lesson, then said, if we can find her, we can have her back. They told me Crisponi would know how to get to her."

George could not believe what he was hearing.

"Then what are you doing, sitting here? We need to go and find him. It looks like the two women are being held together."

Bastiano was pacing the room, clearly agitated.

"It's not that simple. Crisponi's not at the plant and he's not at home. According to his girlfriend, he got a call late last night, said he had to go out for a bit and never returned."

George was puzzled.

"But I saw him in the early evening and he was his usual odious self. What do we do now?" He thought for a moment. "I can talk to the vice questora, I suppose, though this morning…"

Bastiano laughed.

"Who, that poisonous little Capozzi?"

"Well, yes."

"Her father is doing twenty years in Pagliarelli prison in Palermo. He was from a Calabrian crime family, they say. Came over here when he was young and then became a big wheel in the Catania 'Ndrangheta. He was the *capo* who ran the Librino district, until he got caught up in the 2010 super-trials. After he went down, his daughter stepped straight into his shoes. A vice questora *and* a *madrina* – a godmother!. She visits him in gaol every month. It could only happen in Sicily!"

George was shocked.

"Really? Capozzi's a Godmother? Mela, she's not to be trusted?"

Bastiano did not bother to reply. Instead, he looked over at his father.

"But there's something else you need to know. This is why we asked you to come. Dad, tell him about Greco."

Albi then took over.

"There was a Mass the other night, up in Nicolosi. I was there and so was Father Greco. You don't know him, but he's a local priest..."

Bastiano interjected, to Albi's annoyance.

"He *was* a parish priest, but was the victim of gossip, years ago, for 'you know what' with village boys. Now he's a madman hermit type, who lives in the caves on the volcano."

Albi sighed.

"That's not quite true. He's a learned man. He has different views from most, but he's still respected."

"Blah!"

Albi shook his head.

"There're many stories about him, each more fantastic than the last. It's not Father Greco who spreads them."

Bastiano brushed this away.

"Whatever! Anyway, he spends much of his time in the caves and lava tunnels under Etna. He has a chapel in the woods and another in the volcano. Dad and the other Brothers visit them to worship. Now he says he has news for us 'that will raise our hearts!'. He sent a message telling Dad to meet him at the Chapel of St Florian this evening. It's halfway up the bloody volcano! Obviously, with the eruptions, it's suicide going there, but he has to be referring to Benedetta."

Albi looked up imploringly from his chair.

"But we have to! It's the only chance we've got to get Benedetta back, if Crisponi's gone."

George considered the options.

"Either that or find Crisponi?"

Albi shook his head.

"I get the feeling it's a bit late to go looking for him. He screwed up somewhere and now he's paid the price."

———

Albi was absolutely right. Pietro Pomodoro had completed his inquiries and satisfied himself that Roberto Crisponi was indeed a lying piece of shit. Basso had confirmed they had ordered the eco-girl's release weeks ago. People in Malta said the kidnap victim's mother was still weeping in church every day, and masses were being said on Sundays, in Paola Parish Church, for her safe return. There was no trace of any Silvia Camilleri on an aeroplane out of Catania, Palermo or Trapani, and no chapel of rest or morgue had accepted any unknown female matching the woman's description, within the last three weeks. There was no way the Camilleri woman had been dropped off in Palermo. Crisponi was lying, which was enough for Pietro Pomodoro, who had never liked him very much anyway.

When Crisponi had pulled into the car park at the Conad supermarket, on the west side of Randazzo, he had expected his friend Natalino Lelli to be there, waiting to hand over an envelope full of cash. At least, that is what he had been told. One look at Lelli, sitting white-faced and clammy in his Toyota Prius, showed him that was not going to happen. The flash of a full-beam headlight, 20 metres in front of him, then caught Crisponi's attention. Lelli said nothing and looked straight ahead, ignoring his associate, who asked: 'What's going on?' Warily, Crisponi walked towards the parked car, sheltering his eyes from the headlights that masked the identity of the vehicle's occupants.

Suddenly, he became aware of a presence behind him. A hand roughly grabbed at his hair and he was yanked backwards and was held tight, against whoever it was to the rear of him.

Pietro Pomodoro loved the feel of the serrated edge of his 20-centimetre hunting knife severing a throat, particularly when the throat in question belonged to a lying piece of scum like Roberto Crisponi. The slice of the knife was the price one paid for a lie. Without trust, the 'Ndrangheta would be nothing. That was understood by all.

CHAPTER 43

HAKAN TOPRAK
CATANIA PALACE HOTEL, CATANIA

THE CATANIA PALACE HOTEL was ten minutes south of Fontanarossa airport on the coastal plain. From the rooftop bar, Hakan had a perfect view of Etna's south-eastern flank. He appreciated being the additional distance away from the volcano's tantrums – the visit to Nicolosi the previous evening had taken him a little too close for comfort. Here, he could admire the splendour of the fiery rivulets that threaded their way down the mountainside, and join in the exclamations of wonder at the pyrotechnics that intermittently illuminated the summit with showers of sparks and sprinkles of light. Though it was not yet fully dark, the cloudless night allowed for a spectacular show.

At exactly 18:00, Vito Amato arrived, a heavy scarf wrapped around his neck and jaw, and chunky, dark sunglasses concealing his upper face. With amusement, Hakan realised he was trying to disguise himself. Vito stood against the bar and swivelled to face the outside seating area, where Hakan had positioned himself. He raised a glass to attract the other man's attention. Vito hurriedly made his way through the bar and joined Hakan on some all-weather sofas.

"Be quick, I haven't got much time. What's this all about?"

"Be quick? Nothing about this will be quick, Signor Amato. We need to get to know each other first."

Vito glanced over his shoulder, making sure they could not be overheard. Vito leant in, his mouth close to Hakan's ear. He spoke softly.

"I know you, Hakan Toprak. Turkish minister, oil man and banker. You dragged Malta into your clutches and have got them doing your dirty work on the Turkey – Libya maritime concession. You shafted the Greeks, changing international maritime law. Somehow, you have the US in your pocket; you persuaded the Israelis to take out the Iranian nuclear processing centrifuges, to distract them from opposing your military coup, and now, for some reason, you're here, to make my life difficult."

Hakan smiled broadly.

"Well done! And all in 24 hours. I will have to brush up my security if my CV is so easy to unearth. "

"Look, you're obviously no fool and I won't treat you as such. You know who pulls my strings. I've got no room to manoeuvre. There's nothing I can do for you."

"On the contrary, there is everything you can do for me. As I said last night, I intend to become the city's new partner and the powers in Rome are right behind me. I have filled them in on what is happening down here and, it is fair to say, they are not much impressed. The game is up. So, I will need a proper conversation with the top table."

"I don't sit at the top table, and neither does Albi Beneventi."

"No, I know that. What you have to do is to pass the message up the line, to the top table. If any of the middle management decide to take things into their own hands, I will need to know that too. In fact, I should probably send a message first of all. Who is the highest ranker you deal with?"

"It's hard to tell. Some of them look like farmers, but I suppose there's Agostino Basso. He's the main man we deal with."

"OK, good. You do not like him, do you?"

"I don't like any of them, but they've done things Rome and Palermo could never do. Moved quickly, put money where they said they would. They have an investment arm in Rome, they're very switched on."

"Well, that may be true. But I am not looking to usher in a new world of bureaucracy. Rome does not want to dismantle what has been built here – far from it! They think it is wonderful – and, in a way, it is. They just want it out of the hands of the 'Ndrangheta. It looks bad, their model city, getting so much attention, while it is in the hands of gangsters. You understand that?"

Hakan looked at Vito, who just stared at him, the consequences of the conversation rolling around in his head.

"So, you are with me on this? I am the acceptable face of pan-European business. Not organised crime. I am a practical man. I can get you nicely ring-fenced, before you run into serious trouble. If you choose not to help me, I will certainly bring down all manner of trouble on your head, be assured of that. And I will still get what I want."

"If you want me to pass on a message, I'll do that, but you're one hundred per cent on your own. If they think I'm working with you, they'll kill me. It's what they do, if there's even a hint of doubt about someone's loyalties."

"I understand. And, for now, that is reasonable."

"What's your angle here? What exactly are you offering? They've got money, cash, like you wouldn't believe. They pull it in from all over the world. Here, there's a chance to get rid of some of that cash, divert it into long-term legitimate business. You're in the energy industry yourself... I mean, the old stuff, oil and gas... if you can see the appeal of what we're doing here, so can they."

"Signor Amato, what you probably do not realise is that Turkey is in the middle of a currency and debt crisis. The old regime screwed the country. We have had debt defaults, inflation, devaluations, and we badly need new sources of finance. Investors. After the devaluations, the borrowing costs in the international markets are too high for us. We need new partners. Underneath it all, we are still a major industrial power and need long-term partners who believe in our recovery, under the new management, not short-term speculators. In return, we will give them somewhere safe to put their money.

"Incidentally, or perhaps not, Turkey also controls most of the world's heroin trade. That comes from Afghanistan, through northern Iran and into Europe. We can turn it on, turn it off. We decide who benefits, as we always have done. Your associates dropped heroin for the cocaine business twenty years ago. No reason why they cannot get back into it and have both!

"But, most significantly, what has happened here is now too important to be left in their hands. There is too much attention on this project worldwide. Already, questions are being asked. Your associates need to cash out, before too much scrutiny is applied. Rome's anti-Mafia squad arrives on the island next week and they will start turning over all manner of stones, to see what crawls out. I strongly suspect they will start with the mayor's office; they usually do. So, you see? Plenty of scope here for everyone to benefit."

Together they stood and looked northwards, past the distant skyline of the city, at the flecks of light on the side of the volcano. Evening was almost upon them. In farms and homesteads, lights were being turned on and dinners prepared. Brushes and shovels were leaning in readiness against walls, and windows were shut to keep out the malodourous smell of the Mother's exhalations.

Vito was nervous at discovering that this man was serious. He could see his own golden age coming to an end, his reputation tarnished and his legacy destroyed. But Vito had not grown up in poverty in Maletto and risen to own a Maserati and four thousand euros worth of dental veneers, without having some fight left in him. He sensed this strange, implacable Turk had a deal to offer him and he needed to know what it was.

"What can you offer me?"

"I want you to co-operate fully. Give me the information I need so I can squeeze them. Heads need not roll. In fact, I think they will thank me, once they have considered my terms. They will know their profile is already far too high. Our friends across the Straits of Messina are businessmen like me – they do not like making headlines."

"What about me? How do I come out of all this?"

"Well, as for you, my friend, we will keep you alive, out of prison, we will not chase you for your ill-gotten gains and see what we can do to preserve your reputation. But I cannot promise you will keep that office in Palazzo degli Elefante. That is not within my gift." Hakan fixed Vito with his impassive stare. He could smell the fear on him. "But more important than anything, Signor Amato, you will be free of them and able to sleep easy. What is that worth?"

CHAPTER 44

SILVIA CAMILLERI
INSIDE MOUNT ETNA, CATANIA

It took Silvia a moment to believe what she was seeing. Amidst the dust and the flickering of the single light bulb, it struck her that the door had been sprung from the aperture in the rock. The way out was open. She did not move immediately. She and Benedetta still cowered on the bed, while the full might of the eruption raged around them. The main South Eastern Crater, where the major eruption was occurring, was five kilometres to the east. Between them and the jets of magma that spurted up from the chambers beneath, was a mass of hardened basalt rock. In reality they were safe from the flows of magma being ejected on the the southern side of the volcano. None of that was known to the terrified women, though, as it felt as if the violent events were taking place in the next room.

After several minutes, when Silvia had caught her breath and calmed her heartbeat, she got off the bed and went towards the open door. The same cable that brought the power to the single bulb in the cell, stretched away down a smooth-walled corridor, tacked onto the rocky ceiling. Pendant lights hung down its length.

She tried to call to Benedetta, who was still lying on the bed, but the noise of shifting rock and jetting magma drowned out her voice, until she screamed.

"I'm going to see what's down there. Don't worry, I'll be back."

"Don't leave me! Please, Silvia!"

"Just give me a minute."

Silvia walked to the end of the corridor, one hand on the wall to steady herself, past the upturned blue drum of water where she used to wash. She followed the yellow water hose around the corner and, sure enough, there was another solid-looking antique door, that was firmly locked. There was also a table with some old boxes piled on it, plumbing fittings and some lengths of blue nylon rope. The hose and the cable snaked through grooves hacked into the stone, suggesting the exit lay on the other side of the locked door.

She returned to the table and looked through the boxes for anything that might be useful. There was a basic cross-head screwdriver, some wire cutters and two rubber-sheathed torches, held in brackets on the wall. That was it, as far as tools went. She took the torches and slipped the screwdriver into her rear pocket, before returning to the cell. As she approached the cell door, she noticed the corridor continued on ahead of her. She thought there might be another exit going that way.

Benedetta was not going to risk being left behind and had managed to raise herself from the bed and reach the door. Silvia found her slumped against the wall.

"How're you doing?"

"Oh, I'm OK. It just hurts everywhere. Don't leave me. Promise?"

"I won't."

Silvia put a hand on the injured woman's shoulder to reassure her. "Well, there's not much up there. We can wait by the top door and ambush the old man when he arrives, or we can have a look the other way, down the corridor and see what we can find. I've got torches."

She looked down the tunnel, in the opposite direction to the one in which she had just been. It was unlit and forbidding. The dense blackness seemed to suck the light out of the adjacent space.

Benedetta said, "The old guy won't come up here in the middle of an eruption. We might as well have a quick look, if only to rule it out."

The torch beams were powerful and lit the tunnel metres ahead of them. Silvia suggested they should only use one torch, so they could at least preserve enough power to light their way back. The tunnel was several metres high and the floor was smooth. It seemed to be a descending slope, taking them deeper into the volcano. The ceiling dripped with long, smooth red stalactites, caused by lava that had once run from the roof. The rust-red hue of the tunnel made it feel as through the women were walking inside a massive human artery.

They pushed on for several minutes, Benedetta shuffling alongside Silvia, their arms linked. To their left, a narrow gallery branched off the main tunnel. Silvia glanced into the gloom, concluding it probably led nowhere. They kept following the main passage, noticing the heat had started to build. Benedetta's breathing was becoming laboured and the pair of them started to sweat. The background rumbling continued, but the seismic shaking had become less severe. Nevertheless, Silvia was becoming anxious. The clearance above their heads was becoming lower and the tunnel narrowing, as piles of rocks from roof-falls blocked the way. Dust clouds filled the air and the torch beam picked out a million floating particles.

"This is going nowhere. These falls are recent – look at the dust. We should go back. "

Benedetta urged her on.

"We've come this far, let's get to the end. Then, at least we can forget about it."

At that moment, there was a loud rumble ahead of them; the sound of rushing, cracking rock. Then silence. The torch beam searched the blackness ahead. Slowly, a thick spectral fog of material came floating silently down the tunnel towards them. Tumbling particles of rock, suspended in the current of air, were being propelled towards them by the collapsing roof.

The women looked at each other and, without a word, turned around and started to retrace their footsteps. As they made their way back, Silvia remembered the gallery off the main passage. As she passed the entrance, deep in shadow, she flashed her torch into the roof and noticed a darker, regular-shaped area that looked like some sort of door. In fact, they discovered it was the beginning of a staircase, cut into the rock, leading down to a level below theirs.

Silvia looked at Benedetta, then at the rocky steps leading further down into the volcano.

"I don't want to go any deeper. Who knows what's down there."

Benedetta adjusted her bloodied turban and peered down the staircase into the darkness.

"You wait here then – I'll go and look," offered Silvia. "Give me the torch."

"You're kidding! I'm not being left behind. OK... God, I'm scared."

Silvia gingerly started to make her way down the roughly cut, narrow staircase, one hand on the wall. Benedetta put her hand on Silvia's shoulder for support. The treads were narrow and the risers deep, leading to a slow and arduous descent. There were no banister and more stairs than they had imagined, so the descent took them several minutes to complete. When they finished the stairs, their knees aching and their breathing laboured, they found themselves in a large cavern with a high ceiling and the remnants of a mosaic floor, made from volcanic stone and glass. Silvia shone the beam around.

"What on earth is this place?"

At the head of it was a basic wooden table, arranged as an altar, with a silver cross in the middle, flanked by two large candles secured by mounds of wax. In front of the table were about a dozen old wooden chairs, arranged in a semi-circle. Next to the cross was a large stone chalice, maybe 25 centimetres across and forty high, with an elaborate spiral pattern running from the lip of the cup to the circular base. The table was clearly set up for the celebration of the Eucharist.

Silvia went behind the altar and found boxes of candles and matches. She lit half a dozen and placed four on the tabletop, gave one to Benedetta and kept one for herself.

Benedetta peered around. She was immediately certain that this was where she had seen the priest. She knew it, in fact. She walked across to the far end of the cave, some 15 metres away from the staircase, and heard the sound of running water.

"Over here!" she called.

In that corner, there was a pool about three metres across. The water seemed to be bubbling. On the rock wall around it were paintings of figures and old inscriptions. The damp had long-since stripped away the detail and corrupted the text, but the pool obviously had ceremonial significance.

"Look, there's water flowing through it. This must be where I emerged. I recognise it! This is where the priest found me! The watercourse must flow in here, then out again."

Silvia looked at the pool of black water, its surface reflecting the candlelight and the torch beam back up at them.

"You were lucky that priest found you. You could easily have…"

"Died? Yes, I know. He told me I did."

Benedetta looked around.

"Silvia, while you were in the cell, upstairs, can you remember anybody passing backwards and forwards, past where we were held? I'm wondering if there's another way into this place, apart from those stairs. Anybody coming down the way we did would need to pass the cell, but I've never heard any footsteps other than the old man."

"No, you're right. He was the only person who came down that corridor. I lay there for hours, listening and waiting for him to open the top door."

"So, if they didn't come down the stairs, there must be another entrance to this place."

They both started looking around. Their exertions had left Benedetta feeling weak and dizzy and she soon found herself sitting on one of the chairs in front of the altar, behind which there was a curtain hanging from a brass pole. The curtain was painted, or woven, with a bucolic scene featuring the lower slopes of the volcano. Small figures worked in orchards and vineyards, with whitewashed villages and hamlets in the background. The top half of the picture featured the volcano itself, as a dark pyramid, with a thread of grey smoke curling from the crater.

As Benedetta studied the image, she detected the faintest of movements in the fabric – ripple moved across the surface of the image – ever so slightly.

"Silvia! Behind the curtain! The entrance is behind the curtain!"

Silvia put her hand behind it and pushed it to one side. It slid along the pole to reveal a dark, rectangular opening, about the height of a short person. The tunnel behind was narrow and low-ceilinged. Both Silvia and Benedetta had to stoop to escape from the chapel. However, they did not get far. They soon found the way barred by another locked wooden door.

Silvia uttered a screech of frustration and kicked her foot against it. In response, the volcano uttered another growl that reverberated from deep within its gut and squeezed a plug of white-hot rock, through the constriction of the crater, to shoot out then tumble down onto the Valle de Bove, the wide valley on its eastern flank.

CHAPTER 45
SUPERINTENDENT GEORGE ZAMMIT

CHAPEL OF ST FLORIAN, MOUNT ETNA

GEORGE AND BASTIANO joined Albi in his spacious Mercedes and drove for an hour across the back roads that criss-crossed the volcano. The ash and grit deposits made the surfaces treacherous, with sparks and flying cinders starting dozens of smaller fires in the upper forests of the north-western flank. Local Carabinieri and officers from the Vigili del Fuoco stopped the car, on several occasions, as Bastiano negotiated his way around the smouldering upper contours of the mountain but, seeing it was Albi and Bastiano, they offered advice on local conditions and waved them on their way.

George sat in the back of the car, wondering what he was doing, 2,000 metres up an exploding volcano, on his way to meet a renegade priest, risking his life for Gerald Camilleri's niece – of all people. As he looked out of the window, down onto the lights of Catania, he felt a long way from his own family and home.

Before leaving to visit the Beneventis that afternoon, George had received a short-tempered call from Marianna, who had demanded his return to Malta on the next flight. It had been three weeks! She asked him what on earth he thought he was doing, given Gina's wedding was looming and his absence was starting to cause concern. He had promised, on all that was holy, he would not miss the nuptials, but this had only caused more consternation – it had never even entered his wife's mind that George might miss the wedding itself! She had merely been referring to some of the preliminary rehearsals, the reading of the banns, suppers with relatives, final fittings of suits and other crucial appointments. The stunned silence, as she registered the possibility George might not make it back for the wedding itself, was profound.

Then she hissed at him: "If you do one thing to spoil Gina's special day, you'll have me to answer to. And I warn you, you'll wish you'd never have come back." There was a pause. Then she followed up with: "That Abdullah's not with you, is he?"

"No, he isn't, I swear it!" Marianna had a low opinion of Abdullah and, with some justification, considered him to be the cause of all of George's previous prolonged absences from family life.

"Listen, I'll be back as soon as I can," he had told her. "And I'll be a full superintendent again – a senior officer! That'll be something, won't it?"

The line had already gone dead. He had sighed and reached into his pocket for the spare croissant he kept there – for emergencies.

The car climbed up the single-track road and eventually stopped near the woods that concealed the chapel. Albi handed out torches and they made their way across the rocky fields. He followed a faint track between the boulders and outcrops. George was puffing and blowing, as they entered the pitch black under the trees, but soon saw pinpricks of light through the branches from candles placed around the door of a single-storey building.

Albi signalled for them to halt and explained he would go first, to make sure the old priest was not taken by surprise. They watched him approach the wooden door, knock on it and duck inside the chapel. After a few seconds, he reappeared and waved to them. George and Bastiano looked around in amazement at the mural on the wall, lit by dozens of candles, and smelled the rich pine scent from the covering of needles on the floor.

Albi suggested George and Bastiano should sit at the back of the chapel, while he and the priest held their heads close together and talked earnestly. George watched the old priest and got the impression it was he who was confessing his sins, rather than the other way round. Albi seemed to be drawing strength from the conversation and his posture became more erect, as his back stiffened. After a little while, he summoned Bastiano and George over to join them.

The priest sat looking at the floor while Albi said to Bastiano: "We know where Benedetta is." He looked quickly at George. "And the other girl. Father Greco will guide us."

The priest turned to Bastiano and George.

"Please forgive my past silence. I have added it to the list of my many sins. I will pray to receive your forgiveness one day. But, now, we must leave here. It is a good time to go underneath the volcano. There will be nobody else on the slopes tonight."

The priest kicked off his sandals by the door and slipped into a pair of heavy walking boots. He glanced at the footwear of George and the Beneventi.

"Be careful where you stand. There are loose rocks and unstable surfaces everywhere. You will find wet-weather jackets in the box in the corner."

The three of them went and rummaged amongst the dirty and crumpled waterproofs in the box. Father Greco had pulled a rough hooded cloak across his shoulders and fastened three wooden toggles to secure it. He passed Albi a hand-carved hazel walking stick and held the door open, so they could start the climb up the mountain.

The priest set off up the hillside, moving quickly over the rough terrain, seemingly unaffected by the altitude and the sharp incline through the forest. Albi found the going tough. As the priest disappeared out of sight further up the path, he explained to Bastiano what he had been told in the chapel.

"You know the Fratelli Gambino quarries? Well, the Gambino family are the ones who hold the 'Ndrangheta's kidnap victims. It's a long-established arrangement. They feed them, look after them and don't ask any questions."

Bastiano snorted.

"I knew that family were no good. I went to school with Paolo Gambino and he was already a thug then. You should see the house they've built – right in the middle of the quarry! That did not come from digging lava stone."

Albi continued imperturbably, "It's their second business that's truly profitable. Has been for years. They use the caves in the forests above the Rifugio Saletti, south of Randazzo and have one of the families who work for them provide daily visits. Father Greco has one of his chapels in a nearby cavern and their cave systems overlap. He knows what's been going on, but turns a blind eye to it. He said, if he revealed all that he's seen on the mountain, half the population would be in jail. It's how he keeps their trust. He stays with the Gambinos when the weather is bad, so was reluctant to come straight to us. He says they've never hurt anyone before, but the girl in the volcano – the dead girl from Palermo – well, that changed things for him. It was an accident – she tried to escape and fell down a shaft – but still, it happened. They put her in a dark cavern, deeper into the system, as a punishment. She died there of her injuries.

"It was Father Greco who found Benedetta in a watercourse under the volcano, five days ago. She'd also tried to escape and had hurt herself. She was in a bad way. He knew she needed help, but it was only later the Gambinos told him who she was. He said he had some soul-searching to do then, but realised he had to tell me."

Bastiano asked: "He has seen her? How is she?"

"Yes, she's hurt, but alive."

Bastiano grunted.

"Huh! Those Gambinos, they're bastards! They're hard men."

Albi nodded.

"All the quarrymen are. But that's not going to stop us getting her back."

George was struggling up, behind Albi, listening in to the conversation.

"Have they got Silvia Camilleri too?"

Albi shouted over his shoulder: "Yes. That's what Father Greco said."

It took them an hour of climbing through the woods to reach a gully that led to the entrance to the cave system. George had slipped and stumbled in his leather-soled city shoes more times than he cared to count, and Albi, even with the support of the hazel stick, fared little better. The inaccessibility of the entrance from the nearest road, and the fact that, over the years, both Father Greco and the Gambinos had separately kept their access points artfully concealed, meant this system had remained a secret from the amateur speleologists and the tourists who flocked to explore the lava tunnels. Father Greco waited at the end of the path for them to complete the final scramble up to the entrance.

He explained the layout of the system.

"There are two levels. The top one, accessed from a little above here, is where the Gambinos run their business. They have partitioned off some cells to hold people. At the end of their tunnel, there is a cavern, where they hold the more difficult prisoners, or punish those who cause trouble. It's the one where the dead girl in the volcano was held. This cavern collapsed during one of the eruptions yesterday, or the day before, so we have to be careful going into the tunnels. We share a small power plant from a water turbine, so we have light. That is still working. The watercourse runs through the cavern and then into an underground tunnel, to rise in a well in my chapel in the deeper level. That is where I found Benedetta."

George asked: "Mela, and Silvia? Is she being held on this first level as well?"

"Yes. The Gambinos' man told me so."

George was curious.

"And how do you get between these galleries?"

"There is a steep staircase. Those who first showed me the chapel said it was there, even before their time."

"And you have your own entrance to the second gallery?"

"Yes, this is it." He pointed towards the bushes, up against the rock face.

Further conversation stopped, as they were hit by strong tremors. The shifting of the earth beneath them threw the old priest to the ground, causing him to lose his footing and, with a shriek, he slid down the loose scree onto an outcrop below. Albi also fell to the ground, clutching his walking stick like a staff in front of him. George found himself on hands and knees, clinging onto a mound of grass and dirt, eyes wide with terror.

While the earth was still shaking, Bastiano made his way down to the stricken priest, who lay awkwardly, moaning and clutching his thigh. Amidst the roar of the volcano and the strobic lights of its paroxysmal eruption, he decided the priest had fractured his femur. The acoustic blasts made George's head spin and he raised his hands to protect his ears. Bastiano came climbing up the slope, holding something in his fist.

Bastiano had to shout above the cacophony of the blasts and eruptions from the other side of the volcano.

"Dad, you stay here with the priest. He's injured. George, I've got the keys; you come with me. We can't leave the girls locked up in there. They'll be terrified."

George looked at him in horror and shouted over the noise: "I'm not going in there. It's exploding around us!"

"We have to. We're the only ones who can help them!"

"What're these caves called? I'm not going in until you find out. I want someone to know where we are."

Bastiano reluctantly scrambled back down to the stricken priest and George watched him cup one hand and speak into the old man's ear. He seemed to say something in response that satisfied Bastiano, who scrambled back up to join George.

"They're called the Grotta di Santa Maria. Happy now?"

CHAPTER 46

CRISTINA CAPOZZI
QUESTURA DI CATANIA

Vice Questora Capozzi was slumped in her chair. She had spent days at the site of the collapsed tower block at Librino, working alongside the special investigator, Claudia Nardi, to gather evidence on how such a tragedy could have occurred. The city engineers had taken thousands of photographs and exhaustively collected samples of concrete from the failed buildings. Everybody already knew the truth of it. Sicily was blighted by shoddily built apartment blocks, corruptly sanctioned and built by even more corrupt contractors.

In Catania, the situation was compounded by the architects and officials allowing the contractors to build on the exact position where the African and European tectonic plates butted up against one another. It was inevitable there would be problems at some point, but Cristina Capozzi was not going to allow Rome to start a witch hunt on her territory, especially when it was possible her own father and his friends might have been involved.

Librino was built on flat, former agricultural land as a new town to the south-east of Catania and just north of the Fontanarossa airport. It had never been a success. The Catanians preferred the fresher air on the slopes of Etna to the mosquito-infested flatlands adjacent to the airport. However, the area was taken over by the poorly housed from the pre-war urban slums across Sicily. From the early 70s, as was common in Sicily, illegal settlements sprang up on the undeveloped land around new tower blocks. Once it became apparent that the new apartments were never going to be sold into private hands, they were given over to public housing and co-operatives, and the downward spiral began. The city lost interest in Librino, and those in the town started to make up their own rules.

As the third-youngest son in a poor and struggling family, Giovanni Capozzi's own father had encouraged him to leave the poverty-stricken Aspromonte Mountains in the south of the mainland and seek his fortune with his childless uncle in Sicily. Giovanni had ambitions to become a car mechanic at first and moved in with his uncle and aunt, in a rented room in a crumbling block in Palermo's infamous Cascino Courtyard, a stone's throw from the grand Duomo. There, 260 families lived in 210 rooms. After several years of struggle, Giovanni still had no money, but had married a girl from the Courtyard and was in need of a home. He had heard about the availability of free land in Librino and moved his new wife to a rough plot at the end of a dirt track, right at the end of Catania's Fontanarossa runway. There, he quickly set about building a two-roomed dwelling from cinder blocks and red roof slates, stolen from the construction sites of the Librino developments. Cristina was born soon after the roof was completed and her earliest memories were of games, scoldings and conversations, constantly interrupted by the screaming engines of the flights arriving and departing.

Her father set about establishing himself both as the local mechanic and a salesman of locally stolen construction materials. Eventually, he found himself running a significant building materials business, and it was only a short step from that to becoming a builder and developer in his own right. That brought him into contact with other self-made men, who initiated him into the way things were done in Sicily in the 1970s.

Soon, Giovanni had built a second storey onto his house, surfaced the dirt track from the main road with stolen bitumen, and had the municipality grant him the title to the land on which his house stood. He successfully campaigned on behalf of his neighbours for similar property rights and became known as a man who could get things done. He saw the poverty in Librino and protected those who needed to bend a few rules to put food on their table. His transport business grew and he invested in a fleet of refrigerated trucks, taking produce from the rich farmlands of the south, across the Messina Straits to the cities of the north. In time, an ornamental wall with a high metal gate was built to protect the house and Cristina and her brother were told the large black dogs that were kept in the stiflingly hot shed during the day and released to roam the yard at night, were not to be considered pets.

All good things come to an end and, eventually, the name of Giovanni Capozzi was mentioned to the prosecutors sent from Rome to clean up crime and corruption in eastern Sicily. Giovanni was unable to explain where his considerable wealth had come from and why it was that several of his wagons, making the regular trips from the quiet southern ports of Sicily to the mainland, had secret compartments welded onto their chassis that had been found to contain traces of cocaine.

Giovanni realised the game was up and hired a lawyer from Palermo, recommended by his associates. The lawyer advised him to sit in the glass cage in court and say nothing, except confirm his name and plead Not Guilty. This he did and was duly found Guilty and sentenced to twenty years in prison.

Cristina was heartbroken. She found herself trying to pick up the wreckage of their family life. Her brother, who had been the family muscle, had immediately took revenge on the rival haulier he thought had had most to gain from Giovanni's incarceration. Cristina had not approved, but realised an opportunity had presented itself. She had asked a neighbour, who worked within the haulage business, to step up and run their operations, legitimately, for the time being. Another uncle, on her mother's side, was adamant he could run the building materials business, which he did.

Cristina spent her time in her father's office, at the back of the house, to be near the residual smell of him and his rough, smuggled cigarettes. As she looked at the piles of paperwork that littered the floor, to her surprise, she found it included correspondence on all manner of subjects, from requests for rehousing, pleas for assistance for social security support, claims for pensions, appeals concerning school places – all manner of issues where the local community had come to her father for help. He had written letters, paid local lawyers and, on occasion, made small grants from a fund he administered. She saw the compassion he had felt, it was plain enough in his letters, and she admired his quest for justice for the weaker members of society who had turned to him for help.

Cristina had rolled up her sleeves and continued the work he had started. Over time, she realised that, rather than rely on the power of her father's local network and fickle connections, an understanding of the law would be a better way of helping those who came to her. She had never been much for school and becoming an *avvocatessa* required a university degree and years more training. The police force had been the next best thing. She had advanced quickly through the ranks, but never closed her door to the local people who sought her help. Although she made her share of arrests, she was careful how she treated the people of Librino and, more particularly, her father's former associates. On the streets there, she was referred to as the *madrina* – the Godmother.

As the years passed, the building materials company thrived and the transport business went from strength to strength. These days, the secret compartments were sealed within the fuel tanks of the vehicles. Not even the most enthusiastic sniffer dog could detect packages that were surrounded by hundreds of litres of diesel fuel. She was also privy to the activities of the specialised *Direzione Centrale per i Servizi Antidroga* and could easily arrange for the 'adapted' vehicles to be held back for servicing, if the anti-drug agency showed any undue interest in traffic passing through the Port of Messina.

Her father was proud of her and she was a regular and unashamed visitor to Pagliarelli prison, where they held long monthly chats about the family and its business. It was there that she had heard from him of a planned visit to Catania by officers from the Direzione Nazionale Anti-Mafia squad. Giovanni told her that they were going to base themselves at the Questura and were planning to be there for some months. This, he informed her, had not gone down well in certain quarters. He took her hands in his and looked her straight in the eye, saying that when she received a message telling her to be away from the Questura, from a woman called Carla, she should make sure she was very far away! She was shocked by the news, particularly because she had heard nothing about the officers' imminent arrival through official channels. She realised that could not be a coincidence and knew she absolutely had to heed Carla's warning when it came.

CHAPTER 47
VITO AMATO
CARA DI MINEO KNOWLEDGE
PARK, CATANIA

VITO PULLED his Maserati into the car park of the so-called Knowledge Park that was home to the CatTech data centre and Bitcoin mining enterprise. As always, he was struck by the size of the buildings and, judging by the number of vehicles in the car park, how few people worked there. He made his way across from his car to the CatTech offices, noticing his heart rate increased, and the perspiration marks on his thin white shirt. Meetings with Basso always did this to him.

He walked along a corridor with large picture windows, designed so visitors could look out onto the endless racks, housing 800,000 high-powered servers that hummed and flickered away quietly, in a low-humidity atmosphere, constantly held at 18°C by a massive cooling plant to the rear of the building. The executive offices were at the end of the block, and the receptionist waved him through into the stylish boardroom. Sitting at the table, cigarette in mouth, was Basso. Next to him was a red-faced man Vito did not know. Agostino Basso did not introduce them, and Vito was surprised when the man addressed him by name.

"So, Vito, what's up today that could not wait? You frightened of the explosions? Want to close off the power again?"

Vito looked at the grinning red-faced man, his thick farmer's arms bursting from his rolled-up sleeves.

"Who's this?" Vito said to Basso, pointing at the seated man.

"He is my driver, for this trip. He is here on a bit of business himself."

The man gave Vito a knowing look that he did not like.

"Sorry, friend, no offence to you, but I need to speak to Signor Basso in private."

The man looked at Basso, who shrugged at him. With an effort, the red-faced farmer hoisted himself out of the chair and, taking his time, ambled from the room. No one spoke until the door had been firmly closed.

Basso smiled thinly at Vito.

"He will not like that. He likes to think he is somebody."

"Well, he might be somebody, but I don't know a thing about him. What I've got to say isn't for everybody's ears. You know of a Turk called Hakan Toprak?"

Basso sat back in his chair. "I have heard the name. He is a Turkish fixer. Changed sides and did well out of the last coup. Involved with that bunch of relics in Milan. Something in Turkish security before that. Tied up with that bitch in Malta."

"Good, I'm glad you know him. Makes my job easier. He's sent a message – don't blame me – but he says he wants to take over the whole operation."

Vito had never seen Basso look stunned before. His eyes were screwed up in disbelief and his mouth fell open. He would remember that expression for some time.

"What the fuck... he said that?"

"I know. And that he wants to talk."

"Talk? He will be lucky if he can still breathe! What did you say?"

"What do you think? I said nothing, apart from that he must be mad. He's saying he's offering cash, ongoing payments, a money-laundering scheme, facilitated by the Turkish government – even a share of the Turkish heroin route and protection from the heat that's coming our way from Rome. Apparently, he's got Rome onside. He reckons the anti-Mafia agency'll have this whole thing busted open in six months and we'll lose everything. He says we've overplayed our hand and attracted too much attention, of the wrong sort."

"Who does he think he is!" snarled Basso. "If it was up to me, I would have my driver… that is Pietro Pomodoro, by the way… call round this evening and slice his head off. Cheeky bastard! Does he really think we are going to give him it all, just like that?"

"He seems to think his approach is entirely logical."

"Well, fuck his logic! Who is he representing? The Turkish state, the Maltese or that snotnose Milanese Family? From what I have heard, it is hard to know where one finishes and the other starts these days."

"I don't know, I didn't go into it. But what about Rome? He says there's a Direzione Nazionale Anti-Mafia squad arriving, though I haven't yet been officially notified. I'm the mayor of this city, so that's hardly an oversight. Maybe the Turk's right. Maybe there *is* trouble coming."

Basso threw an ashtray across the room.

"*Pezzo di merda!*" He tried to calm himself. "Do not worry about that. I was going to tell you – we heard about it some time back. We are going to give our Roman friends a nice Sicilian welcome!"

Vito knew exactly what that meant and threw his hands in the air.

"For God's sake, don't do anything provocative! You remember what happened after Falcone and Borsellino? Their murders spelled the end of the Cosa Nostra. That was… what? Twenty years ago. They still haven't recovered from the backlash!"

"Are you telling the Provincia what to do, Amato? I'll let them know. The directors will be grateful to you, I am sure!"

Basso left his chair and paced the room. As the ashtray was no longer on the table, he flicked his cigarette end onto the carpeted floor and scrunched the sole of his shoe onto it. Vito looked at him with contempt. The action summed up these people. At least the Mafiosi had good clothes and manners. This lot were not only badly dressed, they behaved like crude, arrogant *cafoni!* Peasants! Even Basso, who should know better.

After a minute spent staring through the viewing window over the server farm, Basso said to Vito: "Do not make contact with him. If he contacts you, ignore him. I have to talk to some people."

CHAPTER 48

SUPERINTENDENT GEORGE ZAMMIT

BENEATH MOUNT ETNA

THE MOUTH of the second-level gallery was barred by a rustic wooden gate arrangement, of the sort found on run-down farm buildings. The rough planking offered no more than token resistance to a serious intruder. A door hung loosely on long cast-iron hinges and was secured by a short chain and a padlock. By the red and orange light that lit the sky over the lip of the South Eastern Crater, Bastiano used Greco's key to open the door and found a switch secured against the tunnel wall. Electricity flowed to a string of lights attached to three car batteries, kept charged by the same hydroelectric turbine that the Gambinis used.

Bastiano stopped to lift away a table that lay on its side and took two torches that had fallen on to the floor, offering one to George.

"Take this, in case the lights go out."

The two men found their way down the short passage to the ancient wooden door that was the entrance to the chapel and tried to open it with an ornate cast-iron key. It turned in the lock, but the door did not budge. George then saw there were two heavy padlocks securing sturdy stainless-steel hasps. He pointed them out.

Bastiano frantically examined the key ring, shrieked and kicked the door as hard as he could. "There are no keys for the padlocks! We will never get past those! Damn that priest."

He was shining the torch along the frame of the stout wooden door when the next eruption struck. It was as violent as the first and, for a moment, they felt the ground tilt beneath their feet, as massive subterranean forces bent and buckled the rock. The background rumbling became a series of loud cracks and creaks, accompanied by a rushing sound, as though somebody had flushed a seismic cistern.

When the tremors abated and they had both picked themselves up from the floor, they noticed water was starting to seep out from under the door. It was then they heard a voice behind it loudly shouting: "Is there somebody there?"

A slight Maltese accent... It was Silvia. George looked at Bastiano and smiled.

"We've found them!" he shouted. "Who are you? Are there two of you in there?"

There was a shriek of excitement and a banging on the door.

"Yes, yes, I'm Silvia Camilleri and I'm with Benedetta Beneventi! We're both here! Please, get us out! There's water everywhere, I think it's flooding!"

A second voice was heard at the door, speaking with more urgency than the first.

"Who're you? Let us out! Help us... please!"

Bastiano pushed George to one side.

"Benedetta? Thank God! It's Bastiano... thank God you're all right. We've got you, it's OK!"

"Madre mia! Bastiano, thank God! Please, please, hurry up and get us out of here, quickly!"

His response was to grab a rock from the side of the tunnel and start manically pounding the door. It was obvious that would not achieve anything. George put a hand on his arm.

"Stop it! Think. Keep talking to them, keep them calm. I've

already called for help. A rescue team should be here soon. Let me go and see what's happening outside. For now, be happy." He smiled broadly and squeezed Bastiano's shoulder. "We've found them. We've done it! All we've got to do is get that door open."

CHAPTER 49
HAKAN TOPRAK

THE BASTIONS RESTAURANT,
GRAND HARBOUR, MALTA

FOLLOWING his meeting with Vito Amato, Hakan had returned to Malta to speak to Natasha. He was annoyed that flights from Fontanarossa had been suspended, due to the ash cloud from Etna. The trip had meant a two-hour drive to Pozzallo, followed by a rough crossing, bouncing around on the high-speed catamaran. Finally, he had disembarked in Valletta, on a mild late-autumn evening, and made his way to the famed restaurant set on the massive defensive walls, high above Valletta's Grand Harbour. It was, perhaps, one of the most magnificent, and romantic, locations in the southern Mediterrean. His dinner guest was to be Natasha Bonnici.

He realised this was very close to the place where they had kissed on the last occasion they had gone out for dinner. On entering the restaurant, Hakan saw that Natasha was already seated at the bar, just behind the reception area. He also noticed that she was wearing the diamond bracelet he had bought her, as an apology for overstepping the line then – and not following through. He made a note he must take care not to find himself in a similar position later that evening.

"Hakan, handsome as ever! So, how was your trip to Sicily? I hope the volcano was not too scary?" she greeted him.

"You are looking gorgeous too, signorina, and I love your bracelet." He raised an eyebrow. "A gift from an admirer? Someone with impeccable taste, perhaps? "

Natasha tutted.

"Don't tease me, Hakan. Tell me about the volcano. Were you terrified?"

"I can assure you, close up, the volcano is very scary. But I am advised it should not interfere with our long-term plans."

"Well, before we eat, I've arranged to meet Gerald, in the bar, just for fifteen minutes. He's rather agitated and I'd welcome your advice on what he has to say."

Hakan was happy to keep the conversation about business.

"Sure, it is always a pleasure to speak with the assistant commissioner. Anyway, I have baited the hook for our friends in Calabria and cast it onto the water. My connections in Rome have proved most helpful and should be delivering a signal next week that will back up my message. Unfortunately, I have not cut through to the right level just yet. I am still rubbing shoulders with the grubby foot soldiers."

"Really? You don't know anybody higher up the chain?"

"No, I'm afraid not. Not yet, at least. What else can I say – rather remiss of me."

"I'm sure I can help with that. We have fairly regular contact, to make sure we don't tread on each other's toes."

"Yes, I had thought of that, but the problem with the 'Ndrangheta is, you never know which limb of it you should be approaching. Some elements are only loosely affiliated to others, and to approach the wrong part of the beast would not help. Anyway, I have stirred the pot and all I can do is to wait for them to come to me. They have a Provincia, a sort of board of directors, and I have put it out that I want to speak to them."

Natasha played with her drink.

"Well, yes, actually, I sent a message of my own to one of the heads of the Italian clans. Southern Italy's organised crime groups have a kind of titular head, more a mascot really. Some crusty old count who's a member of one of those secret societies' you men love so much. He's a fantasist, who thinks he should be the king of Italy, or something. I get the impression the 'Ndrangheta and the others think it gives them some sort of political credence, or blessing. Anyway, the visit by Gerald didn't go down that well but, at least now, they'll know we're serious. That's what Gerald's here to talk about. I'm sorry, I should've told you before."

Hakan was non-plussed by this development and felt his temper rise. This was why he preferred to work alone. You could never trust other people to make the right call. Also, he hated being played, as part of someone else's game. He had been careless again in underestimating Natasha Bonnici.

"What sort of message?" he asked.

Natasha was saved from Hakan's anger by the arrival of Gerald Camilleri, who also seemed to be in a frosty mood.

There was a curt exchange of pleasantries, then Camilleri related the story of his trip to Ragusa.

"I do not know who this count of yours is, but he is the most unpleasant person I have ever met. In addition to that, he tried to murder me and Superintendent Zammit. Fortunately, Zammit used his driving prowess to extricate us from mortal danger and pushed the count's man to the bottom of a Sicilian canyon. The corpse is probably still there. In short, I do not think the count will give you any assistance with whatever it is you have planned."

They sat in silence for a minute.

Finally, Natasha said: "Well, George Zammit saves the day again! That man never ceases to amaze me!" She paused. "Gerald, in many ways your trip was a success. You've rattled the 'Ndrangheta's cage and shown them we're deadly serious about our plans for Catania and Naples. I'm sorry I put you at risk. It didn't occur to me that would ever be a possibility. I thought you two would just have a nice 'knightly' chat. But if he won't play, he won't play."

Camilleri glared at her.

"Natasha, you sent me to see a madman."

"Oh, I agree, he's totally crazy. There's no real basis for his claim to the Bourbon throne. He's not a complete pretender, just there are several others ahead of him with stronger claims. Everybody knows that. He's just that mad cousin that lurks in every family's history."

She smiled sweetly.

Camilleri was confused.

"You said 'rattle the 'Ndrangheta's cage'! What has the crazy count to do with them and where do they come into it? You hinted you had plans to turn Naples into the new Catania. What exactly has that to do with the 'Ndrangheta and the Count?"

"Oh, yes, I should've explained. The count's a bit of a hero, a cult figure for the senior types in the 'Ndrangheta, Cosa Nostra and their like. They dream of the Two Sicilies, with him back in the Royal Palace in Caserta, no doubt doing their bidding. It's all fantastical nonsense, of course." She took another sip of her Dirty Martini. "They'll be so cross we spoiled his day."

She took a moment to swirl the ice-cold vodka around her palate before continuing: "Mmmm, and Hakan, here, has had the wonderful idea that the Family can take a stake in Sicily and southern Italy, that would lead to us becoming the main provider of geothermal energy. All we have to do is make sure the organised crime groups don't ruin his clever idea."

Camilleri sat silent, fury building inside him. Hakan cast his eyes to the floor. Natasha looked at the two men, bemused.

"What've I done?"

Camilleri rose to his feet.

"I am leaving, before I say something I regret."

The Hawk nodded at him, understanding perfectly.

It was warm enough to sit outside, on the rooftop terrace,

overlooking the majestic Grand Harbour that sparkled with a thousand lights. Natasha was dressed in black, shamelessly wearing a fur wrap, with her hair piled on top of her head and loosely pinned. Hakan knew her well enough not to be fooled by her casual manner. She had dressed carefully and deliberately, and she looked a million dollars. He knew he had better watch his step; if she had set out to snare him and failed, she was not likely to take it well. He had seen how badly she took rejection.

He took a sip of water and watched, as she marvelled at the gigantic cruise liner that slowly processed past them, merely metres away, heading out between the breakwaters, its upper decks nearly on the same level as their table. An idiot woman was waving at them pointlessly from the observation deck. They both ignored her.

Natasha looked thoughtfully at the ship.

"You know, call me stupid, but I've never understood how something *that* big can float."

Hakan nodded.

"It's all about displacement. A ship displaces an amount of water equivalent to its own mass. Water cannot be compressed, so it pushes up against the ship, giving it buoyancy."

She laughed.

"Oh, God, don't be such a bore."

"You asked!"

"OK, so is there anything else you need from me for this Sicilian nonsense?"

"Well, first of all, it is not nonsense. If it were, I would not be wasting my time on it. But, given that the hero of the hour, George Zammit, is in Catania, I could do with his help for the odd errand or two I need doing there? Despite getting Gerald out of a hole, I know he is not really the sharp end of law enforcement, but he will do."

Natasha laughed.

"Don't be so sure. George is a crack shot! Remember Abu

Muhammed, the ISIL leader in Libya? George took him out with one shot, from a kilometre away. He sank that Greek naval gunboat for you in Gavdos and crossed the Mediterranean in a migrant raft. Then there was the time he stormed Abu Salim jail in Tripoli and snatched the kid who tried to kill you. I think he's got guts when a situation calls for them. He's also honest and loyal. He worked for me for two years, looking after a pile of Libyan dinars worth three-quarters of a billion US, and didn't steal one of them. I rest my case."

"Yes, I know the man well. I am just not sure he would be my first choice to have my back, if it came to that."

" What exactly do you want from him?"

"Well, I need a bag carrier. Literally!"

"Oh, he's the man for that, definitely. I'll have a word with Gerald, if he's still speaking to me after tonight. I'm sure it'll be fine. Is that our business finished? Come on, Hakan, drink some wine. Don't let me finish the bottle all by myself. You know what happens when I do that!"

"I'll have one glass, Natasha. Remember, I'm on the early fight back to Catania tomorrow morning. It would not do to be fuzzy-headed."

"Spoilsport!"

CHAPTER 50
SUPERINTENDENT GEORGE ZAMMIT
GROTTA DI SANTA MARIA, MOUNT ETNA

GEORGE HASTILY RETRACED his steps out of the cave and onto the side of the volcano. He burst out onto the mountainside, thanking God he had found the women. He was so relieved that he felt briefly tearful.

Albi was still down in the ravine with Father Greco, who did not seem to have moved. George made his way down and was met by Albi's hopeful face looking up at him. George's smile told him all he needed to know. Albi reached up to him and they shook hands.

"Mela, we found them, but they're locked behind a stout door." George was fumbling with his phone. "I've sent for help. Let me check where they are."

Before he had set off under the volcano, he had sent a text to Lucy telling her where they were and that they were hopeful of rescuing Silvia and Benedetta. He had asked her to contact the National Alpine Cliff and Cave Rescue Corps rescue station at Nicolosi and let the station master know that there was a casualty on the mountainside in need of help, and that the rescuers' assistance might be needed again in due course inside the volcano. When Father Greco had told them the name of the cave, he had sent it direct to Lucy, telling her to ensure that Mario Verraci and his CNSAS team knew the location.

Now he scrolled through his messages and, to his relief, read: *On our way. Bringing CNSAS. There soon.*

He read the text again. If anyone could get the girls out of the tunnels, it was the guys from the CNSAS.

He quickly messaged Lucy.

Where are you? Hurry, it's an emergency.

15mins hang on. Have you found her? Who is hurt?

Can confirm we have S and B. I am on surface. But we have an older man with injury broken hip?

Thank God. OK

It seemed to take forever, but, eventually, George could see the lights of the vehicles parking on the side of the rocky track, several hundred metres below. After that, all he could do was wait for the bobbing head torches of Lucy and the CNSAS volunteers to reach them.

Mario and Lucy cornered him and demanded a full update. He felt like a coward, as he told them what had happened, but Mario applauded his quick thinking in ensuring help was called at the earliest moment. George was given a helmet with a head torch on it and asked to lead the party back into the cavern. Now that he had support, he felt massively reassured and confidently strode into the tunnel, beckoning the others to follow his lead.

Mario Verraci stopped by the wooden door that barred the way into the chapel and examined the padlocks. He called for a fearsome set of bolt cutters. One of the team handed him the long-handled tool. George and Bastiano stood back, as Verraci fought to prise the locks free. By that time, the tunnel was running with water that flowed out from under the door. Water that steamed. George felt the stream soak through the thin soles of his shoes and start to burn his toes. He started hopping from one foot to another.

"Ow! This water is hot!"

The tunnel that Benedetta had entered, to emerge half drowned in the chapel's baptismal pool, was now filled with a torrent of heated water from deep underground. Fortunately, it had cooled as it was forced between the strata of the mountain and mixed with cooler water that drained down from the surface. Nevertheless, the pool now appeared to boil, as the pressure of the inward torrent caused it to overflow and flood the chapel.

One of the volunteers stuck a temperature probe into the flow and held his hand there for several seconds.

"It's hot, but it's OK, it won't burn us. Better than being drenched in cold water, that's for sure."

Suddenly, the door burst open and a flood of steaming water gushed out over them. George, Marco and the CNSAS volunteers were drenched to their knees. Bastiano was nearly knocked over by Benedetta as she waded out and fell into his arms. The turban bandage had come away from her head, and steam and sweat had plastered her long blonde hair over her shoulders, rinsing out dried blood so that her face ran red in the light from their torches. Silvia had been leaning on the door. As it opened, she fell to her hands and knees, breathing heavily, in the swirling waters. Lucy dragged her out of the chapel, down the tunnel and onto the mountainside. Benedetta, with her injured arm held across her chest, was supported by two volunteers and laid on the ground by the mouth of the cave. She was shaking, shocked and incapable of speech. Lucy and Silvia held each other tight.

Silvia said, between sobs of relief, "I can't believe it's you! What're you doing here?"

"Looking for you. That's what I've been doing all this time." Lucy laughed with relief. "Are you OK? And why you? What did they want with you?"

"I'm OK, just… you know. I've no idea why me, and I don't care. I'm out. That's all that matters. God, I'm shaking!"

"I've been sick with worry."

Lucy grabbed Silvia and buried her head in her shoulder, laughing and sobbing violently, with relief and shock.

Syilvia was too stunned to speak but was also shaking violently. One of the CNSAS volunteers wrapped a space blanket around her. Lucy, gulping for breath between her sobs, led her away to find a place the two of them could sit quietly. Lucy stroked her hair and buried her face against her neck, also sobbing violently as the relief flooded through her.

Finally, Bastiano emerged from the mouth of the cave, equally bedraggled and exhausted. He comforted Benedetta, as she was strapped into a stretcher and four of the volunteers set off with her, down to the waiting vehicles. Once she had disappeared into the night, Bastiano came and sat beside George on the mountain-side, the eerie glow from the other side of the volcano giving the pair of them blood-red complexions.

George patted Bastiano's shoulder.

"It's so quiet out here. Well done for getting them out."

Bastiano managed a smile.

"No, well done to you. I didn't get them out. You called for help and it arrived just in time. How's the old man?"

George had forgotten about Father Greco and Albi. He looked down to where they had been, but there was no one there.

"I don't know where they've gone. They were just there." He pointed to the spot.

Bastiano said, "I suppose it's not really your concern. You're done here now, I take it?"

"Mela, I suppose I am. I've got a wedding to go to. My daughter's."

"A wedding? Really?" He paused for a moment. "Give me your address. There will be Beneventi wine for everybody. On us, it's the least I can do."

George smiled at him and looked over at Lucy and Silvia huddled together, arms around each other, heads touching, deep in conversation. "At least there's a happy ending on my side. What're you going to do now?"

"I haven't really thought about it. It's all a big mess. But I am not going to work to put money in the 'Ndrangheta's pockets, that's for sure."

It took under half an hour for the CNSAS team to pack their gear, then they all walked off down to the waiting vehicles. Bastiano followed the volunteers through the scree and the scrub, wondering where on earth his father had got to. Once they had reached the Land Rovers and there was still no sign of the two men, Bastiano started to get worried. There was no way his father and Greco could have made their way down the mountainside. After his fall, the old priest could hardly move. As people began to get into the vehicles, Mario approached him, waving a piece of paper.

"This was stuck to the windscreen. I think it's for you."

Saw car lights and went to grotto to help. We have priest and Signor Beneventi. Collect them at Fratelli Gambini building.

Mario Verraci looked suspiciously at Bastiano and said: "Do you know what this is about? You know who the Gambini are?"

"Of course I do. But there's nothing to worry about."

Verraci said, "OK, if you're happy, that's fine. I wouldn't go anywhere near them myself. We can give you a lift down to get your car, but then I'll leave you to sort out any business you might have with them. Ring me when you've got your father. If I don't hear from you in an hour, I'll call it in to the Carabinieri in Randazzo."

It did not take long for the CNSAS Land Rovers to loop around the hillside and drop Bastiano and George back at the Mercedes. Marco insisted on taking the sleeping Benedetta to Garibaldi–Nesima Hospital in Catania, as he was certain she had badly injured her arm. Silvia and Lucy said they would accompany her. Bastiano and George agreed they would join them all there, once they had collected Albi. Bastiano then retraced their route back up the mountain road and soon found the entrance to the quarry belonging to the Fratelli Gambino.

It was a desolate place, with high palisade gates protecting a huge excavated hollow on the mountainside. One leaf of the gates stood open. As they drove through, security lights immediately flooded the entrance and two frenzied dogs leaped out of the shadows, pulling violently on long lengths of chain. To one side of the gates, amidst a car park of huge-wheeled tipper trucks and excavators, was what looked like a replica of Tony Montana's house in *Scarface*.

"My God," laughed Bastiano, "have you seen that?"

George said: "It looks like something out of a movie!"

They sat in the car for a moment, unsure what to do. Then the front door to the house opened and George saw Albi walk out and make his way slowly towards them, limping slightly. A large man and woman stood in the gloom of the unlit doorway, watching him find his way to the car. There was no sign of Father Greco. Bastiano got out of the car and helped his father the rest of the way, then turned to the couple and raised his arm in a gesture of thanks.

He and George then scrutinised Albi, reclining in the back seat.

"Well? What was that about?" Bastiano enquired.

"Nothing. It was about nothing. Benedetta needs to remember it was about nothing. If anybody asks us about what happened this evening, nothing happened."

"You're kidding?"

"That's it, Bastiano. Nothing happened."

He shook his head in disbelief that his father would ask that of them. No Polizia, no trouble. That was exactly how thugs like the Gambini got away with kidnapping.

"Where's Father Greco?"

"He's being cared for by Evita Gambino. He'll stay there until his leg is better. They look after their own."

Albi then addressed George.

"If you want to help this family, remember: this was all about..."

"Nothing happened. I've got the message! We've got what we wanted – the return of Silvia, and you have Benedetta. So, yes, it's all about nothing. I know how things work around here." George paused to reflect, then told them, "I think I must be becoming Sicilian."

CHAPTER 51

VICE QUESTORA CRISTINA CAPOZZI,
QUESTURA DI CATANIA

CRISTINA WAS FINALLY ALERTED by her immediate superior to the arrival of the two special anti-Mafia prosecutors, an hour after they had already unpacked their bags in her office. The Questore himself, Mario Vitali, phoned her, a little after 07:30 in the morning, a rare event in itself.

"Cristina, *buon giorno*, I am sorry to call so early. I have a problem."

"A problem?"

"Yes. Two prosecutors from the *Direzione Nazionale Anti-Mafia* squad have arrived, without notice I should add! I will explain what they want later, but listen, I am sorry, I have had to put them in your office."

"My office! What! Mario? No way, that's not acceptable!"

"I know, I know. The whole situation is unacceptable, but yours is the largest office and to meet their requirements, it is the only one suitable."

"Their requirements? What about my requirements? What about my files and papers? These investigations take months; sometimes years! You've got to find somewhere else for them."

"Cristina, I am in a difficult spot, please, as a favour to me, work with me on this."

"What are people going to think? Two anti-Mafia prosecutors from Rome turn up, at dawn, and hole up in my office. How does that look? I'll tell you, it looks like I'm the one under investigation!"

"Don't be silly! People will think nothing of the sort. We can put that right, don't worry. We will explain everything and we will find you somewhere else."

"Well, get on with it, Mario. Please! I'm not going to sit around in the canteen, like a spare part, while you find me some space. I'll work from home. Let me know when things have been sorted. Is that OK?"

Questore Mario Vitali continued to smooth Cristina's ruffled feathers when she noticed she had a text notification.

"...listen, Cristina, I will be firm with them and tell them they need to have done their work and be out of your office as soon as possible..."

A glance told her the sender's identity was 'Carla'.

"...you know, I am as put out about this as you are. I tell you, Cristina, I will be having words with Rome, mark my words..."

The message was blank other than a request to her to '*rispondere per favore*'.

Capozzi quickly realised what it all meant and said: "OK, Mario, I'll leave you to get it sorted and I'll be in tomorrow. Don't worry, I'll be on my best behaviour and introduce myself to the prosecutors. Any assistance they need, I'll happily provide. Sorry to kick off about it, but it is annoying!"

"That's great Cristina, thanks! I know it is all a pain, but trust me, I will get to the bottom as to what is going on here."

They hung up, and Cristina texted '*ho capito*', 'I understand', back to Carla.

———

The bomb was duly detonated and ripped through the Questura at around 10:00 in the morning. The source of the explosion was a device in a heating duct in the vice questora's office, which had only just been occupied by the two anti-Mafia prosecutors.

The blast blew out walls on the ground floor and the force took out the offices on the west side of the first floor. Fortunately, none of the officers in the building at that time were killed, although there were several casualties, who suffered a variety of injuries; some serious. The prosecutors, who were in the office where the bomb exploded, fared less well. What was left of them was collected, scooped into zip-locked plastic bags and packed in two, black, body bags to make the return journey to Rome.

CHAPTER 52

SUPERINTENDENT GEORGE ZAMMIT

HOTEL CELESTE, CATANIA

GEORGE ARRIVED BACK at the hotel with a sense of anti-climax hanging over him. Lucy and Silvia had returned shortly after him, and he had heard their door slam shut. An hour later, the two women clattered down the stairs and out into the night, in search of food and beer. Bastiano had gone to the hospital with Albi to check up on Benedetta, which left George on his own, exhausted, hungry and lonely.

George thought fondly of home and imagined the family, sitting around the kitchen, doing the dinner dishes, gossiping and making plans for Gina's wedding. It had been some time since he had rung, so he took out his mobile and called the name at the top of his favourites list – 'Home'. Gina answered.

"Dad! Where've you been!" she shrieked, "Listen, we're talking about the wedding and ..."

George relaxed as his daughter excitedly gabbled on, seemingly without drawing breath. He heard about the disaster involving the bridesmaid's dresses, the surly priest, the limited availability of the makeup artist and many other crises that had occurred during his absence. Fifteen minutes later, Marianna grabbed the phone from her daughter. George heard his wife say:

"Enough, Gina. You're making my head spin. You know your father doesn't listen to a word you say. Give it here!"

"George? George? Are you listening?"

"Yes, Marianna, I'm here. How are you, anyway?"

"Never mind that. Your Uncle Edward, from Rabat, you know him? Well, he's accepted. The cheek of it."

George smiled at the sound of his wife's voice.

"But we agreed to invite him. Didn't we?"

"Well, no. I didn't send the invitation. I couldn't bring myself to. The thought of that man with our real guests.... but, anyway, he's heard about the wedding and he rang to say he hasn't got his invite. Well, that's not a surprise, is it? So, he wants to come. If that's not bad enough, he's only bringing *that* woman, *and* her baby!"

"Marianna, *that* woman is his new wife and the baby is theirs."

"He was carrying on with her, way before he left Lina. It's scandalous. And a baby? I don't think it's even his. There's talk, you know. Listen, we can't put them next to respectable people, they'll have to sit at the back, with your brothers.

"And, while I've got you – you listen to me, George Zammit, there's the family meal with the Mifsuds on Friday. Giorgio says his father is going to a lot of trouble and you'd better be there. Do you understand me. Don't you let us all down or, or ... I don't know what I'll do to you. But you won't like it!

"And you haven't been eating too much have you? I've had your blue suit cleaned and I don't want you saying it's too small!"

George instinctively sucked in his bulging stomach.

"No, Marianna, I definitely haven't been eating too much. If only I had!" George's mind immediately turned to thoughts of food. What're you cooking for dinner, by the way?"

"Oh! I've got to go! Good thing you reminded me. The tomato sauce for the rabbit pasta needs stirring. You be back by

Friday, George. Otherwise.... mark my words, there'll be big trouble. Now, mind you stay out of trouble. See you Friday. Early."

George ended the call and wrinkled his nose in disappointment. Rabbit pasta, studded with bright green peas. He was starving. He could see it, he could smell it.

Wearily, he pulled on what was left of his supply of clean clothing. His suit and work shoes had been destroyed by the adventure in the caves. Marianna would no doubt have something to say about that, too, he was sure. His grey slacks, with the elasticated panels, still fitted him and his patterned woollen jumper easily covered the waistband of shame. He slipped on his white trainers and headed out into the night.

There was an eerie sense of calm over the town, a feeling that it had survived the worst. The heavy viscous lava was still squeezing through the fissures and out of the crater, but the flows had slowed and it looked like the depression of the Valle di Bove had saved the eastern towns from destruction. Nicolosi was also safe and the Vigili del Fuoco, supported by the army and a large group of volunteers, including many of the Brothers, were still fighting the fires in the forests.

Groups of people stood around, all looking north, towards the glowing cone of the volcano, starting to believe that life could begin to return to normal. If that was as bad as it was going to get, then the locals started to wonder what all the fuss was about. George walked up a side street, away from the piazza in front of the Duomo, and started to relax. The simple act of walking eased his nerves and calmed him.

Suddenly, his phone rang. Silvia Camilleri had been found and her uncle, the assistant commissioner, was in the best of moods. George spoke to him, while sitting on a low wall opposite a bustling gelateria.

"Silvia called me, George, to thank you and I for our efforts. I told her it was principally you she needed to thank. Listen, I have already told you how much she means to my sister and I. Now, please allow me to say thank you, from both of us, from the bottom of our hearts. You have done a fine job here. Not just good policework, but you put your own neck on the line. I will not forget that. There is no medal for you this time, unfortunately, but if the Camilleri family had a medal, I would certainly give it to you. Listen, I know you had some reservations, but I think we work well together. I would be proud if you would accept a permanent role as superintendent in my own Organised and Financial Crime Command. Come on, how about it?"

George flushed with pride.

"You mean there's a vacancy?"

"Of course, George, there always was! I apologise for pretending otherwise, but I am serious – I would really like you to join me and the team."

"Mela, I'd be delighted to accept, Gerald."

"This is business, remember, superintendent. I am Assistant Commissioner Camilleri to you now."

George thought he detected a hint of humour in his boss's voice nevertheless.

"Oh, yes, sir... sorry, Assistant Commissioner Camilleri. Thank you, sir."

"Good, I am extremely pleased. Welcome to Organised and Financial Crime."

CHAPTER 53
LUISA MARONGIU
PALAZZO DEL VIMINALE, ROME

THE MINISTER WAS BARGING up and down her office, heels ricocheting off the parquet flooring. She was beside herself with rage.

"You suggested this! You said to send in some anti-Mafia prosecutors – stir it up a bit! My God, you succeeded in doing that all right!"

"Minister, let's think about it. The very fact that they brazenly attack us like this proves my point. Catania is in the hands of organised crime. That's what Hakan Toprak told us, and that was the basis on which we acted. So now, we know. There can be no doubt."

"The Prime Minister called... to send me his sympathies. What does that mean, Michele? He sends me 'his sympathies'? I'm going to be fired, aren't I? *I'm* the one to be punished, when it's all *your* fault."

"I really must object, Minister. You've got to remain calm. An inappropriate reaction would play straight into their hands."

Luisa was apoplectic.

"Whose hands? The President's? The Prime Minister's? Those bastards at the Ministry of Justice? That bitch Maria has always had it in for me. Whose hands?"

"The hands of the people who did this!"

"So, tell me what's 'an appropriate reaction'?" she screamed. "Tell me and I'll do it."

"Well, first we should mourn the loss of two of our finest prosecutors."

The minister calmed down a little.

"Hmm. Yes, I suppose so. Who were they, anyway?"

"Parisini and Racani. Parisini is a family man, with connections to the Democratic Party. His wife sits in the Chamber of Deputies."

"Oh! And Racani?"

"Time-serving magistrate from the South."

"I'd better comfort Signora Parisini as soon as possible. Can we get some TV coverage – say of me arriving at the house? Should I wear black or do you think it's too soon? Oh, and send a card to the Raccani household – sincere condolences, that sort of thing."

"You don't need the black just yet. I'll send the card. Do you want to sign it?"

"No, no, just get it sent."

"I do have some good news for you. Hakan Toprak's ready to respond against the perpetrators of this outrage on our behalf."

"If he knows who the perpetrators are, tell him to call the *Polizia di Stato* and have them arrested!"

"It's one thing to know who they are, another entirely to bring them to justice. What Toprak has in mind is some extrajudicial activity. The Turks are masters of the dark arts; always have been. You don't want to know the details, but the man never fails to impress. I think our criminal friends will soon get the message that we're serious about driving them out of Catania."

"Hakan's an impressive man, true. But it was his poor judgement that got us into this in the first place. Can we push some of it onto the mayor... Amato? What's his involvement?"

"I seem to recall somebody saying: 'I will be resolute in the face of adversity. I will not sleep until we have rid the country of the curse of organised crime. I will lead the fight against this cancer that blights our country. They shall not win,' etc., etc."

"Who said all that?"

"You did, in your personal manifesto."

"Hmmm." Luisa turned to face the window. "So, this 'message'? Is it proportionate?"

"Proportionate? What's not proportionate when organised crime feels it can blow up a Questura in one of our leading cities and murder two of our finest public servants?"

"OK, Michele, do it. But remember, I don't want any comeback on this office."

Calmer now, Luisa returned to her enormous Tuscan desk and put on her spectacles.

"Right, that's that. Shall we speak to the Press Office now?"

"Since we're talking about Catania, do you want to know what happened with Mount Etna?"

Sensing more danger, Luisa took off her glasses.

"What do I need to know? Fatalities? Injuries? Destruction of property? Evacuations?"

"Well, there was a very large eruption last night. The boffins who were giving us positive vibes have suddenly all gone quiet and Del Bosco is muttering about the end of the world again. The volcano's still a problem and the signs are the pressure is still building. We can't just ignore it."

"Well, that's all very much as I expected. If he's being a nuisance, shall we dismiss that Del Bosco fellow? Time for wiser heads, and all that?"

"Yes, you could, but it's not going to stop the volcano exploding and you might end up looking a bit silly if he's proved to have been right all along."

"Don't be facetious, Michele. I want only what's best for the country. So, tell me – what *is* that exactly?"

CHAPTER 54

SUPERINTENDENT GEORGE ZAMMIT

HOTEL CELESTE, CATANIA

FOR THE FIRST time since his arrival in Catania, George was feeling relaxed. He was on his second pot of coffee and third plate of pastries, justifying the excess to himself by having to make up for not having eaten the previous day. Well, not eaten that much.

Lucy and Silvia had left a few moments previously, to catch a flight for Rome. Lucy had hugged him enthusiastically and wept on parting, saying to Silvia: "If it hadn't been for this man, you would probably still be in that cave and I would be... I don't know where or what. We owe him everything."

Silvia had taken his hands and asked where he lived in Birkirkara. She had promised her mother she would return to Malta in a week or so and, once George was back in Malta, she wanted to take everybody out for dinner, so they could all exchange stories.

"And I do mean everybody," she said. "You, your wife, Uncle Gerald, Lucy, my mum... It'll be great!"

George was not sure that was his ideal guest list, but nodded along enthusiastically and made Lucy promise that she and Silvia would come to Gina's wedding. After all, the reception was at the Birkirkara Band Club, so it was bound to be a good night!

He was just about to order yet more coffee when he saw Hakan Toprak peek around the diningroom door. He entered and sat down at George's table. George did not say a word. The Turk was immaculately dressed in a dark navy suit with a white shirt and dark tie. Hakan looked George over, taking in the ill-fitting tracksuit he always breakfasted in.

"Sorry to disturb you. Is there any coffee in that pot?"

The last time their paths had crossed, Hakan had blackmailed Abdullah Belkacem and George into raiding a Greek island as part of Turkey's dispute with Greece over territorial waters. George had surpassed himself by accidentally ramming the large commercial trawler that had taken them to the island, into the side of a gunboat belonging to the Hellenic Navy, causing it to sink. On their return, Hakan had sent them deep into eastern Libya, where George had seen terrible things that he would never forget. And, to top it all, Toprak's failure to honour his promise to release Abdullah's son from Tripoli's Abu Salim prison, meant that George had been obliged to accompany his friend on a daring jail break, to effect a rescue. He shuddered at the memory of it all.

Hakan leaned back in his chair and fixed George with his bulbous brown eyes.

"I hear you have had a watching brief over an investigation being led by the Polizia di Stato? How has that gone?"

"We've sorted it out ourselves, with no help from the Polizia di Stato. So, I'm off home now. I've been here nearly three weeks and it hasn't been easy."

"I'm sorry to hear that, but I would not be so hasty, if I were you. MalTech Energy and I need your assistance on a very delicate matter. Given your previous service with MalTech and your unique experience, the assistant commissioner and Ms Bonnici both feel you are the only man I can trust with this assignment. You should be flattered!"

"Flattered? Flattered! You and Natasha Bonnici have nearly got me killed more times than I care to remember. So, no! No! And no! I'm not helping you in any 'delicate matter'. My daughter is about to get married and I'm needed, alive, in Malta, not running fool's errands for you! I've only just escaped from a tunnel in an exploding volcano, thanks to Camilleri's niece. There's no way the assistant commissioner would allow you to ask me to do anything, 'delicate'. So, no, forget it!"

"Right. You had better check with him, then."

Hakan pulled his phone out of his pocket and offered it to George, who kept his hands on the table.

"No? OK, George. Now you have had your say and feel better, here is what you are going to do for us."

Diego telephoned George, an hour after the bomb had detonated at the Questura and ten minutes after Hakan had left.

"I was first in. There was smoke and dust and then there was all this… stuff. I'm telling you, George, I don't feel well at all. I'm still a bit shaky, you know? I have that PMT thing, like the soldiers get."

"Diego, you're in shock. You need to go home and take it easy. Is Capozzi OK?"

"Well, that's the weird thing. It was her office the prosecutors were moving into and she wasn't there. She always locks the doors. I mean, I know she does. But she was at home, on some sort of parental leave thing, and boom! How lucky's that? She never takes any time off. I didn't even know she had a kid! And, how did they even get in there? Sovrintendente Petrucci, the front desk guy, said there're only two keys to that office. Capozzi has one, and he has the other. Weird, yeah?"

George thought it did seem strange, then dismissed it from his mind. There would be an answer to it all somewhere.

"So, these prosecutors. What were they doing here?"

"They were from Rome, from the Direzione Nazionale Anti-Mafia squad. Hey, big stuff!"

"And no one knew they were coming?"

"Well, yeah! Someone obviously did."

"And you're sure this was meant for them, not Cristina Capozzi?"

"If it was meant for her, they would've made sure she was at work. Not the one day, ever, she wasn't there. Right?"

"I've said it before, Diego, we'll make a detective of you yet. So, somebody opened her locked door, planted a bomb, waited for the prosecutors to arrive, made sure she was at home, then set if off?"

There was a pause. Finally, Diego understood George's line of thought.

"What, you're saying it was an inside job?"

"Looks like it, doesn't it? Who wouldn't want the anti-Mafia squad poking around, d'you think?"

"The Cosa Nostra, Camorra or 'Ndrangheta? So, you think there's an insider, a *poliziotto*, who's with the 'Ndrangheta? Never. Not in the Questura di Catania!"

"Or a *poliziotta!* Don't forget the ladies!"

There was a pause on the line, as Diego worked out the implications of what George was suggesting.

"OK, OK, now you're freaking me out! I've got to go."

"Be careful, Diego."

"Really? Do I need to be? Do you think…"

CHAPTER 55
SUPERINTENDENT GEORGE ZAMMIT

PRESTIPINO'S, CATANIA

AFTER THEIR MEETING IN ROME, Michele had telephoned Hakan and told him that Luisa Marongiu had agreed to send the prosecutors, immediately, to begin an investigation into the involvement of organised crime in Catania's 'green miracle'. Hakan had thanked him for the information and assured him the minister was doing the right thing.

Hakan had then promptly placed a call to an intermediary, who had, in turn, got a message to those who mattered in Cittanova, Calabria, that Rome was despatching two special prosecutors, with a broad brief from the Minister of the Interior herself, to investigate all aspects of their businesses in the metropolitan area of Catania. Hakan had suggested to the intermediary that he might advise them to send a message back to Rome, that a 'hands off' approach was required, as was the case when prosecuting magistrates Falcone and Boresllino were killed in two attacks in Palermo, in the early 1990's.

By 'stirring the pot', Hakan planned to give himself the opportunity to raise the stakes and strengthen his own position in the negotiations to come with the 'Ndrangheta. That was where his newly recruited bag-carrier came in. Two days after the explosion, Hakan left word at the Hotel Celeste that George should pack his bags and meet him at Prestipino's.

George found Hakan sitting at a table reading a Turkish newspaper, a cappuccino in front of him.

"Ah! George, how nice to see you. All ready? Packed?"

He was ready and packed. He had been growing increasingly nervous as the days had slid by and the dinner appointment with Giorgio's family drew closer. He did not trust Hakan or Camilleri and certainly not Natasha Bonnici, but felt he had no choice but to do their bidding. As instructed, he had gone to the market and bought a bag of second-hand clothes, including some old denims, a checked shirt, baseball cap and a pair of battered brown boots. He also had to find an old bicycle. At a junk shop near the port, he bought an old mountain bike, with one working brake, for fifty euros, which he had been using to ride around the city.

Hakan slid an envelope across the table which George reached for. Hakan quickly placed his hand on top of it.

"Do not open it here, George! I know you are curious but listen to me for now. Inside are some keys to an old silver Peugeot van you will find in the railway station car park. Ride your bike there and put it in the back of the van. That is important. The registration number is on a tab with the keys. There is a GPS unit in the glove compartment. The address has already been programmed in. Do not touch anything else. There is a case in the back. Leave that well alone. Allow an hour for the drive and aim to arrive for 17:00 hours. The sat nav will take you down a minor road that eventually leads to a very large car park. It should be just about empty. Do not enter the car park, that is important too. Take the farmer's track to the left – it skirts the boundary of the car park and a large industrial building. You will look like a local farmer, off to work in one of the many citrus groves.

"At the rear corner of the large building, you will see a high mast. Park the van by the fence, directly underneath it. That way the CCTV cameras on the mast will not spot you. Then, get your bike out of the van and cycle back, slowly, the way you came. Do not attract attention by pedalling furiously. Remember, you are an agricultural labourer returning from a hard day's work, feeling worn out. Do not look back, do not go back and, most important of all, do not stop. If someone passes you, wave a hand at them. Be friendly.

"You will see a white Fiat two miles down the minor road. The keys are in an old Conad supermarket carrier bag on the verge, on the opposite side of the road. Leave the bike and drive the car back to the Fontanarossa airport long-stay parking. Throw the keys away. We have copies. Go to left luggage. There is a key in the envelope to a numbered locker. We have a duplicate and will deposit your case inside it. There is also an envelope containing your boarding pass for the evening flight back to Malta. There should also be a thank you present, which should just about cover the expense of a daughter's wedding. Take it. Camilleri will never know anything about it."

George looked at him suspiciously.

"What's in the van? You said no one'd get hurt. You're not asking me to plant a bomb, are you? Because I'm not doing it. Full stop. And I don't want the money. If it's there, I'll just throw it away."

"Please yourself, it is your loss. And no, no bomb. You are just leaving something, for somebody. That is all."

"So no explosions?"

"No. You have my word."

"And if I ring Camilleri, he will back you up?"

"He has no idea what we are doing. But he would tell you to trust me."

"But why can't I drive away? I'm not sure pedalling a bike is the quickest way to escape. If that's what I'm doing."

"Because sometimes low tech is best! Trust me on this."

———

Later that day, everything was going according to plan. George drove the old Peugeot van towards Mineo, 50 kilometres south-west of Catania. As he followed the instructions on the sat nav, and drove down the Strada Statale past Sigonella US air base, he found himself humming along to the radio, thinking of his return to Malta that evening. He felt he had been away for too long. The idea of being back with the family made him smile with pleasure. He even began to get excited about the idea of Gina's wedding. He had to give a speech, of course. Gina told him that Marianna had already written something for him to say, but he had his doubts about his wife's speech-writing abilities, so passed the journey composing some suitable lines in his head.

Eventually, he turned off the major highway and found himself making his way up a rolling back road through an agricultural landscape. On either side of it, there were orchards, so he wound down the window to see if he could detect the fruity, citrus aromas of oranges and lemons, but it was getting too late in the year for that. The road flattened and ploughed fields opened out ahead of him. After a kilometre or so, on the left-hand side of the road, George saw a small white Fiat parked on the grass verge. He craned his neck as he passed it; he was sure that this was his escape vehicle.

His pulse started to beat a little more quickly as, in the distance, he made out the low, flat grey buildings of an enormous business park, which included the longest building he had ever seen. He checked his watch and found it was nearly 17:00. He slowed, as he approached the entrance. The road led directly into the car park, which only contained about twenty vehicles or so. The entrance was unbarred, but he saw the whole complex was surrounded by a high mesh fence, with a topping of razor wire. As he swung the van off the road, onto the unmade track, he noticed the CCTV cameras at the entrance to the car park pointing away from him. He was satisfied he had arrived undetected.

He was jolted around in his seat, as the van bumped along the farmer's track, following the boundary fence. To his left, just ahead of him, he saw the communications mast on the other side of the fence. It rose at least 30 metres into the air and resembled a giant Christmas tree, decorated with all manner of dishes and aerials.

George parked the van to one side of the track, underneath the mast, and put on the baseball cap and a pair of cheap sunglasses. A touch of his own. As he took the bike out of the back of the van, he looked down at the silver metal case strapped to the deck. It was the sort used to keep a power tool in, but this one was about two metres long. When he had first seen it, he thought it could be a bomb. On a second inspection, he was even more convinced that whatever was inside that case was definitely not a set of power tools. George tentatively tried one of the catches on the side, but found the box locked. Deciding that what he did not know, could not hurt him, he tucked the bottoms of his jeans into his socks, sent a text to Hakan Toprak confirming he had done as asked, climbed onto the bike and negotiated the rough track back around the boundary of the Cara di Mineo Knowledge Centre.

CHAPTER 56

HAKAN TOPRAK
MALTA INTERNATIONAL AIRPORT

Hakan Toprak was used to the good things in life, so, for him, the budget airline flight from Catania to Malta International airport was an ordeal, albeit a short one. The cabin smelled of sweat; there were crumbs and empty water bottles under his feet, as the rapid turnaround meant there had been no cleaning. To cap it all, there was no ice to chill his plastic cup of sparkling water.

He checked his watch, noting that George should now be on his way to Fontanarossa airport and that there were only three minutes to go before the detonation of the device in the back of the van. Given the anticipated impact of the events he had set in motion, he felt it best to remove himself temporarily from the arena, until tempers had cooled and more reasonable counsel prevailed. He had booked a suite at the Athina in St George's Bay, Malta. It was pleasant enough; he just hoped they had found a decent mixologist. The cocktails had been a major disappointment during his last stay.

He watched the second-hand tick down and tried to suppress the satisfaction he felt in dealing such a blow to the amateurs in Calabria. When the hands signalled the exact moment of the small explosion, he imagined the blast in the back of the van, blowing out its windows and throwing open the doors. The explosion, however, was not designed to damage any nearby building, or to incapacitate any person, but to generate sufficient energy to power the microwave device within the high-powered electronic e-bomb.

There were many advantages to having the Americans as allies of the Turkish military regime, an alliance he and Natasha Bonnici had created only twelve months previously. Hakan managed the uneasy relationship, effectively blackmailing the Americans from time to time, using his possession of one of their nuclear warheads that he had had stolen from their Turkish base at Incirlik. The Americans were terrified that the loss of such a weapon would be made public, or that Hakan might make good on his threat to auction it on the Dark Web. They had accordingly been forced into making a number of important political concessions, favouring the Turkish state and, on occasion, MalTech Energy. One other benefit the Turks enjoyed was access to American weaponry, not readily available on the international arms markets, such as the highly effective, and highly expensive, e-bomb.

———

People working inside the Knowledge Centre were blinded momentarily by an intense burst of energy in the form of a flare of light. The short, and very intense, power surge was equivalent to tens of thousands of volts. It ripped through the semiconductors in the servers, corrupted all the computer data, including the back-ups, and completely fried all the electric and electronic equipment.

Following that, the deep buzzing and low reverberations from 800,000 fried servers eventually faded away to silence. The emergency lighting failed and the damage to the control systems in the back-up generators meant they failed to kick-in. The whole of the 75,000-square-metre windowless building was plunged into darkness. The transformers and distribution systems sat idle, unable to direct the incoming current through any of the switches and relays. Inside the building, the lifts stopped between floors, the cries of the three women within shaft 4B echoing around the silent west side. People's phones, laptops and tablets were all frazzled. Even the computer chips in the vehicles in the car park were so compromised as to render them useless. The coffee machine dribbled its last drops of cappuccino into the drip tray.

The businesses of ReachAd, the CatTech Data centre and the Bitcoin mining enterprise were destroyed in a flash. Literally. All promises of systems security and integrity exposed as false. Those inside were so completely stunned, it took them a while to work out they had been hit by an electromagnetic bomb. Never in any of their security scenarios had they envisaged anything like it.

At the same time, George was making his great escape, legs slightly bowed, wobbling along the track, negotiating the potholes on the lane that led towards the white Fiat, parked outside the 400-metre range of the electromagnetic burst.

He, of course, had no idea of the mayhem he had just caused at the electronically scorched Knowledge Park. All he knew was that he was going home to Malta and, later that night, he would eat with his family, sleep in his own bed, and need no longer worry about volcanos, tunnels, rivers of fire or shady groups of priests and criminals.

He had wanted to say goodbye to Diego. He had grown attached to the boy during their time together, but doubted they would ever see each other again and, if they ever did, that Diego would have risen much above the rank of Agente in the rough and tumble of the Catania Questura.

He found the keys where they were supposed to be and opened the door to the car. Before he lowered himself into the seat, he looked around at the green hills to the north where the deciduous planes, oaks and chestnuts were well on their way to showing their late-autumn colours. The oranges had been harvested, but the windfalls and spoiled fruit lay on the ground, creating a sun-bleached, tawny carpet under the regular rows of fruit trees. Malta was a limestone rock, with only a few centimetres of topsoil, and was largely devoid of trees, so he took a minute to soak in the feel of the rich, verdant landscape around him.

He was just about to get into his car when he heard his phone ringing. He retrieved it from the pocket of his jeans and looked at the screen. The caller was Vice Questora Cristina Capozzi. He held the phone in his hand, a tremor of fear running through him every time it shrilled its alert. George felt a flood of guilt wash over him. What had he done and how had she found out about it so quickly? Finally, the phone stopped ringing. He looked at it for half a minute, holding his breath, waiting for it to spring back to life accusingly. He looked around, turning a full circle, expecting to see Polizia hiding behind every tree, weapons out and pointing at him. Leading them, he imagined Capozzi, her accusing gaze fixed on him. Of course, there was nobody in sight

Then, suddenly, like a fist to his chest, a text arrived.

Superintendent, where are you? Ring me. VQ Capozzi

He physically leaped into the air in shock. *What did she want? What had Hakan got him into?* It was several minutes before he began to relax. There was nothing much to know. He had not actually done anything, other than park a van on a country track. The explosion of the e-bomb was a fairly minor blast and the sound had escaped him entirely. After giving it some thought, he concluded Capozzi probably wanted to wish him well and say her goodbyes. It had actually been rude of him to leave without saying farewell. But then again, she had formally ended their relationship when she had kicked him out of the Questura. There was nothing to be worried about. He would set off for the airport as planned. Marianna might be making rabbit pasta, in honour of his return. That would be something!

An hour later, he had parked the Fiat in Fontanarossa Airport and went into the terminal building searching for the left-luggage locker that matched his key. As he was pulling his case out of it, he became aware of someone behind him and turned to find Cristina Capozzi standing a metre away, with the familiar bulk of Sovrintendente Andrea Lamieri just behind her.

"Well, George, I assume you didn't get my message?"

"Er, no. What message?"

"Let's not play games, George. I know exactly where you've been and what you've done. But what I don't understand is why you did it. There're some very, very angry people who would love to talk to you. So let's take a walk. I'm sure the *Polizia dell' Immigrazione e delle Frontiere* will let us use their facilities."

CHAPTER 57

VICE QUESTORA CRISTINA CAPOZZI

PREFETTURA DI CATANIA

THE DAY after the devastating explosion in the Questura, Cristina Capozzi was occupied trying to fit a staff of 130 officers, plus administrators, into the Prefettura, the government offices of the state. It was a grand building, its four sides built around a large central courtyard, which seemed to Cristina to be at least a third empty. Despite the fact that both the Polizia di Stato and the Prefettura reported to the Ministry of the Interior, the Prefect himself was so far proving to be remarkably unsupportive, obstructive even.

The police inquiry into the bombing of the Questura, which had only just got going, and was being hampered by the destruction of their offices, plus the fact that Cristina herself more or less knew who was responsible, but had no intention of bringing them to justice. Inquiries into the causes and culprits in the construction disaster at Librino had been similarly diverted, sidetracked and muddied. At that moment, she had a lot on her plate and could have done without the message that had caused her to reprioritise her day.

Fifteen minutes after receiving the emergency text, she was sitting in her car, using a burner phone, in another area of Catania. If anyone ever decided to trace the call, they would place it as coming from the tower near the Stadio Angelo Massimino football stadium in the north-west of the city. The caller told her of the disaster at the Knowledge Park in Mineo. The chief technical officer had guessed what had happened and run to a farmhouse a kilometre away to find a working phone. On his way across the fields, he had spotted the bombed-out Peugeot van. He had the wit to find the number plate, which lay a little distance away. Cristina copied the registration details into her phone.

She immediately understood the magnitude of the loss and was shocked that anyone had the balls to make such a bare-faced attack against the 'Men of Valour', as the 'Ndrangheta liked to call themselves. It took her about ten seconds to realise that this was retaliation for the murder of the two prosecutors. The events had to be linked, but she could not believe the state would ever be involved in such a sophisticated move. She also knew that nobody in the Polizia di Stato or the ministry had any idea what really went on behind the scenes in the grey, faceless building at Mineo, so it would never occur to them to attack it. She wondered whether it could be the start of a turf war of some sort.

Cristina looked at the number plate and realised all she could do was check if the van was stolen or not. She could not access data from any of the road-traffic CCTV. Their systems were still down and it would be some days before new kit could be set up, back-ups installed and networks re-established. She thought about what lay between Mineo and Catania. It was a reasonable guess that whoever did this had approached the Knowledge Park from the city. She called up Google maps and, seconds later, banged the dashboard with satisfaction. If her guess was right, there was a good chance that the van would have driven past the main gate of the US Naval Air Station at Sigonella, on the Strada Statale, 15 kilometres south of Catania.

She rang the head of security at Sigonella, a hard-nosed red-cap who was a long-time contact of hers. He spent valuable minutes commiserating with her about the recent terrible bombing and the loss of her colleagues. Cristina played along, until frustration got the better of her.

Finally, she said: "Listen, Jake, we have a lead on a vehicle we think may be involved. Our systems are still down and we need your help. Can you check your gate and any perimeter cameras covering the Strada Statale, between these times, and see if you can get a visual on a silver Peugeot van with this registration?"

Fifteen minutes later, a photograph had arrived on Cristina's phone. It showed the Peugeot cruising along the highway, past the base's high wire fencing. It was accompanied by a second file, containing a blown-up, but unmistakable, image of the driver.

————

She marched George to the offices of the airport police and they were shown into a windowless holding cell, with a table and three chairs. Sovrintendente Andrea Lamieri leaned against the wall and looked at George, with the lazy menace of a resting Bengal Tiger. Capozzi took out her phone and showed him the picture. George's eyes flicked between the picture and Lamieri, who was cracking his knuckles, one by one.

"I don't care whether you're the main man from Scotland Yard or the head of the CIA – you're in big trouble. In fact, it's probably worse than you imagine. First, let's see what you're prepared to tell me. Why did you do it?"

"Do what? I only drove the van…"

"Don't go down that line. It'll end badly. Do you know who owns the businesses you've just ruined? Have you any idea how much money you've cost them?"

"I didn't realise…"

"George, we're all professionals here. Please show me some respect. Are you going to talk or are you not? If not, fine, Andrea will take you to meet the people you've just badly upset and I'll treat your missing persons file with the same contempt as I treated Silvia Camilleri's. If you're going to talk, start now!"

George knew when he was beaten and started to talk. He told her about Hakan Toprak, about Natasha Bonnici and Gerald Camilleri. He said he had no idea what was in the van, but had been assured that, whatever was in the metal box, was not a bomb. He was told somebody would collect the van from where he had left it and that was all that was expected of him. As soon as he said it, he realised how stupid it sounded.

She asked him if he had Hakan Toprak's mobile number. He had. Cristina pondered for a moment and left the room.

She rang the number on his phone and it was answered promptly in accented English.

"George, good to hear from you. You should be ready to board about now."

"I'm sorry, Toprak *bey*, but it's not the superintendent speaking. George is with us and is helping us with our inquiries. Someone was stupid enough to destroy a perfectly legitimate technology business. He's been most helpful."

There was a lengthy pause, as Hakan Toprak collected his thoughts.

"I assume I'm speaking with Vice Questora Capozzi?"

"That doesn't matter."

"OK. Well, first, I am glad I have finally got your attention. Second, you seem quite content to murder two investigating magistrates, risk the lives of your colleagues and destroy a Questura, but you are complaining about a few bytes of data being scrambled? I think you are missing the point."

"And what is that, Toprak?"

"The point is that you should be asking me what I can do to prevent the Ministry of the Interior declaring war on you, and making this whole situation a total financial write-off. Killing two prosecutors was a very bad move. Rome is not happy. I need to speak with your directors – the Provincia, I believe you call them? You will have to write off the losses at Mineo as the cost of ignoring my initial overtures. Decline my offer this time and I will make sure there is nothing left in Catania for you to sell."

Capozzi was quiet. It was her turn to pause the conversation.

"Are you there?" he asked.

"Yes, I am."

"Good. Now can you please let the good superintendent go? He is a civilian in this and we did rather twist his arm. And he has a flight to catch. You have my number. I will be waiting for the call."

CHAPTER 58

LUISA MARONGIU

PALAZZO DEL VIMINALE, ROME

"IT'S WONDERFUL, Michele! I wish I could've seen their faces. The bastards! Hakan is such a genius. How on earth did he get his hands on a weapon like that?"

"That, minister, is a very good question. It's been noted, at the highest levels, that the Turks seem to have the Americans wrapped around their little finger. I suspect that device came straight from some secret US weapons program."

"That's all well and good. But it still leaves us with a problem of presentation."

"Presentation?"

"Yes, Michele, presentation. We've got to be seen to be doing something. It's fine for Hakan to creep up, and let off his computer bomb, but what about us? Do you think the press gives a damn about a computer centre in the middle of nowhere? And we can't even mention it to them, can we? But I've got two unavenged public servants and I have to be seen to be doing something about that. Something dramatic. We need some arrests. Headlines! A maxi-trial. A round up of these people. The public needs to know we can protect them."

"Minister, this isn't China! You can't just have a 'round-up'!"

"Oh, Michele, at times like this, people expect us to grow a pair! Think what Hakan would do."

"He's from Turkey, he probably could have a 'round-up', if he wanted one."

"We could ask around for some soft targets and go for them, all guns blazing!"

"I hope you don't mean literally?"

"Of course not. We could ask Direzione Nazionale Anti-Mafia to formulate a plan to bring in some 'Ndrangheta types and hold them for a while? Let people think we've caught the perpetrators."

"Hmm. Yes. That's a possibility. Operation Strike Down."

"Yes, yes, good! Can we call it that?"

"I don't see why not."

"I think I might call the Prime Minister and see what he thinks."

"About the plan? I wouldn't – it's still a bit vague."

"No, silly. To see if he likes the name!"

CHAPTER 59

VITO AMATO
CITY HALL, CATANIA

THE DAY FOLLOWING the incident at Mineo, the papers reported that a freak electrical surge, caused by a serious volcanic tremor, had impacted the power supply to the Knowledge Park. The damage to the infrastructure of the businesses that operated there was said to be substantial. That same morning Cristina Capozzi, called a meeting at Vito's office in the Palazzo degli Elefanti on the northern side of the Piazza del Duomo.

Vito had been irritated by the tone of the vice questura, demanding time in his diary without providing a reason, or even an apology, for the short notice of the meeting

"Well, Cristina, what's this all about?" He didn't raise his eyes from his desk, pretending to be engrossed in the papers in front of him. "I'm busy this morning."

When he glanced up, he noticed Cristina Capozzi had a cold, unsmiling look on her face. In fact, Vito suspected there was the hint of a sneer, as she dropped the corners of her mouth, while she coolly appraised him.

"I have instructions for you Vito and, for Agostino Basso, on our response to the attack on our assets at Mineo."

Vito nearly fell off his chair, all pretence of studying his papers, now gone. The idea that she intended to 'instruct' them implied she was a senior member of the... no, that could not be right? He could not just lie down and accept this from her. He said, slightly hesitantly: "What on earth are you talking about? Have you gone mad?"

"I'm sorry, I know this must come as a shock but you'll get used to it. Basso will explain it all. Ring him."

Vito hesitated, unsure how far he should go in acknowledging the vice questora's assumptions about his knowledge and involvement.

"I'm not sure I know..."

"Yes, Basso, ring him. You know who I mean, the man you meet almost weekly to keep this show on the road. Text me a time to meet you both later. And please don't mess around with me, it wouldn't be clever."

With that, she left him sitting stunned, in his office.

Basso was equally shocked when he got a call from the vice questora. He had long known of the existence of an unknown supervisor, which the Provincia had made no secret of, but he would never have guessed it would be the unassuming Vice Questora. Yet, the more he thought about it, the more sense it made. He remembered her father had been a *capo* and, by all accounts, he was now one of the main men in Pagliarelli. It was not unheard of for family members to step up when an elder was forced to move aside.

Basso placed a call to a farmhouse in Cittanova, in the heart of the Aspromonte National Park, in Reggio Calabria, right on the toe of the Italian boot. That was his contact point with the Provincia. Basso spoke in coded terms to his main contact, a man he had often called, but whose name he did not know.

"I have been contacted by the woman I understand supervises some of our work. Is it OK for me to meet her and discuss our repairs at the Knowledge Park?"

"Meet her and do what she says. But there's something new

to be done. We need to value our interests in the Green Catania project. There's a possibility we'll sell, if the price is right."

"What, everything? Even the geothermal plant and hydrogen facility?"

"Yes, everything. Not that the Knowledge Park businesses are worth much, now!"

"Can I ask why?"

"There seems to be an imminent increase in regulation that'll make it more difficult for us to operate the assets."

Basso thought of the myriad businesses and operations they owned as part of the Green Catania project. It would usually take months for him to get all the accounts inspected and undertake a proper valuation.

"If I am going to do this, we need to move fast or word of a sale will get out. I have to warn you, the valuation will be very rough and ready. I will do it myself."

———

Early in the evening, the vice questura met with Vito and Basso, in City Hall, in the Palazzo degli Elefanti. Cristina Capozzi led the discussion. The two men sat uneasily, as she began the conversation without the usual niceties.

"I've made inquiries. We've been played by the Turk. He's working with Rome and must've given them enough information to justify sending in the prosecutors. Then he suggests to us we should send a signal to Rome, to make them back off, '*come Falcone e Borsellino*' – his words. So, like fools, we murdered two special prosecutors from Direzione Nazionale Anti-Mafia, which we should have known would open the doors for reprisals from Rome. Mineo is just a taste of what they're prepared to do. He has set us up nicely.

"Now we've proof that Rome is working with Toprak, it makes our position difficult, which is exactly how he intended it to be. The Provincia has decided to test the Turk, to see how serious an offer he'll make. If he's not serious, we'll destroy him and the Maltese who work alongside him. The murder of the prosecutors was an act of stupidity that was carried out without thinking through the full consequences."

Basso looked at her in horror.

"But that's not right. I did what I had to. Cittanova knew what was planned."

"Yes, but it was *your* idea, *your* plan, both of which were wrong and shortsighted. You could go to Cittanova and explain yourself, but I wouldn't suggest it. The best thing you can do is complete the valuation of the capital plant and revenues. Then, maybe, you can restore Cittanova's faith in your judgement. Until then, you talk to me only. Cittanova don't want to hear from you directly."

Basso was speechless. Behind his large leather-topped desk, Vito slumped back in his chair, desperately calculating what it meant for him, for Catania.

"So, Vice Questora, say there's a sale. What does that mean?"

"It's simple Vito. If there's a sale, it means the contracts will transfer to the Turk and the Maltese. It also means you won't receive the private financial support you've grown used to. Still, your mayor's salary should be enough, and I'm sure you'll scrape enough together to bankroll the next election, won't you?

"At the moment, I'm only including you in this discussion because Hakan Toprak made the initial approach through you, and so that you agree to providing any information Agostino needs to make his valuation. Also, I want you to hear this directly from me. If anything, and I mean anything, about this matter becomes public, you'll pay, whether it's your fault or not. Basso understands our rule of strict responsibility, don't you, Agostino? When you've got a quiet moment, perhaps you can explain the code to Mr Mayor. In the meantime, Vito, forget all about this and get on with cleaning up your city."

Cristina Capozzi did what had to be done, as she always had, but there were occasions when she hated herself for doing so. The minute she knew, or guessed, about the plan to bomb the Questura, she would swear her heart had stopped beating. It was her second home. The people inside it were her people. Right up until the last moment, she was not sure if she could let it happen. Even while she hid in her house, her fingers had lingered over her phone. An anonymous text to the Anti-Mafia Confidential phone number would have saved lives, saved their ongoing work, preserved a cornerstone of the community. But she could not do it, for all the usual reasons. Her daughter Luciana would be at risk; her imprisoned father was an easy target; her own career would be finished – they would make sure of that. And she would be prosecuted and then jailed with no protection. Once she was behind bars, it was certain that she, too, would never leave prison alive.

It was ironic that she only got into it all, in the first place, in order to help the people of Librino, picking up her father's burden. When the state was absent, the void had to be filled by other means. Yes, life was unfair. Sometimes the end justified the means. But, with the arrival of drugs, the game had become more complicated; the money at stake too much for her to ignore, and, by then, she was already in too deep. It had started slowly at first, just to help get the business back on its feet after her father's imprisonment. Soon, her 'specially adapted' wagons were rolling across the Messina Straits on every other ferry. Now, her bosses owned an entire city. Those small-minded people, stuck on a hill-side in the mountains of southern Italy, owned *her* city. For the sake of its citizens, maybe it was no bad thing that change was on the way.

CHAPTER 60
SUPERINTENDENT GEORGE ZAMMIT

CUSTODY SUITE, POLIZIA DELLE
FRONTIERE, CATANIA

WHEN THE VICE questora left to go to her meeting in City Hall, she did not release George from the Polizia delle Frontiere custody suite at the airport. She thought causing him a little inconvenience would do no harm and was only mild punishment for destroying property worth over a billion euros. It was a well-known tactic of border forces across the world to hold people they were not going to prosecute, but suspected of wrongdoing they could not prove, just long enough so that they missed their flights.

A few hours later, at Malta International Airport, Marianna, Gina and Denzel stood in the Arrivals area. Gina held a pink balloon with 'Welcome' written across it. As time went by, her disappointment turned to anger.

"No message, no call, nothing... and the family meal is tomorrow. It's just too much, too much!"

Denzel, who served Assistant Commissioner Gerald Camilleri, had a slightly different view. He knew his father was not the sort to leave them standing there and he also knew how important it was to their mother that the meal with Giorgio's family went without a hitch. The young man was worried, but did not want the women to see that. As his sister and mother walked back to Giorgio's car, Gina let go of the pink balloon. It drifted silently away into the night sky. Denzel lagged behind to phone Camilleri and ask whether there was any reason for his father's no-show at the airport. The assistant commissioner remained quiet for a moment, while he thought it over. He agreed it was strange, but told them not to worry, that he would look into it and get back to them.

Back in Catania, the Polizia di Stato were in chaos, as they tried to relocate themselves into three floors of the western block of the Prefettura. It was true that there was not a lot of room, but there was even less organisation. Vans had delivered load after load of filing cabinets from what remained of the old Questura, boxes of papers were stacked against walls, technicians stood around awaiting instructions on the installation of computers and telephones, but of course there was no master plan and Capozzi seemed to have vanished. The Questore himself paid only a brief visit. He took one look at the bemused expressions of his officers and exited quickly, demanding that somebody find the vice questora and tell her he wanted the mess sorting out at once.

Sovrintendente Andrea Lamieri had returned from Fontanarossa airport and was lounging around near a table with a kettle, a stack of plastic coffee cups and a jar of instant coffee.

"We can't be expected to drink this filth. Where's the proper coffee machine? Someone should go out and get coffees. Hey, *ciccone*, come here!"

Diego was trying, but struggling, to set up six desks for the Criminal Investigation Unit, when he heard Lamieri shout to him across the room. He sighed and put down his electric screwdriver, and walked across towards Lamieri, seeing the other officers grin at the use of the derogatory nickname.

"Sovrintendente, it's OK to ask, if you want me to do something. But, please, I'd prefer you use my rank and proper name, Agente Diego Russo, if that's OK with you."

A huge "Whaoooo!" went up around the room, as the assembled officers waited to see what Lamieri would do, in the face of such cheek!

Lamieri roared with laughter, then mimicked Diego's voice.

"If that's OK with you? You *ciccone* – you fatso!"

He looked around, encouraging the others to join in the mockery.

Diego had had enough. As he turned to leave, he deliberately brushed the plastic cup of hot coffee off the trestle table and into Lamieri's crotch. The sergeant leapt to his feet, as he felt the coffee soak through to his skin, desperately pulling it away from his scalded groin.

"*Sei fuori di testa*, Russo? Guys, did you see what he just did?"

A wet stain spread over the front of Lamieri's trousers. He was more shocked than hurt, but the uproar in the office, as he became the target of general derision instead of Diego, was worse than being doused with a thousand cups of hot coffee.

He rounded on Diego.

"You've had it now, *figlio di puttana*, it's just you and me. Your Maltese superintendent can't protect you now. Hah! He's locked up in Fontanarossa. Capozzi saw to that. And, you know what? You're next. You're finished, Russo. Now get out of my sight."

Diego looked at him.

"A pleasure, Sovrintendente, at once! But I think you should, er, change those trousers. It's not a good look."

A cheer went up, followed by the banging of metal desks and a round of raucous applause, as Diego quickly made an exit.

The encounter had rattled him. It had taken a lot for Diego to stand up to the bullying sergeant. He was shaking and breathing heavily, as he scuttled down the long staircase of the Prefettura and out into the Piazza dell'Elefante. Across the square was

Prestipino's. Diego remembered the many conversations and meetings there, over the previous weeks. He, George and Lucy had been a team. He had enjoyed working with them and he had been shown a measure of respect. A month ago, there was no way he would have been able to stand up to Lamieri as he just had.

Diego thought about what Lamieri had said to him. George was locked up at Fontanarossa? That could not be true. He sat on the steps of the fountain and took out his mobile. It was dark and the tourists had thinned out. There were still a few visitors standing around, looking up at the Duomo and the dark mass of Etna, but otherwise it was quiet. Taking a deep breath, he rang the Polizia delle Frontiere at Fontanarossa and identified himself. He asked if they were holding a Maltese policeman, Superintendent George Zammit. The desk officer confirmed they were. Diego forced a laugh.

"How pissed off is he?"

"Oh, very! His flight left ten minutes ago!"

After they had both enjoyed the joke, Diego said: "Serves him right, poking his nose in where he's not wanted. Listen, Vice Questora Capozzi has asked me to pick him up and bring him back to town. I'll be there in twenty minutes, that OK?"

"No problem. I was going to get him a *panino*, he was whining he was hungry! But I won't bother, if you're coming for him. Saves me a job."

Diego did not really know why he was interfering, just that George being held in custody did not feel right. It was something to do with their conversation about an insider being involved in the explosion at the Questura. George had said: *Or a poliziotta! Don't forget the ladies!*

The only lady he could be talking about was Capozzi and, here she was, holding George back from getting his flight to Malta. Suddenly, Diego felt worried. Was he doing the right thing?

He drove to the airport and parked the little red Fiat.

Mustering what confidence he had, he strode into the grubby, badly lit reception of the Polizia delle Frontiere to pick up his prisoner. He decided to make a show and handcuff George, so pulled the cuffs free from his belt and slapped them on the reception desk. The officer's mouth was full of food so he could only nod to acknowledge Diego's arrival. He brushed some crumbs off his chest and placed a paper bag, containing something in flaky pastry, under the counter for later.

George appeared, the border policeman yanking him by his upper arm. George's face was twisted in anger. On seeing Diego, his expression turned to one of surprise.

"What on earth are you doing here?"

"You're coming with me. No messing around, yeah?"

Checking on the desk officer, who was retrieving George's personal items, Diego gave George a theatrical wink and told him to hold out his arms. To George's further surprise, Diego put the cuffs on him and then, for some reason, he signed the custody book in the name of Sovrintendente Lamieri. Showing more confidence than he felt, he hustled George and his suitcase out into the car park.

They looked at one another.

Diego said: "What's going on?"

"I couldn't begin to explain it all, but Capozzi is definitely the insider. She's 'Ndrangheta. I need to get off this island as soon as possible."

Diego was thoughtful.

"So, does that kind of make me your accessory in the eyes of the 'Ndrangheta?"

"Well, springing me from custody – for which, thank you, by the way – does seem to put you on the other side of the fence. Don't you think?"

"Yeah. That's bad. I mean, good you're free, but bad 'cos they may not feel good about me helping you. You know?"

George shook his head to clear it.

"Listen, stick with me for the time being. We'll sort things out for you later. First, I'm going to make a call."

He rummaged in the bag of possessions the border officer had given him, found his phone and pressed the number for Hakan Toprak. Hakan answered.

"Yes, Vice Questora. Have you released him yet?"

"What? It's me – George. What are you talking about?"

"Well, the last person to ring on this number was Vice Questora Capozzi herself. So, have you been released?"

"Mela, yes, I'm out! No thanks to you."

"Good."

"No, not good. I was arrested by Cristina Capozzi, who's part of the 'Ndrangheta. I've been held in a detention cell at the airport and have just managed to escape with the help of a friend. I need help – now!"

"Oh! How dramatic. I asked them to set you free. I am surprised they did not. I suppose simply getting on the next plane is not on? They will be waiting at the gate for you. And the same with the catamaran service to Malta. So, where are you exactly?"

"The airport car park. Listen this is all your fault. You said there was no bomb in that van. That wasn't true, was it? You lied to me!"

"Well, it was not totally true, but there was no high explosive device that was a danger to life. I assumed that is what you meant by a bomb? So, my answer to you, was partly true but, anyway, the airport carpark is not the best place to hang about. I take it this friend has transport?"

George turned to Diego.

"You've got the car?"

"Er, yeah, the red one you don't like very much."

Hakan was speaking.

"I am going to send you a GPS pin and an address. I will speak to Rome and get some proper security to meet you. We will make sure we get you safely on a flight. Tonight, stay at the address I am sending you. You will be fine. In fact, you will be more than fine. I am quite jealous, actually. Tomorrow, I will have Gerald organise trustworthy security."

"If you're speaking to Camilleri, ask him to tell my wife... I don't know what, but make some excuse, anything! There's a family occasion tomorrow. If I miss it, I'd rather be at the mercy of the 'Ndrangheta than her!"

"Do not joke about things like that. Just get going!"

They drove north for an hour, following the GPS on George's phone, until there was a turn off for Taormina. A small side road wound through the coastal hills for another few kilometres, until they saw a sign outside some large ornate, wrought-iron gates: *Privato, Villa Genovese.*

Diego was uncomfortable.

"I don't like it, George. I know this place. Well, I know *of* this place. The Genovesi are a big Mafia family. They went to America after the war and became one of the Five Families. You've heard of them, right? They were like Goodfellas, you know? But still, a lot of the family have come back to live here. They're not nice people!"

At that moment, the automatic gates noiselessly swung open, to reveal a long drive cutting through dark woodland.

"Well, Diego, we haven't got a lot of choice, have we?"

Small up-lights along the edges of the road guided Diego's Fiat until they saw the floodlit villa ahead of them. As far as they could tell in the moonlight, the garden was classically ordered, with fountains, ornamental parterres and geometrically trimmed bushes and hedges. The villa was a huge, three-storey, late-Renaissance building with colonnades and a huge portico, giving it a classical look.

Diego was stunned.

"Wow, look at this! Do you think it's got a pool?"

As they pulled to a halt, the huge front door swung open and two suited men stood back to allow a tall, elegant woman to emerge. She seemed to be wearing a flowing evening gown or silky dressing gown, George could not tell which. The light was behind her, but she did not need clever lighting to reveal the fact that she was a beautiful woman, with the movement and poise of a ballet dancer. She addressed them from the top of the stairs.

"Welcome to Villa Genovese. I'm Baronessa Orsini. I assume you are Hakan's friends?"

Diego stood bowing his head, rubbing his hands together.

"Yes, Madam, your Baronessa, thank you, thank you. We're looking forward to our stay. Aren't we, George?"

The Baronessa arched her back and tilted her head so she could look down her nose at the two oddballs on her doorstep, or rather, under her portico. However, as friends of Hakan, she could not turn them away.

"There is guest accommodation to the rear, Klaus will see you round. There is a kitchen and a drinks fridge, please help yourselves. Once Klaus leaves you, please do not wander. We take security very seriously here. If the dogs do not get you, Klaus probably will. He is under orders: shoot first, ask questions later. I know, it is all very dramatic but there it is. Cannot be too careful.

"So, tell me. How is Hakan? Still a man of mystery?"

George could not help but suppress a smile. "Yes, man of mystery just about sums him up. But he's well."

"That's good to hear. And still single?"

"I'm sorry," said George, "I've no idea."

The Baronessa sighed.

"Hmm. We were to be married once. But he was a Muslim and I, a Catholic. Neither of us would, or could, change. But that is another story. Anyway, good night. Please do not linger in the morning. It upsets my routine. Give Hakan my love, tell him I often think of Kalkan."

With that, she turned away, ball gown or dressing gown

swirling behind her, and disappeared inside the villa. One man shut and noisily locked the enormous double doors behind her, leaving them to face the formidable, shaven-headed Klaus, who stood looking down at them with undisguised contempt.

"Bring that heap of junk round the back, out of sight."

CHAPTER 61
HAKAN TOPRAK
CASTELLO BONNICI, MALTA

IT WAS windy and very wet in Malta. Natasha and Hakan were sat in the breakfast room, watching the rain bounce off the flagged terrace. The storm had started several hours before dawn and showed no signs of abating. Hakan was in his shirt sleeves, peering through his spectacles at his laptop, a look of intense concentration on his face. Natasha had decided to breakfast without any makeup and selected a simple grey cashmere leisure suit, hoping to show him how at ease she felt in his company. So far, Hakan was too engrossed in his spreadsheets to notice anything other than the size of the enterprise in Catania.

He pushed his glasses on top of his bushy hair and rubbed his eyes.

"It is impossible to put an accurate value on the Catania project. I do not have any of the data or a team to do research, due diligence, anything. I cannot imagine they are going to hand over a pile of financials either. I am shooting in the dark, here."

Natasha took a bite of melon and shook her head.

"That's the problem when you're dealing with criminals. They don't play by the rules."

"I would like you to make sure the Family are onside with this. I do not want to find we have overpaid and for there to be negative feeling among them. When do you next meet the Committee?"

These were the senior members of the Family, who met at Natasha's behest to agree all major decisions. It had been noted that, after murdering her way to the head of the table, she now managed the Committee with openness and even-handedness, something that had surprised the men of Milan.

"I can call them any time you need me to."

"First we need the 'Ndrangheta to get in touch and say there is a deal to be done. They are taking their time."

"They're probably doing what you are – wrestling with the numbers. I can't imagine their bookkeeping is up to much. Anyway, do you want to go out for lunch? I know an excellent little place in St Paul's. Honestly, it does the best fish."

"Natasha, can you not see what I am doing here?"

"Ooh! You're no fun sometimes, Hakan Toprak."

As it turned out, they did go out for lunch and the fish was superb. It was mid-week and the restaurant was quiet. They sat by the window and watched the wind whip foam from the incoming waves. Through the mist, they could just about make out the shadowy, low-lying mass of St Paul's Island, a kilometre or so offshore. The island was so called because the saint had landed there after he was shipwrecked, while being returned to Rome from Cyprus to face trial. Natasha had read accounts of the event and believed it was more likely the wreck occurred on the south-east coast, but did not really care. As the rain ran in rivulets down the windows, they shared a pile of fresh shellfish, served over a bucket of ice, followed by fillets of line-caught sea bass in a herby white wine sauce. Just as they were about to start the main dish, Hakan's phone rang. His expression changed.

"It is them."

He stood up and walked towards the door, where he stood in the porch to avoid the rain. Natasha watched him through the glass. His back was turned towards her, so all she could do was study his body language. He was gesticulating with his left hand, seemingly making a point. Then he slouched against the door, head back, listening carefully, his eyes shut. After a minute or two he was heading back to the table.

"They want to talk. They will make all arrangements through Zammit."

Natasha's mouth dropped open.

"George? Why him?"

"I really do not know."

"What did you say?"

"What could I say? I agreed."

"I'd better speak to Gerald Camilleri, tell him to get George prepared. What else did they say?"

"They want the meeting to be in Cittanova, Aspromonte. Their home patch."

"Oh my God! I don't like the sound of that."

"I suggested somewhere more convenient and on neutral territory, but they said if I wanted to meet the Provincia, that is where I would find them. Also, I can only bring one other person, the policeman. Nobody else."

"George isn't really made for that sort of thing."

"I suspect that is exactly why they have specified him."

"This is all getting too dangerous, Hakan. We should think it through. It's also too much to lay on one person's shoulders."

"I agree, it is becoming disconcerting. But this is an enormous opportunity for me personally that will not come around again. If I pull it off, it will cement my position in the Family and silence those who see me as an *arrivista*, only tolerated because I enjoy your protection."

"What? After all you have achieved with the oil and gas deal in Turkey and the way you manage the Americans? Nobody would dare think that! They look on you as Superman, just like I do. Never doubt yourself, Hakan."

She leaned across to plant a lingering kiss on his cheek.

IT WAS GOING to be a difficult morning for Luisa. She had a meeting with her arch-rival, Maria Sarti, from the Ministry of Defence. As Minister of the Interior, the Polizia di Statoreported to Luisa, but the Carabinieri were part of the armed forces and so came under the control of the Minister of Defence. If they were going to mount operation *'Strike Down'*, they needed her co-operation, and Maria Santi was proving difficult. Michele had tried to use his charm on her advisers, so far without success.

Had Luisa been prepared to share the real story behind her request, as she was advised to do by Michele, she might have got further. Luisa, however, did not want to risk Maria Santi taking all the credit for ridding 'Green Catania' of the 'Ndrangheta and clearing the way for the 'Green Naples' project. Luisa maintained that, if she told Maria the depth of the 'Ndrangheta's involvement in 'Green Catania', she would surely leak it, just to embarrass a rival minster – she was that type; no scruples and all naked ambition.

Unfortunately, Maria controlled the assets needed for the 'Strike Down' project. As the Carabinieri were military, rather than police, they had formed up the Squadron Cacciatori di Calabrin, or Calabria Hunters. This specially trained unit, based in Vibo Valentia, less than an hour's drive from Cittanova, had sharpshooters, rock climbers, dog-handlers, specialised trackers and, most importantly, tunnellers, all ready to perform military interventions against organised-crime groups. Michele had said that to ask a police unit to undertake such a dangerous operation would be negligent, whereas the crack Hunters were based only 50 kilometres away from Cittanova. To clinch the argument, he told Luisa that, were there to be any casualties or, God forbid, fatalities, they would be laid at her door, and she certainly would not want that."

So, to deliver 'Strike Down', she had to make her peace with Maria.

The Minister of Defence was a short, top-heavy, sixty-some-thing woman, with bad veins in her legs and a terrible collection of handbags. As Luisa had remarked to Michele: "They are just so garish and large. What does she keep in there? I mean, they are all designer and must cost a fortune, but really? At her age?"

Michele was used to such outbursts and was pleased when he had the diversion of answering a ringing phone.

"She's here. I'll bring her in. Remember, she can help us. So be nice."

"Hmmpf."

As Michele headed for the door, he noticed Luisa quickly dive inside her desk and pull out a handbag, wrapped in large sheets of tissue paper. She unpacked the bag and placed it on the desk-top. Michele was no expert in handbags, but this was unlike anything he had seen before.

The bag seemed to be made of white crocodile skin, and had been dyed, or treated, so it looked like driven snow. It was in fact a Hermès Crocodile Himalayan Birkin bag, made from the white skin of a crocodile. The idea was that the skin was treated to emulate the snowy peaks of the Himalayan mountains. It retailed in the designer shops of Via Condotti at well over one hundred thousand euros. Luisa casually adjusted the angle of the bag, so the white-gold hardware faced in the direction of the guest seat, then stood back to admire her work.

Michele watched, with one hand on the door handle.

"What're you doing?"

"Shut up. I've borrowed it."

He shook his head and swiftly disappeared, to return with their guest. The two ministers air-kissed enthusiastically and Luisa gestured Maria towards the seat, nearest the bag.

Maria Santi could not fail to recognise such a provocative item, especially when it had been placed right under her nose.

"Oh, I say, you've got a Hermes Himalayan! I mean, it's last year's, but who cares these days? It's lovely!"

Luisa gritted her teeth.

"Have a seat, Maria, take the weight off those legs. They must be killing you."

"Oh, no, darling, doing 'Couch to Five', you know! Fit as a fiddle these days. You should try it, might do you some good – looks as though you've put on a kilo or two. It's all these meetings and conferences. I understand how easily it can happen when you get to your age."

The women flashed their fake smiles at each other.

Hostilities completed, Maria turned the conversation towards business.

"So, my people have heard from Michele that you want the Hunters for some daring, clandestine raid, but aren't prepared to tell me why or what it's for. Have I got that right? How mysterious!"

"No, no! The Prime Minister and I have both agreed 'Strike Down' is an excellent idea – he congratulated me on the name actually. But, between you and me, there've been some internal security concerns about what's happening with the 'Ndrangheta and we all feel they need to be taken down a peg or two. A raid on Cittanova would send a clear signal to them that we won't put up with it any longer!"

"What 'concerns' are these? Who's 'we' in this context? And precisely what 'won't we put up with any longer'? You see, you're not really telling me anything, Luisa. That's why I'm not playing ball with you."

"Well, the PM…"

"I called the PM and he said he'd heard something was going on, but he doesn't know any details, other than you've given it a silly name. He's asked me to find out exactly what you're up to. So, darling, spill it."

There was an awkward silence. Then, realising she was beaten, Luisa said: "Michele, tell Maria what she needs to know."

Luisa put on her glasses and started ruffling through some papers on her desk.

For the next ten minutes, Michele carefully, and selectively, laid out how they had discovered a serious organised-crime presence within the 'Green Catania' project, and how the Polizia di Stato had tried to force the hand of the 'Ndrangheta. The result had been the murder of the two prosecutors, a disgraceful and cowardly act that had angered the entire country and warranted a severe response. This was why they were asking for the support of the Hunters, to raid certain properties in Cittanova where their intelligence sources believed senior 'Ndrangheta lived. He conceded it was primarily a fishing expedition and they might never be able to win a conviction, but if nothing else, it would show the 'Ndrangheta they could be struck down at any time, by the combined forces of the Polizia di Stato and the Carabinieri. Ministerial teamwork. The PM would love it!

Maria Santi listened intently.

"OK, that's better. Now I understand, I'll authorise it. You see, Luisa, it's amazing what a little candour can achieve?"

Luisa took off her spectacles and pushed the papers to one side. Maria continued: "My people will be in touch and we can agree an operational plan." She was about to lift herself out of the chair when she said: "Oh, and by the way, Luisa, haven't I seen Mina Mattei with a Hermès Himalayan? You're good friends with Mina, aren't you? You know, you needn't have bought one really. I'm sure she'd let you borrow hers, if you ever needed to impress." She smiled sweetly and sprang to her feet, with more ease than Luisa would have liked.

"See you both later. *Ciao!*"

Once the door had closed, Luisa spat out: "That appalling woman, what a cow! There was no need for that."

Michele said nothing, but had to turn his back, screw up his eyes and try desperately to quell his shaking shoulders. It was deeply satisfying when the minister got a taste of her own medicine, and there was none better at dispensing it than Maria Santi. Once he had gathered himself, he blinked the tears out of his eyes, took a deep breath and asked: "Minister, if we're going down a military course of action, should we alert Hakan Toprak? After all, he could be in the middle of delicate negotiations. I'm wondering if launching 'Strike Down' is entirely wise, just at the moment?"

"Absolutely not. Nothing must get in the way of my operation! We need to keep things tight. Both the PM and Maria Santi are expecting me to be decisive. I can't back down now. Anyway, Hakan will thank me for it. Giving those Southerners a taste of something nasty can only strengthen his position."

"If you say so, Minister. Just wanted to be quite sure we'd factored in everything."

"Yes, quite so – and Michele?"

"Yes?"

"Stop calling the operation, 'Strike Down'. It was a rather silly idea of yours to give it that name!"

CHAPTER 63

SUPERINTENDENT GEORGE ZAMMIT

THE STABLES, VILLA GENOVESE, TAORMINA

KLAUS HAD SHOWN George and Diego to the old stables, which had been converted into luxurious accommodation for the Baronessa's guests. He showed them round their apartment and gave them a lecture about the intelligent lighting, as well as using the spa baths and steam room. He told them not to drink any of the wines on the bottom shelf of the temperature-controlled glass cabinet, as each bottle cost more than a policeman's annual salary. If they wanted anything, they just had to ring him.

"But, remember, I'm not a fucking butler."

Diego wandered around, open-mouthed with astonishment at where he found himself. He kept picking up items, or playing with the automatic curtains, saying: "Look at this! Look at this!

"So, the Baronessa talked about a guy, this Hakan. You know him. Yeah?"

George nodded.

"And he could've married her, and like, she's beautiful of course, but he could've had all this, too?"

"I suppose so."

"And he said no?"

"I don't know what happened."

"Wow, it's all too much!"

George went into the kitchen and rummaged around in the fridge, finding eggs, cheese and bread. He decided to make them an omelette, but that idea came to nothing, as neither of them could manage to operate the white glass induction hob. Finally, after making sandwiches, they decided to have a swim in the indoor guest pool to relax themselves, then head for bed.

George was conscious of the Baronessa's warning about not lingering and set his alarm for earlier than he would have liked. He had been contacted by the Anti-Mafia squad in Palermo, who were going to accompany him back to Fontanarossa airport and make sure he got on a plane to Malta. To his great relief, he thought he had a good chance of making the dinner with Giorgio's family that evening. He had also spoken to the Anti-Mafia people about addressing Diego's situation. They had agreed a plan of action, but George was not sure it was what Diego had in mind.

George watched him, messing around with something by the picture windows, no more than a boy really, and realised Diego assumed he would be coming to Malta too. The boy was wearing a white towelling dressing gown that only just covered his torso. He was playing with the automatic curtains again, which seemed to massively entertain him. He had crossed Capozzi, sprung George from custody, but still seemed incredibly relaxed, or perhaps unaware of the possible consequences of his actions. Diego joined George around the table in the kitchenette, where he decided to broach what was weighing on his mind.

"So, Diego, what's your plan?"

The boy was chewing a mouthful of left-over cheese sandwich from the previous evening.

"My plan?"

"Yeah, will you be OK back at work? How do you think it'll go with Capozzi?"

Diego made a huge effort to swallow the lump of bread and

cheese in his mouth, then gave George that thunderstruck, open-mouthed look he had come to know so well. Diego flicked at the lock of straight black hair that always seemed to stick to his brow.

"What? Go back to work there?"

"Well, yes, unless you've thought of something else to do?"

"But I'm coming with you, aren't I? I can't go back."

This was what George had feared. Diego had no plan at all, other than to accompany him to Malta. Anxious eyes were fixed on George.

"But... you can't just leave me. Not after what I've done for you."

George had no answer to that.

"Diego, I can't take you to Malta. What would you do over there?"

"I don't know. Wait until this all settles down. Work, maybe?"

"As a policeman? You've got to *be* Maltese and able to speak the language!""

Diego got up off the stool and walked around the kitchen.

"Look, the Assistant Commissioner... he's important, isn't he? He said if I ever needed something, I only had to ask. Remember? He said that. He said he was very grateful for what I'd done. Didn't he? So, now I'm asking that you take me back with you. Speak to him and sort something out. Yeah? You can't leave me here – that's not fair. And you promised you'd try and do something, remember?"

Diego's round eyes were desperately seeking a sign that George might be ready to capitulate. If he wanted to, of course Camilleri could resolve the situation. George recalled what he had done for Abdullah when he had fled from Libya. But somehow, George could not imagine Camilleri being too concerned about Diego's fate, no matter what promises he might have made to the young man's face.

"Look, Diego, we can talk to someone senior in Sicily – explain your situation."

"Well, Capozzi's pretty senior and she's 'Ndrangheta – you told me that. So that's no good."

"Have you any friends or relatives outside Catania who could put you up for a while?"

"No! They're all here. I've got to come with you, that's what I'm telling you!"

George felt weighed down by his young friend's unrealistic expectations.

"OK, Diego, if there's no other option. But let me handle things, please. You'll have to do it my way. I'll try and speak to Camilleri very soon, but these things take time and they're above my pay grade. I can't take you with me tomorrow, you understand that, don't you? Trust me, I'll try my best to sort something out for the longer term."

He saw the hope spreading across Diego's face.

"Do you promise? You won't just leave and forget about me?"

"Yes, I promise, I'll try and get you out. But for now, you've got to trust me."

George sucked his teeth. This was a mess. He would have to stick with his original plan, then see what he could do for Diego later.

George and Diego met the two officers from the Anti-Mafia squad at the bottom of Villa Genovese's drive. As they approached, the large gates automatically swung open. George imagined Klaus glowering into a CCTV screen, somewhere in the back of the villa. A BMW estate was parked on the opposite side of the road. The two officers had been asleep, having driven from Palermo overnight. They got out of the car, stretching and urinating in the roadside hedge. Once they had finished, George told them to follow the red Fiat. One officer looked at Diego dubiously.

"Is he the one for the safe house?"

Diego spun round, banged his fists on his fat thighs and stamped his left foot.

"No!!!!"

"Sorry, Diego. Just until things settle down," said George. "I told you, you've got to trust me. Now shut up and let's get on with it. Otherwise, I'll get in the car with them and leave you on the roadside."

Diego sulked all the way to the airport. They drove for forty minutes without a word being said. The nearer they got, the greater the tension and the worse George felt.

Finally, Diego broke silence.

"You're sending me to a safe house?"

"Yes, that's the plan."

"Who arranged it?"

"The Palermo Anti-Mafia section, so it should be safe."

Diego turned in his seat. His face was very pale and beaded with sweat, despite the early hour.

"You don't know their reputation, do you?"

George did not say anything. His mouth had gone dry.

"They stink! They're...they're bent and total bastards! Everybody says so! No one trusts a word they say"

George was shocked to hear this.

"It's just until we can arrange something else. Believe me. Listen, you're not a big trial witness or anything. You've got nothing to fear. You're a policeman, one of their own, nobody'll lay a hand on you."

But Diego's protruding bottom lip and tearful eyes told him otherwise. George felt sick; he just wanted to get away, to get it over with. He hated the way Diego was making him feel. He had done what he could, even though he was not responsible for the boy. There was nothing else he could arrange now. He had made the decision and the Palermo officers were following them, to take Diego to the safe house once George had departed – it was a done deal.

At the airport, George got out of the car, as did Diego. He shook the young officer's damp hand and thanked him for what he had done. He told him once more, promised, to make sure he was all right. With a half-hearted wave, Diego turned his back and morosely approached the first officer, who said with a laugh: "Come on, *ciccione*, get into the car."

By the time George realised the implication of what he had heard, the car had gone and he was accompanied by the other officer to the airport check-in desks. George felt like a dishonourable coward. He should have done more. Been braver, pushed Camilleri harder. He sighed, comforting himself in the knowledge Diego was most likely going to be fine.

George was home in Malta later the same afternoon. Camilleri had sent his own black BMW to meet him airside and he enjoyed the inquisitive looks, as he descended the aircraft steps and made his way straight for it, the Malta Pulizija pennants resplendent on the shiny bonnet.

On arriving home, he found the house in chaos. The women were having their hair washed and coloured in the kitchen. He had to bang on his own door for minutes before Gina finally appeared with her hair in clingfilm and the hairdresser's gown billowing around her. With a shriek of pleasure, she grabbed him and hair colour ran all down George's face onto his collar. He was quickly rushed to the kitchen sink where Gina and Marianna started dousing him with water and scrubbing his neck and cheek.

When they were satisfied with their efforts, Marianna gave him a peck on the cheek and said: "It's just as well you're back. I thought you and I might be having words. Anyway, your turn in the bathroom. I want us all ready by six, for the photographs."

"Photographs?"

"Yes, you agreed last time you were home. Photographs of our family, then of the two families together. They'll be here soon."

"But there's a wedding in two weeks, there'll be a thousand photographs!"

"Well, this is a special night. It'll be nice to have photographs to remember it by. Anyway, you agreed when Gina was cutting your hair. Now, go and get a quick bath, a shave and try on that blue suit. It looks to me like you've put on a bit of weight. I'm glad you didn't go near that volcano thing. You could've been killed! We saw it from the shops, remember? The TV pictures were awful. I kept saying: I hope my George isn't anywhere near that. It would be just like you to fall into it!"

George went upstairs to run his bath, vowing never to fall asleep in his chair again, especially not when Gina was discussing the budget for her wedding plans.

———

The evening turned out to be a great success. Photographs were taken, sparkling pink Lambrusco was drunk and the decibel level around the table increased as the evening progressed. Giorgio's large, red-faced father, Joseph, owned Mifsud's Butchers on Birkirkara high street and the table was a farmyard of meat. The starters included trays of home-cured peppery salami, thick slices of prosciutto dripping in olive oil from their groves west of Rabat. There was pistachio-studded mortadella, blood-red bresaola... all washed down with litres of rough Italian red wine, or Coca Cola for the ladies. For the main course, Mrs Mifsud produced roasted ribs of beef, rolled and stuffed loin of pork, and enough chicken pieces to fill the average oven. Marianna looked on in amazement.

George sat next to Denzel. It was good to catch up with Pulizija gossip and escape from the hysterical shrieking coming from the women at the top of the table. Joseph sat on George's other side and, after producing a bottle of best Maltese red, proved to be jolly company. He won George over to the Mifsud family by promising him Gina could bring home as much free meat as the Zammits could eat. George replied, with a wink, he could not give him free meat but, if he ever needed a favour, in a legal sense, then he was always available to him. The pact was sealed. They all agreed over shot glasses of Joseph's brother's home-distilled, ice-cold *grappa*, that it was going to be a great marriage and the families would always be the best of friends.

CHAPTER 64

SUPERINTENDENT GEORGE ZAMMIT

BIRKIRKARA, MALTA

GEORGE WOKE LATE the next morning and the house was in a flap. They were due at St Mary's Parish Church for ten o'clock for the reading of the marriage banns. He had missed the first of the three readings and Marianna was determined the whole family would be there for the second.

George was not a big drinker and had a terrible headache. Denzel felt the same.

"It was that *grappa*, Dad. Did you smell it? It was home-distilled and not even drinkable. I've used better spirit to clean the chain on the motorbike."

Marianna was merciless and ushered them into the car in time for an early arrival at church so they could get a good seat for the busy ten o'clock Mass. George did not remember much about it, except his undying wish for it to end. Finally, he escaped into the fresh air and walked slowly around the seventeenth-century building. On one side were bullet holes from the battle when Napoleon's troops had hidden inside its walls, while on the other, was ancient graffiti, going back to the time of the Knights Hospitallers. George, however, was only aware of two things.

One was his pounding head and the second was the black

BMW parked at the kerb outside the main door. He looked around for the long thin figure of Gerald Camilleri. Sure enough, there he was, talking to Denzel and Marianna. George walked across to join them.

"Ah! George, the man of the moment. I have just been extolling your bravery and heroics to your lady wife and Denzel. I have told them they should be very proud of you. I had dinner with Silvia and Lucy last night – they are over for the weekend, visiting my sister. They tell a remarkable story. I have already thanked George, Marianna, but really, this time he has been truly heroic. I do not want to seem overdramatic, but his driving skills and quick wits saved me from certain death, and his detective work saved the life of my niece. I truly do not know how to thank him enough."

Denzel smiled with pride and Marianna was aghast.

"What've you been doing, George? I thought you were out there looking for a missing person?"

Camilleri interjected.

"He was, Marianna, he was. And he found her – in a secret tunnel under Mount Etna – and saved her, just as the volcano was erupting around them. Remarkable! But I have come to expect nothing less from him. Now, Marianna, would you mind if Denzel took you all home? I'll follow with George. I just need a few moments with him."

Camilleri's expression altered, as he ushered George towards the BMW.

"Listen, I have some bad news for you. The worst, I'm afraid. Look, sorry but it concerns the young Agente, Diego Russo. I am afraid he is dead."

George laughed nervously, shaking his head.

"No, that's impossible. I handed him over to the Anti-Mafia squad yesterday afternoon. He was fine then. Off to a safe house… it was all arranged."

"I know. He never made it. He never made it inside the safe

house. He was confronted by a police officer, or someone in a police officer's uniform, outside the safe house and he was shot. They have the guy in custody, but he is saying nothing. That is all I can tell you at the moment."

George grabbed hold of the roof of the car to steady himself.

"Oh God, forgive me," he muttered to himself, "this is my fault. I arranged it. He didn't want to go. He wanted to come here, with me. He knew he was at risk. He was practically begging me – he said he was going to rely on you to get him to safety."

"Me?"

"Yes, you said, if he ever needed anything, then all he had to do was ask. You *did* say that. He was going to ask you to arrange for him to come here!"

"That would never have worked out. I am sorry, George. Listen, do not blame yourself. There was nothing you or I could have done. In Sicily, you cannot trust anyone. They play by different rules. Not your fault."

"But the Anti-Mafia squad… you've got to be able to trust them, surely?"

"Obviously not. Get in the car, there's more."

"More?"

George felt awful. He had let his friend down, handing him over like that. He remembered the look on Diego's face when he had realised what George was going to do. George should have known when he heard the officer calling Diego *'ciccone'* that something was not right. He had trusted George, and George had sold him out. He would never forget that look. Diego was an innocent, a child really, just finding his way in life. George thought of Denzel – how he would feel if someone had betrayed him. George felt cheap, dirty and unworthy. He realised there was no way to put it right, no apology he could make, no redemption for him. He would have to live with this for the rest of his life and it would always haunt him.

They sat in the back of the car. The driver nodded to George, in recognition. George had known Mizzi for years. He was not a bad bloke. His fellow officer then turned away to look straight ahead, pretending not to listen in to the conversation.

"I am sorry, George, details are scant. I will try and get more information for you in due course."

"We worked so closely together, with Lucy. The three of us."

"I know, she told me. You all did an excellent job. I know what it is like to lose a colleague. You never forget it. I am genuinely sorry. It will get easier with time, but it will always be there. It is just one of those things that you chalk up against yourself."

George rested his head against the cool glass of the window. He felt tearful.

"Mela, I don't understand how it could happen."

"No, neither do I. Listen, I know it is hard, but I need your full attention. Can you give me that?"

"I'll try."

"I need you to go back to Italy. Not Sicily, but into Calabria. Mizzi? Why don't you go and have a smoke or something, just for ten minutes? I will sound the horn when we are ready."

The driver nodded and took another look at George. Mizzi could remember when George had been known as the 'use it or lose it inspector'. Not that many years ago, George had been a sergeant in the Immigration Division when an inspector's post had fallen vacant. The superintendent at the time had been told to fill the post quickly, or lose the position, as part of an ongoing budget review. George was the sergeant with the longest time served, so he had got the promotion. Hence, the 'use it or lose it inspector'. Now, he was a superintendent running secret missions for the assistant commissioner, no less. It just went to show, in the Pulizija, anything could happen. He reached for his cigarettes and got out of the car.

Usually, when Camilleri wanted George to do something

unpleasant, he would cajole, threaten and try to bribe him. This time, he simply asked George what he could do for him, to persuade him to go to Calabria.

"I can arrange most things, George. Money, promotions, business trips to nice places... all those things are within my power."

After thinking for a few moments, George decided. Yes, he would go. But this time he would go and look after number one. He was damned if he was going to risk his neck again for no good reason. George agreed to go to Calabria, with Hakan Toprak, on condition that Camilleri promised to support Denzel's application for the rank of sergeant, once he had passed the sergeant's examination. The boy deserved a leg up and George had no compunction about using the opportunity to ensure he got it. This was Malta, after all.

Camilleri shrugged and said: "If that is all that you want, then I gladly give it. The boy is good police material in any event. He is lucky to have such a considerate father."

George felt the guilt flood through him. He knew he could never watch Denzel progress through the force without thinking about Diego and what his life, and his career, might have been, had George acted differently.

George found the shock of hearing about Diego's death had made him light headed. In the background, he was only just aware of the assistant commissioner saying: "Before you go, be sure to sign out a handgun. I think it would be wise."

The words cleared his head and he responded: "I'm not going as security! You said driving and bag-carrying only! I'm not going to fight with the 'Ndrangheta!"

Camilleri looked at him, all the previous camaraderie gone.

"Superintendent, I expect you to do whatever is necessary! Take the gun and be at the VIP Terminal at the airport tomorrow morning. You fly at six. Remember who you are speaking to."

"Tomorrow? I've only just got back!"

"Tomorrow at six. Be there!"

CHAPTER 65

THE CALABRIAN HUNTERS

WOODLAND OUTSIDE CITTANOVA, ASPROMONTE MASSIF, CALABRIA

THE NAME ASPROMONTE literally means 'Wild Mountain'. The Calabrian range was known for its inaccessibility, the absence of mountain paths, the prevalence of dangerous landslides and its deeply incised valleys. These features had long conspired to make it the perfect hiding place for those living beyond the law. Ever since the Unification of Italy, in the late nineteenth century, the ordinary people of the forgotten South had refused to follow the ways dictated to them by their remote masters in Rome. This cultural obstinacy manifested itself in the rise of the Mafia and the other southern criminal communities, who chose their own path.

Commander Alfredo Balsamo had wet boots. In fact, he was wet down from his Goretex camouflage jacket, through to his white cotton undershirt. He and his platoon of ten men had spent all night labouring through the dense forests on the Aspromonte hills to the east of Cittanova, with the aim of being in position before the dawn of the coming day. The Commander's boots were wet from the heavy dew on the forest floor and the streams they had crossed; his undershirt from the hard physical effort of negotiating the ten kilometres of rough mountainous

forest. Each man carried a 20-kilo pack, a machete, plus whichever weapon they had been allocated.

The Hunters were an elite, highly trained squad who stalked
and captured members of the 'Ndrangheta in their own heart-
land. Rather than arrive at their destination by helicopter and
fast-rope down onto the hillside, or drive their blue Land Rovers
past the spying children of the criminally complicit villages of
the region, they had hiked in the darkness, unobserved, to take
up their concealed position.

They were a much-feared outfit, and their successes over the
last twenty years had helped them recruit the fittest, most skilled
officers, all with a full range of prior military experience. Much
of their work was observation, watching deserted farmhouses,
remote caves, abandoned shacks, where the leaders of the
'Ndrangheta met and even lived. In the villages, the bosses travelled between houses using tunnels, often so tight a person had
to slither, snake-like, to get from one end to the other. Being in a
crime family was an act of fate, you were born to it. For most of
them, there was no escape. In San Luca, a village of 4,000 inhabi-
tants, over 1,000 were currently under arrest, such was the
strength of the 'Ndrangheta in the Aspromonte Mountains.

As the sun came up, the squad was dotted over the hillside,
deep in the vegetation, with their binoculars trained on a traditional single-storey stone farmhouse that seemed to be abandoned. There was a long, gated access drive through the forest, a
few kilometres out of town, which crossed several watercourses,
making it inaccessible to anyone not in a four-wheel-drive vehicle. An earlier patrol of two Hunters had revealed there had been
some significant activity at the farmhouse recently. A long table
arrangement, with at least a dozen chairs, had been set up. Also,
a side table had appeared, plus a gas ring and a bottle of fuel.
The Hunters reasoned there must be a meeting, imminently. You
could not hold a meeting without coffee.

The Commander had been told that an order had come from

the Minister of Defence herself, no less, that a strike against the 'Ndrangheta leadership was required, in reprisal for the recent murder of the two special anti-Mafia prosecutors in Sicily, and they had been chosen to execute it. They had even given it a name that made him laugh: 'Operation Strike Down'. It sounded like a cheap TV show. Notwithstanding the stupid name, he thought the meeting at the farmhouse provided an excellent opportunity for them to hit back at the 'Ndrangheta. His team had carried out a full reconnaissance of the surrounding area, as well as the meeting place itself. He would have some surprises in store for them once they arrived. Meanwhile, the men watched and waited like the dedicated hunters they were.

CHAPTER 66
HAKAN TOPRAK
LAMEZIA TERME INTERNATIONAL AIRPORT, CALABRIA

NATASHA'S DASSAULT Falcon whisked them away from Malta International towards their destination of Lamezia Terme International Airport in Calabria. Lamezia Terme was an unremarkable town, 50 kilometres north of Cittanova, famous only for its lido and railway connection to Rome. On the flight George waited for Hakan to outline what was expected of him.

Hakan had bidden him 'Good morning', then resumed tinkering on his laptop. He had seemed more interested in working than talking, so George gave up on any attempt at conversation. Finally, Hakan closed the lid on the laptop and turned his brown unblinking eyes on George.

"Well, here we are. Are you enjoying your trip, so far?"

He waved his hands around the cabin.

"I used to fly back and forth to Libya in this plane all the time, so it's no novelty to me," George responded coolly. "It would be useful, though, if you could tell me what we're doing and what I can expect."

"The 'what we are doing' part is easy. I am meeting some senior members of the 'Ndrangheta to try to buy some businesses from them. Before you ask, we have been given guaranteed safe passage. What can we expect? That is a different question. What is the expression… 'expect the unexpected'?

"Just watch and listen, George. Keep an eye on my face. You can tell a lot about what is going on by watching a person's face. I am watching yours and I see your suspicion and fear. That is fine. Stay alert and this will all go down with no problems."

They landed a little after 07:00. The plane rolled to a halt and cut its engines. Silence descended in the cabin. Hakan sat and stared straight ahead. Then, as if he had just made a difficult decision and resolved to get on with it as soon as possible, he stood upright and exited the plane. Waiting to meet them was a man with a tan-coloured Land Rover Defender. Hakan scribbled a signature on a form and pointed at George. The man threw over a bunch of keys that George managed to drop onto the tarmac. As he retrieved them, he noticed all eyes were on him.

"What?"

"Shall we go?"

George had brought a hooded waterproof jacket, which he put into the boot. He noticed Hakan wore his usual dark suit, with a white shirt and navy tie. George had received a WhatsApp message with a date, a time and some coordinates. Hakan agreed this was the set-up for the meeting. George programmed the coordinates into the sat nav from the instructions on his phone, and they set off, driving in silence. They were directed south, down the Autostrada del Mediterraneo, along the narrow coastal strip. To the right, they glimpsed the slate-blue sea, while the rocky edifice of the Aspromonte Massif rose on the left. The day was drizzly and overcast. The wipers scraped grime across the windscreen every fifteen seconds, with an irritating screech. After thirty minutes, they turned east, off the autostrada, onto a regional road that crossed the widening coastal plain. The sat nav told them they only had another ten kilometres to travel. By now, rain was falling heavily. After they passed through the old town of Cittanova, the roads became increasingly narrow and more remote. George started to feel a little nervous.

"Do you think this is the right way?"

Hakan pointed at the sat nav screen.

"All we can do is follow it."

They turned onto a single-track road that eventually descended, by a series of narrow hairpin bends, into a deeply wooded valley. At the bottom, the road had been washed away and a narrow stream ran between loose rocks. On the other side of the stream, about ten metres further on, the road was intact and climbed up into the trees. George came to a halt.

"Mela, I can't drive across that! You'll lose your deposit."

"This is why we have got a Land Rover. It has a low-range gearbox." Hakan pressed a button on the dashboard and smiled at George. "It's OK, drive."

He crawled the vehicle over the rocks, the water half way up the wheels and arrived safely on the other side. He smiled at Hakan.

"Wow! That was fun!"

"Let's hope we encounter nothing more dangerous than that today! Pay attention, I think this is where we leave the road."

About 100 metres up the hill was a turn to the left, into some dense woodland. There was a five-bar gate, locked with a chain and padlock.

"Is this it?"

"We are on the red pin, so I think so."

"What do we do now?"

"We wait."

George got out of the car to stretch his legs and went to the gate, to try and spot the path ahead. As he rested his arms on the top bar, he became aware of a rustling sound, a little up the hill above him and to his left. As he turned his head, a man appeared. He was dressed in a green hooded waterproof jacket, brown corduroys and a flat cap. Rain ran down the waterproof and dripped onto thick canvas trousers, but the automatic pistol in his hand looked perfectly dry. He waved the gun at George, signalling him to return to the vehicle.

As he walked back, three other men crossed the road behind them. One opened the padlock on the gate. He waved George onward. By now, the others had surrounded the car. Hakan sat inside impassively. George joined him.

"It looks like we have arrived. Be cool. They are only the reception committee. They will search us. You have not done anything stupid, by the way, like bring a gun?"

George swallowed.

"Yes. It's in my coat pocket."

Hakan shook his head in disbelief.

"A very good way to get us both killed."

The man in the green waterproof circled the car and checked something on his phone. He tapped on the window with the tip of his gun barrel.

"Name, please, date of birth and passport."

He checked their passports and scrutinised their faces.

"Welcome, Toprak *bey*. If you would care to get out of the vehicle."

He scowled at George.

"And you."

Happy with their identification, he addressed Hakan.

"We're now going to do a thorough search for listening devices and weapons, as you'd expect. You can put all electrical items, everything with a wire or a battery, into this basket. Also, any weapons: guns, blades, hand-to-hand fighting aids. Please don't forget anything or it'll look bad when we find them, which we will."

They handed over their phones, the laptop, headphones, even their watches. George sheepishly placed the Glock pistol in the basket. A bearded man in a knee-length waxed jacket held a plain back golf umbrella over their heads, as they were thoroughly searched under the canopy of dripping trees by the road-side. Once the men were happy, one took the keys for the Land Rover and reversed it into the field. Two of the remaining men walked on ahead, the third followed behind.

They walked back the way they had come for 100 metres or so, crossing the stream that George had driven across. On the other side, they found an outcrop of white rock, covered with a heavy growth of moss and riparian vegetation. Amongst some fallen boulders, to the right of the outcrop, was a small fissure in the rock, just high and wide enough to squeeze through side-ways. Unless you were George, who had to suck in his stomach and force his large girth through the tight entrance.

Without a word, the line of men pushed themselves through the fissure into a damp, musty cave that smelled of rotting plant life. At the rear was an eerie yellow glow that marked the entrance to a passage, hewn into the rock, that started to climb uphill. A series of bulkhead lights ran along the wall. After a few metres, the uphill passage turned into a staircase and their ascent became steeper. Soon, more light appeared above them and pairs of hands pulled them up the last metre, onto the stone floor of a one-roomed building. It was bare except for a long table covered in a ruby-coloured damask cloth, a dozen wooden kitchen chairs, and a side table with a large kettle and a stand alone gas ring.

They saw a group of mainly, older, men, unsmiling and unwelcoming. Basso stood out; he was the only one dressed in a suit, under a knee-length grey woollen overcoat. George noticed his shoes and trouser bottoms were wet and his coat covered in dust and cobwebs from his trip through the passage. In the middle of them, wearing a pair of jeans and a navy puffer jacket, was a woman. Vice Questora Capozzi. George did not know how to react on seeing his suspicions confirmed. Here was the woman who was responsible for Diego's death. He had thought about how close he had probably come to meeting the same fate. Had he not been whisked back to Malta, he ,too, could have been lying in a morgue somewhere.

No hands were shaken and the group of men quietly made their way to the chairs around the table, leaving one unclaimed at the bottom and the top. Capozzi stood looking at George, with a half-smile on her face.

"Bet you didn't expect to see me."

He returned her stare.

"I had my suspicions."

She turned to Hakan Toprak.

"I'm glad you brought George. He's quite competent as a driver and someone to fetch your coat, but it's good we already know his limitations when it comes to security. Now he's got you here, he can wait outside." She turned to face George. "After all, George, you're still a policeman, so we can't have you hearing too much, because, on this occasion, we've promised not to do away with you."

There were a few smiles around the room, but everything went quiet when Basso spoke.

"*Allora*, to the table. This is the man who destroyed our data centre, then thinks he can walk in here and buy our city. Let us hear what he has to say."

George quickly scurried out of the door, to stand under the small porch out of the rain. He had a feeling he would be there for a while so picked up a log from a pile waiting to be split, gently lowering himself onto his new seat.

CHAPTER 67

COMMANDER ALFREDO BALSAMO

WOODLAND OUTSIDE CITTANOVA

So FAR, it had been a wet and uncomfortable stake-out for the commander and his squad, and it was approaching midday. But their intel had been correct. The meeting was on. The first sign was when he noticed four armed men appear from the cover of the woods, to stand outside the farmhouse. One stood very still, scouring the wooded hillside with binoculars. Balsamo was confident in his squad; they were well trained and would have seen the threat too, instinctively dropping their heads behind cover, remaining still and silent. Their green and brown Kevlar jackets and helmets melded into the autumn foliage; their hands and faces were covered in camouflage paint. A casual sweep of the binoculars would never find them.

The other three men made their way up the hillside, through the thick greenery on the forest floor, checking the ground cover. They were slack, though, randomly poking and prodding the bushes and undergrowth. Commander Balsamo smiled to himself. This casual approach to making a search meant they were in for a shock later that afternoon. As they drifted away, Balsamo made a series of hand signals to one of his men on the flank, telling him to track the men and see where they went. He would need to keep eyes on them at all times, to ensure they did not wander back and inadvertently spoil the party.

An hour or so later, he became aware of a subtle change within the farmhouse itself. The windows were shuttered and his men who had made the earlier reconnaissance had reported they were blocked with slats of wood on the inside. Now Balsamo could see a glow inside the building. Somehow, the lights had gone on. This could only mean that those inside had gained access though a secret entrance. He clenched his jaw. That created problems. Not knowing how many people were inside or how they were armed posed a risk to his team. He would have to wait and gather more information, but that meant taking a chance that those inside might disappear in the same fashion they had arrived.

One hour turned into two. Then, to his surprise, the door opened and a man appeared; slightly overweight, with light brown receding hair. He sat forlornly on a log, in the shelter of the porch. He scratched his head, poked a finger in his ear and was sublimely unaware of the eleven pairs of eyes drilling into him from the forest. The commander passed an instruction down the line. *Take him.*

Balsamo watched, as the bushes and some of the longer clumps of grass rippled on the squad's right flank. Two of the Hunters were crawling to the rear of the farmhouse so they could creep around the perimeter of the building and surprise the man sitting on the log. The commander saw his two men leave the cover of the woods and silently make their way behind the house. One held a roll of silver tape, the other a 20-centimetre hunting knife.

George lifted himself up and decided to stretch his legs. He flapped his arms around his body to stimulate some circulation and walked over the rough ground that separated the farm from the edge of the woods. He had no idea how it happened but, seconds later, he was on his belly, his face covered in tape and his hands secured behind his back.

Out of the corner of his eye, he saw a savage serrated blade appear near his cheek. He felt the cold steel pressing just under his eye socket. A voice hissed in his ear.

"Silence, you scum, or I'll flick your eyeball out!"

George's eyeballs were half out of his head already, with the shock of what was happening. He was gasping for air. The Hunter's knee was on his back and tape covered his mouth and, partially, his nostrils. He thought he was going to suffocate. Once he was secured, he was dragged into the bushes, a little way up the hill, out of view of the house.

With the knife still hovering near George's eye socket, the Hunter gently peeled the tape off his face.

"*Silencio!*"

"I'm a policeman – I'm on your side!" George said desperately.

"Oh, yeah, sure you are. How many people inside? Details, now!"

"Check my ID. Inside pocket, brown wallet."

The Hunter beckoned a colleague over, whispering: "Check this joker's ID. Wallet, inside pocket."

The second man found George's wallet and asked him his name, date of birth and Maltese Pulizija number, which were all on his ID card. "So, you memorised the details on a forged card?" he said. "Very clever."

"Listen, ring that number and ask for Assistant Commissioner Gerald Camilleri. He'll verify we're here on police business. Look, there's his number." George pointed to the number of the Organised Crime Squad on his ID.

"Ring and ask."

The second Hunter said: "I'm getting the commander. I need to check you out. Even if you're who you say you are, what I want to know is – what the hell are you doing here? Meanwhile,

Maltese copper or not, tell him all you know about who's in that building and what arms they've got, otherwise we'll kick the door down and push you in first. In fact, we'll probably do that, anyway!"

Fifteen minutes later, George was telling Commander Balsamo everything he knew. Well, nearly everything. He explained Hakan Toprak was with Turkish Intelligence, MIT, *Millî İstihbarat Teşkilatı*, and that the Italian Minister of the Interior knew all about their mission. That caused trouble and the commander disappeared further up the hill to make more calls.

On returning he whispered: "Well, the Ministry of the Interior has confirmed it was aware a meeting was to take place, but they didn't know where and when, but they also joined with the Ministry of Defence in authorising the operation to arrest the 'Ndrangheta leaders. It's a complete political clusterfuck, but our minister's orders are to proceed with the arrests. We can sort this mess out later. Describe this Turk to me, so we don't shoot him."

"It's easy, there're only two men in suits and he's the Turkish one."

"That improves his chances – slightly."

George told the commander about the tunnel leading to the farmhouse and said, if he was taken back to the road, he could lead them to it. The commander checked that the squad had fitted suppressors to their automatic rifles. George led four of them back down to the stream and, after ten minutes, found the entrance to the cave. The three men who had originally met him and Hakan were lingering by the opening, smoking and chatting. Within minutes, the Hunters had them surrounded, disarmed, gagged and handcuffed. A wire cable was fed through the cuffs and looped around the trunk of a young oak tree so the three of them were going nowhere.

One of the Hunters said: "We've got to remember where we left them. Wouldn't be the first time we drove off and forgot a prisoner. Ha!"

CHAPTER 68
HAKAN TOPRAK
THE FARMHOUSE, ASPROMONTE
MASSIF, CALABRIA

HAKAN HAD TAKEN a seat at the head of the table. As a whole, the group were much as he had expected them to be. Stunningly ordinary – clothing from discount chain stores; cheap scratched spectacles; contempt for anyone who chose to look or act differently from them; pathological distrust of anyone who attempted to push them into a corner. Underlying that, was the virulent racism and Islamophobic hatred that was prevalent in so much of the undeveloped areas in the South of Italy. It radiated from them. In some ways, it made Hakan's task easier. He need not try to make them like him, they never would. On the contrary, he could be totally direct and unemotional about the whole situation, safe in the knowledge they knew Rome was on to them and motivated to do them damage. They had been entrapped into a display of power that was self-defeating. They knew, if they were not careful, they could end up with nothing. Hakan's first play would be to reinforce that message.

There were only three of the group doing any talking. The business type in the suit and long wool coat, Basso, the woman, Cristina, and an old man who wore braces attached to his trousers with leather thongs, and a small black beret. He had crooked teeth, thin white hair, his eyes half hidden by pouches of skin that hung over his eyelids, and a heavily veined nose. The rest sat there, lumpen, brooding and chain smoking. It took Hakan a little while to read the room.

Basso was definitely for a deal of some sort and knew the numbers and financials. Cristina seemed more interested in how the project would be completed and what a combined MalTech Energy and Turkish sovereign wealth fund hoped to achieve out of the arrangement. The old man, who Hakan had more or less discounted to begin with, had now come to life. He was quizzing Hakan about how, in the event of a deal, the Turkish government would secure them the right to traffic Afghani heroin from Syria, through Turkey and into Europe, and how the Turkish authorities would help them launder their money.

But, unlikely as it seemed, it was the woman who appeared to be the lead spokesperson. When someone made a point, the others would incline their heads in her direction, to gauge her reaction. When she spoke, nobody contradicted her. There was definitely a deal to be made here. Hakan detected no sign that anybody was against cashing out.

It was then that there was a timid knock on the door – not threatening in itself, but sufficient to make everybody freeze. Pistols and rifles appeared from beneath the table. There was a communal exhalation of breath when George popped his head in, a sheepish grin on his face.

"Sorry, sorry, I just need Hakan for a minute."

The Turk frowned at him and tried to shake his head, signalling that now was not a good time. He felt they were getting close to the point where the deal would be agreed in principle. But, too late. There was a general relaxation around the table and several side conversations broke out. The woman took out her phone and started messaging.

Hakan made his excuses and he and George went back outside.

George took his arm and led him as far away from the door as he could.

"Mela, listen, we are surrounded. There's a military squad in the woods waiting to go in and take them, they've got the tunnel covered."

"What are you talking about?"

"I've just told you. It's a bust! The Carabinieri have a special unit, the Hunters – you've heard of them? They're here; in the woods, waiting for you and me to make a run for it. They took out the welcoming committee who were hanging around by the gate. I'm telling you; they're going to burst in very soon – take them or kill them."

"Who the hell is behind this? We have to stop it!"

"Stop it? Why would we stop it?"

"Because we have not done the deal yet, that is why! If this lot are all arrested, how on earth are we going to get legal control of the businesses? It cannot happen! We are so close. They will think we tricked them!"

"It's going to happen and you've got to get out of the way. These boys mean business, I'm telling you. Come on, quick!"

George put his hand on Hakan's arm, to try and steer him towards the woods. The Turk brushed it away.

"I am going back in. Tell them to give me fifteen minutes. Then, when they come in, I will be under the table. There are ten of them in there and they are all armed. Take it from me, they are not going to lie down and make it easy. The Hunters are fools to try."

Hakan turned away and went back inside. George went around the side of the farmhouse, where there were no windows, and slid into the woodland to talk to Commander Balsamo.

He was not impressed with the outcome.

"We've got to go in, those are our orders. But, if there're ten armed people in there, I'm going to have to use smoke grenades and stun grenades, to shake 'em up. So, your friend's in for it now. He's had his chance!"

"But you can't do that. He's working with the full knowledge of Rome, the Minister of the Interior herself!"

"Look, maybe you're right, I've spoken to Rome and it looks like a right cock-up but, here and now, I'm working on the direct orders of the Minister of Defence and they're very clear. Best thing you can do is lie low. On the off chance one of them manages to make a break for it, can you shoot?"

"Yes, I'm a qualified police marksman."

"Good, good. We've got the MP5s. Can you handle one of them?"

"Yeah, I've seen service against ISIS in Libya, with US Special forces, so semi-automatics are no problem."

George could have bitten his own tongue, as soon as had spoken. He had promised himself he would not brag like that, but, sometimes, he just could not help himself. It was not actually a lie, more of a half-truth. He had done all of those things, but usually as a reflex or in a state of blind terror – kill or be killed.

"OK, wow, welcome to the team! You take cover up there and, if any one of them comes out carrying a weapon, well, you know what to do."

Balsamo positioned George 20 metres up the hillside and got him lying, sniper-stye, in a shallow trench, filled with loose rock and old sodden leaves and bark. He had the perfect view of the door to the farmhouse, although he doubted he would be able to pull the trigger unless his life depended on it.

Balsamo's men approached the door, one carrying a short battering ram. The commander held up his hand and indicated they could simply turn the handle, given the door was unlocked. One of the Hunters opened it slightly and another gently rolled in a flash grenade, followed by a smoke grenade. The flash was an explosion of magnesium, emitting a burst of light equivalent to seven million candles. The light overwhelmed the receptors in the eyes of those around the table, leaving them temporarily blinded.

The bang of the detonating ammonium nitrate was thirty decibels louder than a fully revved jet engine, causing temporary deafness and adding to the disorientation of those inside. The Hunters ran in, firing their guns in the air, to add to the chaos and cacophony. Bodies were already tumbling down the staircase, in a vain attempt to make their way back the same way they had come in. The Hunters were waiting in the cave below, with their protective goggles and earplugs, ready to use more flash-bang grenades in the confines of the passage.

George lay still, imagining the panic inside the farmhouse. Suddenly, he saw the shutters of a window fly open. Someone had managed either to remove or kick through the slats and open the internal catches. A figure in a blue outdoor jacket climbed through, to squat on the sill and then, in one graceful movement, spring down to earth. Capozzi.

She was still struggling with the effects of the flash and was rubbing her eyes like some night-time creature, cast into the light. George watched her down the barrel of his rifle. She was zeroed, sighted perfectly. He thought of Diego, ruthlessly killed. For what? He had not hurt anyone, but she had ordered him shot. George's finger tightened on the trigger.

"Halt! Stay there, Capozzi, or I'll shoot." But he knew he could not kill her in cold blood, tempted as he was.

She raised her hands and George stood up, his gun still trained on her. He was steady now, in control, feeling none of the confusion of a moment before.

"On your knees or I'll put a bullet in your leg. Nobody would blame me."

He kept walking towards her, gun steady against his shoulder, his eyes only on her. He kept his footsteps high and deliberate, to avoid tripping. His focus was total. Somewhere, from in front or behind, he did not know, he heard a voice saying, "Calm yourself, George."

"I'm calm, as calm as she was when she ordered my friend killed."

He advanced towards the small figure, head bowed, now kneeling on the ground. His gun was still trained on the centre of her skull.

Hakan and the Hunters' commander stood at the door, watching him.

"George, leave her be." Hakan's voice shattered his concentration.

George lowered his gun and looked at her. "I don't know how you can live with yourself."

Capozzi stayed very still.

"I'm a cog in the wheel, George. It's family. This is the way it's always been. I didn't have anything to do with Diego's death, if that's what you think. It was a stupid, wasteful thing. It upset me, too."

"So you say. Who shot him then?"

"Believe it or not, it looks like it might have been an accident. An argument got out of hand and a gun went off. Lamieri had had an argument with him in the Questura and Diego made him look a fool. After that, Lamieri decided to go after him. He heard about the safe house – he has a cousin who works as a protection officer – and tracked Diego down there and waited for him. After that, I'm not sure what happened. Lamieri isn't talking. Typical stubborn Sicilian… but he's in custody. He must have lost it. Maybe the protection officer drew his weapon, who knows? Diego ended up on the floor. I'm sorry, George, but it was nothing to do with me. It wasn't a hit. I'm telling you the truth. "

George tried to imagine the circumstances she had described. There was something about Capozzi; when she spoke to you, you always felt she would not lie to your face. Behind them, Hakan was in earnest conversation with Balsamo. He walked quickly over to the prisoner and squatted down on his haunches, so his head was level with hers.

"Listen, you have to go with them," he jerked his hand over to the Hunters. They want their moment, but if you and Basso sign the paperwork, and we complete what we were just talking about, I will see what deal we can do for you both in Rome. Understood?"

Capozzi raised her head and looked him in the eye. After a moment, she sighed deeply and said: "OK. I'll trade. Only because I've got a daughter to think about. I'll do what I have to so I can get back to her. But you've got to cut in Pino Cuore Nero too, or there's no deal."

Hakan said, "Who is Pino Cuore Nero?"

"He's the one in the moleskin trousers, braces and black cap; the old man with the blue nose who was doing all the talking. He's the head of the Aspromonte clan. Don't tell the Hunters, otherwise they'll find an excuse to knock him about. He's caused a lot of trouble in his time. Include him and I'll sit and serve my time. Just get his name on the papers from Rome."

"What's his real name? I can't call him Pino Black Heart."

"Giuseppe Capozzi. He's my grandfather."

CHAPTER 69
THE WEDDING OF GINA ZAMMIT AND GIORGIO MIFSUD

THE BIRKIRKARA BAND CLUB, MALTA

GEORGE RETURNED HOME from his impromptu trip to Sicily and slept for fourteen hours straight. He woke up, spent fifteen minutes on the phone to the assistant commissioner and then entered the kitchen, to announce he had been given the following week off, as extra holiday, and was available to help with the final preparations for the wedding.

He enjoyed his extra time with the family, including running Gina down for the final fitting of her wedding dress at the bridal boutique. George tried not to think how much money the fussy, middle-aged woman, with the man's haircut and enormous pink spectacles, was charging them. She pulled and tugged at Gina's dress, huffing and puffing as she did so.

"Your mother did tell me to cut it tight, sweetie, because you were going to drop a dress size. Remember? Well, that hasn't happened, has it, dear?"

Gina had looked as though she was going to burst into tears.

"Never mind, let me fix it for you. Don't get upset. I think we've got time to let it out, here and there."

On the day itself, she looked fantastic. The white satin train was enormous, in length and width, and her two friends and

Giorgio's sisters, who were all bridesmaids, struggled to wrestle it through the church door and down the aisle. The episode took so long, the organist had to slot in an extra chorus of 'The Wedding March'. George's main fear, however, was that the bride would topple off the enormous white wedge platform shoes she had insisted on buying. He had visions of having to take his weeping, white-clad daughter to Mater Dei to have her ankle put into plaster.

However, they all survived the ceremony and had just finished eating a feast of meat, courtesy of the father of the groom. An enormous joint had been placed on each table, with a huge carving knife and fork. External wood-fired ovens, usually used to roast whole pigs, had been called into service. Trays of roast potatoes appeared together, with serving plates of roast peppers, courgettes and onions. The meal was accompanied by Beneventi wines, which were exceptional. George could not believe his eyes when the courier had arrived at his house, with case after case of sparkling white and full-bodied reds.

He had telephoned the winery to thank Bastiano, who was not around, so instead he had his first conversation with Benedetta, who tearfully thanked him for his heroics in saving her from the tunnels. George asked how she was getting on and she told him work was the best cure, but the nights were the worst time for her. The doctors had told her the claustrophobia she suffered from would go eventually, with time, but, right then, it was hard. Her father had recently announced he was taking a long-term leave of absence due to ill health, though he seemed much happier, and Basso, whom she had thought a bit of a bully, was nowhere to be seen. George held his tongue about the reason for that, as he had been asked to do.

When George told Marianna that he had invited Lucy and Silvia as extra guests, she had gone into a tailspin. She had demanded to know if they were bringing husbands or partners as well, because that would be four more seats! And, if they were as important as he had said, they would have to seat them near to the top table.

George had explained that they were a couple, who lived together. Marianna had taken a while to grasp the implications and had said that was all very nice, but quickly decided she did not want to make a fuss, that would only draw attention to them. She decided to seat them at the back, next to George's drunken brother and the long-lost uncle from Rabat, and his new wife with the illegitimate child. She remarked that they should all get on very nicely.

In fact, they did indeed. George's brother was a former fisher-man, who now had a boat that took tourists around the island and on deep-sea fishing trips. He was highly sociable and he and Silvia both had a love of the sea and its preservation. The long-lost uncle was a retired bus driver, with a repertoire of jokes and stories that had the table weeping with laughter. His new bride, with the illegitimate child, was young, glamorous and hopelessly in love with him – as she had been with her two previous, now deceased, elderly husbands. George spent more time on that table than on any other.

As the party progressed, George spied an all too familiar figure entering the hall, clutching a large box tied with a white ribbon. The assistant commissioner stood at the door, looking uncomfortable, a late arrival at a party in full swing. George nodded to Silvia.

"Your uncle is here."

"Well, Superintendent 'Father of the Bride', go and bring him over!"

George got to his feet and ventured across the dance floor, where Marianna was jiving vigorously with a red-faced, heavily sweating Joe Mifsud. Reluctantly, George accepted Camilleri's congratulations. He thought about fetching Gina, but saw her spinning madly around with Giorgio, as the brass band changed tack and started to pump out an Abba medley.

"Gerald, how good to see you!" he shouted above the noise.

Camilleri pressed his mint-scented mouth to George's ear.

"Well, I could not let the beautiful Gina's day pass without leaving a small gift. She certainly seems to be enjoying herself."

"It's been a good day. The family are all very pleased with how it's gone."

"Good. Then your recent absences have all been forgiven, Superintendent?"

"If that new posting has been officially confirmed and an invitation to the Christmas drinks party is in the post, I'll be out of the dog house."

Camilleri flashed his reptilian smile and produced three envelopes from his pocket.

"Can we go somewhere quieter for a moment? I find this music a little disorientating. "

They walked out onto a large balcony, to the rear of the room, which was half full of people smoking and cooling themselves from the rigours of the dancefloor. George had to shake off numerous approaches by effusive guests, well tanked with complimentary Beneventi wine, who wanted to share a moment with him.

"George, I do not want to take too much of your time, I can see you are in demand," Camilleri put in, when he had a chance. "These three envelopes... I wanted to give them to you personally. One is formal confirmation to your new role as Superintendent in the Organised and Financial Crime Division, with an enhanced salary. My personal congratulations to you, of course." He formally handed over the first envelope. "Envelope two is an invitation to the Commissioner's Drinks Party at the Phoenicia Hotel in three weeks' time." He passed the second envelope over. "Maybe you should just give that to your wife!" He glanced over at the dance floor, where Marianna had a sweaty Joe Mifsud staggering around to the band's version of 'Waterloo'. "My word, she has some energy, that wife of yours. Thirdly, well... I'll let you read it."

It was a letter to Assistant Commissioner Gerald Camilleri from Michele Tommasini, principal adviser to Luisa Marongiu, Minister of the Interior.

The Minister has asked me to write, in confidence, commending the role played by your officer, Acting Superintendent George Zammit, in a number of successful operations over the last several weeks. Not only did his investigative skills lead to the successful rescue of two kidnapping victims, whose lives were saved in hazardous circumstances, he also alerted us to a significant organised- crime operation at the centre of one of our major cities. Acting on his own initiative, he then single-handedly dealt a blow to infrastructure belonging to the criminal organisation, placing the assets in question beyond future use. Then, with the support of this department, he aided and assisted a covert operation, with our own Calabrian Hunters, 1st Air Assault Squadron, Cacciatori di Calabria, *ambushing and capturing a criminal clan, closely associated with the 'Ndrangheta crime organisation.*

The minister thanks the superintendent for his assistance and regrets that, due to the confidentiality of the operations in which he was involved, she cannot make the public gesture of acknowledgement that would otherwise be appropriate. However, she invites Superintendent George Zammit to a reception at the Italian Embassy in Valletta, with his family, on a date to be arranged, where it will be our honour to present him with the Civil Medal Cross, in recognition of his service to the Republic of Italy.

Distinti saluti,

Michele Tommasini
For and on behalf of Luisa Marongiu, Minister of the Interior

George looked askance at Camilleri.

"Wow, I wasn't expecting that!"

"George, next week I am going to set some time aside and you can tell me what on earth has been going on. As you know, I am sorry about the loss of the young Sicilian Agente who was assigned to help you. I have thought a lot about it, and concluded there was nothing that you or I could have done about it. Most upsetting, but best put behind us.

"I must say though, for the record, I was a bit alarmed about the bit in the letter where it said you acted on your own initiative, destroying some major piece of infrastructure. I shall need assurances that will never happen on this island! But, congratulations, George, the Pulizija is proud of you. It is just a shame we cannot make more of it publicly. Then again, I suppose you will be taking Marianna to the presentation of the medal. That should do it!

"And I thought you would be interested to know Natasha Bonnici sent me an article from the *Giornale di Sicilia* about a nasty explosion at an old *palazzo* in the centre of Ragusa. It says in the paper, it was at the family seat of the last of the Bourbons, if you can believe it. The poor Count's assistant was an eminent Knight of Tripoli, a Professed Conventual Chaplain no less. He was found dead at his desk. He had been handcuffed to a gas cylinder that exploded. Horrible way to go. Apparently, he was known to the Holy Father. Not that it did him much good though, eh?

"The Count himself survived. Apparently, he was handcuffed, too, but forced himself behind his assistant, who bore the brunt of the blast. The Count suffered some of the blast and has some nasty burns, but will probably live. I cannot imagine who would want to do such a thing, can you? Anyway, the word amongst several chivalric orders, including my own, is that no one is too distraught about what has happened. Apparently, he was not the most popular of individuals. The world moves in mysterious ways, does it not?

"Enjoy your evening. I am going to have a moment with my niece. Ah, yes, and my sister is baking this week. I fear you will receive an invitation to join us, before Silvia goes back to Rome and Lucy returns to Catania. I will tell her you and Marianna are delighted to accept, shall I?"

———

George did receive an invitation to Gerald Camilleri's sister's house. So, the Friday after the wedding, they made the trip to Paola, to the three-bedroomed townhouse in a working-class suburb, populated by many of the families who had previously relied on the docks and shipyards for a living.

George stood with Gerald and his sister, Carmella, on the front step, while she smoked a cigarette. She explained that Gerald and she had been born in that house. When their father had died, Gerald was only twelve, but was forced to leave school soon after, to work with an importer of fresh fruit and vegetables, and support their mother. She casually slipped an arm around her brother's waist as she told the story. Once he was eighteen, his father's friends found him a place with the Pulizija, at a wage sufficient to support the family comfortably. From then on, she remembered things getting better.

Camilleri smiled at him,

"You see, George, I have not always enjoyed an easy life. Times were hard then, certainly, but in some ways, simpler. And, despite there being no money, I think the three of us were happy. Do you agree, Carmella?" She nodded.

That evening, Gerald was in his shirt sleeves, without a tie, and, although he still wore grey pinstripe trousers, there was a pair of well-worn moccasins on his feet. It was a privilege to see the man George had feared and despised all these years, talk so freely and be so relaxed in his company. And Camilleri had more to say.

"You know, George, there are times when I envy you."

George was taken aback.

"Mela, really? Me? How so?"

"Well, the joys of family – a wife and children – now the possibility of grandchildren. I am not saying it is all a bed of roses, Lord knows, there must be moments, but, yes, on balance, you are a lucky man. It is a regret of mine that these things never happened for me."

George took a moment to reflect.

"Well, yes, I suppose I am lucky. It's just... I never really think about it much."

"Well, George, you should. Most definitely, you should!"

They returned inside, where Silvia was once again regaling Marianna with tales of George's bravery. His wife was stunned to silence when Silvia told the full story of her and Benedetta's kidnapping. Marianna had not really heard the details when they had met at the wedding. The dancing, the noise of the band and the effects of the Beneventi wine, had all proved too much. If George had alluded to his adventures before that, she had not really bothered to listen. After all, there was a wedding to think about.

"Well," she said, "it's just like my George – you should see the medals he has back home. You've got to watch him. The quiet ones are always the worst! Isn't that right, Gerald?"

"Quite so, Marianna, absolutely!"

"So, Gerald, will Madam President be at the Commissioner's drinks party? You know she wrote to Gina, congratulating her on her engagement? We met at the Grandmaster's Palace when

George got his first medal. I did send her an invitation for the wedding... just to be polite, I didn't want her thinking we'd forgotten about her... but she couldn't make it. Too busy, I'm sure."

Over the years, Camilleri had come to know Marianna well, but this time even he was taken aback.

"It is not usual for the President to grace us with her presence at the Christmas drinks event. And I would not take offence at her not being able to visit the Birkirkara Band Club – she does have a lot of very boring, formal state occasions to go to."

"I know, I know, that's what I said to myself. Well, to make it up to her, if Gina and Giorgio have a family, God willing, perhaps she might like to be a godmother..."

"Marianna!"

George looked daggers at her.

Across the room, he saw Lucy beckoning him outside. They stepped onto the small traditional balcony that overlooked the front street.

It was the first time George and Lucy had had the chance to talk quietly together about Diego's death. They found themselves embracing, tears rolling down their faces. George told her he had enquired at the new Questura in Catania about the address to which flowers should be sent. They told him that, given the circumstances, the family had made it known they wanted no Polizia representation at the funeral, nor any expressions of sympathy from them. So, unfortunately, they thought it best for all concerned not to pass on the details.

George was more deeply affected by Diego's death than people realised. If he had not gone into the Questura interfering in things that were really none of his business, Diego would still be alive. He had been funny, innocent, well-meaning, harmless, still strangely childlike. George wondered, had he been given the chance, what sort of man he would have become. George thought then about another young man, also embarking on a police career. How different his life was turning out to be, compared to that of the young officer in Catania. George had touched both lives, Denzel's for the good, Diego's very much for the worse. He felt the guilt of that, like a knife twisting in his guts.

IT HAD TAKEN two months of Hakan's time to sort through the mess left after the arrests at the farmhouse at Cittanova. The way it had ended was that he had all the information and leverage with which to negotiate, while Basso, Pino Cuore Nero and Capozzi had all the anger, resentment and conviction that they had been deceived and royally ripped off. Hakan had appointed some wellknown Sicilian lawyers, who understood Pino Cuore Nero's clan and their *avvocati*. He let them blow off steam for a while, until he introduced them to a second set of lawyers, from Rome, who were working with the Ministry of the Interior, preparing to seize the entire assets of their criminal enterprise in Catania. Hakan told them, if they did not play ball, he would pick up the whole lot for a couple of cents in the euro, once they had been convicted. It was not quite as simple as that, but the point had been made.

An agreement was reached quickly after that and at a much-reduced price. Hakan knew he had won, but he also knew that, even though the Aspromonte clan had been broken, the power of the 'Ndrangheta extended far beyond those remote Calabrian hills. He had to appear as though he had offered a fair price, in the circumstances. Nobody liked a cheat. So, once the numbers had been settled by the lawyers, Hakan took the Dassault jet from Malta to Reggio Calabria and onwards, to the new prison facility in Arghillà, on the outskirts of town. The three-storey detention blocks contained spacious six-person cells of up to 30 square metres and the governor understood the special requirements of the 'Ndrangheta. The Aspromonte clan members enjoyed a six-person cell each, along with numerous other privileges, including free association with each other.

The governor cleared the staff canteen and the lawyers from Palermo and Rome gathered there, together with representatives of the Ministry of the Interior, led by Michele Tommasini. The three remand inmates were ushered into the room, without ceremony. It was Hakan who first noticed their arrival, as he had been standing at the back, not involved in arranging the dozens of piles of papers relating to each of the businesses in 'Green Catania'. He walked across to Capozzi and stood in front of her, without saying a word.

She looked at him, the muscles in her face twitching. Her hair was lank and even the few weeks of incarceration had turned her skin prison-grey.

"Well, you've got what you wanted," she spat out.

"I have. I think you have, too, in the circumstances."

She glared at him.

"You haven't lost a child."

"I know any separation is hard for a mother, but this is the life you chose. You have not lost her for long. Just two years and you are free. Without me, it would have been thirty. When you come out, you and your daughter will be set for life."

It was a condition of the settlement that some of the monies paid to the clan members would be ring-fenced and not subject to any recovery proceedings So, when they had served their reduced sentences, they would at least be able to see out the rest of their days in comfort. The government lawyers had baulked at the suggestion, but Hakan pushed it through. In exchange, he had gained an assurance that he need not spend his time looking over his shoulder for the rest of his life, either.

"We were comfortable, anyway. I had a job and we lived together in an ordinary house. In her world, we looked like normal people. Now, that's finished, I'm disgraced Pulizija and 'Ndrangheta."

"That is what I do not understand. Why do it?"

"I was born into it. My father did it, and his before him. It was expected. For many years, the South had to look after itself. Rome and the North didn't care. Underneath the drugs and the money, there's something else – an independence, a pride. We look after our own. That's what counts."

"You have made arrangements for the child?"

"She's got a name, Luciana. And yes, I've made arrangements."

"You have money?"

"What do you care?"

"If you have problems, contact me. I will help."

"Why should I believe that?"

"You have my respect. I do not give that easily."

She snorted her contempt for him.

"It's time, Hakan Toprak, let's go and sign some papers."

They started the laborious process.

During the negotiations, Basso had proved himself difficult and Hakan felt, despite the assurances he had been given, would potentially be the most vengeful of the clan, were he to be released in the near future. Michele agreed and, in exchange for an agreement to release Pino Cuore Nero after twelve months' token imprisonment, they decided they would throw Basso to the wolves. The prosecutors guaranteed he would receive a sentence of at least thirty years. All Pino Cuore Nero had to do was put his name to several hundred documents.

———

Vito Amato had given Michele Tommasini a particularly thorny problem. The minister wanted him hoisted on a scaffold in Piazza dell'Elefante and publicly whipped, but Michele had managed to talk her out of any extreme punishment. He was keen to preserve an element of continuity and Rome needed to front the changes happening in the 'Green Catania' project and avoid any loss of face, in so far as the government was concerned. Following Capozzi's fall from grace (due to 'accounting irregularities' discovered by the auditors from Rome), Michele was also keen there was someone who would oversee the rebuilding of morale within the Polizia di Stato and the reconstruction of the Questura. It was agreed Vito would be allowed to finish his term, focusing on these objectives, and then announce he would not be standing for re-election in the next Mayoral contest. He was more than willing to avoid years behind bars and be humble in his acceptance of the arrangement.

———

Back in Malta, Hakan found himself at a table in the formal oak-panelled dining room of the Castello Bonnici for what Natasha had promised would be a celebratory dinner. The Family had been delighted by Hakan's success; the prospect of being the supplier of the energy needs of Catania and, in time, Naples, was considered a major coup. The associated benefits from the geothermal power stations were immense and Natasha had ensured Hakan Toprak had been the toast of the Committee at their last meeting in Milan.

There was a damp chill in the *castello* and the seventeenth-century fireplace was ablaze with what looked like a huge pile of imported logs. Malta had few enough trees and none of the local wood was as regular in shape, or as resinous in aroma, as those currently throwing an orange glow around the room. Hakan had insisted on taking a suite at the Athina for himself, rather than stay as her guest, which he thought just as well, since Natasha's celebration dinner was looking very much like an entrapment into a romantic situation.

The private chef in the kitchen had been flown in the day before, on the Dassault, from Milan, and Katia had been stressed out for a day before that, searching for items on his long list of ingredients. The tasting menu of seven dishes was fantastic. One delight followed another and, before they knew it, two bottles of wine had disappeared and balloons of brandy were being cradled in their hands. Natasha suggested they spend the last part of the evening outside on the terrace. Hakan resisted, saying it would be far too cold. Natasha smiled knowingly and led him out to a double swing seat, placed in front of a circular, stainless-steel fire pit, alive with dancing flames. She took a large blanket from a wicker basket and ushered him into the seat.

As they swung gently backwards and forwards, watching the sparks fly up into the night sky, she folded herself into him. The glow from the embers lit her face, expectant, challenging and knowing. She dared him not to kiss her and he fell for it, the whole seduction. He had seen it coming but had failed to avoid the trap closing. There was no way back. She had him. He tried one last play.

"Natasha, you are the most beautiful woman I have ever met and no man could ever say they did not want you. I know I do. But you do see the reason you and I can never be together?"

She kissed him slowly on his cheek, her lips lingering on his skin.

"Tell me."

"I am a traditional man. If I give myself completely to a woman, it will be when I want to marry her, to have children, a family home. I want my children to be Muslim, to meet my parents and do all those traditional things that would bore you in seconds. You are a rare creature; you would be smothered by living in the way I want."

She put her mouth close to his ear and whispered: "That's a lie. You could've had that any time you wanted. Why hasn't it happened yet? I tell you what – I'll offer you a deal. Let's try having sex first, then swear to me you want to settle down with a nice wife and become a family man. You don't fool me, Hakan Toprak!"

He had lost the game. The Hawk had been snared. They dropped the blanket on the stone flags and went upstairs, hand in hand.

CHAPTER 71
GIANNI DEL BOSCO
NATIONAL INSTITUTE OF
GEOPHYSICS AND VOLCANOLOGY,
ROME

It was late on a Friday afternoon and Gianni Del Bosco was deciding the shifts of his disgruntled staff to cover the weekend. It seemed there was a growing sense of panic at the Observatory in Catania. Stress had been building all week and now the situation was becoming critical.

Lucy Borg had returned to Catania Observatory earlier that week, after taking some time out in Malta. It was just as well. She and Ornella Mancini had been sending twice-daily reports that had rekindled Gianni's anxiety. Etna was on the verge of a cataclysmic eruption, he was convinced. Gianni knew his stock was low with the minister, so had held back from reporting the bad news until he was absolutely certain there had been a step-change in the data.

When he telephoned on the Wednesday, Michele Tommasini had told him the minister was still refusing to speak to him since his previous scaremongering had caused her political embarrassment.

"You know how sensitive she is about these things, Gianni. She calls you Peter... you know, after the boy who cried wolf!"

Del Bosco had snorted his contempt and slammed the phone down. His latest call, mid-afternoon Friday, had gone no better.

Michele had listened to him calmly state his case. Del Bosco then asked if he could meet the minister to go through the data with her.

"Gianni, she's left for the weekend and has asked not to be disturbed."

"She has a phone, doesn't she?"

"She's in Capri. And, Gianni, she won't want to speak to you, I can guarantee it!"

"I don't care what she wants! This is not some casual briefing! You'd better get back to me in the next few hours, because, if she doesn't listen to me, I'm going straight to the press and will call her out in front of them. This is serious, thousands of lives could be at stake. I'm not going to lie down and stay silent, just to protect her precious self-image. Do you hear me?"

With that he slammed the phone down for the second time in a week. He made a note, he would have to stop doing that. It was another hour until he expected the next report from Catania. He could not wait that long; his nerves were shredded.

He rang the Observatory and spoke to Ornella and Lucy on a conference line.

Lucy was first to speak.

"It's happening, Gianni. We don't need to look at the data, it's off the scale now. We've only got to look out of the window."

Ornella's voice was shaky and he could hear her shallow breathing.

"In the last six hours, the noise and the lava flows haven't stopped. The whole south side is ablaze. Nicolosi is just about empty – people have abandoned their houses. They're talking about 1669, you know, when lava flows hit Catania and rocks and dust fell all over Sicily, only except this one is going to be bigger. We're scared, Gianni."

He looked up at the ceiling for inspiration.

"Listen, Rome is giving me a hard time. We have to take this on ourselves. Do you think a general evacuation of the area is called for? If so, we've to get to Vito Amato. He'll be able to see what you see. I'll try and get Rome to put resources on standby, but Vito can mobilise local emergency services and get the local radio and TV broadcasters to issue evacuation advice. That'll shake Rome into action."

"Gianni, it's Lucy here. Let's wait another six hours. We can't call for an evacuation in the middle of the night, it'll be chaos. It's bad enough already. People can see, hear and feel what's happening. They're not stupid. Let's talk again in the morning. Ornella, perhaps you can talk to Vito and tell him what we're thinking?"

Her shaky voice came on the line again.

"What about us, Gianni? We've got families and they are asking us what they should do."

Del Bosco was losing patience with the *direttrice*.

"Ornella, you're a public servant. You'll stay in post until the evacuation order is given. If I were you, I'd tell your families to head for Palermo. I'd keep a car on the west side of the city, on one of the quieter roads, and a scooter at the Observatory. The main roads are going to be a nightmare."

"Too late, Gianni, you can't get out of Catania, the traffic is already jammed solid," said Lucy.

CHAPTER 72

VITO AMATO
CITY HALL, PIAZZA DUOMO, CATANIA

WHILE LUCY and Ornella sat fretting, looking at live raw data from the measuring devices located across the volcano, Vito Amato had just finished a round of meetings with the emergency services, Church volunteer groups and the major utility suppliers, to prepare Catania for the disaster they could see looming. He too had spoken with Michele Tomassini in Rome, who by now realised he had a major problem on his hands. The minister, however, had turned off her phone. Michele knew she was staying at the villa of an American film producer, who was hosting a party on the island, but had no further contact details, as Luisa had failed to provide the required information for the ministerial log.

Vito was exhausted and deeply worried. He had arranged for his elderly mother to be taken out of her care home, on the outskirts of Maletto, and transported to another church-run home, in Palermo. There was nothing he could do now but wait. Like most of the residents of the Metropolitan Area of Catania, he spent his time watching the flanks of the volcano, eyes drawn again and again to the rolling smoke and gas leaking from a dozen vents and craters. He had heard that the Sapienza barrier had collapsed and the tourist facilities and chair lift at Rifugio

Sapienza had been destroyed by the inexorable force of the lava flows. He watched the red, orange and black of the molten rivers of rock inching below the treeline to ignite the forests. It was terrifying.

He sank back into his leather chair and pondered his future. He had another eighteen months of his term left, unless the volcano destroyed him first. Then he had to step down. He felt regretful about leaving office, but it was a far better outcome than years in a state prison. The thought of that made him shudder. He had heard Capozzi had done a deal with the prosecutors, and good for her. In his opinion, she did not deserve a long stretch, after all the good work she had done in the Librino investigation. They had shafted that bastard Basso, though, something that brought a grim smile to Vito's lips.

If he ever got out of this, maybe he should make a real attempt to get Benedetta to get together with him. Possibly, if he married her and joined the Beneventi family, there was something he could do around the winery... managing director, maybe? Everybody knew Bastiano did not have what it took. Vito was sure Benedetta would have forgiven his part in it all. At the end of the day, he was only trying to help her father and brother. Given what they had been through together, it was natural there should be bonds between them...

Then, he realised his own stupidity. What was he thinking? He had to learn to face reality and accept his fall from grace, make his way again, as an ordinary citizen. He had already been granted that second chance. It would have to be enough for him.

His thoughts were interrupted by the ringing of his phone.

"Buonasera, signore. Sono Paolo Gambino. Come sta?"

Vito wondered what on earth Paolo Gambino wanted with him, at that time of night.

"I'm sorry, it's late for me to be calling, but the old man needs you. Can you come to the house?"

"Paolo, have you seen what's happening outside?"

"He may not have much longer. He wants to go and rest."

Vito was about to suggest Evita should take him to his bed, when the true meaning of the words hit him.

"What... now? It's impossible. What's it like where you are?"

"We can take one of the big trucks. It can be done. But he wants you to be there."

Vito closed his eyes and sighed.

"I think I understand. I'll be with you as soon as I can."

Vito climbed into the Maserati and left the underground car park of City Hall. He headed north, against the flow of the traffic and towards the volcano, passing the lines of stationary cars, loaded with possessions, that were attempting to flee the city. The police roadblocks were unmanned, so he was able to work his way along the back roads, towards the Gambini's quarry on the western side of the blazing volcano. Several times, fires in the forests forced him to turn back and, on one occasion, when he stepped out of the car to move a barrier, he noticed that the paint on the Maserati's bonnet had blistered under the rain of hot ash. The small rocks that intermittently rattled down on the car had scratched and dimpled its bonnet and roof panels. He was surprised to realise he did not care. He would hand it back, anyway, when his term ended. It was just a car.

―――

Eventually, Vito drove into the Gambini's yard. Light from the fires further up the hill cast an eerie glow over the enormous white house, almost as though the sun were rising behind the mountain in the middle of the night. There was activity in the yard, despite the hour. An enormous yellow dump truck, with wheels higher than a grown man, stood by the main front door. The dogs were still, lying on their haunches, chains slack, watching the men moving the more expensive equipment onto low-loaders, getting ready to evacuate.

Paolo walked across the expansive yard and ran his hand over the Maserati's damaged paintwork, before wiping his dusty hand against his trousers.

"I know someone who'll fix that for you."

"I'm not bothered, Paolo. Where's the old man?"

He gestured towards the house, saying: "With Evita. He's talking mad stuff. Wants to go up the volcano. He says it's time."

"Are you going to take him?"

"I'll do whatever Evita tells me to do. She knows what's best."

Vito left him to load a giant drilling machine that looked like a crouching dragon, silhouetted against the orange glow, that shimmered above the rim of the quarry. Inside the house, he was surprised to find Father Greco and Evita sitting in the hallway, in large armchairs with floral print covers and gilded feet. As catastrophe unfolded around them, they appeared peaceful and relaxed. It looked as though they had been waiting for him to arrive.

Vito grabbed a chair from the opposite side of the hall and joined them.

The old priest was simply dressed, in his grey woollen cassock, belted around the waist with plaited cord. On his feet, he wore high woollen socks up to his knees and his lightweight Gortex mountain boots. Resting against the wall behind him was a pair of wooden crutches.

"Thank you for coming, Vito." The old man reached out his papery hands. Vito leaned across to clasp them, briefly.

"It's time – you'll help me, won't you?"

Vito thought he knew what the priest meant, but still was not sure.

"Time for what, father?"

"For me to make my peace. You remember when you were a young *scugnizzo*, I talked to you about the mountain? You know my teachings, you come to the Brothers' masses."

He asked the questions, as though he was interrogating Vito at the Sunday School, in the back room of the church in Maletto.

"Why do we pray to the Mother, Vito?"

He looked at the priest's pale watery eyes and heavily wrinkled face. The years spent living on the mountain had weathered his skin and aged him beyond his years. His hermit's life had not been kind to him. Vito responded patiently.

"We pray that the Mother will keep us safe, like the Greek Empedocles prayed. And we pray that the Mother will give us eternal life, once we find perfection."

"Ha! When we find perfection. But Empedocles cast himself into the flames, in the hope of returning to us as a god. What vanity!"

The priest looked at Evita Gambino, sitting stoically by.

"Evita, do you seek to become a god?"

She furrowed her brow and shook her head.

"No, of course not. That is not our way."

Father Greco looked up at the ceiling, as if for inspiration.

"So, in my years of solitude on the volcano, I have asked this question again and again. What must we do to be redeemed, to gain eternal life? It is not to become a god – that is vainglorious thinking. Only God is God and sufficient unto Himself. Our sufficiency comes from Him."

Evita said: "*Corinthians.*"

"Yes, Evita, correct. *Corinthians.* The only action we can take is to intercede with Him, speak with Him through prayer. Now, it is time for me to speak with God. I need to make amends for the wrongs I have done and if I am forgiven, receive his blessing."

Evita stirred in her chair.

"What wrongs can you have done, father?"

"Oh, there were many. You, Paolo, and I have done many wrongs, I am sorry to say, Evita. I turned away too many times from wrongdoing being carried out before my eyes. And I have surrendered to temptation when I should have been stronger. I lost the love and friendship of those in the towns, because of it. I have tried to do penance for these sins but have not felt His forgiveness. I feel there is one more thing I can do, to be forgiven, saved even. And, not just save myself, but all of you, too. Time is short, Vito. We must go. Will you help me find peace?"

The old man struggled to his feet and Evita passed him the crutches. Vito reluctantly raised himself, wondering if what was happening was real or just some terrible dream. He followed the priest to the door. Behind them, Evita took a handkerchief to her eyes and started to sob quietly.

———

The enormous yellow dump truck ground its way up the tracks towards the volcanic wasteland of the summit. Its huge wheels rolled smoothly over the hot ash deposits and its sturdy frame absorbed the constant clatter of bombardment by rocks and cooling lava that fell from the sky. Paolo worked the gears and drove where he knew the tracks should be. The landscape was changing around them, as the pressure beneath lifted the surface and fresh lava oozed through the fissures. In time, God willing, it would cool and start to form new cones and calderas.

The heat had started to percolate into the cab, as did the rotten egg smell of the sulphurous gases. Paolo produced some dust masks, used by those operating the drilling machines, and he and Vito covered their faces. Father Greco waved the offer away. They pressed on, drawing nearer and nearer to the rim of the South Crater. Approaching from the north avoided most of the new lava flows, but Paolo was starting to become concerned.

"How much further, father? If we get cut off, we'll soon all be talking to God."

As if to prove the point, a huge boulder, jettisoned from the crater itself, crashed onto the bonnet of the truck, nearly jolting them out of their seats.

"Just a little further, Paolo, please. Is that the rim ahead?"

They trundled on for another ten minutes. The truck's engine strained, attacking the steepest part of the climb at a little over walking pace. Paolo peered through the smoke and dust.

"I think this could be it."

He stopped the truck and, with Vito, gently lifted the old man down onto the rocky surface.

The priest balanced himself on the crutches and then approached each of them in turn, laying his palm on their forehead.

"Bless you both. You go now, do not wait. It is too dangerous. And do not worry, my faith has never been stronger."

Paolo was confused. He looked at Vito, who said to the departing priest: "We understand, father. God bless you. And thank you!"

Vito laid a restraining hand on Paolo's arm, as together, they watched the old priest pick his way up towards the rim of the crater. Hot flows of lava tumbled down the incline around him. The rim was nearer than they had realised and it only took a few minutes before the silhouette of the priest was intermittently visible, in between the banks of drifting smoke, standing on the edge of the crater, high above the pit of lava. The heat was incredible. Sweat was streaming down Vito's face and his clothes were sticking to him. He could not imagine how hot it must be at the rim itself.

Vito saw the distant figure of the priest drop his crutches then raise his arms skywards. With a smooth action, he lifted off his cassock and his skinny naked form was immediately enveloped by a swirling mass of white smoke, as he disappeared from view. Suddenly, an intense flash of white light burst out of the crater, blinding the two men. This was immediately followed by a roar, as a jet of white and blue flame shot high into the sky above them. Paolo fell to his knees, muttering to himself, as Vito reached back to steady himself on the wheel arch of the truck.

The hot metal seared his hand. He snatched it away. The smoke cleared and there was no longer any trace of the man on the rim of the crater.

Vito and Paolo looked at each other.

Paolo said, aghast: "What's he done?"

Vito felt emotionally drained. Grief and pain for the man who had changed the whole course of his life would come later.

"He's gone into the volcano. Not to become a god, but to surrender himself to the Mother, as a sinner, to save us all from our sins. That's what he was trying to tell us."

AT EXACTLY THE same moment as the Mother shot her white flame of redemption high into the air, the sensors across the volcano started to record a dramatic decrease in her activity. Lucy was later to say it was like watching a balloon deflate in front of her. The fires on the flanks continued to burn for many days and, of course, the smog of ash and tephra hung heavily in the sky, waiting to fall down to earth, but the pressure in the chambers dropped dramatically. The lakes of lava, upper and lower, shrank back in on themselves, as if a gigantic geothermal plug had been pulled, and the swirling lakes of molten rock disappeared down a huge sink, back beneath the earth's crust. All that happened within hours of the priest's disappearance.

Lucy and Ornella were amazed by what was occurring. Every number, every measure, did not just fall, it tumbled. They tried repeatedly to call Vito, but he was nowhere to be found. Ornella said, "The toad has probably done a runner. I don't know what I ever saw in that man."

Lucy spoke to Del Bosco, who could not hide his tears of relief. He thanked God, the gods, everybody he could think of. Del Bosco immediately telephoned Michele Tomassini, to share the good news. Michele, who never liked being woken up in the early hours, frostily told him he was in big trouble this time. He had cried wolf once too often.

"It was just as well we didn't listen to you before, Gianni, or we would have evacuated half of Sicily. I don't want to prejudge what Luisa is going to say when she returns, but if I were you, I'd be considering my position."

This time Michele put the phone down on a shell-shocked Gianni.

Gianni Del Bosco then placed a conference call to Ornella and Lucy, to vent his anger at the unfairness of his treatment. They were the only two people he knew who were awake at that moment. While Gianni raged in Rome, in the conference room in Catania, Ornella Mancini made the sign of a knife being slid across her throat. She put the palm of her hand over the microphone and silently mouthed to Lucy: "He's finished. Gone."

Lucy nodded and shrugged. Ornella continued silently mouthing to her, as Gianni chuntered on in the background.

"Do you want to work for me?" Ornella pointed to the floor with her index finger. "Here?" she mouthed, "Permanently?"

She raised her eyebrows and rubbed her thumb and first finger together, the universal sign for 'plenty of money', looking at Lucy enquiringly.

If Gianni was going to be sacked, Lucy's secondment in Rome would also finish. A permanent job, studying Etna? The most exciting volcano in the world! Why not? She was sure she could get Silvia to join her there. She had been offered a post at the Institute of Biological and Marine Sciences, at Catania University, in the recent past, but had turned it down in order to stay with Lucy in Rome.

She mouthed back silently: "Yes, please!" and gave her new boss a thumbs up.

EPILOGUE

THE WEEKS FOLLOWING the wedding were anti-climactic for George. Giorgio and Gina squeezed their considerable combined bulk into a three-quarter bed in Gina's old room, which still featured the One Direction wallpaper and pink emulsion walls. A redecoration project had been planned, which entertained his wife for a week or two, but George could tell Marianna was missing Gina's shift of attention away from her, to her new husband.

George liked Giorgio and got used to seeing him at the kitchen table, eating prodigious quantities of cured meats, roast joints, fried offal, braised cuts, grilled meats... in short, meats cooked and prepared in ways George had never heard of. Every evening, their son-in-law would return from the shop and slap a bulging carrier bag in front of Marianna, who would grimly accept the challenge of preparing the latest farmyard selection for an increasingly weary, overfed family.

Denzel had met his father for lunch in the Pulizija canteen in Floriana and the pair of them had simultaneously picked up a plate of salad. They both dissolved into laughter.

"I tell you what, my bowels haven't moved since that lad moved in with us!" George said.

"I know, I don't understand where he puts all that meat! When're they moving out? We'll all be dead with coronaries if it's not soon!"

They set about their salads, enjoying the fresh flavours and textures. The assistant commissioner approached and asked if he could join them, for a moment. Now the house was so chaotic, George saw less and less of Denzel, who spent as much time as he could out and about. It was not that he had fallen out with the family, he said, it was just the incessant noise. George enjoyed time alone with his son, particularly when it was in the canteen and they could talk 'shop', a subject banned at home. He grudgingly waved Camilleri towards a spare seat.

"Actually, George, it is Denzel I wanted to talk to." Camilleri settled himself in his chair and rested his folded arms on the table top. You have served with us for, what, three years now?"

"Three and a half, actually, assistant commissioner."

"You passed the sergeant's exams at the Academy for Disciplined Forces?"

"Yes, sir, I did, got the results last month."

"Good, good. They are currently interviewing for a sergeant's post in one of the Investigation teams. You are eligible to apply for it. I have sent the interviewing inspector a letter of recommendation, which should help. You will be hearing from him soon. I just wanted to let you know and wish you good luck."

As Camilleri stood up and turned away, he caught George's eye and bowed his head, ever so slightly.

George saw the expression of excitement on Denzel's face. Then, it changed slightly, to one of puzzlement, as though something had suddenly occurred to him.

"Dad, that thing with Camilleri that just happened. Did you have something to do with it?"

George laughed out loud.

"Mela! You're kidding? I have zero influence over that man! It is purely down to you, son. Don't disappoint him. He'll be watching you."

George smiled and clapped his son on the shoulder. As he did so, he could not help remembering another young police officer, bright-eyed and keen, whom he had promised to help – a young man he had failed, who would never now be making the rank of sergeant, no matter how many favours were called in.

ABOUT THE AUTHOR

AJ Aberford is a former corporate lawyer who moved to Malta several years ago. He is enthralled by the culture and history of the island that acts as a bridge between Europe and North Africa. Its position at the sharp end of the migrant crisis and the rapid growth of its tourist and commercial sectors provide a rich backdrop to the Inspector George Zammit series.

To keep up to date on AJ Aberford's fiction writing please subscribe to his website: **www.ajaberford.com**.

Reviews help authors more than you might think. If you enjoyed *Fire in the Mountain*, please consider leaving a review.

You can connect with AJ Aberford and find out more about his writing and George's upcoming adventures, by following him on Twitter, Facebook, Instagram or better still, subscribing to his mailing list.

When you join the mailing list you will get a link to download a novella, *Meeting in Milan*, a prequel to the Inspector George Zammit series.

ACKNOWLEDGMENTS

Writing books is a solitary enterprise, so those few who join me in the work deserve my heartfelt thanks.

My wife, Janet, is my number one fan and backs that up with forensic attention to detail when it comes to reviewing the early drafts. She also acts as my publicist, because getting books written is only the beginning of its journey.

Lynn Curtis is my editor, who reviews the first draft manuscript and patiently advises on plot structure, themes, and characterisation. Later she will look at the technical aspects of my writing, making sure the manuscript is as good as it can be. I thank her for all the great work she has done on all the books in the series.

Finally, I hand the manuscript to Rebecca and Adrian, at Hobeck Books, who publish the Inspector Zammit Series. They turn the manuscript into the book that you have bought, investing their time and money to format, advertise and distribute my work. Without their faith and support the manuscript would still be on the shelf in my study. I thank them for enabling me to call myself a 'published author'. I still get a kick out those words!

THE GEORGE ZAMMIT CRIME SERIES

Meeting in Milan (short-story prequel)

Bodies in the Water
Bullets in the Sand
Hawk at the Crossroads
Fire in the Mountain
The Knife of Mercy – coming soon

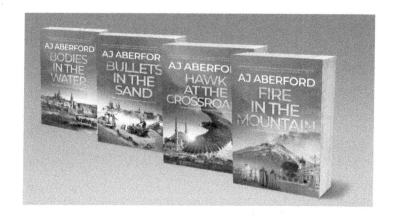

MEETING IN MILAN

Short-story prequel available for free: www.ajaberford.com.

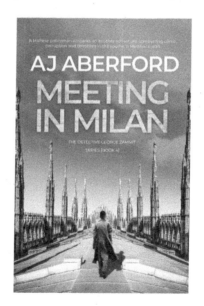

How did Marco and Sergio first meet? What brought them together? How was their lifetime of friendship and loyalty forged?

To find out more, go onto AJ Aberford's website, subscribe to his mailing list and download this novella for free: www.ajaberford.com

THE KNIFE OF MERCY

George Zammit returns in *The Knife of Mercy*

In the midst of the civil war in the Middle East, the UN has a problem. Millions of euros are going missing. The man to find out what is happening is Superintendent George Zammit. The search leads George into war-torn territory, where danger lurks around every corner. His investigation uncovers a web of deceit and leads our reluctant hero into the hunt for a dangerous and powerful old enemy.

Back home in Malta, George faces fresh problems. Turmoil and conflict in an ancient organised crime family places George at the heart of a dilemma. Old crimes and past secrets have come to light and the time has come for someone to pay. George finds himself in an impossible moral quandary. What does a good policeman do in a land where the truth is bought and sold? How can George keep order, when all around him is chaos, crime and madness?

Subscribe to AJ Aberford's website to keep up to date on the release date of *The Knife of Mercy* and news of further books in the series to come: www.ajaberford.com

HOBECK BOOKS – THE HOME OF GREAT STORIES

We hope you've enjoyed reading this novel by AJ Aberford. To keep up to date on AJ Aberford's fiction writing, please subscribe to his website: **www.ajaberford.com** and you will also be able to download the free novella *Meeting in Milan*.

Hobeck Books also offers a number of short stories and novellas, free for subscribers in the compilation *Crime Bites*.

- *Echo Rock* by Robert Daws
- *Old Dogs, Old Tricks* by A B Morgan
- *The Silence of the Rabbit* by Wendy Turbin
- *Never Mind the Baubles: An Anthology of Twisted Winter Tales* by the Hobeck Team (including many of the Hobeck authors and Hobeck's two publishers)
- *The Clarice Cliff Vase* by Linda Huber
- *Here She Lies* by Kerena Swan
- *The Macnab Principle* by R.D. Nixon
- *Fatal Beginnings* by Brian Price
- *A Defining Moment* by Lin Le Versha
- *Saviour* by Jennie Ensor
- *You Can't Trust Anyone These Days* by Maureen Myant

Also, please visit the Hobeck Books website for details of our other superb authors and their books, and if you would like to get in touch, we would love to hear from you.

Hobeck Books also presents a weekly podcast, the Hobcast Book Show, where founders Adrian Hobart and Rebecca Collins discuss all things book related, key issues from each week, including the ups and downs of running a creative business. Each episode includes an interview with one of the people who make Hobeck possible: the editors, the authors, the cover designers and other industry experts. These are the people who help Hobeck bring great stories to life. Without them, Hobeck wouldn't exist. The Hobcast can be listened to from all the usual platforms, but it can also be found on the Hobeck website: **www. hobeck.net/hobcast**.

OTHER HOBECK BOOKS TO EXPLORE

The Rock Crime Series by Robert Daws

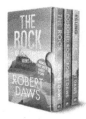

The magnificent Rock crime series from acclaimed British actor Robert Daws – includes free bonus story *Echo Rock*.

'An exciting 21st-century crime writer.'
Peter James

'A top crime thriller.'
Adam Croft, crime writer

Detective Sergeant Tamara Sullivan approaches her secondment to the sun-soaked streets of Gibraltar with mixed feelings. Desperate to prove herself following a career-threatening decision during a dangerous incident serving with London's Metropolitan Police, Sullivan is pitched into a series of life-and-death cases in partnership with her new boss, Detective Chief Inspector Gus Broderick. An old-school cop, Broderick is himself haunted by personal demons following the unexplained disappearance of his wife some years earlier. The two detectives form an uneasy alliance and friendship in the face of a series of murders that challenge Sullivan and Broderick to their limits and beyond.

The Rock Crime Series transports readers to the ancient streets of the British Overseas Territory of Gibraltar, sat precariously at the western entrance to the Mediterranean and subject to the jealous attention of neighbouring Spain. Robert Daws shows his mastery of the classic whodunnit with three novels rich in great characters, tense plotting full of twists and turns and breath-taking set-piece action.

The Rock

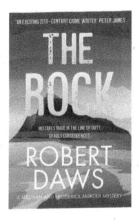

Exiled to Gibraltar from London's Metropolitan Police after a lapse of judgement, DS Tamara Sullivan feels she's being punished – no matter how sun-kissed the Rock is.

But this is no sleepy siesta of a posting on the Mediterranean. Paired with her new boss, DCI Gus Broderick, Sullivan will need all her skills to survive the most dangerous case of her career.

A young constable is found hanging in his apartment. With no time for introductions, Sullivan and Broderick, unravel a dark and sinister secret that has remained buried for decades.

Are they prepared to face the fury of what they are about to uncover?

Poisoned Rock

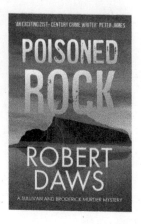

As the bright lights of a Hollywood movie production shine into the dark recesses of Gibraltar, murky secrets emerge from the shadows of the Rock's past.

It seems the legacy of wartime spying, sabotage and treachery runs deep on the Rock.

Past and present collide plunging detectives Tamara Sullivan and Gus Broderick into a tangled web of intrigue and murder, and their skills and uneasy working relationship are about to be tested to the limit.

Killing Rock

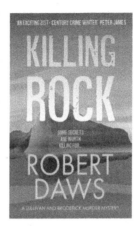

A wealthy household massacred in Spain.

Unidentified mummified remains found at the foot of the Rock.

A US Congressman's run for President hangs on events in Gibraltar.

What's the connection?

Detectives Tamara Sullivan and Gus Broderick face the most dangerous and elusive murder investigation of their lives, and for Broderick, it's about to become all too personal, with his career in real peril as his past comes back to haunt him.

Will Sullivan and Broderick's partnership survive this latest case, as killers stalk the narrow streets of Gibraltar?